THE EXHIBIT

Dianne Neral Ell

Printed: August 2016

ISBN-13: 978-0692287194

ISBN-10: 0692287191

Printed in the USA.

SUN

Fifty priceless Egyptian art objects—made of gold—were
coming to New York for the first time.

Claudia, Peter, Charles, and Sharon thought they could find a way
to remove some of them and escape detection.

They thought they knew how to get a million dollars apiece
out of the theft.

And they thought they could trust one another.

They were mistaken. Sometimes fatally.

FRIDAY, FEBRUARY 11

Warm and secure in her black mink, Claudia Betancourt swept through the frosted glass doors etched near their top with the single word *Sirocco*. She was carried along by a current of snowladen air that rushed ahead of her, then disappeared into the crowded restaurant while the gentle warmth of the room that greeted her began to soothe the sting in her cheeks.

The front doors opened to a well appointed reception area where customers waited for tables in the dining room. Claudia stood a moment, unbuttoned her coat and flipped her dark hair from the collar. The dining area was to the right. The bar and lounge to the left.

She stepped inside the lounge's entrance where smoke from Asian incense burners rose toward the ceiling and the din of voices crowded the room. Mixed in with the sound of voices, in a corner, surrounded by small parquet cocktail tables, a pianist played to half interested listeners who were engrossed in their friendly Friday-after-work conversations.

Unable to see her companions, she remained motionless, looking over the heads of the people milling about. Holding onto a large brown envelope, she tucked it more tightly under her arm as tiny drops of water falling from the surface of her fur left dark stains on the carpet around her black boots.

After a minute, she began making her way across the room. Seemingly unaware of the heads that turned as she passed., she walked by the bar where customers were lined up shoulder to shoulder, then skirted the tables with comfortable lounge chairs until she came to a booth along the far wall. A flicker of recognition crossed her face. Finally, when she reached the booth, her look of concentration gave way to a smile.

"Treacherous out there," she said. She nodded to the three occupants of the booth. "Sorry I'm late."

"I slipped on the ice coming down the street," Sharon Hiller said. "I know what you mean." A young, curly-haired woman, she sat close to Peter Mandel, a man in his late-thirties. Across from them, alone on the other side was Charles Green, a heavyset, well-dressed man who started to get up but was stopped by a gesture from Claudia. Instead, he squirmed back into the corner, making room for her on the outside of the seat.

Claudia placed the envelope on the table and took off her gloves. She draped her damp coat over the back of the booth and pushed it along towards Charles Green as she slipped into the seat.

Charles saluted the arrival of the coat by lifting his glass. "Cheers," he said in a voice that was surprisingly high coming from his stocky body and thick neck.

She acknowledged his gesture with a nod as she moved the envelope in front of her.

"How are things at the museum?" Peter Mandel asked, not taking his eyes from the envelope.

"Hectic—" Her reply was interrupted by a waiter who had come up to the table to take her drink order. She hesitated only for a moment. "Extra dry, Tanqueray Gibson, please."

The waiter left with the angry eyes of Charles Green on his back. "He must think you're alone," he complained.

"Still snowing?" Sharon Hiller asked.

"Yes. Snowing, blowing and typically New York in February. If not for the exhibit and your program. I'd be drinking Daiquiris and listening to the surf right now in Barbados," Claudia answered.

"Is that all that's keeping you busy at the museum?" Peter asked.

"Isn't that enough? I've got to help you and Sharon with the broadcast, answer Charles' questions about security, work on the invitation list for the opening, put together the catalogue and stay as far away as possible from the curator," she concluded as the waiter arrived with her drink.

He put the glass down in front of Claudia, taking care not to touch the envelope. Next to it he placed a small glass full of cocktail onions. He beamed proudly as he stood erect, waiting for Claudia's reaction to his little surprise. Her smile of appreciation was sufficient praise. He bowed and left.

"I don't understand it," Charles said. "If I ask for two olives in my Martini, I get a lecture about the lack of rain in Italy."

"Don't be bitter, Charlie," Peter laughed. "He probably remembers your quarter tip."

Sharon Hiller joined in the laughter and reached across the table for one of the small onions. Still holding it gently in her fingers, she rested her hand on the envelope in front of Claudia. "Curiosity is killing me," she said. "Is this what I think it is?"

Claudia smiled warmly. "Yes. They arrived today." She bent the metal clasp upward and peeled back the flap. Several copies of a magazine-sized booklet slid out of the envelope and onto the table. "Here they are," she announced. "Two weeks late, but worth the wait."

The cover of the booklet was a thick paper coated with a glossy film of plastic. In the center of the cover, on an all-black background, was the picture of a golden statue. The dark eyes and plaited hair identified the statue immediately as being Egyptian. Above the head of the statue in gold script were the words "Golden Age of Egypt—3500 to 1000 B.C." Below it, in the same gold script, smaller words read, "New York Metropolitan Museum of Art—April five through June thirty."

For a long moment, all four stared at the booklets. Claudia ran her finger over a cover in a gentle, caressing movement. "The photography is beautiful," she said. "I hope your television cameras will do as well?" She looked across at Peter Mandel.

"Well ..." he hesitated. "Perhaps not exactly. These were done in a studio under perfect conditions. We'll be shooting in the museum and the lighting may not be as perfect. But it's going to be fine, don't worry."

Claudia took the top copy and turned it to face her. She opened it and turned to the first color photographs. Each picture filled half the page, and under each there was descriptive copy. She turned several more pages, passing pictures of statues, urns, weapons and jewelry. Each item had the same yellow color. The text described the pieces as either being fashioned of solid gold or covered with a gold leaf.

"The name certainly doesn't lie," Charles said and whistled softly. "The Golden Age is right. There's enough of that bright stuff to fill every tooth in Puerto Rico."

Peter looked ground quickly to see if any of the waiters were nearby. He was relieved to see none.

Taking the copy she had been leafing through, Claudia slid it across the table towards the curly-haired young woman. "Sharon, there are about fifty pieces in here," she said. "It's up to you and Peter to decide which ones you want to concentrate on during the program. Those are the ones you'll have to write about in your script."

"It's going to be a bitch deciding," Sharon said. "They're all beautiful. Is there anything special about any one of them, some mystery, or a legend—even a curse?

Can't we tie this together in some way with the King Tut treasure they had here a few years ago? Anything that I could use to put a little drama in the script. That knife, for instance." Sharon pointed to a jewel-encrusted dagger. "It would be interesting if it was used by someone called Ra the Ripper to carve up a few ancient prostitutes."

"Wouldn't it be poetic justice if he used to do away with female television scriptwriters?" Charles said.

Sharon continued to turn the pages, paying no attention to what Charles had said. Suddenly, Claudia reached across the table and placed her hand on the book, not allowing Sharon to turn the page. "Some of these pieces do come from the time of Tut, and I suppose there are superstitious people who think anything connected with ancient Egypt is cursed, but this exhibition is much bigger, there are articles from many kingdoms. Here, for instance, look at this."

She was pointing to a small rectangular box on four small ball feet. The top and sides of the box were covered with hundreds of tiny gold granules arranged in intricate patterns. Sharon read the text and looked up at Claudia. "It says here that this is one of a pair of boxes. It is beautiful. The other one is supposed to be an exact duplicate and is in the private collection of ..." She paused and bent further over the page only to look up again and beam across the table at Claudia. " ... In the private collection of Mr. and Mrs. Maurice Betancourt of New York City. That's you!" she laughed. "That is you, isn't it?"

"Yes," Claudia said quietly. "That box is one of the most important pieces in my collection. I've always felt badly about not having the set. They should be together."

"Then why not donate yours to the museum?" Peter asked.

Claudia's head snapped around to face Peter. Her eyes narrowed as she searched for an answer to a question that, to her, was absurd. Finally, when she could think of no simple explanation, she said, "It would be just as easy for them to sell theirs to me."

Peter seemed taken aback as if sensing he had stumbled onto a delicate subject.

In the awkward silence they became aware again of the piano. Sharon tapped the rim of her glass in time to the beat of the time, while Charles raised his empty glass in the direction of a passing waiter and signaled with a circular motion of his hand for another round.

"Same for everyone?" he asked.

They nodded.

"These things are all very valuable, aren't they?" Sharon asked, pointing at the book.

The question was not directed at anyone in particular, but Claudia chose to answer.

"Priceless, is more like it," she said. For confirmation, she looked at Charles. "How much is the museum insuring them for?" she asked.

"Three hundred thousand dollars for each piece is the price we agreed to with the museum," Charles said, stating the numbers matter-of-factly. "The whole collection comes to fifteen million dollars."

Peter whistled softly. "You mean if the plane bringing these things from Egypt goes down in the Atlantic, you pay the Met fifteen million?"

"If it happened that way, we'd end up in court arguing about who had possession. No," Charles went on, "our insurance is written on the exhibition once it goes on display here."

"I can see why you keep asking Claudia about security arrangements during the broadcast," Sharon said.

"When the museum agreed to let them televise the opening night ceremonies, there was an added risk and a higher premium." He smiled at the last thought as the waiter arrived with the tray of drinks. There was no extra glass of onions.

"See what happens when you order," Peter said. "At least I didn't get my lecture on Roman drought," Charles said seriously.

"Why is there an extra risk because of the television show?" Sharon asked. "The place will be a mob scene for months anyway."

Charles lifted his Scotch and peered at Sharon through the gold-colored liquid. "With Peter's goon squad running all over the place with their cameras and lights and cables, who knows what might turn up missing?"

"What happens then?" Sharon asked.

"When?" Charles replied.

"Oh, hell, Charlie, any time!" she said.

"You mean once the stuff has been put out for show at the museum?"

Claudia winced visibly at the reference to the exhibit as "the stuff."

"It's treated the same as any robbery. The police investigate, we investigate and eventually, we pay the museum."

"Oh." Sharon sounded disappointed.

"What did you expect?" Peter asked.

"Something more dramatic. These are priceless antiquities and Charlie makes it sound like someone broke in and swiped a TV set."

"It's all the same," Charles said. "If someone steals a TV set or the Mona Lisa, someone collects, if they're insured."

Sharon shrugged. "I can see a TV set being ripped off. You can sell it or use it, but what do you do with a statue or a gold box?" She gestured at the pictures in front of her.

"You can sell it, ransom it, or..." Charles started to answer.

"Or keep it," Claudia finished.

"Wait a minute." Sharon edged forward. "Sell it to whom?"

"Lots of people buy stolen art," Charles said.

Sharon looked at Claudia for a moment, hoping Charles' remark had not offended her.

"He's right," Claudia said. "Many do. I've been approached often and I've been tempted, but it's a risk Maurice and I don't choose to take."

"All right," Sharon brightened, "but what about ransom? I can't see someone getting a note made of newspaper clippings that says 'pay me or I'll kill your television set'."

Charles laughed. "A lot of people would pay to have their TV sets killed, especially after watching one of Peter's programs." He glanced in Peter's direction but saw no reaction on his face. "The stakes are so high with artwork," he continued seriously, "that any price demanded below the insured value would be considered by the insurance company."

"Why all these questions about a robbery?" Peter asked Sharon.

"Plot. It's all plot material."

"Plot for what? We're doing a documentary, not a whodunit."

"My book isn't going to be a documentary," Sharon said.

"What book?"

"The book I'm turning into a screenplay."

Peter stared at the young woman sitting next to him. His mouth was slightly open, his eyes wide.

"You know," she continued, "the screenplay I'm adapting from my Broadway play."

Peter slapped his forehead. "Oh, God, am I a fish. You really had me going. Look, when you're all through, just make sure you adapt your play, movie, and book into a television documentary. O.K.?"

Sharon raised her glass to Peter. "Yes, master." She smiled at him over the rim.

They sipped their drinks in silence, the melody from the piano drifting towards their table through the waves of conversation nearby. Claudia's head was bent, her dark hair falling forward as she stared at the booklet on the table. She seemed fascinated by the picture of the statue on the cover.

"Exquisite, isn't it?" she asked.

There was no answer.

"I guess, as a collector, I see it differently." She fell deeper into her thoughts, and when she continued speaking it seemed as if she was explaining something to herself in a place far removed from this setting. "I suppose that's why I chose to work in the exhibition department of the museum and put up with their bickering and politics. It's just to be close to such things." She traced the outline of the statue with her fingers and then suddenly pulled her hand away from the book. "We got together tonight for two reasons," she said in a businesslike tone. "First, I wanted you all to have a copy of this," she pointed to the books. "And second, I wanted to find out from Peter what the next steps were."

Peter clasped his hands on the table around his drink, assuming his professional role of television producer. "Sharon and I will go over the catalogue, pick the best pieces and rough out a talking script. Then we should get a floor plan from you, Claudia, to block out a shooting script."

"And then you can give me an idea of the number of men in your goon squad," Charles added.

"Anything you want, Charlie," Peter said.

"And an affidavit from you stating that none of your crew will steal anything." Charles laughed.

"I still find it hard to imagine one of these things disappearing from the museum," Sharon said. "Even with all the confusion of a TV show and the thousands of people who are going to come and go after it opens. There's so many guards and precautions, it sounds impossible."

"Just difficult, not impossible," Charles said.

"Tell me again what would happen if one of these things did walk out of the museum?" Sharon asked.

"A three-ring circus the likes of which you've never seen before," Charles said. "City police, investigators from the museum, the insurance company, the feds and probably the Egyptians. These are the crown jewels of the Arabs we're dealing with, not chopped liver."

"I guess this is one time the exhibit is safe," Sharon sighed. "Who wants to get involved with all of that?"

Claudia looked at them all and smiled.

"You find this all so amusing?" Charles asked.

"No, not at all ... it's just something Sharon said that reminded me of an incident at one of the local museums. I think it was during the exhibition of some rare gem collection."

"What was that?" Sharon asked.

"There was a robbery that caused absolutely no fuss. No police, no investigators, no commotion at all."

"I find that hard to believe," Charles said.

Claudia fiddled with the edge of the catalog. "You remember the old question about the tree, don't you?" she paused. "If a tree falls in a forest and no one's around to hear it, does it make a sound?"

"What's that got to do with anything?" Sharon asked.

"It's the same thing with a crime. A crime isn't a crime unless someone can prove that it happened. If something did walk out of the museum, as Sharon puts it, who would know about it if nothing was missing?" Her voice trailed off. As if reacting to an unseen command, the three people at the table leaned back, away from Claudia, and concentrated on their drinks.

"This sounds like a riddle game we used to play," Peter said. "I wasn't very good at it then, and I'm not going to try this one."

"I love it," Sharon said.

Charles said nothing. Now he was trying to look at Claudia through his nearly empty glass.

Claudia realized that she had caught them all up in her daydreaming. "I'm sorry," she sighed. "I've had so many things going on that I just let my mind wander, and look what I've done."

She could see they were all caught up in their own thoughts.

"Let's get back to work. Everyone take their copy. Peter, you and Sharon work on the scripts, and I'll get a floor plan for you." They took the offered books and let them sit on the table in front of each of them.

"We should get together again soon," Claudia continued. "I'll call you all towards the end of next week to set up another meeting. Is that all right?"

"Sure," Peter said. Catching a waiter's eye, he made a writing gesture in midair to signal for a check. Although no one objected to his calling for the check, he volunteered, "Don't worry, this all comes out of the production budget."

In a few minutes the check had been paid and they moved in a group across the room, toward the steps that led to the frosted front door. Charles walked close to Claudia, hoping that some of the eyes would include him in their jealous stares. Once outside they separated. Charles went in search of a taxi to take him to Grand Central Station, while Sharon and Peter moved off in the opposite direction, not wishing to advertise the fact that the taxi they sought would take them to Peter's apartment.

Only Claudia remained outside the frosted doors of Sirocco. She pulled the tall collar of her coat up against the cold wind. Perhaps, she thought, a walk would help clear her mind.

She turned east towards Park Avenue and began walking, slowly at first, then at a faster pace as the cold began to reach her. The faster she walked, the more her thoughts came in rapid succession. The booklet and its golden pictures flashed through her mind, followed by her memory of the gem robbery of over a year ago.

If Sharon could make the same connection, it would give her all the plot she needed.

But Peter Mandel was key to what lay ahead. UBS senior producer of documentaries. Savvy. With the understanding of the ins and outs of the network and what it took to pull together the type of program needed for the *Golden Age of Egypt Exhibit*. Sharon was the way to hype his enthusiasm. Reel her in. The rest was easy. The only problem was Charles Green. Perhaps it wasn't fair. Maybe it just stemmed from her general dislike of insurance people.

WEDNESDAY, FEBRUARY 16

The small crystals hanging from the lighted chandelier moved almost imperceptibly, creating a pattern of iridescent shapes that floated atop the dinner table. Claudia leaned forward in her chair, appearing to be absorbed in this play of light, but her thoughts were actually focused on the man sitting across from her. He appeared to be devoting his full attention to the last slender slice of veal on his dish. Tonight's dinner was as so many others had been, with silences far outnumbering the bursts of conversation. Her husband wasn't distant—he just wasn't there. Claudia watched him, debating what to say next. Maurice had a way of avoiding a conversation if he wasn't interested. Lately, he seemed to be doing more and more of that.

She ran her fingers up and down the stem of her wine glass, thinking...looking for an opening. Claudia looked across at Maurice's plate. It was empty. Suddenly, as if she had been watching from one of the darkened recesses of the room, the housekeeper appeared and carried away the dinner dishes.

"Dessert?" the woman asked. "We have a kirsch torte." She spoke with an English accent.

Maurice looked at her and then tilted his head back until he was looking up at the ceiling. "Mrs. Britton, you are a devil. You could tempt a saint."

"One very small piece for me, and an even smaller piece for the doctor," Claudia snapped out the order.

The woman returned quickly carrying the dessert. "Would you like some coffee?" she asked.

"No, thank you, Mrs. Britton," Claudia answered. "I'm going to have brandy." She looked in Maurice's direction and he nodded. "We both will, and I'll get it myself. Why don't you go ahead and leave...it's late."

Claudia placed her hands on the arms of her chair and started to get up.

"Stay, please," Maurice said as he rose and walked to the mirrored cabinet above the buffet to pour two glasses of Hennessy.

"I'm glad we were able to have dinner tonight," Claudia said. "We haven't been able to do much of that lately. I guess...it's our work. We really devote too much time to it."

Maurice's round face with its thick brows melted into a frown as he set her brandy glass on the table. "What would you like to do, leave the museum? And me, what should I do, give up my practice?"

"We could, you know. We don't need the money." She saw the instant darkening of his eyes and quickly busied herself with a cigarette.

"I'm afraid I'm not ready to settle down to a life of travel, carrying your suitcase around the world."

"That's not what I meant." She saw that explanations would only bring on an argument. The same argument that was beginning to plague their lives. Even if the words were not said aloud, the feelings were there. After ten years of marriage, she was sure that Maurice had begun to resent her money and everything it did for them, especially their travel and collecting. Rather than argue, he would leave and go to his study to work late until she was asleep. Tonight she wanted to be with him. "I'm sorry, Maurice ..." She tried to change the subject. "By the way, I marked the evening of April fifth on your calendar. It's the opening night reception at the museum."

"How is the exhibit coming?" he asked. His tone was still cold.

"No one knows exactly what will happen when the pieces for the exhibit arrive, and the guest list for the reception is a shambles. However, I'm sure no one is panicking—yet. Not with Miriam Gottfried in charge."

At the name of the curator, Maurice grimaced. "The old dragon probably had everyone too scared to notice any problems," he said.

"They're also complicating her life on opening night with a television broadcast from the museum."

"With the way she feels about anyone interfering with her collection, I wouldn't want to be a part of that television show."

"I'm afraid I have to be," Claudia said matter-of-factly.

"Oh, really? Tell me about it," he asked. But before she could answer, he got up. "First, let me freshen your drink, then we can go into the library."

They left the dining room together and walked down the hall to the double doors of the library. Maurice took a key from his pocket and opened the doors. Once inside, he turned on the lights.

It would be impossible for anyone to enter the Betancourt library for the first time without being affected by the room. The books, the ancient treasures, the dark colors ... everything worked together to make one feel that one had stepped across a threshold into a different time and place.

The room was large, fifteen by thirty feet. Three of the walls were lined with display cases and the fourth with bookshelves which continued upward, overhead, past the first story, then expanded covering all four walls of the second story. The bookcases higher up were accessible only by a balcony which ran around the perimeter of the room and connected with the first floor by means of a staircase.

High above the display cases on the west wall, at the juncture of the first and second stories, were three small windows unnoticeable except during the late afternoon hours when the sunlight, filtering through the small stained-glass panels, sent shafts of colored light throughout the room.

The glass-enclosed display cases were framed, as were the bookshelves, in a dark wood, and the indirect lights hidden in the walls and shelves of the cases could be controlled from a wall panel near the door. Each piece on display caught and reflected the lights in a different way. There were gold jewelry, ivory boxes, statues inlaid with lapis and jewel-encrusted weapons. Some objects absorbed the light, others sent it dancing about the room in a dizzying kaleidoscope of colors. As the lights were turned up, the pieces shimmered and glowed as each became a light source of its own.

There was little furniture in the room. A large desk near the center, two identical black leather club chairs near the desk, and a large world globe set in a wooden cradle which stood in front of the desk.

The floor was dark parqueted wood covered with three identical area rugs, which were a deep red color shot through with gold threads in a geometric pattern. The rugs were rare Mamchikes, the Egyptian equivalent of the Turkish or Ottoman designs.

This room was Claudia Betancourt's favorite. It was her pride. It had taken her most of the ten years of her married life, and much of her fortune, to complete it.

Maurice settled himself into one of the leather chairs next to the desk while Claudia sat at the desk. He began to read over the manuscript of an article he had prepared for the American Journal of Psychiatry. She busied herself slowly turning the pages of the exhibit catalogue she had received several days earlier, and waited for Maurice to pick up on the conversation.

They remained quiet, absorbed in their reading for a long time. When he finished rereading his article, Maurice got up and stood behind his wife watching as she turned the pages. After some time he broke the silence. "They're beautiful pictures," he said. "The trouble is they don't do the real thing justice."

"You're right," Claudia answered, looking up from the book. "But can you imagine what one of those pieces would look like in this room—in one of our displays? Or even in here." Claudia got up from the desk and moved over to the bookcases. In a quick movement, she reached behind a book and released a catch. Two rows of books swung away from the wall as lights went on revealing a small opening the size of a medicine cabinet. It was empty save for a black felt-covered pedestal.

"I still don't know why we bothered to have this built, we have nothing that we want to keep hidden," Maurice said.

"Not yet," she whispered, pushing the bookshelves back into place and closing the cabinet.

"Why do you say that?" he asked.

"Oh, I was just thinking out loud. What would we do with a very important piece if its provenance were questionable?"

She walked back to the desk and reached across the leather desktop to pick up her cigarettes and lighter. She lit one, drew in deeply and blew the smoke up at the expanse of air over her head. The smoke curled, eddied and disappeared somewhere in the second story. Again she picked up the catalogue and started flipping through it slowly, taking her time, looking at each item carefully. Suddenly Maurice reached out and touched her hand, stopping her. On the page in front of them was the gold box covered with granulation work. Claudia was carefully watching the change in his expression.

"You never mentioned that this box was going to be part of the exhibit."

"I didn't see any reason to. If anything, I thought my bringing it up would have made you angry."

"Why would it make me angry?" He frowned and placed the catalogue back on the desk. "I only asked why you never mentioned it. You're the one who's angry, not me. You've never really gotten over our passing up the opportunity to buy that second box, have you?"

Claudia's eyes turned dark. She stared down at the desktop. "Don't use the word 'we'," she said quickly, without looking up. "It was you and your inhibitions."

"My inhibitions? Refusing to be part of a crime is not an inhibition, Claudia. You've never understood that."

"Buying something that has had a questionable past is not participating in a crime."

"I agree. That is not the bone of contention and you know it. What I object to is the method by which one comes into possession of these objects. Half the time they're stolen either from Egypt or from some museum. That is a crime, Claudia, and in a crime, there's always a third party—the person who is selling the objects. And I refuse to have a third party know I conspired in a crime."

"So that's it," Claudia said, getting up from the desk. She swept across the floor to the far wall and stood in front of the bookshelves that hid the secret cabinet. She pointed her finger at the spot where the cabinet was.

"You wouldn't mind putting something in here as long as we were the only ones who knew it was here. It's not your conscience at all that bothers you. It's merely the existence of this third party. So, all we have to do is eliminate the third party. Right?"

"No!"

"But Maurice, you just said that if we could eliminate the third party, you'd have no problem buying stolen merchandise."

"That's not what I meant at all. I refuse to argue the point any further." He returned to the black leather chair and sat down while Claudia went back to leafing through the catalogue. At the end of the book was the section she had written about the reproductions that were being made of selected artifacts, and the cities in which they'd be on sale.

"Maurice, did you know that reproductions are being made of some of the artifacts in the exhibit? They're supposed to be perfect in every detail."

"So ..."

"Would you settle for one of them?"

"Why would you even suggest such a thing?"

"Well, one of the pieces I've always loved and would give anything to own is this." She turned the catalogue for Maurice to see. Facing him was the cover picture of the statue of Sekhmet, the goddess with the head of a cat and the body of a woman. The light emerald eyes, a relief from the gold head and body, stared directly at him.

"It's one of the pieces being duplicated. Since we can't have the real thing, would you settle for this reproduction?"

"Certainly not. Everything we have here is genuine. I would not adulterate this collection with fakes. I don't care how perfect they are. I'd know they weren't real, and that's what's important."

"But what if you didn't know it was a fake, then would it make a difference?" She spoke slowly, measuring each word. "If everyone visiting a museum were shown a collection of replicas and told they were the real thing, they would accept it and believe it. Their reaction to the exhibit would be real. There would be no difference. I don't think even Miriam Gottfried would know if the museum was full of these replicas."

Maurice was watching her closely. Her eyes spoke for her. They had changed from dark and pensive to gay and flashing as she spoke of the curators' being fooled by counterfeits.

"Are you thinking of substituting a duplicate exhibition for the real thing?"

"Oh, I'm not thinking anything of the kind."

"Then let's be done with this conversation."

Before she could say any more, Maurice rose and stretched.

Claudia jumped from her chair and held his arm. "Are you leaving?"

"Crime tires me and I have early rounds tomorrow. Don't forget to lock up before you come up," he said coldly.

"But Maurice...I thought tonight..." She stopped in mid-sentence. He waited for her to finish but she said no more. Finally, she let go of his arm and sat in the chair. He turned and left the room.

Claudia stared at the closed door and after several moments emitted a sigh as she let her body sag in the chair. By now she thought she should have become resigned to Maurice's coldness, but it still hurt to know that she was not the woman he wanted. There were others. None were serious and none were lasting, but they were there, living examples of her failure as a wife. All that remained between them was their collection.

Claudia again idly turned the pages of the catalogue. She stopped at the cover picture of the statue of the goddess Sekhmet, then went on until she came to the box that was the twin of hers. Maurice is right, she thought. I've never really forgiven him for not letting me buy the second box. It should be here!

It was sometime later that Maurice Betancourt looked across at his wife's bed before turning off his reading light and saw that it was empty save for Karma, her white cat, curled up at the foot. Whether she was there or not made little difference to him. He fell asleep quickly giving no further thought to her empty bed. There were other women in other beds, in other rooms.

FRIDAY, FEBRUARY 18

The snow, after falling for several hours, had begun to accumulate. Charles Green stepped off the train platform and started across the parking lot. Everything now had a thick white cover that muffled all sounds except the soft hissing of the tiny flakes as they drifted down. As he walked, he stared down behind him at his tracks. The wet, black marks on the pavement fascinated him.

At this late hour, most of the commuters had come and gone, leaving few cars in the lot. Charles made his way to an old white Volkswagen and opened the door. He threw his case onto the right-hand seat, got in, and turned the key in the ignition. There was a faint grinding sound from the starter, and then silence. He tried again. Nothing. He pulled the headlight switch. A pale, yellow glow appeared in front of the car. He tried for a third time and quit.

"Shit!" The sound of his own voice in the quiet startled him. He got out, slammed the door, and retraced his steps back to the platform and a pay telephone.

"Hello," a boy answered.

"Terry, this is your father. Is your mother there?"

There was a long pause before a woman's voice came on. "Charles? Where are you?"

"I'm at the station with a dead car. Can you come down for me?"

A pause. "Sit tight, I'll be there in ten minutes."

"Listen, take it easy, the streets are lousy."

There was no response. Charles hung up slowly. The coin box clicked. He started out of the booth, turned and stuck his finger into the coin return. Now, for the second time, he walked across the lot to his car and got in. He stretched his legs out as far as he could, leaned his head against the back of the seat and closed his eyes. He was not looking forward to seeing his wife. What he had to say was not going to be easy, and he didn't know how she would handle it. He was having trouble himself in accepting the fact that his professional life was floundering. For Charles Green to admit that all was not perfect was bitter medicine.

The early seventies had been good and fruitful years. The money rolled in and rolled right out again. The home in Connecticut was purchased to provide the perfect setting for Pat and the boys. There were private schools for the boys, vacations, decorating the house, entertaining, the country club, household help and an orthodontist.

The Greens lived at a level that was becoming progressively harder to maintain. Charles knew that eventually there would be a day of reckoning. But he had kept painting with broad, firm strokes, never looking back. Then slowly, almost imperceptibly, business slowed. Things were not bad, they were just not as good. Charles began to worry. Not aloud and not for long, but there were quiet moments on the train going home, like tonight, when his mind began to create a scene where he was forced, for the first time, to say no to his wife. It was a blow to his pride, yet he did not need an expert in financial planning to show him that he was moving slowly, yet surely, towards financial chaos.

For the first time in his life, Charles Green now hesitated before reaching for a check. For the first time in his life, he avoided the windows of men's clothing stores. For the first time in his life, Charles Green was afraid.

It had become a habit, or as he preferred to think of it, a family tradition, to stay home over the Christmas holidays—there was too much entertaining to do. Then in February, when the snow and cold had become tiresome, the Greens headed to the Caribbean. It meant taking the boys out of school, but it was worth it.

Each year they selected an island where they could swim, play golf and tennis, ride, and sail at a pace that returned them to Connecticut more tired than before they left. The suntan he got in February was worn with pride and spoke for itself. Charles relished it.

This year, reservations had been made and final plans for the trip were moving ahead. Charles had sat at his desk in the office today and figured out that the trip would cost about $18,000. After taking care of the holiday bills, the hard truth was that the Greens' finances could not stand a $18,000 vacation. But how do you tell your wife and sons that the trip is off? He had never said no before. He had never had to. How do you explain it? How do you live with your pride?

He was jolted out of his thoughts by a sudden brightness in the car as his wife's station wagon pulled up beside him. He reached for his case, got out of the Volkswagen and slipped into the right hand seat of the station wagon beside her. He leaned over and kissed her cheek.

"I guess it's a dead battery," he said in greeting.

They drove in silence for several blocks. Charles was grasping for some way to broach the subject of money. For years he had told his wife very little about their finances, they were his responsibility and she never pushed him about it.

"I've been thinking about our trip..." he began.

"So have we," she interrupted him. "The boys are really excited. Michael has been reading up on scuba diving and he wants ..."

He cut in, "That's just it ... the boys, I mean. I don't think either one can afford to lose two weeks of school right now."

His wife did not answer immediately. When she did, she remained looking straight ahead, concentrating on the road. "You may be right, Charles, but isn't it a little late to think of that? After all we're almost all set to go."

"Well get unset!" he snapped at her.

"You don't have to get angry," she said, turning to look at him.

"Keep your eyes on the road, damn it."

She said nothing for several minutes and then asked in a soft voice, "Did anything happen at the office today?"

"No, nothing happened at the office," he shot back at her. "It's just time someone around here began thinking a little more practically."

"Practically?" There was a touch of hurt in her voice.

"Yes, practically. Every time I turn around we're up to our asses in something that doesn't make any practical sense—like this trip." He knew that if he stopped now he would never find a way to tell her, so he plunged on.

"And it's not only the trip, it's a lot of other things. The carpeting for the den. I think that was unnecessary. What you pay that cleaning woman for the work she does is a crime, and all those lessons, golf, tennis, guitar, between you and the boys, we're keeping half the instructors in Darien alive."

"I never realized you were against the lessons," she said, "but you never mentioned money problems before."

Charles was on the defensive now. Just the sound of the words 'money problems' made him cringe. "I didn't say we were having money problems. I said it's time we acted more practically."

"What do you want me to do?" she asked.

Charles was beginning to burn inside. He wanted to grab his wife and shake her, make her understand. Why couldn't she see that every word he was saying to her was a blow to him—a bad mark against his record as a provider?"

"Do?" he repeated. "I don't want you to do anything." Suddenly, he felt drained. It would be so much easier if she fought back, he thought.

They were nearing the house now, and Pat took one hand off the steering wheel and patted Charles' leg. "I guess we can put the trip off until Easter. That way the boys won't miss any school."

They pulled into the driveway. She started to get out when he reached for her arm. "It does make more sense to hold off for a while, doesn't it?" There was almost a plea in his voice.

"I guess it does," she answered, but there was no conviction in her voice. "I was going to give you a preview showing tonight of the two new bathing suits I bought for the trip. Now I guess that can wait too."

Bitch...rotten bitch...he thought. What are you doing, getting even? No trip, no fuck, is that it? He let go of her arm and got out.

Later that evening, after his wife had gone to bed, Charles sat alone by the fireplace in the den. He leaned down and poked half-heartedly at the glowing logs.

Suddenly, the red embers shot up into flames. He sat back in the chair and watched as the small triangles of fire quickly traveled the length of the logs, warming his feet and hands.

What do I do now? he thought, and reached for his glass of Scotch and water sitting on a table beside the chair. The vacation was a promise and it was also a symbol of what a successful provider did for his family. The canceling of the trip was the same as canceling their lifestyle. But the money just wasn't there any more, or at least not enough of it. He knew the day was coming, he hadn't realized it would get here as soon as it did. He could feel himself being crushed by the weight of it.

He could probably sell some stocks, but they were for the boys' education. He could borrow money, but when would he repay it? What do I do now? The question remained long after the fire died and left him staring at the cold grey ashes.

TUESDAY, FEBRUARY 22

Peter Mandel lay back with one arm behind his head looking up at the ceiling, listening to Sharon Hiller as she sighed contentedly. Their lovemaking had been direct and urgent. There was no coy ritual. The mating dance had been performed, but the music was rapid. She was demanding. At first he had been puzzled, then gradually the surprise turned to delight, and the delight gave way to his own demands. Both their demands had erupted finally in a synchronous, physical explosion, an earthquake complete with slowly diminishing aftershocks.

Now, lying together, in the first quiet moments, she felt drained, but alive, physically tired yet mentally awake—more alive and awake than she had felt in a long time. She wanted to talk now. He wasn't ready. He was spent, euphoric, playful. He wanted to tease her.

"Sharon, could you answer one question for me?"

"If I can."

"You're a responsible woman. Right?"

She offered no answer.

"You're a wife and mother. Right?"

She paused again. The words seemed to have a special meaning. Finally, she answered quietly.

"So... ?"

"I want to know how you do it? What do you tell Clayton?"

"What difference does it make?" She was defensive.

"I don't know." He lifted himself on to his side, facing her, his head propped on his hand. "We've known each other for a year, ever since you came to work for the network. When we went out of town together we knew something would happen. Nights like that were inevitable. I'm a horny bachelor and you're a bored, frustrated lady, out of the house for the first time in years. Sure it's going to happen. We let it happen. We wanted it to happen. I just wonder what kind of bullshit you feed them at home to get away with this."

"You mean when a guy says he's working late and goes and gets laid it's one thing, but when a woman says it, it's something else. Is that what you mean?"

"Don't get uptight."

"Oh, don't worry. I'm not. I just think that under all that horny bachelor shit you're hiding a shred of gallantry."

In response, he flicked his tongue out and touched her nipples. She shivered.

"That's not fair," her voice had dropped an octave.

"Do you think dragging me here and raping me was fair?" he demanded.

"It was not rape. It was two consenting adults."

"I was brought here under false pretenses. You said you wanted to talk. Is this your idea of talk? You know how easy a make I am. You took advantage of me."

"Um huh, I certainly did." Her smile was wide, self satisfied.

For a moment they were quiet. The room was bathed in a grey-pink glow from one small lamp on the dresser. The evening traffic sounds filtered up to the windows, asking to be heard.

He snuggled against her breasts. She stroked his hair and let her fingers idly trace a line across his shoulder.

"I've been offered a bigger job by the network," she said finally.

He turned and bent his head back to look at her. "That's terrific," he said.

"They want me to go to California to work for at least three months—maybe longer."

"Aren't you pleased?"

"Yes, and scared."

"Nonsense, there's nothing to be afraid of, you can do it. The writing you've done on my shows is good."

"It's not the work I'm scared of. It's the change, the new career, the big chance."

"Isn't this what you wanted? You keep saying you want to cut loose and do your thing."

"It's my chance, yes."

"Then do it." He turned over onto his stomach, supporting his head on his hands.

"I want to do it, but it's going to turn my whole life upside down."

"You can handle it."

"It's easy for you to say. You could pick up tomorrow, go to North Dakota and become a cowboy. Who'd care?"

"You would."

"Only until I found another apartment to sneak up to after work."

Suddenly she became serious. "This offer to go to the coast is make or break for me. I can't pretend any more. Do I really want out? I have a dead marriage that refuses to get buried. I have two little girls that I love but who are strangling me. If I say no to this chance, then I might as well go home and bake bread. If I say yes, do I cut all the strings, Clayton, the girls, the house?"

"Me?"

"Probably even you."

"This is deep."

"Maybe after a while, if I'm fairly successful and doing some good writing, I'll come back for the girls."

"That might be tough."

"I don't think so. Clayton is selfish, and his mother would push him to get rid of them since they mess up her house. It would be a short time for the girls, and then I would want them with me. I really would."

"Why not cut out and take them now?"

"Too complicated. I'm supposed to go out and go to work. With them I would have to worry about cooking, cleaning, schools, clothes. It's too much. It would be terrific if I could afford to rent a big place, hire a nanny and do my thing while someone else worries about the nuts and bolts."

"So why not do it that way?"

"Without money? The minute I leave, Clayton takes me off his payroll. I'm on my own. Suddenly there's rent, food, the whole package for me, the girls. There's no way I could swing it. What the network is willing to pay me doesn't include this other very complicated lifestyle."

"Isn't there any other way?" he asked. "Can't Clayton lend it to you? Repayable in about four hundred years?"

"No, I won't ask him for a cent. I can't."

"That's too bad. How much of yourself can you put into your writing wondering what the girls are up to?"

"Well, that's the way it's going to have to be unless I can come up with some way to rob a bank."

Peter lay back again with his arms behind his head. "No matter what. I'm sorry I'm going to lose you," he said.

"Hey," she answered quickly, "we're a number. We can't go cold turkey. Even if I do go. I'll see you here, you'll see me there. Who knows, we may go on forever."

"Until some producer dangles a film deal in front of you."

"She sat up and rolled off the bed. She stood next to it looking down, her legs slightly spread, her hands on her hips. She was angry, and he knew it.

"You're a prick, Mandel. You think that I jumped into your bed because you're a producer. Well, bullshit on that. I needed someone and you were there. I still need someone and you're good for me, damn it." She was fighting to keep back the tears.

"I'm sorry. It was a dumb remark. You know I didn't mean it. I was trying to be funny." He reached for her. She sniffed and her look softened to one of sadness. "When do you have to give the network an answer?" he asked.

"In a few weeks."

"Did they tell you what they wanted you to do?"

"Two projects. One is working on scripts for stuff that's on the air now and the other is really a come-on."

"What's that?"

"Take a swing at a made-for-TV movie script."

"Your own or an adapt?"

"My own. They know my little passion for mystery and suspense, so they said give them an outline of something in that line. If they like it, they'll ask for a script."

"Well, do you have anything?"

"I didn't until last week."

"What happened last week?"

"Don't you remember? The remark that Claudia made."

"What remark?" he asked.

"You know, the thing she said about a crime not being a crime."

"I don't know, was I supposed to think about it?"

"Come on, didn't that intrigue you at all? That someone could commit a crime and no one would know about it?"

"I suppose. But I'm not really sure what she was talking about. I don't see how you could use it."

"It's the beginning," she said.

As quickly as it had come, her sadness was gone. Instead she was pensive. All she needed was a push, some head start on an idea and she could go to work. Almost, without thinking, she sat down on the bed and was brought back to the present by Peter pulling her down beside him.

WEDNESDAY, FEBRUARY 23

A light mist was falling as Claudia arrived at the Partridge Galleries on Madison Avenue and crossed quickly under the green and white-striped canopy that extended from the curb to the ornate brass and wood door.

Once inside, she was escorted to a small elevator that carried her slowly to the third-floor office of the gallery owner, Harry Partridge, Jr. The tall, thin young man who rose to greet her from behind his desk was the grandson of the gallery's founder and bore a striking resemblance to the gaunt-faced man in the portrait hung over a couch against the far wall.

Although Harry, Jr. bore a physical resemblance to his grandfather, his business practices were decidedly different. In the pursuit of art he was unscrupulous. If the object was something he had to have, he often closed his eyes to the ethics his father and grandfather before him had so steadfastly maintained. Auctioneers could be bribed or threatened, private sellers browbeaten into accepting offers scaled directly to their financial needs. If Harry Partridge, Jr. told one of his important clients that he could deliver at a specified price, he made the delivery as promised. Harry Partridge, Jr. was highly successful and universally disliked. Claudia Betancourt did not relish doing business with him, but he had been responsible for many of the pieces in her collection, and a call from his office usually aroused sufficient curiosity to bring her quickly, if not willingly.

He took her coat and hung it in a closet near the door and walked to a small bar where he poured two glasses of brandy. She accepted the crystal snifter and remained standing while he returned to the desk.

"I dragged you out of that nasty museum into the cold for a very good reason," he said. The smile spread across his face.

"I'm sure you did, Harry. I'm anxious to hear why." The flat tone of her voice hid any anxiety.

From the top drawer of his desk, he took a photograph and laid it on the blotter. "Recognize this?" he asked.

Claudia walked to the desk and looked down at the picture. Her eyes brightened. "The Osiris scarab," she said, trying to keep the surprise out of her voice. The picture showed a gold ring on which a beetle, carved in black stone, sat amid a cluster of colored stones. Claudia knew that every second she spent staring at the photograph betrayed her interest, but she was helpless. The ring was fascinating.

"Yes, yes, indeed. The Osiris scarab."

The ritual game had begun. Claudia was the fish and Partridge was the fisherman. The picture was his bait.

"How do you like it?" he asked expectantly.

"Beautiful," she said. "The detail in the beetle is beautiful."

"I knew you'd recognize it," he said. "Only a few true connoisseurs would recognize what a rare treasure we have here."

"Do I take it that it might be for sale?" She knew the question was ludicrous, but she did not want to show the emotion that was building inside of her.

"It might be, if we can get it authenticated in Switzerland and brought here to the States."

"That would be interesting," she said, proud of having used the most noncommittal word she could think of.

"Is it something you might bid on?" It was his ludicrous question.

"That depends on several things."

"And they are?"

"The authentication. The number of bidders. The price and how my husband feels about it."

"Oh, yes, dear Maurice. And how is he?"

"Busy, as usual."

"Not too busy to take part in our little auction, I hope. That is, if he wants to."

The gallery owner was testing his fish. If Claudia was hooked, she would find a way to act with or without her husband.

"How many know about this? I mean, prospective buyers?" she asked.

"Probably three, at most four."

"Any museums?"

"I'm afraid your own Metropolitan knows. Miriam Gottfried has ears everywhere. She hasn't said anything to me in an official capacity, but I'm sure the minute we hear from Switzerland I will get a call and an offer."

Claudia turned from the desk and walked across the thickly carpeted room to the couch. She sat down, took the case and lighter from her purse and lighted a cigarette. This was the moment in the game when she had to be careful. Harry Partridge was an expert. He set his prices on the look in a client's eye or the tone of the voice. The highs and lows in this price war depended on her ability to playact.

He had teased her about handling Maurice but that was an obvious ploy. The museum was a different complication. She wanted the ring, and Harry Partridge knew it. The remark about Miriam Gottfried was a test. If Miriam wanted it, that made it all the more desirable. But did Partridge know that?

"You know that I could be accused of conflict of interest if I bid against the museum?" she said, putting a touch of humor into her voice.

He shrugged his shoulders and spread his hands apart, palms up. "A moral issue and almost unheard of in our little world....eh?"

She had to express herself carefully. It would require a fine line drawn between real interest and mere curiosity.

"Well, not to waste any more of our time," she said, as she tapped out her cigarette and rose from the couch. "Everything is premature at this point, but I would appreciate you doing one thing for me."

"And what is that?" He, too, rose, and walked to the closet.

She waited until he had helped her into her coat. "If the ring is authenticated. I'm sure you'll hear from the museum. Before you answer them. I'd like a chance to consider a bid. By then I will have talked to Maurice, and we can decide if we want it and how much we're willing to spend."

He held her arm as they walked to the door. "That's fair enough. I'll certainly do it. You'll hear from me. Give my regards to Maurice."

He closed the door gently behind her and smiled up at the portrait over the couch. "Well, grandpa," he said aloud, "I think we've hooked a fish—a big fish."

On her way out of the gallery's main lobby, Claudia paid little attention to the crowd of people waiting to go into the evening auction. Off to one side, a tall, heavyset man, wearing a tan raincoat and holding a soft tan rain hat and brown leather gloves, watched her exit with interest.

A few minutes earlier, the tall man in the raincoat had given Harry Partridge's secretary an envelope. In it were ten twenty-dollar bills. The money was in exchange for information, and the information had to do with Claudia Betancourt. The man in the raincoat had asked what Harry Partridge had offered to Claudia, and since the secretary added considerably to his income by knowing what the gallery's prominent clients were up to, he was in a position to answer his questioner.

The man who had waited in the lobby followed Claudia outside. The direction she took on foot, down 76th Street towards Park Avenue, satisfied him that she was going home. He waited until she disappeared into the darkness altogether. Then he entered the nearest bar and took out his phone.

* * *

Barnard Simms had been assistant to the curator since Miriam Gottfried arrived some five years back. Like everyone else on her Staff, he lived and worked in fear of the gaunt, grey-haired tyrant who ran the department of Egyptology as a personal fiefdom.

His summons to her office that afternoon forced him to participate in another of her inquisitions concerning the preparations being made for the Golden Age of

Egypt exhibit. The cross-examination continued until the ringing of her telephone provided blessed relief. The instrument in her weathered hand now replaced him as the target for her cold interrogation.

She spat questions into the telephone, knitting her thick, grey eyebrows, and listened to the lengthy answers while staring at Barnard Simms with dark eyes set in deep sockets. Her fingers drummed impatiently on the desk top.

"Yes, that is fine and you will continue to call me. Yes. Anything else that is important. Yes. But you must be discreet, do you understand? She must not know of your interest." There was the slightest trace of an accent in her speech, a lingering reminder of her German birth and early training at the University of Berlin.

Again, a pause. She listened, stared at Simms and drummed the desk.

"All right. Goodbye."

She replaced the telephone slowly. The tight skin around her mouth wrinkled as she pursed her lips.

"It seems, my dear Barnard, that we have a traitor in our midst." She did not look at her assistant as she continued. "A Judas is trying to outmaneuver me for the purchase of a small item I wish to add to my collection."

Dr. Miriam Gottfried never referred to the museum's collection. Officially, she was acting in the museum's behalf, using public funds, but in her mind it was always her money, for her collection.

"Do you know who it is?" Barnard Simms asked, grateful that her attention and venom were aimed in another direction.

"Yes. I know."

For a second, Simms thought he saw a sparkle in her eyes. My God, he thought, what would happen if she smiled? Her skin is so tight it would split, like a grape.

"Yes. I know," she repeated. "And I think it is time that I rid myself of a sore that has been festering since I came here."

She got up from the desk and walked to a wall lined from floor to ceiling with bookshelves. She moved slowly down a shelf of books, touching each one with her finger, her lips moving silently as she mouthed each title. Her finger stopped. She took a book from the shelf and began to turn the pages, her back turned to her assistant. She had found her place and began to read. After several minutes she stopped, closed the book over her finger, and returned with it to her desk.

"It is all here," she said.

"What is that?" Simms asked.

"The history of the trinket our disloyal friend is trying to get. It's all here."

She sat down, deep in thought, again ignoring the visitor to her office. After several minutes she looked up.

"I think we are through for now, Barnard. I will see you tomorrow. Goodnight."

Without waiting for him to leave, the curator opened the book again. The page bore a photograph which she stared at for a long time. It was the picture of a ring, and the caption under it read *Osiris Scarab*.

FRIDAY, FEBRUARY 25

In the days that had passed since the four had met at Sirocco, Sharon Hiller had made several false starts on the broadcast script. The reference books cluttering her small office told the histories of the kingdoms of Egypt, but they failed to produce the theme—the dramatic focal point for her narrative.

She, like Peter Mandel and Charles Green, had received a floor plan of the exhibition hall. She sat staring at it glumly, fascinated by the priceless treasure and frustrated by her failures with the script. She turned, picked up the phone, and called Peter. He agreed, this time, to call Claudia and suggest another meeting at Sirocco.

"I guess you better call Charles," he had said. "I can tell him more about the size of the television crew and some other arrangements."

Each had come to the restaurant tonight unwilling to admit, even to themselves, the extent to which the subject had been on their minds. Tonight's conversation, sprinkled with Charles' sour commentary and Peter's good-natured sarcasm, seemed strained. The laughter, what little there was of it, was forced. They seemed more like actors reading from a script. Their business talk was perfunctory.

Peter estimated the number of cameras and men to operate them, while Charles made notes in a small pad.

"We'll have to run cables from a control unit parked in the rear courtyard," Peter said.

"I'll get you a parking permit," Claudia answered flatly.

"Better make it three," he said. "There'll be two equipment vans."

For nearly thirty minutes, they had avoided admitting that there was something else they wanted to talk about.

The soft notes of the piano sent Sharon's mind back to the conversation of nearly two weeks ago. She was like a child wanting an adult to repeat a favorite story, and like a child she feared embarrassment if she asked. Finally, when business talk had been exhausted, she could no longer contain herself. Trying to be offhand and casual, she said in a slightly amused manner, "I've given it all the thought I'm going to."

Her remark was met with apprehensive stares. "Given what thought?" Peter asked.

"Claudia's riddle," Sharon said.

There was a sigh of relief from Charles' corner. He hid behind his raised drink.

"Oh, that," Peter said nonchalantly. "I'd forgotten." He did not sound convincing.

"Well, just to remind you," Sharon said. "Claudia asked us how a crime could be committed without a crime actually taking place?"

"And the answer was, if no one knew it had happened, then it never happened," Charles spoke from behind his glass.

"I'm lost," Peter shrugged. "It's too deep for me."

"What about it, Claudia?" Sharon asked. "Could you be more specific?"

"We were talking about the exhibition and what would happen if something disappeared," Claudia said.

"Not disappeared," Sharon corrected. "Walked out."

"Well, yes, walked out," Claudia continued. "I merely said that there would be no commotion if nothing was missing."

"That's it," Sharon said. "How could something walk out or disappear and not be missed?"

"If it looked to everyone as if it was still there," Claudia looked across the table into the faces of Sharon and Peter, She was greeted by puzzled stares.

"I think I understand." Charles had put his drink on the table, and was staring intently at his fingernails. "If someone wanted to take a statue or something from the museum, they could get away with it if they put something in its place."

Charles looked up at their intent faces. "The so-called undetected crime, as you put it, would go unnoticed only until someone looked closely. If that happens immediately, your criminal has the whistle blown on him right away."

"Not if the thing they left behind looked a lot like the thing they took," Sharon said. Suddenly her eyes opened wide and she slapped the benchseat beside her. "That's what you were talking about when you mentioned the robbery at the gem museum."

Claudia nodded as Sharon continued. "I remember the story now. Someone replaced one of the big diamonds with a paste duplicate, and the switch wasn't discovered until long after the exhibit closed. The fake stone was tested because they were going to cut it up or sell it or something. Isn't that it?"

"Yes, that's the story," Claudia said. "I'm surprised you remembered it. It never got much press. The museum was embarrassed, especially since they never got the stone back."

"It caught my eye because I thought it might have the makings of a good story," Sharon said. "I still do."

"But how does the puzzle apply to this exhibit?" Peter asked.

Charles answered before Claudia could begin. "Something could be taken from the exhibit and go unnoticed, at least for a little while, if the thief replaced it with something that looked like it. Am I right, Claudia?"

"Yes, exactly, Charles," Claudia said.

"But this exhibit isn't diamonds that all look alike," Sharon said. "Each of these pieces is different."

"That's right," Peter said. "You couldn't take a gold statue and leave a wooden Indian in its place, and where could you find a dagger that even comes close to the one in the catalogue?"

"You could," Claudia said flatly. "If you were serious, you could find what to leave behind."

"Where?" The question came from the others.

"Right here," Claudia said. She reached into her pocketbook and took out several folded sheets of paper which she spread open on the table. They looked like pages torn from the exhibit catalogue, but in this case, each glossy page contained only one color photograph of a golden object. There were ten pages in all.

Sharon reached across and took one while Charles and Peter watched her. They seemed reluctant to pick up a page themselves. She finished reading and whistled softly.

"It says here," she began, "that this candle holder is a replica of the one in the Golden Age exhibit. That it's made of ten-carat gold while the original is pure. In size and color it's an exact duplicate including precisely positioned dents and scrapes and that a chemical test is the only way to tell the difference. This piece is being sold through the Metropolitan Museum Art Reproduction Department at selected museums and jewelry stores throughout the country. And, get this, it states that this little number is made to retail for five thousand, yes, folks, five thousand dollars."

Peter had listened intently. Now he shook his head, "No shit. Five thousand. What the hell is the real one worth?"

"Insured for three hundred thousand," Charles said. "The fake is a bargain, isn't it?"

"What are these things, Claudia?" Sharon asked, pointing at the sheets of paper spread on the table.

"They're pages from a catalogue we'll send to everyone who's a member of the museum, and members of other museums. We also arranged to have it sent to the mailing list of Tiffany's and several other stores whose customers might like to own one of these pieces."

Peter and Charles reacted as if a curse had been lifted from the sheets of paper. They each took one to read.

"Hey, there's a dagger," Peter said. "And it's only thirty-five hundred."

"Here's a gold collar for only twelve hundred," Charles said.

Sharon placed a page gently on the table and looked at Claudia. "Here's your favorite," she said. The picture was the same as the cover of the original catalogue. It was the cat-headed goddess, Sekhmet. "I'm afraid this one goes for seventy-five hundred. Too bad," she laughed. "I was thinking of two for bookends."

The chatter subsided. They did not talk again until a waiter had approached, taken their drink order and brought it to the table. Charles picked up his fresh drink and saluted Claudia.

"Here's to you for coming up with a non-crime." He took a long drink. "The problem is, it would take a rich thief to do it." Charles looked as if his own remark had surprised him. "I take it back. This thief would only be making a short-term investment." Again, his own statement silenced him. He closed his eyes and for an instant saw a glowing log. The log was burning in his den fireplace, and he was there once more feeling lost, afraid, and desperate to return to that comfortable time when money was never a problem, when the checkbook and the day-to-day savings account were always there to cover the clothes or vacations or whatever minor extravagance Pat and the boys discovered. Earlier in the evening, as he had half-listened to the conversation around the table, he had thought ahead to when they would get up to go home and had hoped Peter would pick up the check again. The thought had disgusted him. Charles Green wasn't like that. His thoughts returned to the present. God, how simple Claudia made it all sound. You invest a few thousand dollars and walk away with a few hundred thousand. Almost without being aware of his own voice, he began asking questions.

"Are those pieces for sale now?" he asked. "And if you had one and did what you said you could, how would you turn it into money. Fast. Big money?"

"You said they were worth three hundred thousand. You're the one who set the price," Sharon answered sharply.

"That's the insurance money that would go to the museum," Charles said. "But don't forget, the museum doesn't even know anything is missing."

"That's right," Sharon said. "How do you turn your little trick into a profit?"

They turned towards Claudia. The answer that came to her immediately was not one she wanted to share. As she began talking, a picture of the small, safe like cabinet in her library flashed through her mind. It was not empty as it was in reality. Now the small fluorescent bulb shone on a gold statue of a woman with the head of a cat.

"You'd look for an unethical dealer, tell him to find a customer, and decide on an asking price," Claudia answered quickly.

"Is it that easy?" Sharon asked.

"There are dealers and there are buyers. Yes, it would be easy."

Charles picked up one of the sheets of paper and studied it. After reading the description several times he threw it back on the pile. "Suppose you didn't try to sell it? Suppose you told the insurance company what you had done? Then what?"

He pointed a stubby finger at the picture on the table and continued. "I'll tell you. The insurance company would find out that the piece in the museum wasn't real. No one would want to go public with the information, so the company would settle with whoever took it. That's what would happen."

Charles leaned back feeling and looking satisfied. Claudia might know all about crooked art sales, he thought, but he knew how insurance companies worked. "If the asking price was two hundred thousand, the company would feel it had a bargain, and would very quietly pay up."

"Everyone wins, right Charlie?" Peter said. "The museum gets the piece back, the insurance company saves a hundred grand and the thief gets two hundred. The company writes off the two hundred as a loss, so it really comes out of Uncle Sam's pocket."

"That sounds easier," Sharon said.

Peter and Charles began exploring details of this last scheme, but Sharon lost the drift of the conversation. Her mind had flown off to California where she suddenly became a young, curly-haired mother, sitting by a sliding glass door, overlooking a swimming pool. In the pool, two little girls splashed and played under the watchful eyes of a white-uniformed nanny. No sounds came through the double-thick, glass doors to disturb the work of the mother—the famous novelist and screenwriter who lived and worked there.

Sharon was silently putting together a budget. What would it cost, she wondered, to rent a house for one year and hire a full-time housekeeper-nanny? If the rest of her expenses could be covered by her salary, what was she talking about in real live dollars? The house might be three thousand a month and the woman, one thousand. That's forty-six thousand for the first year. But things cost a lot more in California, she thought, and I don't want to strangle myself. No worries about money for one year. Just time to write.

"Fifty thousand dollars," she said aloud, startling everyone. "That's what it would take. Fifty thousand."

"What would take fifty thousand?" Peter asked.

Sharon became embarrassed by the stares. "Just doing some mental arithmetic," she said. "I'm a piker, I guess. If I had one of those pieces. I'd ask for fifty thousand dollars. That's all I need. I really wouldn't know what to do with the rest."

Charles and Peter both slapped their foreheads.

"I can't believe this naive broad," Peter said. "What are you trying to do, save the insurance company money? You might as well go all the way. Fifty, a hundred, two hundred, what's the difference? You can't be half-pregnant. If you're caught, it's goodbye anyway, no matter what the price."

"Speaking of getting caught," Sharon said. "What kind of a crime is this?"

"Robbery. What else?" Peter answered.

"I don't think so," Charles said. "Robbery, I believe, is done at gunpoint. This is burglary."

"I think you're wrong," Peter shot back. "Burglary has to do with breaking-in, and this isn't a break-in, is it?"

"But what about the ransom, or selling stolen goods? Aren't those different crimes?" Sharon asked.

"That's grand larceny, or extortion. I'm not sure which," Charles said.

"Well, whatever the legal terms, this isn't small, is it? If you get caught, it's more than a lecture and a fine," Sharon said.

"A lecture, a fine and twenty years," Peter concluded.

Claudia listened to the conversation with growing impatience. Finally she cut into them. "Are you finished joking?"

For an instant they each felt angry. They wanted to protest that they weren't finished. That they needed this forced foolishness to keep from saying what was really on their minds. They were more at ease talking about the scheme as if it were a game, not a reality.

Claudia obviously felt different. She looked around the table and, in turn, they met her cold glance. It was a moment of decision. Right now, the slightest remark could change the course of their relationship. Claudia could scoop up the papers and end it. Peter could call their attention to the muted melody coming from the piano. Sharon could mention the script, or Charles could call for another drink. Anything foreign could break this fragile concentration, but no one spoke. No one wanted to speak.

At what point does a game stop being a game? At what point does interest become a commitment? If, in looking back, any one of them had asked the same questions, the answer would have to be now, this moment, at the table in Sirocco, on the night they first saw the pictures from the catalogue. That was when it became a conspiracy. At the precise moment when Claudia bluntly brought them back across the line to reality, and by silent acquiescence they crossed the line together.

Claudia had to know if her fish were hooked. She was sure they each had tasted the bait and found it appealing. She knew they were toying with the hook. In order to make them swallow it, she had to convince them of how good it tasted and how easily it would go down.

"Ransom or sale, my friends," she said. "What you see here," she gestured at the pictures, "are ten items whose worth is measured in millions. Not the few thousand dollars it would cost to buy them, but the millions their original counterparts represent."

Her voice still held an edge, but it was an edge softened by the need to soothe them, to enlist their help. Gently, almost secretively, Sharon sought Peter's hand on the bench between them. She grasped in tightly. Charles clasped his own hands together on the table in front of his drink. He squeezed them together, released them, squeezed them together again. Claudia played with the photos, turning them to glow in the light then leaned over the table. The others came forward almost imperceptibly, drawn to her.

"It is ridiculously easy," she began. "I've seen these pieces. It's virtually impossible to tell them from the originals. And I saw them in the bright lights of the photography studio. In the darkness of the museum, there is no way that anyone could tell. Once the switch was made, the change would be undetected for as long as you want. Forever, perhaps."

"That's all fine ..." Charles found that his voice was not totally under his control. It cracked, then squeaked. He cleared his throat and began again. "That's all fine once a switch is made, but how do you arrange it? How do you pick one thing up and put another down and then just walk away?"

In her fantasy, Claudia had watched herself walk up to a display pedestal and lift up the goddess Sekhmet. From somewhere another goddess materialized and she placed it on the stand. Just as easily and mysteriously she found herself in her library holding her newly acquired statue.

She looked at Charles. "How? Sometime between the morning that the exhibit arrives from the airport and the official opening to the public, there's going to be ample opportunity. I'm sure of that."

Charles looked at her doubtfully.

"If making an exchange is as easy as that," Peter said, "it looks to me like you can do all ten of these." He pointed to the pictures.

"Oh, come on, Peter," Sharon said. "Be reasonable."

"Sharon is right," Claudia said. "There is the problem of coming and going. Ten would be out of the question." She thought for a moment and then said, "Four or, at most, five."

Charles seemed shocked. "Are you serious?" he asked, staring in amazement at Claudia. "At the gem museum, one diamond was taken and that's tiny compared to any of these things."

They waited for Claudia to answer. Only two objects interested her, and neither one would be sold or ransomed. But she could not admit this to them. She had to make it a grand design with all their needs in mind. To this end she began to describe a plan which was part truth and part fiction. "There is one piece that I want very much, and I do not intend to sell it. If we limit ourselves to four pieces, then only three would be sold."

"For how much?" Charles asked. He seemed to have forgotten the difficulty in removing more than one piece.

"The insurance company says three hundred thousand for each one," Peter said, looking at Charles.

"That's a negotiated number to keep the premium from getting out-of-hand," Charles answered. "There is no real value. That's up to the buyer and seller. What will they bring?" he asked Claudia.

Claudia thought for a minute. "I'm sure the three pieces, sold individually or as a package, would bring no less than three or four million. Maybe more."

She let the number roll out of her mouth and fill the air around the table. The results were as she had expected. Everyone drew back and gaped. Now all she had to do was reinforce their need. "Even if they bring only a million dollars, that might work with only three people sharing it."

No one spoke.

Claudia sat back, satisfied, and signaled to the waiter to repeat the drink order.

When the drinks came, they raised their glasses in a wordless toast. No one voicing the project or its future.

Peter stirred. He would think back later and come to the conclusion that it was only the remoteness of it all that kept him from running in fear. The other three had real needs or, at least, what they thought were real needs. But what of himself? Big money? What for? A racing car? Flying lessons? A country house? These weren't needs, they were luxuries that he had lived and enjoyed life without. Perhaps it was the intrigue or the tantalizing possibility of being caught that hypnotized him into dismissing every logical and moral argument that came to mind. For whatever the reason, he had to know more.

"Do you have any idea how you're going to get four pieces in and out?" Peter asked.

Claudia had not given this any more thought than she had to when to do it. But again, she could not say so. "I've thought of several ways," she lied, "but none seem right. I'm open to suggestions."

Peter laughed aloud. "A fine gang we are. We don't know when and we don't know how, but we're ready to split the loot." Then he had a sudden inspiration. "Claudia," he said, "what do you know about the day of the broadcast? Will the museum be closed?" Claudia thought for a moment before answering. "The museum will be closed to the public because that's the day everything will be moved from the vaults to the exhibition halls to get ready for the opening."

"And that's the time we'll be setting up for the program," Peter added.

"Yes," Claudia said pensively. "There will be a lot of people. A lot of people milling about and commotion."

"Yes, ma'am," Peter said. "A perfect cover. With my people and the museum people moving in and out all day, the opportunities will be there."

"There might be a way for the TV crew to bring more things in and out than just cameras and lights," Sharon said.

Peter turned in his seat to look at her. "Wait a minute," he said, "I can't get anyone else involved." There was a note of surprised anger in his voice.

"I didn't mean it that way," Sharon said. "I just meant that there's going to be so much moving of equipment in and out of the museum, the crew might be a cover,"

"Oh, didn't know what you meant," Peter said apologetically. "You might have an idea there though," he said.

Claudia sat and listened, gratified. Her fish were writhing on the baited hooks, setting them deeper. But it was time to take the pressure off. Time to let them think about the rewards and savor the future. It would be unwise to push them any further now. There were too many weeks to go and too much time for them to change their minds. It was well that no real plan had been developed. That could come easily and in small doses over the next few weeks. In the meantime, she had things to do. Things that these people need not know about. It was time to go home.

Peter called for the check after Claudia announced that she had to leave. When the bill came, Charles tried unsuccessfully to take it, and when he realized what he had done, he smiled to himself. How different he felt now! The desperate sadness that had been with him when he came in was replaced with a tingle of excitement. When he stood up to leave, he no longer felt choked. The air seemed to rush into his lungs in a way that he had not felt in a long time. His step seemed lighter, too.

Charles was not alone. Sharon, too, felt different. She could almost tolerate the trip home and what she knew was waiting for her because there was an end in sight. The last day of her prison sentence was at hand. Claudia had come to her with a pardon in her hands. She wished she could stop at Peter's apartment before going home. That would really set the world right. No, tonight she would go home, take whatever they wanted to throw at her and hide in the den after they had all gone to bed. Yes, tonight, while it was all fresh and alive in her mind, she wanted to begin to put it all down on paper. Everything was coming together beautifully.

FRIDAY, MARCH 4

"Mr. Green, Mr. Edwards would like to see you."

Charles Green looked up from his desk. He had not been concentrating on the insurance plan with its columns of premiums, tax deductions and yearly equities. Concentration, he found, was growing more difficult every day, and a summons to Edwards' office was not what he wanted. He closed the folder, and as he did he became aware of the dampness on his hands, in his armpits and down his back.

"Just a minute," he called out in a loud voice. Then he saw the secretary who had called standing next to his desk and he gave her a sick smile as he stood up, took his jacket from the back of the chair, and started towards the corner office. Not too long ago, he thought, I would have gone in there without a jacket.

He threaded his way through the maze of desks in the large room to the glass-enclosed corner office. He hesitated for a moment, and went in.

As Charles' immediate supervisor, Donald Edwards received an override on the commissions earned by everyone on his sales staff, for a long time he had basked in the reflected glory and income of Charles Green. However, things were no longer as they had been. Donald Edwards once referred to the swimming pool he had built behind his home in New Jersey as the Charles Green Memorial Pond. They had all laughed at the remark. But now the time for jokes was past. It was time for hard management.

As Charles entered, Donald Edwards got up. He was well over six feet tall, thin, with a craggy face. A beardless, square-jawed Lincolnesque figure, with steel-rimmed glasses.

"Come in. Sit down, Charles." He gestured to a seat across from the desk. "I've been going over your 101." He patted the orange file on his desk. This was the income review kept for each man by the district manager and updated monthly. In it was a record of continuing commissions on existing business, new commissions and monthly salary withdrawals. Every six months, the salary was adjusted to compensate for the commissions earned. If commissions were up salary was increased, and one had to run just that much faster to keep the salary from going down six months later.

"It reads like a roller coaster, doesn't it?" Charles said more rhetorically than as a question.

"Not exactly, Charles. A roller coaster has its ups and downs. Granted, your earnings through the last few years are still good enough to keep you in the top five per cent of the country, but their trend line makes it painful to look ahead."

Charles tensed. "Well, you know my specialty, Don. The networks, and they're tough."

"I'm well aware of that, Charles."

"Hell, Don, there's no one else in the organization who would even touch the category."

"Perhaps it's time, Charles, that we gave someone else a crack at it."

The words fell like hammer blows. Before Charles could recover, Edwards went on. "I think for your sake you ought to take on a different category. Perhaps something a little easier."

Charles felt clammy. No matter how he phrased it, Edwards was offering him a demotion. How should he react? As he fought to sort out his options, he realized that Edwards was still speaking.

"It's not just a matter of income for the company. Please understand, it's for your own financial well being. Based on the business you've produced in the last six months, your salary draw has far exceeded your commissions. If I adjust your draw on April first to reflect your production, do you have any idea what you'll be earning?"

Charles offered no answer.

"Well Charles, I'm sorry to say that on April first you'll begin to drawing twenty-five percent less. That's quite a comedown from where you were just a year ago. But what I'm offering you is a chance to build that number back up to where it was...and quickly."

All that was sane and rational in Charles fought to have him accept Edwards' offer. Yet inside that sane and rational person was someone else—the same demon who made the sarcastic remarks when Charles wanted to say nothing.

"I'm afraid I can't accept another category, Don." The words were as much a surprise to Charles as they were to his boss. He wanted to remain quiet, but he continued.

"I've been a valuable asset to this company for a long time. I built the category up to the point where it was one of the most profitable in this office. Now I've hit a bad time and as soon as the goose stops laying those golden eggs the farmer gets all nervous. Well, I'll tell you it's not fair. Not fair at all."

"No one is blaming you for anything." Edwards' tone was soothing. He could see that Charles was emotionally overwrought, and he was embarrassed by the outburst. "We're trying to give you a safe harbor to ride out this economic storm."

The demon in Charles pushed him forward in his chair and made him grasp the edge of Edwards' desk with both his hands. He leaned even closer and looked directly into Edwards' eyes as he spoke. "I'll tell you what's really behind this. You're worried about your override. You don't give a damn about me. It's your own nest you're worried about."

Edwards was shocked. He leaned back, away from Charles, as he searched for an answer. "Now see here," he said levelly. "That is very unfair of you, and entirely untrue."

Charles interrupted him. "Oh, I can see the picture. You're tired of having just a swimming pool behind your house, and you've decided to put in a tennis court. Sure, that's it. You want a tennis court, and old Charlie, the old golden goose, isn't producing on command so you're all set to send him to the butcher. Well, I don't think I want to play your little game."

Donald Edwards stood up, a muscle at his jaw working, and squared his shoulders. When he spoke his voice was cold, detached.

"Your accusations are completely false. If you feel that way then perhaps you would be more comfortable at another company."

Charles' mind was crying out. What in God's name have I done? I've been carrying a chip around on my shoulder, but how did I let it come to this? He had jumped from the precipice and now in midair he wanted to turn around and fly back.

Thoughts rushed at him like waves, pushing him further and further away from the reality of Donald Edwards' office. He had been here dozens of times before. This was unreal. It would go away. His wife's image rushed at him. She was smiling, opening a Bloomingdale's box. Then it was his younger son in a scuba mask. Then it was only fragments that flew at him--his railroad commutation ticket, his handicap sheet on the locker room wall at the country club. Suddenly, they were gone. There was nothing except Donald Edwards standing next to his chair, his hand outstretched.

"I'm sorry our talk had to end this way, Charles. But you know, I think it is all for the best. Sometimes a change is needed. Some men dry up if they stay in one place too long. A change of scenery, new challenges, that's what's needed. There's no way in the world that I could say I'm happy to lose a man like you. You've done a job here, a good job, no, a great job but it's time to move on."

He took Charles' hand, which was limp and wet, and practically lifted him out of the chair. They took the few steps to the door together with Edwards' arm around Charles' shoulder. At the door Edwards reached down and opened it. His face was serious.

"I'm glad we took this step to clear the air. I think we will both sleep a little better now that it's all out in the open. You take your time deciding on your next move and please have anyone you want call me. I guess we can figure on an April first cut-off. That should make it nice and tidy." He dropped his arm, stepped back into his office and closed the door.

Charles stood outside Edwards' office door. His eyes scanned the large room, the people busy at their desks, talking on the phones, getting up to fetch a file. He did not belong here. They were working. He was unemployed. How quickly the fact took root.

He walked back to his desk and sat down. The rational Charles was fighting to take control. There was a lot to do now. Lists of people to call had to be made. Appointments for interviews had to be set up. He opened the top drawer of the desk and took out his personal phone book. He moved a yellow pad in front of him and opened the first page of the phone book. He stared at the page for several minutes and wrote nothing. He turned the page ... still nothing. After several more minutes, he closed the book, put it back into the desk drawer, got up and walked out of the office.

Had this scene been played a week before, Charles Green would have gone to the nearest bar and, in bitter despair, drunk himself into oblivion. This afternoon he walked slowly and in deep thought to Sirocco. Once inside this place that seemed to offer him familiar refuge, he stood at the bar and offered to buy a drink for the stranger next to him. It was not the behavior he would have expected from someone who had just been fired.

TUESDAY, MARCH 8

The two hours she had just spent with Peter after work had left Sharon feeling warm and contented. It took all her will power to dress and leave for home. If it weren't for the girls' dental appointments in the morning, she thought...shit! She really should have canceled them and stayed with Peter. In spite of the cold, she could still feel his mouth, his hands, the warmth of his body.

Now, standing in the station parking lot, her feet wet from the slush, her hands chapped and cold from the ice she had scooped from the windshield, she felt anger and frustration. Peter's apartment had become a haven. There she felt comfortable. Home was drudgery.

Inside the car, she stamped her icy feet in anger. Once the sluggish engine had started, she turned on the lights and the windshield wipers and continued to stare through the streaky triangle made by the dry rubber of the blades.

On a nice day, the drive from Green Haven Harbor to the train station took about fifteen minutes. Tonight, Sharon thought, she would be lucky to make it in twice the time. Grimly, she headed out of the lot.

This is the most god awful weather, she thought. God, I can't stand it. I think I'm starting to lose my mind. She began to sing out loud. "It Never Rains in Southern California ..." she fairly shouted.

It was almost thirty minutes later when she pulled up to the front door of the house. Fuck the car, Sharon thought as she defiantly disobeyed Clayton's rule about putting the cars in the garage. It can sit out front all night. And I hope it freezes.

Inside the hallway, she shed her hat, coat and boots and looked around for any kind of greeting. It came in the form of Sandy, the Scotch terrier. She knelt and petted him. "Where is everyone?" she said to the dog. "Where's Clay? Where's Fern and Debby?"

The dog ran towards the playroom, stopped, and waited for her to catch up. Sharon could hear the sound of the television coming from the den. She walked into the din. The TV was on and Clayton was stretched out on the sofa, fast asleep. She hesitated, then retreated and followed the dog into the playroom, where her older daughter, Debby, was sitting on the floor coloring, while the younger girl. Fern, was asleep on a pillow on the floor.

"Why aren't you in bed?" Sharon demanded of the older girl.

"Because we haven't had our dinner yet," the girl answered.

"Haven't had dinner?" Sharon repeated, her voice a high shriek.

The little girl nodded her head emphatically.

The Exhibit

Sharon ran into the kitchen. It was a mess. Dirty dishes were on the table, pots were in the sink. Food that should have been in the refrigerator stood on the counter tops. The stove was caked with whatever had boiled over during the day.

Her daughter had followed her into the kitchen. Sharon turned to confront her. "Debby, are you telling me the truth about not eating? Whose mess is this?"

"Honest, mom," she said, tears welling up in her eyes. "Me and Fern just had some crackers. Daddy and Grandma ate."

Sharon fought to calm down. "Debby, take Fern upstairs and get into your pajamas. Then come down and mommy will fix you something to eat. O.K.?" She turned and walked back into the den and stood next to the sofa with her hands on her hips.

"Clayton," she said in a tone loud enough to wake him. "What the fuck is going on here, Clayton?"

Her husband opened his eyes and looked at her. There was a woozy smile on his face. "Hi, Sharp... ," he started.

"Have you seen your daughters lately, sleeping beauty?" she broke in. "Have you looked at the kitchen lately? Have you done anything lately except lay on your back and drink?" she continued. "Oh, yes, you did eat dinner. You and your souse of a mother turned the kitchen into some kind of a pigsty. What about your kids? Did you think they were going out for dinner? Did you let the dog out? What would have happened if I hadn't gotten home tonight? Would you lie on this fucking couch until the girls starved to death? I don't see why I have to come home to this crap, night after night. You and your mother are as useless as ..." She turned and walked out. What was the use? This wasn't the first time, but soon, very soon, it would be the last. April fifth was right around the corner. She wondered if she'd survive that long.

THURSDAY, MARCH 10

Claudia Betancourt watched a small industrious spider stretch thin strands between a yellowed lampshade and a stone statue which stood on Miriam Gottfried's desk. It served her right, Claudia thought. But then Miriam Gottfried was the only person she could think of who would dare use an ancient Egyptian artifact as a paperweight, especially amid a pile of clutter.

As she sat waiting in the curator's dimly lighted office, wishing it was a tarantula that was building a home on Gottfried's desk, the curator strode into the room and immediately sat down at her desk.

She began rifling through a stack of papers. "How are you?" she asked, without looking up and immediately continued. "I've read your memos. Everything seems to be moving ahead with those television people."

Claudia waited, not sure if a reply was called for.

"I don't approve of this whole idea," she continued, "I'm certain you're aware of that." She looked up at Claudia over her half-rimmed glasses. "It's disruptive to the museum routine, and God only knows how destructive it may be with all those wires, cameras and clumsy men tripping about." Gottfried continued to look at Claudia with her head half bent over the desk. The lamplight threw shadows across her thin face, making her eyes look like empty sockets.

"These men are professionals," Claudia said irritably. After all, the museum had approved the broadcast months before. "They do this for a living. They've been in the White House, the Kremlin, Westminster Abbey. They're not about to destroy anything!"

"I hope you're right," Gottfried concluded, pleased at the edge in Claudia's voice. She took off her glasses and slowly set them on the desk. At the same time she looked up at Claudia, narrowing her eyes to adjust her focus.

After several seconds of silence she said, "I understand that you intend to bid on the Osiris scarab."

Claudia, who had been half watching the workings of the spider, was taken by surprise.

"The Osiris scarab?" she repeated, stalling for time. How had Miriam found out? Perhaps she was just on a fishing expedition.

"Come now, Claudia. The scarab is an enormous find. One of the best ever. I have undisputed proof that Harry Partridge has given you a chance to bid on it." Harry Partridge wouldn't have told her, Claudia thought to herself. He didn't even deal personally with the museum. It must just be a fishing expedition, she reminded herself, but Gottfried did seem to be very sure of her information.

"Wherever you got your information, Miriam, it's incorrect," Claudia replied crisply.

Miriam Gottfried's eyes turned mean. "You're bluffing. You know it and I know it. So we'll proceed from there. The scarab is being authenticated in Switzerland. Once its provenance is established, I would like you to tell Harry that you've reconsidered and do not wish to bid on it." Gottfried paused, letting her words sink in.

Claudia was fighting to control her anger. Then, as she opened her mouth to speak, Gottfried raised her hand.

"Let me finish. Should the provenance of the scarab be determined, it would be one of the greatest finds of the century. Utterly priceless...and you know what something like that would mean to the museum's collection. You must realize, Claudia, that if we bid on it, we will get it. The wealth of the Betancourt, or should I say the combined wealth of the Betancourt and the Fields, cannot compare with the wealth of the museum."

This last comment went through Claudia like a knife. The old woman was bringing her inherited wealth into it. She was rubbing a raw sore.

"Your bidding would only drive the price up," Gottfried continued, "and, as I said before, this is one battle you cannot possibly win. You could only make us pay more than is necessary."

She got up and walked around to the other side of the desk. "There is also something more important to consider here. You and Maurice are responsible only to yourselves. I, on the other hand, am responsible to the board of directors and the trustees of this museum. And, my dear Claudia, I really believe that art treasures like this scarab belong in museums where all can enjoy them, not shut up in the library of a private collector."

Claudia had heard enough. Her anger was about to surface. She began speaking in an icy tone. "You may be right about one thing. If we were to have an interest in the scarab, we could not outbid you. But don't start dragging out your so-called obligations to the museum or the board or the public! You have one obligation, to yourself! You're no different than I am. You have an all-consuming interest in Egyptian antiquities. The difference is that I can afford to own them and you can't, and that's what's eating you alive. You're jealous because you can't have them. You use the museum's money the same way I use my own. 'For the good of the public' is something you, and others like you, invented to camouflage your personal greed."

"That is your opinion." The curator shot at her, her voice raised in a way Claudia had never before heard. "I warn you. You are still an employee of this museum. Remember that. I believe the phrase is 'conflict of interest'."

Her eyes blazed in their deep sockets. "Should you buy this thing. I'll make sure you're not only removed from the Department of Exhibits, but from the museum entirely. I'll use my influence to make sure that you never work here or in any other museum ever again. I'll make you an outcast, a renegade in the art world. Believe me. No one will have anything to do with you!" The jealousy and hatred that had been held in check between these two women was now out in the open.

"I don't know where your information comes from," Claudia said, "but you may tell your source to watch closely. If the scarab proves authentic, I'll buy it. I'll hang it on a chain and dangle it in front of your nose, and dare you to do anything about it. You have pushed too far this time. I warn you...if you get in my way again."

The sentence was cut off by the ring of the telephone. Gottfried glared at the instrument and then at Claudia. After three rings she grabbed it from its cradle and shouted into it. "Yes ...hello ..."

The voice on the other end had a sudden quieting effect on the old woman. Her eyes focused on some point across the room. Her responses were softer. "Yes...I see...yes..."

Claudia stared at the grey-haired woman for several more moments. Then without saying any further, got up and walked out.

As she strode back to her office, debating whether to call Harry Partridge and tell him of the incident, another idea came to her. Miriam had said she'd have her removed from Exhibitions. Did that mean she could also have her removed from the Department of Egyptology? To do that, Gottfried would need to have proof of wrongdoing.

Proof! Where? Someone had once told her that all personal data was filed with the Personnel Department, and Miriam Gottfried kept the most trivial things about everyone in it. She looked at her watch. It was 7 p.m. No one should be around now. It was certainly worth a try.

THURSDAY, MARCH 10

The corridor leading to the Personnel Department was empty and silent. Overhead, the night lights burned dimly. Claudia's only fear was that she might run into a security guard. How could she explain what she was doing there if she did?

She reached the large walnut door and turned the knob. As she slowly pushed the door open, the hinge creaked. She stopped and listened. No voices. No footsteps. She slipped inside closing it quietly behind her.

The room had no windows. Its solid door cut off any chance of light or noise from the hallway. Claudia found herself enfolded in blackness, her eyes totally unable to distinguish the solid objects from the air itself. The flame from the cigarette lighter she took from her purse created enough of a glow to help her find her way about the room. As small as the glow was, she did not risk turning on even a desk lamp.

The filing cabinets at the rear of the room seemed to contain only correspondence and resumes. Nothing whatsoever to do with employment records. Those were undoubtedly kept somewhere else.

Against the opposite wall were four doors. Through previous visits, she knew the far two doors belonged to the director and her assistant. The third also bore a name, but next to the fourth a metal tag embedded in the wall read 'Records.' She tried the knob and found it locked. Damn! She should have known she couldn't just walk in, take what she wanted and leave. Nevertheless, the key had to be nearby, and judging from the type of lock, it was old and large. A quick check of the secretaries' desks yielded such a key. In a minute she had unlocked the door and stepped into the records room.

She felt safe enough to flick the light switch. The bright glow of a single bulb overhead forced her to shield her face with her hand while she looked about her. The large room was filled with floor to ceiling shelving where manila file after file was stored.

The active records seemed to be in a section by themselves and she found that the B's could be reached without using one of the awkward ladders. After a brief search she found the folder labeled *Betancourt/Fielding*. Curious, she thought. Why include her maiden name?

She sat down and began to read. At the back of the file were two envelopes. The first was marked 'Fielding' which she opened and read. It was a complete list of items her father's gallery had bought over the years including those for which the museum had competed.

The second envelope was marked 'confidential' and was sealed. Very carefully,

Claudia lifted the corners and worked her way to the tip. The envelope flap didn't open cleanly, but she hoped no one would notice. She pulled out the contents and began to read, becoming so absorbed that she failed to hear the footsteps coming from outside in the hall. She was oblivious to the creaking hinge of the door to the outer office. It was only the muffled sound of voices that brought her head up.

She froze. The voices continued, then stopped. She prayed that whoever it was could not see the light under the door. The waiting continued. She strained to pick up any other sound. Whoever they were, they were not moving about. Her heart raced. After what seemed an eternity, there were footsteps again. Then the click of a light switch and the dull thud of a door closing.

She sat listening, hoping the silence was permanent. After another moment she drew in a deep breath, picked up the letter from the table and began to read again. It was from Doctor M. Gottfried, addressed to Wallace Miller, Chairman of the Board, and was marked 'confidential'. It was the original letter, not a carbon, and it was undated. Claudia read with increasing wonder.

"As you know, as a condition of my employment, I reserved the right to employ people of my own choosing. Where possible, I have retained those previously employed in the Department.

One of these employees is Mrs. Claudia Betancourt. Mrs. Betancourt's private collection of ancient Egyptian art is world-renowned. And it is a given fact that the interests of the private sector of collecting are diametrically opposed to those of the public sector.

In my judgment, I feel I could not employ Mrs. Betancourt. However, based on the fact that she is currently assistant director of acquisitions, perhaps she is that rare breed of person who has learned to serve two masters.

After an investigation of her activities, I believe I can state unequivocally that Claudia Betancourt has, whenever possible, used her position to further her own private interests, and she has willfully deprived the museum of the right to preserve for posterity certain objects used in ancient Egyptian life.

Therefore, I feel that she should not only be removed from the Department, but should be refused the right to serve on any staff function since her activities can be labeled as nothing but treasonous. The attached documents fully support my this. I regret that this entire incident has occurred, but in the long run the department and the museum shall be better off."

Claudia reread the letter, then looked through the attached sheets of paper. A cold chill had taken hold of her. She couldn't begin to imagine how Gottfried had gathered the information. But she had, and it was quite damning. And worst of it all, Gottfried was right.

Claudia placed the letter in its envelope, but instead of returning it to the file, she put it in her purse. The file was returned to its original spot on the shelf. She turned off the light and stepped back out into the main office. The darkness was soothing and comforting. Gottfried was evil, there was no doubt about that in Claudia's mind. She had almost managed to destroy her—but what had stopped it? Perhaps Gottfried simply didn't want that type of embarrassment for the department.

Before opening the door to the hall, Claudia hesitated, held her breath and listened. There were no sounds. She stepped out, closing the door gently behind her, and began her walk down the corridor. She was deep in thought. The words in the letter appeared again, and her sense of chagrin heightened. Her footsteps grew faster and louder. She knew now, and for certain, that she was going to get even.

SATURDAY, MARCH 12

As her taxi crossed the Manhattan Bridge, Claudia realized she had never been in Brooklyn before. There had never been a reason to visit the borough. Now, on her way to a street with the unlikely name of Schermerhorn, she concluded that the most she could say was that she had flown over Brooklyn many times on her way into or out of LaGuardia Airport or JFK International.

The area she was entering was called Brooklyn Heights. It was close to the bridges spanning the East River between Brooklyn and Manhattan. The Heights had once been an elegant neighborhood of brownstones, hotels and apartment houses, and later had been a slum. It was now in the throes of a renaissance. Many new buildings had replaced the three-and four-story townhouses. Many of the inhabitants were young and creative and would have looked at home in Greenwich Village. Others were fixtures in the neighborhood, living out their lives on fixed incomes.

The taxi slowed, then stopped on a block of rundown townhouses to let its passenger out. Cars lined both curbs. Claudia threaded her way between two parked cars, and stood looking up at a building that was typical of the street. She shifted the carefully wrapped package in her hands, pushed open the rusted metal gate and started up the steps. Suddenly, from under the steps, a voice growled, "You Fleischman?"

Claudia stopped and looked over the railing, down into a face that did not match the deep, scratchy voice. The head was round and devoid of hair. The eyes, behind large round glasses, were also large and round. The nose was large and red, and the lips were pursed so that the mouth looked like a round hole.

Humpty Dumpty, Claudia thought.

"Yes, I'm Mrs. Fleischman," she answered.

"Come on down," the round ball said.

Claudia turned and retraced her steps, around the front stairs to a basement entrance. She followed the man down three steps into a basement room that obviously was both living quarters and workshop.

"Are you Mr. Roncalli?" she asked.

"I'm Roncalli. You like coffee?" He gestured to a stove in the back corner on which a percolator was bubbling. He was small, she saw now, hardly five feet tall and slightly hunched. The head was much too large for the small body, giving him the look of a comic strip gnome.

"No, thank you. I'd like to get down to business."

"Hey, coffee ain't gonna hurt. So you talk while I drink."

Claudia stood as the man waddled to the stove. As he paused over the coffee pot, she looked around at the furnishings.

The large room was low-ceilinged and smelled of the dampness that seeped from the raw concrete wall. An old coat of whitewash had long ago flaked away, leaving the sand-colored foundation streaked with dark water stains and mildew.

To one side was a minute kitchen with a four-legged gas stove and a chipped porcelain sink flanking a small refrigerator. Nearby was a table and four chairs that had, in better days, graced a dining room. The table stood on a rug that had started as an oriental. Years of feet treading on it had left it threadbare, with more cording showing than design.

Against a long wall, adjacent to the kitchen, stood a three-cushion couch covered with greasy, torn upholstery, still wearing a dirty lace doily on one arm. Next to the couch was a heavy black credenza. Its scratched surface bore three photographs...one, a wedding picture of a round-faced, smiling bridegroom standing next to a solemn young woman who was half a head taller than her husband. The other pictures were studio portraits of a boy and a girl in their Confirmation clothes.

Across from the living room area was the work space. The workbench was well made, large and fully outfitted with gas tanks, pickling vats, polishing wheels and dozens of hand tools.

"I see you do your work right here at home."

"Sure," he said, waddling towards her with a steaming mug. "I ain't exactly ready to open on Fifth Avenue, next to Tiffany."

"I'm told your work is beautiful."

"Lady, I'm an artist. What I can do with gold only Cellini could do. When I die, people who got my stuff are gonna be famous. Like it was paintings."

"I'm sure, Mr. Roncalli. The reason I'm here is that I understand you can duplicate any piece of jewelry."

"Sure, that's how I make a living. I make fakes so that ladies can put the real stuff in the vault and wear what I make for 'em. You got something you want made?"

"Yes," she said. "Here."

She walked to the kitchen table and began to unwrap her package. When she was through, she pushed the papers to one side so that the little man could fully appreciate what she had brought.

It was an oblong box, no more than six inches long, three inches wide and less than three inches high, standing on four tiny feet. It was gold. On its surface, worked into intricate patterns, were hundreds of tiny gold pellets.

The man peered at it carefully and finally let out a long whistle. "Whooee.

What is it?"

"A box. It's very old. It belonged to a queen who kept medicines in it." In part, this was true. Claudia had no intention of telling this man the story of the duplicate boxes.

The jeweler whistled again. "Whooee. I ain't seen granulation work like that in a long time. There ain't too many left can do them tiny pellets. This what you want done?"

"Yes."

"It's tough. I don't know what gold that is without testing it. It almost looks pure. But I would have to do it in ten or twelve so that the whole thing don't melt when I start to fool with them granules."

He picked up the box and turned it over and over. Claudia stared at his hands, holding her breath. If he drops it. I'll kill him, she thought. I'll drive one of his jeweler's spikes into his skull.

He set it down again and suddenly gasped for breath, grabbing the front of his shirt.

"Sorry, lady," he gasped, "my bum heart. Once in a while it grabs me."

He hurried to the sink. Claudia followed him with her eyes, watching as he hunted among the stacks of dishes until he found a pill bottle. He shook two small white pills into his hand and washed them down with the last of the coffee in his mug. Then he returned to the table and looked down at the gold box.

"This ain't a quick cheap job, Mrs. Fleischman."

"How long and how much?"

He paused, rubbing the back of his round head. "About three weeks."

"And the cost?"

He picked the box up, and moved, crablike, to his workbench. There he placed the box on a scale, and began setting counterweights until the two sides balanced. As he worked he mumbled to himself.

"Labor and gold," he mumbled, "labor and gold...um, um. Thirty-five hundred," he blurted.

"Fine."

He seemed not to have heard her as he again said, "Thirty-five hundred. Even alloyed way down, that's a lot of metal."

"I said fine. I'll pay it." She paused. "Just so long as it looks like the real thing, but I must have it by April first."

"Hey, lady, didn't I tell you? Nobody can tell when I get done."

Claudia reached into her purse and withdrew an envelope containing hundred-dollar bills. She counted out ten and handed them to the little goldsmith.

"I'll be back in three weeks."

"If I need you, where can I call you?" he asked.

"There should be no need for that, should there?"

"No, I guess not." He turned back to the box, still resting on the scale. "This should be a real interesting job."

"It could be your pièce de résistance, Mr. Roncalli. Your masterpiece." Claudia smiled warmly.

MONDAY, MARCH 14

When Sharon arrived at her office at 9:30 Monday morning, she found a telephone message. Mrs. Betancourt of the museum asked that Sharon meet her at her house that evening after work. Sharon saw no problem. At five minutes to six she got out of a taxi at Madison Avenue and 74th Street, and started down the block. This section of the upper east side was known for the brownstone townhouses that were not only owned but occupied by single families, unlike areas where these beautiful old homes had been subdivided into several apartments. Sharon had always loved this part of the city and, at one time, had tried to talk Clayton into taking an apartment near here. He would not.

It was the fourth house from the corner of Fifth Avenue, a three-storied building of beige sandstone with a curving, black, wrought-iron staircase leading from the street to the front door. When she rang the bell, the door was opened by a stocky, grey-haired woman. It would have been a disappointment if Claudia had opened her own door, she thought.

"I'm Sharon Hiller," she announced. "Mrs. Betancourt is expecting me."

As she stepped into the foyer and handed her coat to the woman, Sharon was impressed, against her will, by the elegant simplicity around her. The floor was a geometric pattern of black and white marble squares, and the three-tiered crystal chandelier created tiny reflections of light which danced on the cream-colored walls.

"This way, please." The woman led her into an intimate sitting room. "Mrs. Betancourt will be with you in a few minutes."

Sharon did not sit down on the blue-striped, velvet sofa. She could not help comparing this room with the garishly furnished home she lived in. It was difficult to tell the exact color of the pale walls, because the only light came from a delicate figurine lamp. Everything in the room had been chosen with care and taste. Along one wall shelves held Egyptian and pre-Colombian artifacts. Sharon began to feel uncomfortable, as she sometimes did in Claudia's presence. It was disturbing to know that she could not even begin to put a room like this together.

"Sorry to keep you waiting."

Sharon was startled by the sound of Claudia's voice. "I was admiring the collection," she answered, gesturing toward the shelves.

"These are just odds and ends," Claudia laughed. "The real collection is in the library."

The grey-haired woman reappeared with a tray and glasses of wine.

"Thank you, Mrs. Britton." Claudia dismissed her and handed Sharon one of the glasses. "Here's to our shopping trip."

"Shopping trip?" This was actually going to happen. Sharon sipped the wine and watched Claudia over the rim of the glass.

"I've decided on a total of four pieces," she began. "The Sekhmet statue, the dagger, the burial collar and the candlestick holder." Claudia thought of the little box, but it was her secret and these people were not to know about it. "I called jewelry stores around the country to find that all four pieces are available. The problem is the logistics. We'll have to do some traveling. That's why I felt it was best if two of us went. We can split the list. As it turns out, we have to go to four different cities."

When Claudia saw that Sharon was not going to question her, she continued. "Actually, doing it this way is best. Buying each piece in a different store, we won't arouse anyone's curiosity. And later, if anything should get into the newspapers, it will be impossible to make a connection. Please sit down."

Claudia sat down next to Sharon on the couch and offered her a cigarette from her gold case. She moved close to her with a lighter. Sharon leaned back from her hostess. This was a different Claudia from the one she had seen in Sirocco. The cold, businesslike aloofness had been replaced by a warmth that was frightening.

"Can I see the rest of your collection?" Sharon asked, too abruptly, she knew.

"Of course."

Claudia led Sharon out of the room and down the hall. She unlocked the tall double doors of the library, and stepped back to let Sharon walk into the room. Claudia came in behind her, and turned on the lights.

Nothing had prepared Sharon for what she saw. The dark paneling, the indirect lighting, the many pieces poised throughout the room on glass shelves or pedestals. A fragrance, subtle, but detectable permeated the warmth of the room. Claudia had seen many react in the same way. As the beauty around them became a reality, they wanted to touch everything, and talk about what they saw.

Now Sharon slowly walked towards one of the display cabinets. She moved as though in a trance, looking at the ancient necklace almost hypnotized.

Claudia reached out and lightly touched Sharon's arm trying to get her attention and steer her to take in all the collection.

Sharon sighed then turned suddenly. "This room, all of these pieces, it's all so incredible. This must have taken many years."

"That's why what we're doing is so important," Claudia said. She led the way back into the living room.

Once they stood again with their glass of wine, Claudia picked up a piece of paper and handed it to Sharon. "Here is an itinerary of where you're going and what you'll be buying. I don't want to make our trip sound too mysterious or melodramatic, but it would be best if we transacted all our business in cash."

"That's fine with me. Can we travel under other names?" Sharon laughed.

Claudia missed the humor entirely. "I'm afraid I've already booked airline tickets and hotel reservations."

"Damn!" Sharon said. "I wanted to be Mata Hari."

Claudia opened the drawer of the end table and took out a large manila folder. Inside was an envelope. She handed it to Sharon.

"Inside are the hotel reservations and again the names of the stores and addresses. The airline tickets will be at the counter when you go. I'm sorry, I nearly forgot, you leave on Wednesday morning and should be back Thursday night. I hope this is all right."

Again, Sharon nodded.

"There's also cash in the envelope. Enough for the trip and the purchases."

Sharon took the envelope, and stood silently for a moment before Claudia said, "I guess that covers everything. I'm sure you're anxious to get home." She steered Sharon to the entrance foyer. "I'll speak to you on Friday."

Sharon turned to find the housekeeper standing at the door holding her coat. She glanced back at Claudia who had walked down the hall to the staircase. A white cat was waiting on the landing, and rose to its feet when Claudia approached. She stopped for a second, turned and smiled noncommittally at Sharon, then disappeared up the stairs. The cat followed.

WEDNESDAY, MARCH 16

Private family dwellings lined both sides of 74th Street. Shrubbery and trees along the sidewalks were still barren in March. It was a difficult street for anyone to loiter on without calling attention to themselves. Especially in the early morning.

The large man in the tan raincoat, standing several yards down and across the street from the Betancourt residence, had made his own compromises with the difficulties. In the two months he'd been following Claudia Betancourt, he had sometimes not picked her up until she left her office for lunch.

For the past week, however, he had begun his vigil early, outside her home. He had a feeling that she was up to something, and he had better be ready when it happened.

The wind gusting down the street blew the front of his raincoat open. He hated standing around like this. If something didn't break soon, he fully expected to be greeted one morning by a blue-and-white New York City patrol car.

The door to the Betancourt home remained closed. He shifted his weight from foot to foot, blew into his cupped hands, and checked his watch. It was 7:30. Then the front door opened. Claudia Betancourt closed it behind her, and quickly walked down the iron staircase. She was carrying a suitcase.

The large man moved quickly towards Park Avenue and hailed a passing cab. He got in and told the driver to wait. In a minute, Claudia Betancourt reached the corner. She waved to the first passing taxi. As she got in, the detective leaned forward and told his driver to follow her. They headed uptown, onto the Triboro Bridge, and past LaGuardia. When the expressway split and the driver followed the Van Wyck Expressway, the detective knew his destination. He checked his cash and credit cards. He knew he would be taking a plane, only he didn't know how far.

Unaware that she was being followed, Claudia Betancourt paid her cab driver and entered the Delta passenger terminal at Kennedy Airport. She bought her ticket, then headed for the ladies' room. Her only companion was the cleaning woman, who was sweeping the floor. In front of the mirror she combed her dark hair smoothly off her face, and wrapped it around her head. The wig she pulled out of her case was ash blond and short—reminding her somewhat of Sharon Hiller's hairstyle. After securing it in place, she pulled out a small leather bag and skillfully applied makeup to blend in with her new hair coloring. It was 8:30 when she emerged and headed for gate number eleven. She had her airline ticket and a driver's license that bore a vague resemblance to the way she looked.

The man in the raincoat had decided to wait at the departure gate, since he knew from the ticket desk she'd be on the 9 a.m. flight to Los Angeles. At twenty minutes to nine, he was beginning to regret that he hadn't waited for her outside the ladies' room. What on earth could be keeping her, he wondered. As the seat numbers began to be called, he grew more anxious. Somehow he' had missed her. Where could she have gone?

He reluctantly stood up and looked around. Suddenly he spied the suitcase. "Damn," he muttered. Twenty years in the business and he had almost allowed this female to fool him. The clothing and the luggage were the same—only the face and hair were different. And that's what he had not been looking for. What was she up to?

The first-class section was the last to be called. Claudia Betancourt picked up her bag without looking around and started toward the plane.

Behind her, clutching his ticket, the detective rose to follow.

* * *

Sharon Hiller shoved the money into the cab driver's hand then hurried into the LaGuardia terminal. Security check-in was crowded and slow, and by the time she got through, she had added something else to the list of irritations that were slowly turning the morning sour. Clayton had been difficult, her train had been late and her cab to LaGuardia had gotten stuck in a traffic jam. She was now almost an hour and a half behind the schedule Claudia had given her. Fortunately, there had been some slack time. If everything else went smoothly, she should still be able to make the 3:30 flight from Washington, D.C. to New Orleans.

She picked up her ticket and walked over to the departure gate. She looked at her watch, then at the clock overhead. 9:46...9:47...9:48....Her anxiety was increased by the twelve thousand dollars in cash that was lying in a secret compartment in her carry-on suitcase. The cash, given to her by Claudia, was to cover all expenses during the two days she'd be gone.

Claudia's plan seemed simple enough. Sharon would go to Washington, D.C., buy the dagger, then on to New Orleans for the statue of Sekhmet. Leave Wednesday morning, back Thursday afternoon. When she arrived back at Grand Central Station, she'd rent a luggage locker and place the two items in it. That was all there was to it! Right now, however, it was becoming increasingly frustrating.

An hour and fifteen minutes later, Sharon Hiller stood in front of a mirror in the ladies' room at the Baltimore-Washington Airport, pulling a beige turban over her hair. As she re-did her makeup and put on tinted glasses, she wondered about the disguises. Why? Was Claudia merely exercising caution? Or was there some danger that Claudia wasn't telling her about? They always tell you to assume the worst, she thought, picking up her suitcase and walking towards the exit. If that's the case, I may as well do exactly what she wants.

* * *

The first-class section on Claudia's flight to Los Angeles was spacious. Seats and tables could be turned to accommodate the passengers.

Claudia had finished breakfast and her second glass of orange juice and champagne. She had finished her book as well. There was only half an hour to go before landing. She decided to freshen her makeup. As she moved towards the restroom, the door opened and a large man came out. In the semi-darkness, Claudia saw him stare at her. She returned his gaze. She was used to men staring at her, but this one made her feel uncomfortable. She stepped into the tiny room and dismissed him from her mind.

* * *

A soft warm breeze and blue skies tinged with a yellow layer of smog greeted Claudia as she stepped out of the Los Angeles International Airport. The change in weather made her feel good. For a little while, at least, she could try to forget Maurice. Her energies, right now, were centered on what she had to do before she returned to New York. She thought for a moment about Sharon and how she must look in her disguise. The frown came and went quickly.

The Beverly Hills Hotel was her usual stopping place in Los Angeles, but this time she couldn't chance anyone recognizing her. The Sheraton, near the airport, was not luxurious but it was convenient. She stopped at the hotel long enough to drop off her suitcase before going on to the jewelry store.

Ferrier & Furman Jewelers was situated with other expensive shops along Rodeo Drive in Beverly Hills. It reminded her of Cartier's with its private sales rooms off the main showroom area.

She stepped inside the store and was stopped immediately by a voice.

"May I help you? I'm Mr. Morton." He was in his fifties, with wiry grey hair.

"Yes. I'm Mrs. Bennett. I called on Monday regarding the purchase of a collar from the Golden Age catalogue."

"Please come this way."

Claudia followed him across the thickly carpeted floor into a small room furnished with a desk and several chairs.

"Make yourself comfortable. I'll be back in a moment."

Claudia sat down and waited. She felt edgy. There was no reason for this nervousness, but she could not shake it.

The man returned in a few minutes, carrying the gold collar. It was just under two inches wide with a band of bright stones running around the top and bottom edges. The collar was hinged at the back and had no catch in the front. It was as

Claudia had expected—a beautiful reproduction.

She took an envelope out of her purse and paid for the collar in hundred-dollar bills. The salesman showed no surprise. Customers in this neighborhood often paid large sums in cash.

The transaction had gone so quickly and easily that Claudia began to feel more at ease. The package in her purse, she detoured into a side room to look at a fascinating collection of antique jewelry. At least fifteen minutes passed happily. Feeling secure, she decided to ask the salesman about the candle holder she wanted. Surely she had been overly cautious in her plans. If she could make another purchase here, she could forget about Chicago and go straight home.

She left the little side room and began to walk around the store looking for the salesman. Not seeing him on the first floor, she went up the steps to the second floor, turned the corner, then stopped suddenly. From where she was standing she could clearly see into the room without being seen. The salesman stood on one side of a desk, head bent down as he spoke. Seated on the other side, with his back towards Claudia, was a large man wearing a tan raincoat.

He turned slightly, and Claudia could see his profile. Immediately, she knew she had seen him before—on her New York to Los Angeles flight. She stood frozen to the spot. What's the matter with me, she thought. This is ridiculous! He has as much right to be here as I do. But Claudia continued to stand in the archway, watching.

The salesman disappeared into a back room. He reappeared carrying something—another copy of the gold collar she had just purchased.

What did the man in the raincoat want, she wondered? She had the feeling that he wasn't a dealer or collector. Then what was he looking for? Did it have anything to do with her? Or was it just a coincidence?

Claudia watched the salesman as he lifted his hands and then shrugged his shoulders. Obviously, the man in the raincoat was not going to purchase the collar. Suddenly Claudia was convinced that they were talking about her. She backed up against the wall, hidden in the shadows, and watched the men for a few more seconds.

Then she realized that she had to get out of the store before someone discovered her. Quickly she walked back down the stairs, her footsteps muffled by the thick carpeting, and out the front door.

WEDNESDAY, MARCH 16

It was almost 7:00 p.m. when Sharon Hiller entered the Highlander Hotel in New Orleans, two hours late because her plane was delayed in Atlanta due to mechanical difficulties.

She registered at the front desk, then went straight to her room and sat down on the bed. It was only 7:30. She didn't feel like reading, and she certainly didn't intend to watch television. Exhausted, she collapsed on the bed. Her last thought as she fell asleep was, what a waste of an evening in New Orleans!

Sharon knew she was awake, but she wasn't sure how long she had been that way. The room was dim. She wasn't certain, at first, where she was.

She looked around. New Orleans! She'd gotten the dagger in Washington, and had it and the money for the statue safe in her suitcase. She'd fallen asleep in her clothes. Yuk! What she needed was a shower. Sharon looked at her watch. It was only 6:30 a.m. She had plenty of time.

She let the hot water beat on her body, stimulating the muscles, massaging the mind. She turned the shower, knob. The cold water taking her breath away. After several seconds she turned it off, toweled briskly, dressed, and went down to the restaurant to get something to eat. Then she returned to the room to finish her preparations. The last touch today was the wig she had packed. The hair color was the same as hers, dark brown, but the style was different—shoulder length, with bangs. A softer, more delicate look than she could achieve with her own curly hair. She wondered what Peter would think if he saw her in it.

She closed her luggage then gave herself one more glance. Satisfied, she took the elevator to the lobby where she checked out, then headed out to her destination, a small antique shop.

It was located on a narrow street in the French quarter. Sharon found the store easily, and was browsing through the merchandise when a tall, grey-haired man asked if he could be of any help.

"Yes," she said. "I'm Mrs. Wilson. I called on Monday regarding the statue of the goddess Sekhmet from the Golden Age catalogue."

"Of course, Mrs. Wilson. I'll be right back."

The photographs of the statue had not prepared her for the real thing. The almost real thing, she corrected herself. The salesman brought it on a navy blue velvet cushion. Sharon felt an actual chill when she reached out to touch it. It was beautiful, but eerie. The emerald eyes seemed to stare right through her.

"It's a little larger than the original, isn't it?" she asked.

"No. It has exactly the same dimensions. The duplication is so perfect, it would be difficult to tell it from the original."

Sharon smiled. "It's beautiful," she said softly. "Have you ever seen the original?"

"No. I'll have to wait until the exhibit comes here to New Orleans."

"I saw the statue once—a very long time ago in Cairo."

"Is it satisfactory?"

"Yes, quite," Sharon answered, lifting it with both hands. "It's so light. I would have thought it would have been much heavier."

"The real one is slightly heavier. Different purity as you know. I'll have it packed, Mrs. Wilson."

The salesman picked it up and took the statue to the back room.

Five minutes later he returned, carrying a box tied with cord.

Sharon paid for the statue with hundred-dollar bills, lifted the box from the counter and left.

* * *

On the flight back to New York, Sharon's thoughts were a jumble of hope and disbelief. Could she really pull it off? The thought was both exciting and frightening. If she could do it, and get the money, then she'd be free. Free of Clayton, his mother, the house. She'd have a new life, a new job. She could take the girls and leave.

It was 6:15 p.m. when the taxi from LaGuardia dropped her off at Grand Central Station. The baggage lockers were over by the Hudson Line train platforms. She selected one of the larger ones, put both packages in it, and slammed the door. She leaned against it. It's over, she thought. I've done it. She went to the ladies' room, took off the wig, and waited for the next train to Connecticut.

* * *

That Thursday morning, the dining room of the Drake Hotel was filled with early morning risers. The traveling business people were anxious to get their work done and get out of Chicago.

Claudia Betancourt sat by a window finishing her coffee and waiting for time to pass. Outside, the snow was swirling across Lake Michigan. The sky was grey and cold and the buildings to the north were dissolving into the freezing mist.

In a half hour, she would make her last purchase. Meanwhile, a fresh cup of coffee was in order. As she turned her head to find a waiter, the thought flew from her mind. He was there, then he was gone. The man that just left the dining room was the man she had seen in Beverly Hills. The cold seemed to invade her body.

On an impulse, she got up and went into the lobby. "Excuse me, but I think I just saw a friend of mine leave the dining room. Could you tell me if he's staying here?"

"Yes, ma'am, surely. What is his name?"

"Well...he's an actor. He travels incognito. You know how those Hollywood people are."

"Yes. We get them here frequently." The man behind the desk gave her an edgy smile. "They don't really give you their real name."

"I know. I don't know what name he's going by, but I can describe him. He's rather large, over six feet. Dark hair, greying at the temples. He usually wears a tan raincoat and hat. You know, sort of the rumpled Humphrey Bogart look."

The clerk's face brightened. "I did see him. He checked out earlier this morning. I didn't wait on him, and the man who did isn't here at the moment. But I saw him."

Claudia thanked him and walked back to the dining room. As she sat down at her table, the morning paper spread out just as she left it, the waiter hurried over. Claudia asked for a fresh cup of coffee.

As Claudia picked up the cup her hand shook. The anxiety she had felt in Los Angeles returned. She hadn't been mistaken after all. No, she was becoming convinced it wasn't all coincidence. How much coincidence could she buy. On the plane, then in Beverly Hills, at the same store, looking at the same piece of jewelry. Now Chicago! Same hotel? The realm of coincidence didn't extend that far. Why would he be following her?

She paid her bill, then went upstairs to collect her luggage and checked out. Outside, the snow was still coming down. She looked out the cab's back window. In this weather, it was impossible to tell if she was being followed. As much as she didn't want to admit it to herself, she was frightened.

MONDAY, MARCH 21

A pencil-sharp cone of blue flame moved across the gold box imbedded in a round sand pot on the jeweler's bench. The flame did not move in a regular pattern, but darted, beelike, in and out of the intricate designs formed by hundreds of granules of gold.

The man holding the torch perched on a tall stool. One of his small feet rested on the bottom rung, the other hooked around the second. His bent head moved from side to side, following the torch, ducking to avoid a round magnifying lamp. The cold, blue-white glow of the lamp reflected from his hairless head. It looked like a pink and white egg.

Roncalli moved his hands with the practiced assurance of a surgeon. He held the torch in his left hand while his right, holding a long, thin tweezer, positioned each tiny granule as the heat fused it in place. The goldsmith's eyes squinted through thick magnifiers hooked to an eyeglass frame. After each sweep he would. hold the torch away from the work while he looked up and over the half-glasses at another gold box standing on the workbench next to the sand pot.

Nodding in apparent satisfaction, he moved the torch away with a dramatic flourish, threw the tweezers onto the table, and reached across to turn off the burner. The flame disappeared with an explosive pop that echoed across the dingy half-lit basement.

Across the room a chipped porcelain coffee pot gurgled on the stove. The gnome like man trotted across the room and around the table covered with the remnants of his lunch, filled a mug with coffee and returned to the workbench.

The gold box in the sand pot had cooled a little, enough for him to pick it up. He turned the small object over, checking it from every angle. Next he picked up the other box and held them next to each other, comparing each of the like sides. His face softened into a smile. Deep in his throat he gave a satisfied chuckle.

His inspection was interrupted by an insistent banging noise. He turned, staring into the far corner where a black metal door opened into a small vestibule under the front steps of the house.

The banging came again—three quick, hard raps in a row, then silence. The old man shuffled across to the door. He did not open it immediately but stood facing it, waiting. The raps came again, this time in front of his face, making his eyes blink in rhythm to the knocks. He reached up and turned the knob on the dead bolt allowing the door to swing open about two inches before the chain on the safety lock pulled tight.

Through the narrow opening, the little man saw the middle of a long tan raincoat, standing very close to the partly open door.

"Yeh?" he asked, staring directly at the coat.

The voice from above the coat was deep. "Mr. Roncalli. I'm looking for Vito Roncalli."

The old man hesitated before answering. "That's me." He paused. "Who wants him?"

"I want to talk to you."

Vito Roncalli peered upwards. In the grey dimness of the late afternoon he could make out only a pale area, obscured by the shadow of a tan rain hat.

"You're doing some work for a friend of mine. A woman," the deep voice said.

"What work? What woman?" he asked the lapels of the coat nervously.

A brown-gloved hand disappeared inside the raincoat, and emerged holding a piece of paper that was offered through the crack of the door. The goldsmith stepped back in surprise, then took the paper. It was a grainy machine copy of a newspaper photograph. A photograph of a woman. The goldsmith nodded and handed the photograph out to the waiting glove. Glove and picture disappeared once more into the folds of the raincoat.

The voice asked, "Do you recognize her?"

Again, a pause. "Yeah."

"I'd like to come in and talk to you about what you're doing for Mrs. Betancourt."

"For who?"

"Mrs. Betancourt, the lady in the picture."

Betancourt? The little man looked startled. "Listen, could you tell me what you want?"

The raincoat fidgeted, then said weakly, "She wanted me to see what you were doing for her."

"Yeh? Why?"

"Because I might have some work for you, also." The voice held the edge of frustration.

"I don't need no more work. I'm busy. And anyway, she's gonna get it back soon. Ask her then."

"Well, I would like to see it now."

"Ask her when she gets it back. You'll like it. It's gonna be perfect. An exact copy."

"When did you say she was coming back?"

"I didn't. She's gonna call to see if it's ready. Listen, it's cold here by the door."

"Are you sure I can't come in to see it?"

"Yeah, I'm sure."

The door chain drew tighter, as if some weight were pushing against it from the outside. Then, just as quickly, the tension eased.

"Thanks anyway. Goodbye, Mr. Roncalli."

"Yeah, goodbye."

The jeweler closed the door and turned the dead bolt. He walked back to the workbench and looked at the small boxes resting side by side. As he studied them, he began to nod again.

"Yeah," he said aloud. "Perfect."

Out on the street, the tall, heavyset man in the raincoat was walking briskly toward the subway. He would have liked to have seen what the old man was making, but he had learned several things. The runt had recognized the picture, and whatever he was making, it was a copy of something else. Also, he would deliver it soon.

These little pieces of information would probably fit nicely into whatever else the old lady knew. No, he thought, the trip had not been a waste. He pulled his collar up against the chill of the fading day and continued down the street.

FRIDAY, MARCH 25

The eyes staring out of the bathroom mirror at Charles Green were red, alcoholic red. At the home of a friend this evening, Charles had consumed two extra dry Martinis before dinner. At table he had finished most of a bottle of Chablis, and later several brandies. He'd insisted on driving home, and had maneuvered himself upstairs to his bedroom, undressed, and entered the bathroom before he realized that he was only one or two drinks away from passing out. He contemplated going downstairs to finish the job, but it seemed like too much effort. Now, if Pat were to volunteer to go fix a couple of nightcaps, he thought, and the thought made him smack his lips as he walked into the bedroom.

Pat was standing at her dresser taking off her jewelry. She had removed her dress and was wearing a bra and panties. Charles started to say something about the drinks but changed his mind. He stood looking at his wife's back until she turned around.

At thirty-five, Pat Green was losing her girlish slenderness and gaining, in its place, a sexy sag. The round behind was just a bit rounder at the bottom. There was a hint of stomach, and the breasts were taking on the shape of champagne goblets. Her face maintained the clear smoothness it had in college where, at the prodding of her parents, she became engaged to an Ivy League boy named Charles Green.

Charles put his hands on her shoulders. "You looked nice tonight," he said, trying to remember what she had been wearing. The smile on his face was foolish. He dropped his hands and rested them on her hips. The smile remained. His pulse became noticeably faster.

She turned back to the dresser and finished removing a bracelet. As she bent forward to open her jewelry box, she pushed back into Charles who stood close behind her. His excitement was evident.

"You drank a lot tonight," she said, without turning, trying to move forward slightly.

"So?" he slurred, moving forward against her.

"You know how you get when you drink too much and try to make love."

She looked up into the mirror over the dresser and saw a puzzled frown on Charles' face. "You try so hard and nothing happens, and then you get very frustrated and end up mad at yourself and me."

"I'm not that drunk as you can tell," he snickered.

She slid sideways out of his grasp and walked to the bed where her nightgown lay, and without turning she quickly took off the underwear and pulled the nightgown over her head. When she turned to face him, the straight lines of the gown hid all but the faintest outline of her figure. The pounding that had started in Charles' chest slowly gave way to burning—a feeling of indigestion accompanied by anger. Charles was doing a slow burn. He wanted to rip the gown from his wife's shoulders and push her, naked, back onto the bed. Instead, he sneered at her, his lips pulled back.

"What's the name of this little game, Pat? I remember when you would get all excited if I came near you, and now...lately...I'm the plague."

"Charles, what happened with Don Edwards?" She put her hands on her hips and was looking at him with intensity. It made him nervous. "In the last few weeks, your hours are crazy. Sometimes you don't go into the city. You've made rotten remarks about Edwards and the company. It's all strange—not like you. You hinted at money problems. Is there a job problem too?"

"How nice to see you're concerned," he snarled. "Worried about your paycheck, your vacation, your dresses, your lessons. You need fucking lessons, not tennis lessons."

Her mouth fell open. Charles walked up to her and stood very close.

"Yeah ... I got a problem. I got no job. Your friend Edwards offered me a little comedown and I told him to stick, it. Pretty soon I'm off the payroll and we start living on my profit sharing." He reached out, touched the tip of her breast with his finger. "In the meantime, I'm still collecting my salary, so you can lift up your nightie and let old Charlie in." He reached down for her nightgown and tried to pull it up. She slapped his hand away.

"No, Charles. Go sober up, and we'll talk about it. I don't think I deserved what you said."

"Oh, fuck off, Pat. Ever since I put a hold on your vacation, you've had this bug up your ass, and now that I told you about Edwards, you'll probably go down to the doctor's tomorrow and get the damned thing sewed up."

She started to turn away and he grabbed her shoulder and spun her towards him. His grip was tight. She winced as he leaned close to her face.

"You're nothing but a whore, a goddamned whore. Play for pay! So long as daddy keeps the bread on the table you'll spread your legs on command. But now it's off limits, huh? No tickee, no shirtee? Well, just you wait. I may show up with a lot of money. A million bucks! How's that? Is that enough? Will that buy me a piece of ass? You bet it will! But you'll beg for it first."

He let go of her, turned and stumbled towards the stairs. He'd finish the job of getting drunk.

THURSDAY, MARCH 31

Peter Mandel filled two wine glasses, killing the bottle, and joined Sharon Hiller on his living-room sofa.

Sharon reached up for her glass. "Have you spoken with Claudia and Charles?" she asked. "How did they take it? Did they think the ideas were good?"

"Yes, I'd say so." Peter leaned back and stretched his legs across to the coffee table. "Claudia thinks your idea for getting the real stuff out of the museum is fine, and she's pleased with the plan for moving the big piece in and out."

"Pleased?" Sharon asked, "Is that all? Pleased?"

"Come on, now. You know Claudia. Her range of emotions is zero. She's always all business."

"Is she taking care of bringing in the smaller pieces?"

"I assume so," Peter replied. "The only problem was the statue and we've solved that."

"I hope getting it out is going to be as easy as you two think."

"With a little help from Charles, don't forget that."

"What does he think of the whole thing?" Sharon took a sip of her wine.

"I haven't told him about that part. He's better off knowing as little as possible. Speaking of Charles, what was the name he wanted to use on his pass?"

"Meyer. Better write it down so you don't forget."

Suddenly Peter turned to face her. "Tell me honestly ... do you still want to go through with this?"

Sharon lowered her eyes. "It's not a matter of wanting. It's a matter of having to. I'm like Charles— there's so much riding on it. And to be quite truthful, I find it exciting. No, that's not even the right word. It's sexy. What about you?"

"I don't know," he answered. "Sure, it's exciting and scary and there's a hell of a lot of money for doing very little. For sure, Claudia is crazy...but what the hell!" He raised his glass, "Here's to the fifth and to us, as nuts as we are." He leaned across and kissed her.

* * *

This trip to Brooklyn seemed shorter than the last, more direct. Claudia dismissed the taxi at the corner and walked to the jeweler's brownstone. Once inside, Roncalli took her right to the workbench to see the two gold boxes. She looked at the little goldsmith, and he smiled complacently. "Go ahead, look 'em over. Which is which?"

They were startlingly similar, not only in design, but in color of the gold.

Both pieces had the look of antiques, the soft patina of a highly polished, bright metal worn by time and the warm sweat of many hands.

"My own little aging process." He chuckled, then hiccoughed, patting his chest. "Palpitations," he said in explanation.

Claudia put her elegant leather totebag down on the workbench, opened the top and withdrew a long brown envelope. She offered it to the little man, but he waved it aside.

"Not yet, Mrs. Betancourt," he said.

"What did you say?" she asked.

"I said Mrs. Betancourt."

Claudia stood absolutely still.

"Hey, what's the matter? Did you think little Roncalli was a dope? I know that Fleischman name is a phony."

The third party. Maurice's remark hammered inside her head.

He said, "Don't worry. It don't make no difference who you are. So long as your money is good." He paused, studying her. "And speaking of money, the price of gold went up since we last talked. So this piece will cost you ten thousand instead of thirty-five hundred."

How right Maurice was. Claudia could hear his words over and over ... *"I refuse to have a third party know I conspired in a crime ..."*

"I don't have enough money in that envelope," she said.

"Hey, so you pick up the box next time." He shrugged and hiccoughed again. This time his eyes opened wide. He stared at Claudia and blinked. "Madone, what a rap." He slapped his chest.

"I can guarantee my money is good, Mr. Roncalli." Her voice was a whisper.

"Lady, I know your money is good." The little man began to laugh richly. Suddenly, he was staring at Claudia with a look of pain on his face. He drew a deep breath and grabbed at the front of his shirt. Claudia watched him, her eyes riveted on the hand pressed against his heaving chest. It was an ugly hand, with dirty fingertips and cracked nails.

He backed away until he touched the kitchen table. A wineglass shook, spilling the red liquid. The little man's hand swept the air, searching for the chair back. He found it and fell heavily into the seat. His voice, when he spoke, was a low rasp.

"Please, lady ... on the sink ... my pills."

Claudia moved closer to the table and stood looking down at the jeweler.

"The pills ... over there," he repeated, pointing toward the sink.

Slowly, Claudia walked to the sink, where she stood for a long moment staring at the clutter of dirty pans and dishes. Then she saw the plastic pill bottle. Without removing her leather gloves, she picked it up and looked back at the table. The little goldsmith was slumped in the chair, his irregular breathing punctuated by gulps and low moans. His bluish lips were moving, but she could not distinguish any words. She stared at the bottle in her hand. Holding it closer she read the pharmacy name and prescription number. There were about twenty small white pills in the bottle. She turned it slowly in her hand, becoming totally absorbed in the pills' tumbling motion.

The noises from the table faded as did the sight of the messy sink. There was nothing in her mind now except the slowly turning bottle and the rattle of its contents as they moved from side to side.

It could have been one minute or ten. She had lost track of time. When she stopped turning the bottle and again looked at the table, the little man was quiet. As she watched, his lips moved. He was still alive, even though his eyes were closed and his round head hung limply with his chin resting on his chest.

She put the bottle down, back in its place on the sink top, and walked past the table to the workbench. Placing the envelope on the table, she picked up the gold box nearest the totebag and placed it inside. From a side compartment in the bag, she took a folded sheet of tissue, wrapped it around the other gold box, then placed it inside the bag.

For a moment, she looked down at the goldsmith. His position had not changed, but now his lips were not moving. One hand rested on the table, the other hung limply at his side. There was no sign of life.

When she finally pulled her eyes away from him, she thought about leaving the money. But doing so could cause problems even she couldn't foresee. There was nothing she could do for him.

"Thank you," she whispered. She placed the envelope with the money in her bag and let herself out.

The Exhibit

EARTH

MONDAY, APRIL 4

The U.S. Air Force cargo jet carrying the Golden Age exhibit to New York landed at La Guardia Airport at 2:00 on the afternoon of April 4th. The date, time, and place of arrival had been treated like a military secret, and like a military secret, the information had leaked.

As the plane taxied to the cargo terminal, virtually everyone on the field knew what was on board.

On hand to meet the plane were an unmarked white van, two blue-and-white New York City police cars, two motorcycle policemen, and a black Mercedes sedan in which sat a very nervous Barnard Simms.

Transferring the aluminum crates from the airplane to the white van took an hour and thirty minutes. The fork lifts paused only long enough for Simms and the two Egyptians who had accompanied the flight to read the shipping tags on the cases and check them against the manifest on their clipboards.

When each crate had been accounted for and loaded, the procession moved out of the airport and into the afternoon traffic on Grand Central Parkway, heading for Manhattan and the Museum.

The trip from the airport took eighteen minutes—probably a world's record, thanks to the police escort.

The welcoming committee at the museum was small—the director himself, a few members of the general staff, and a dozen men who would move the crates from the truck to the second basement vault. The move took over two hours and was watched closely by Miriam Gottfried from her second-floor window. Simms and the Egyptians—a boring Mr. Ali and an even drearier Mr. Kamil—cross checked to make sure each of the crates that had arrived at LaGuardia also arrived at the door to the vault.

At 6:30 p.m., the vault door in the second basement of the Metropolitan Museum of Art swung shut with a resounding thud. The work was finished for tonight. Tomorrow would be another day.

TUESDAY, APRIL 5

The morning of April 5th dawned grey and threatening. At 7 a.m. the streets of New York were quiet. Fifth Avenue, in front of the Metropolitan, was deserted save for a lone jogger, wearing a green running suit, who trotted past the broad stone steps and faded into the mist. Seconds later, a black Mercedes appeared, moving slowly down the avenue. It turned right into the museum driveway and disappeared behind the south wing. There, a ramp curved around behind the building, ending in a large courtyard surrounded on three sides by museum buildings. The fourth side was lined with trees and shrubbery that shielded the museum from Central Park itself. The Mercedes' door opened. Bernard Simms got out and entered the museum. Gottfried had given him most of the responsibility for today's events, and it weighed heavily on him.

The first workers to arrive would put the finishing touches on the exhibition hall—hanging signs, checking electrical systems—and, most importantly, adjusting the lighting arrangements. These final adjustments to the lights—changing the angle of a spotlight here, using a different-colored gel there—could be made only after the exhibit was in place. Thank God, Simms thought, that they were not his direct responsibility.

The museum staff, those who would bring the pieces from the vault to the exhibition hall, would not arrive until 8:30. Even then, nothing would be done until Barnard Simms orchestrated the entire movement with his clipboard. He had prepared a schedule for the day. He loved making schedules, they gave him a feeling of confidence that nothing could go wrong.

His secretary had typed the schedule and Miriam Gottfried had approved it. Now he sat at his desk and looked it over again.

8:30 a.m.	Arrival at museum
8:45 a.m.	Proceed to vault area
9:00 a.m.	Commence unpacking and examination
12:00 noon.	Unpacking/examination of all pieces completed
12:00-12:30 p.m.	Lunch
12:30 p.m.	Commence movement of pieces from vault area to exhibition hall
2:30 p.m.	Movement of all pieces from vault area to exhibition hall completed
4:30 p.m.	All pieces in proper location in four chambers of exhibition completed

6:30 p.m.	Final lighting arrangements completed
6:30-7:30 p.m.	Dress for evening
8:00 p.m.	Arrival of guests
9:00 p.m	Live UBS telecast begins

The staff had been sarcastic about his 'generosity' in allowing thirty minutes for lunch and an hour to change into formal attire required for the evening. The museum was not providing facilities for change of clothing, so there had been a scramble among those who did not reside near the museum for some place to change. Those with nearby apartments found themselves taking in guests complete with hanging plastic clothes bags and toilet kits.

Simms was unsympathetic to sarcasm. His personal checklist ran to six pages, each one covered with his own small, precise handwriting.

Yesterday the staff had set up the pedestals in their proper places in the exhibition rooms and bolted each one to the floor. Affixed to each pedestal was a white plastic plaque engraved with black lettering. Last evening Simms had checked each room of the exhibition hall, just to make sure. After dropping Mr. Ali and Mr. Kamil at their hotel, he had gone home to his immaculate bachelor apartment on the upper West Side, taken one Valium and gone right to bed. Nevertheless, this morning he felt tired and nervous. He checked his watch. 7:00. He got up, clipboard in hand, and headed for the vault. He'd have time to get the crates in order before the staff gathered at 8:30.

* * *

At precisely 7:03 a.m, Claudia Betancourt left her house, softly closing the heavy oak door behind her and walked the half block east toward Fifth Avenue. The sun, although above the horizon, was well hidden behind a curtain of grey clouds. The air was expectant with rain and the damp breeze made her pull her coat closer together. Over the shoulder of her raincoat hung an elegant leather totebag.

At the corner of Fifth Avenue she turned north. The museum was only a few short blocks away and the walk would give her a few minutes to pull her thoughts together.

In the weeks since the scheme had begun to take shape in her mind, she'd never dealt with today as a reality. April 5 was a date on the calendar, not a day when she got out of bed, dressed, and went to work. The installation and reception were items on an agenda, not actual events. Yet today was April 5. All the conversations at Sirocco, the trip to California, to Brooklyn, all came together today. There was nothing more to say. No more fencing with Maurice or Miriam

80

Gottfried. No more tempting Peter or Sharon or Charles. Today, the exchange would take place and it would all be hers.

Thank God, Barnard Simms was a predictable man, she thought, waiting for the light at 80th Street. She knew that when he set 8:30 a.m. as the starting time, he'd be there at 7:30, if not sooner. She was counting on that. Because she needed him to get into the vault before the activity started. He'd be there going over his predictable checklist, on his predictable clipboard.

Somewhere she had arrived at a conclusion when she first saw the perfect gold box that Roncalli had made. She would make that switch first. The Sekhmet statue was the prize but she knew if she could switch the little box, everything else would fall into place. That was why she wanted to be at the museum early. Just a few minutes alone in the vault would do it. The duplicate of the gold box sat in her leather bag on top of the other replicas, ready to come out first. The dagger, the collar and the candle holder were there, too, and their time would come.

The grey granite walls of the museum loomed in front of her, appearing out of the early morning mist which brushed across the tops of the trees. At the back entrance, the officer on duty nodded to her and buzzed her in. Inside the museum, on the first basement level, it was still night. The dim lights peering from the high ceiling, created shadowy monsters of the most innocent of objects.

A narrow staircase led down to the vault level on the floor below. She stopped and listened. At first there was only silence. Then she heard it—sounds coming from the second basement. Quickly she started down the worn marble steps, holding the handrail and clutching the leather bag tightly.

At the bottom, as she had hoped, she saw that the vault was already opened. Two guards stood outside the wire caged area. She walked up and looked in and smiled. Barnard Simms was inside, alone, trying to arrange the gleaming crates along the walls in some kind of order.

"Good morning," she called softly to Simms, smiling past the two guards. Startled, Simms spun around. "What are you doing here so early, Claudia?" He glanced at his watch. "It's only 7:30. You have a whole hour yet before you have to be here."

"I know." Still smiling, she walked past the two guards into the vault. "It's just that I'm excited and couldn't sleep. After all, this is the day we've been waiting for. The months of planning...of work ... "

Simms nodded in agreement. "Yes. The Tutankhamun Treasure made nervous wrecks of all of us and this one is just as bad. I've got a funny feeling about this exhibit. I won't be happy until it's in place and all the guests and TV people have gone home."

He looked down at his clipboard, then at the crates, "Claudia," he began, "since you're here, there's something you can help me with."

Claudia's heart began pounding. Helping Simms was not a part of her plan.

Simms detected a frown on Claudia's face but he ignored it and went on. "I have to run upstairs. What I'd like you to do is to take this sheet," he lifted the clip and extracted a sheet of paper, "and compare the descriptions on the crate with those shown on this sheet. When you find a match, number the crate according to the number marked here, indicating the numerical sequence on the typed form. "I've gotten down to number eleven. You see, there are over forty to go. It will save time for all of us later, not to mention the confusion we can avoid. And you know how Miriam is ... " He lifted his eyes towards the ceiling and sighed.

He glanced back towards Claudia to see the kind of argument she was going to give him. Her eyes had brightened, and her lips moved into what he assumed was a smile, although he wasn't sure.

"Of course," she answered, "I'll be happy to. Remember—that's why I came early—to help. I knew there would still be a million details for you to take care of."

"That's good of you, Claudia. Here." He handed her the sheet of paper and took the black marker from his breast pocket. "I'll be back in a few minutes."

He turned and walked out of the vault, through the caged enclosure, and disappeared. Claudia could hear his footsteps as he climbed the stairs. Then the sound was gone.

Dozens of aluminum shipping crates were scattered about the vault floor. Each crate was sealed with two straps that released at the top through heavy metal buckles. Black stenciled markings on each crate indicated in abbreviated lingo, what was inside.

It was now 7:42.

Claudia removed her raincoat and her camel-hair blazer and hung both on a rack in the corner. The vault was warm and large with beige plaster on the two-foot thick walls and four long fluorescent lights on the low ceiling.

She began with the crates nearest to her, finding a marking, and checking off the first two. The same with the third, fourth, and fifth. By the time she got to the sixth, she was beginning to worry. And by the time she reached the tenth, with nothing to show for her efforts, she was scared. She began to check the markings with desperate speed. The letters dag and col appeared— the dagger and the collar—but not the box. Several crates later she read the letters Sekhmet. There was her statue.

Suddenly she saw it—the thirtieth crate. She stopped in mid-motion and stared at it. Two hyphenated words— GRAN-BOX. That was it!

The small black face of her watch read 8:08. Simms' few minutes had stretched into a half hour. But even if he didn't come back shortly, others from the staff would begin arriving in the next ten minutes. She looked over her shoulder, the guards were safely facing outward. Then as deliberately as she had walked away from Roncalli, she knelt down and turned the front of the crate to face her.

She pulled up on the strap to release the buckle, but it wouldn't budge. In fact, the strap had tightened as the buckle teeth bit into the rubber strap. She tugged, the teeth held the strap securely in place.

No wonder they never open the crates this way, she thought. There's got to be another way to do it. She tried to relax.

Then a smile brightened her face. It was easy after all. She pulled on the first strap, stretching it around the side of the crate, and then yanked it off. The second strap came off just as easily. Without tension on the metal teeth, the buckle lifted up easily releasing the strap. She spread the two straps open, ready to be replaced on the crate.

The rest went quickly. By 8:19 the duplicate box was hidden well within the crate in its shockproof bed of styrofoam pellets. The ancient gold box, which had once held jewelry for a queen, was inside Claudia's leather bag.

As she picked up the first strap, a distant sound reached her ears. She listened carefully. It was getting louder. She looked at her watch—8:20. Probably Simms, and possibly others gathering upstairs.

Quickly Claudia buckled the first strap, and grabbed up the second. As she was struggling to get it in place, the teeth of the buckle slipped and grabbed at her finger, tearing a 'V' in her skin and sending droplets of blood onto the smooth aluminum surface.

She continued to work. At last the strap was in place. She slid it over the area where the blood had fallen.

The footsteps were closer now, coming down the stairs. And there were voices. Claudia pushed the crate back into place with the others. She was fumbling around in her bag for a tissue to stop the bleeding when Simms and Miriam Gottfried walked into the vault.

"How far did you get, Claudia?" Simms asked, then added, "is something wrong?"

Claudia continued rummaging in the bag. "Some of the markings were hard to make out. I turned one of the crates around and I guess the edge was sharp. I cut myself. That's all."

She stood up and looked at them. "When I finish marking the sheet. I'll go up and get a bandaid."

Miriam started to reach for the sheet, but Claudia pulled it back. "No, really. I'm fine. I'm sure you must have something better to do." She could not allow Gottfried to see where she had stopped.

Gottfried looked at her suspiciously, then stared down at the crates. They were all still sealed and in order. She let the sheet remain in Claudia's hand.

"You're right," she said sharply, "I do have more important things to do. Thanks," she added grudgingly. She marched off to the opposite end of the vault.

When Claudia had checked off the rest of the crates, she walked over to Simms who was standing near the doorway and gave him the sheet. She picked up her bag and started towards the doorway, just as other staff members started coming in.

She turned to greet them and as she did, she spotted several styrofoam pellets on the floor under the table. There was no way she could go over and scrape them up unobserved. All she could do was to cross her fingers.

TUESDAY, APRIL 5

A little after 9:00 a.m., the television crew—totally oblivious to the drama in the vault of the museum—began to arrive.

They came in three red, white and blue vans emblazoned with the United Broadcasting System shield. The larger of the vans was the remote control room with its racks of electronic equipment. It served as the working headquarters for the director and his audio and video engineers.

The other trucks contained cameras, microphones and the cables which were the arteries connecting the vital organs of broadcasting. They also held dozens of small wooden crates bearing the three-colored network shield. They were indistinguishable from one another, and from the crate which sat in the hallway of Claudia Betancourt's home.

Only six television crewmen arrived with the vans. The rest would arrive over the next hour or two.

While a crewman was directing the parking of the network vans, the first of the caterer's trucks arrived. It contained the chairs and tables to be set up inside the reception hall. There were several more trucks to come. They contained an electrically operated portable buffet, dishes, silverware and table linens, flowers, musical instruments and a portable bandstand. The food trucks would arrive late in the afternoon. The caterers had learned that if they arrived early, there was a migration from the television trucks to the food trucks...not unlike ants at a picnic.

The cocktail party and buffet would take place in the main rotunda of the museum. There the reception guests could circulate freely without interfering with any of the exhibits.

Two halls extended off opposite ends of the rotunda, the north hall ended in the wing which had been built to house the Treasures of Tutankhamun. It was modern, triangular-shaped and glass-enclosed, allowing natural light to filter in.

The setting had seemed inappropriate for the Golden Age Exhibit, and the museum staff had decided to evoke the mysterious quality of the artifacts. A replica of a Middle Kingdom tomb, complete with entrance passage and four separate chambers, was constructed. To reach the tomb, visitors had to climb a staircase to the second floor and descend a narrow passageway to the entrance, then enter each of four rooms, seeing the artifacts in their natural environment. The tomb would be dark, lit only by overhead spotlights fixed directly on each object. Tonight, however, the tomb would have the added illumination of the television spotlights.

At the very rear of the museum's great rotunda was a hall which led past a great marble staircase to doors opening into the rear courtyard. These doors were to admit the television men and caterer's staff. There, Thomas McIlhenny, a museum security guard, was posted. It was his job to make sure that everyone entering belonged. But he knew he couldn't stop everyone coming in and ask for identification, especially if the person had his hands full of cables, cameras, chairs, flowers or food. Nor was he going to check every piece of equipment on the way out.

As the chief of security had said yesterday, "The real job don't start until the public gets in on Thursday, them are the ones you gotta watch. These working stiffs what's gonna be here tomorrow ain't gonna steal nothin'. And the bigwigs at the reception ain't takin' nothin' but some of the silverware."

McIlhenny stretched and yawned.

By 9:00 a.m., work in the vault area had shifted into high gear. There were fifteen people in the room adjacent to the vault, hard at work unpacking at the three tables including Barnard Simms, Miriam Gottfried, Claudia Betancourt, Mr. Ali and Mr. Kamil.

Guards hand-carried shipping crates from the vault and placed them on the tables. Once the retaining straps were cut, eager hands removed the foam rubber padding and then the loose styrofoam pellets that were packed around each piece. With the protection of the aluminum and plastic wombs gone, the pieces stood bare under the hard glare of the lights. The work proceeded in silence, the atmosphere was one of awe.

The crates came in the order prescribed by Barnard Simms' list and, as each box came to the table, Claudia greeted it with nervous anticipation. The first crate contained a small gaming table.

The *Book of the Dead* said that the Egyptians had loved board games, and in fact, many of the rich had taken such games with them into their tombs. The gaming table that Claudia began to unpack was a rectangular ebony frame two feet long by six inches wide. She peeled back the new foam-rubber sheet, revealing a rectangular board of thirty ivory squares, separated by ebony strips, set in solid gold. It was in fact a gold box supported by four legs, each leg seven inches in height, ending in an ivory-clawed bail.

As each piece became visible there was a subdued chorus of oh's and ah's. These gasps brought either Barnard Simms or Miriam Gottfried hurrying to stand and watch like a grandparent outside a nursery window until the next sharp noise turned their attention to the next table.

Miriam Gottfried carried a thick, loose leaf binder containing a detailed description of every piece, including dents and flaws. When satisfied that no damage had been done during the trip, she checked it on a master inventory sheet clipped to the front of the binder, and got Mr. Kamil to initial it as well. It was this sheet Barnard Simms would use to oversee the movement of the pieces from this room to the exhibition chambers upstairs.

Claudia removed the protective pellets from the game board with tenderness as a mother might clean the residue of birth from her infant child. She neither gasped nor clucked at the finally revealed object. To her, it was a reunion with a familiar friend. Her mind automatically recited at the litany of the piece. What it was, its purpose, where it had been found, the details of its history that she could recall. There was a jealous flash in her dark eyes when another pair of hands at her table touched the piece to pick off a stray pallet. This look intensified when Miriam Gottfried began to examine the piece. The atmosphere at the table when the two women were together, heads bent in examination, was charged. The others moved back a fraction of an inch as if they could feel the electricity.

The floor of the room was soon covered with small foam rubber pads and styrofoam pellets. Moving from one area to another, Miriam Gottfried lost her balance and grabbed at the edge of a table to keep from failing. "Didn't anyone think to order garbage cans for this mess?" she snapped, looking directly at Barnard Simms.

For a moment Simms panicked before turning to one of the security guards. He whispered some instructions and the guard hurried off. He cursed himself for omitting this detail, but the sudden flare quickly subsided as Miriam Gottfried moved to the next object with full and undivided attention. And so the unpacking continued.

The plan was to hand carry from the vault to the exhibition hall all the pieces that could be lifted easily. Simms had planned to avoid the stairs by using the freight elevators. These elevators opened into the anteroom of the "temple." To cut down further on the possibility of slips or falls, Simms had insisted that everyone wear sneakers or other rubber soled shoes today.

The unpacking and examination were proceeding according to schedule, and should, he thought, be completed before noon. After his staff took their lunch break, he would oversee the placement of the pieces in the exhibition rooms while keeping an eye on preparations for the reception. So far, with one exception, his plans were unfolding with clock like precision, but the time for self-satisfaction would come much later, when the last guest departed.

TUESDAY, APRIL 5

In his apartment across town from the museum, Peter Mandel stood staring into the bathroom mirror. He had just stepped from the shower, tied a towel around his waist, and was preparing to shave. The room was hot and still steamy from the shower. Droplets of condensation hung from the ceiling and clouded the mirror. He reached out and cleared a spot so that he could see his face.

After ten years in broadcasting, he no longer felt nervous on the day of a show. He had decided that this was due to his position behind the cameras and not in front of them. Seasoned performers had readily admitted to him that they still experienced everything from minor headaches to major diarrhea before going on. Once Peter felt secure with the script, the ability of the on-camera people and the flow of the action, he usually looked forward to the day of the program eagerly.

Today was different. The prerequisites that he needed were there. Sharon's script was good, she had caught the mood. When the network had agreed to use a well-known newsman as narrator, with an equally famous actress as a roving reporter, he was ecstatic. The ninety minutes blocked out well. The movement through the exhibition chambers would be intimate and mysterious due, in part, to his insistence on the use of hand-held, light-sensitive cameras. With the famous voice reading Sharon's words, the viewer would be transported back in time to the Valley of the Kings to relive the breathtaking revelations that greeted the archeologists who had discovered these treasures. It was Emmy material, he thought.

He opened the bathroom door, peering out to see the clock on his night stand. 9:15. I should be at the museum by ten o'clock, he thought, to make sure we set up correctly. Shit, they don't need me to set up. I'm excess baggage at this point. He stepped back into the bathroom and began shaving. As he splashed water on his face to remove the last traces of soap, he remained bent over the sink, both hands cradling his head. I'm scared, he thought. *If Claudia screws up. I'm in a lot of trouble. That kooky broad could put us all in jail forever.*

Only a joke. Your Honor, he pleaded before an imaginary judge. *All I did was get her a crate and an I.D. badge for a friend, that's all.*

The judge's verdict made him skip breakfast entirely.

* * *

If nerves were the order of the day, the winner and absolute champion was Charles Green. It had taken every bit of his persuasiveness to arrange to be alone at home. Pat had resisted the idea of flying up to Boston to see her mother. She had agreed only after he had arranged to farm the boys out with friends. But he had done it. He was alone in the house at 7:00 a.m. this Tuesday morning, free to wear his Saturday working clothes on a weekday, and free to take Pat's station wagon instead of the VW.

Leave at 8:30...Christ! What the hell am I doing dressed and ready to go at 7:00? I'll make some coffee. An hour and a half to make coffee? I guess I could wash the car. I don't think Pat has had it cleaned since before the winter. No, a clean car in New York is too noticeable. Maybe the morning paper is here.

The paper was there, on the front steps. He opened the door cautiously, grabbed it, and stepped back into the house with the speed of a fighter throwing a jab. Back in the kitchen he fixed a cup of coffee and sat down. *New York Times*, Tuesday, April 5th. A time of infamy, he said to himself. He could almost hear the voice of Franklin Roosevelt, castigating the Japanese attack on Pearl Harbor. Only now, Roosevelt was condemning Charles.

Charles couldn't concentrate. Not one word of what he read penetrated to his brain. He had started into the second section of the newspaper when an article headline stopped him. "Gala Fete at Met to Herald Opening of Golden Art Exhibit".

Charles sat for several moments, his finger resting on the article. Then he got up and walked to the front closet where he took out his jacket. He returned to the kitchen, poured the untouched coffee into the sink, washed out the cup and went out the back door into the garage. A moment later the grey station wagon backed out. The parking permit with the red, white and blue UBS shield lay on the kitchen counter where he had left it.

* * *

In the Hiller household, the day was beginning normally. It was after 7:00 a.m. Sharon Hiller was making sandwiches for her girls' lunch. Upstairs, Clayton Hiller was still in bed. He never got up before 8:00 a.m. The girls were in the last stages of dressing. The only noticeable difference today was the fact that Sharon was still in a robe and not dressed for work. Today she was not going to her office. Today she had to be at the museum some time before 2:00 p.m. for a walk-through of the program. Then she would go to the room at the Park Lane Hotel on Central Park South, reserved for her by UBS to change for the evening. She could have gone to work and left her office after lunch, but that would have been a waste of time. She was so keyed up. Any thought of her office, her job or even her home was just ludicrous. There was no way that she could try and blend Sharon the working mother, the wife, into the writer Sharon, the criminal Sharon.

Tonight a famous man would speak her words and millions of people would be watching and listening. And still later tonight a part of the greatest, richest collection of Egyptian treasures would be gone, and she would be part of it, an accessory ... .. Oh, God, she thought, let no one know. Today, she thought, today there is no Clayton, no Deborah, no Fern. Today, it's me.

"Mommy, we're ready," seven-year-old Deborah said. "Fern can't find her other shoe."

Fern who was five, limped into the kitchen wearing just one shoe.

"I can't find my other shoe," Fern announced. "Can I have Sugar Pops for breakfast, instead of an egg?"

"That's fine. Fern," Sharon said. "Deborah, pour some Sugar Pops for yourself and your sister. I'll look for the shoe. And hurry the bus will be here in ten minutes."

Sharon raced up the stairs into the girls' bedroom. The room looked at if it had been in the path of a tornado...clothes, books, toys in every direction. Every drawer pulled open with its contents strewn about the floor. A shoe thought Sharon? She'd be lucky to find the beds in there.

She kicked at the clutter on the floor, hoping a shoe would appear. None did. She yanked open the closet door. A shoe bag was fastened to the inside of the door, the sixteen Douches were empty. On the closet floor were four or five odd shoes. She grabbed a small brown one and headed for the kitchen. She arrived in time to see Fern spooning sugar into her bowl of cereal and milk. Sugar on pre-sweetened cereal, she thought. Well, this morning whatever suited her was fine. She laid the shoe on the counter and jammed the sandwiches into the small lunchboxes. By this time she had forgotten who had the peanut butter and who had the cream cheese and jelly.

A horn sounded in front of the house. "The bus is here, girls, let's go."

The girls ran for the front hall closet. Fern's limp reminded Sharon of the shoe, and she ran back to the' kitchen to retrieve it from the counter. When she got back to the front door and gave Fern the shoe, the girls were struggling into their coats. Sharon handed each a lunch box, kissed them quickly, opened the door and shoved them in the general direction of the bus. Fern carried her shoe with her lunch box as she limped down the front walk. Too late, Sharon saw that Fern was destined to go through the day wearing two right shoes, one black and one brown. Sharon shrugged wearily. It was Fern's contribution to her mother's career.

TUESDAY, APRIL 5

Just after 9:00 a.m., Charles entered Manhattan. The traffic coming off the Triboro Bridge onto the East River Drive was, as usual, frustratingly slow. Charles exited from the Drive at 96th Street, drove west to Fifth Avenue, turned south past the Metropolitan Museum and turned into 74th Street, stopping in front of the three-story granite house at exactly 9:20 a.m. The trip of forty miles had taken just over an hour and a half. It could have been worse.

He sat still for several minutes gathering the courage he needed to begin the next step. Finally he got out and climbed the wrought iron steps to the front door and rang the bell. Almost immediately, as if she had been poised on the other side waiting, a short, grey-haired woman opened the door.

"Good morning," Charles said. "Are you Mrs. Britton? My name is Green. I came to pick up a box."

"Yes, Mrs. Betancourt told me, Mr. Green. The box is down at the end of the hall," she said holding the door wider.

Charles walked past her, his eyes riveted on the small wooden crate. The UBS letters seemed to vibrate. They were vivid in the dimness. He grasped the handles on either side and lifted the box. It came up so easily he almost lost his balance.

My God, he thought, is there anything in it?

Carrying it in front of him, he walked back to the front door.

"Thank you, Mrs. Britton, I'll be going now."

"You're quite welcome. I'm sure." The last word was almost lost as she closed the door. Charles carried the box down the steps and to the back of the station wagon, swung the tailgate out and lifted the crate in. He pushed it gently, but it only moved an inch or two before jamming to a stop. He pushed it hard. It slid back into the car with the ripping sound of metal tearing into wood. Charles bent to one side and saw the reason—the handle of his tire iron. As he pushed the crate in, the pointed edge of the iron, which was used for prying off wheel covers, had caught on the side of the crate and had taken a long gouge out of the side of the box as it slid past. The red and blue paint now had a long, deep white scar cut almost the entire length of the box.

Charles quickly shut the tailgate and got into the car. He reached into his shirt pocket, pulled out an I.D. badge bearing the name Charles Meyer, pinned it on his shirt front, and drove off.

As the car pulled away, Mrs. Britton turned from the front window where she had been watching and walked quickly back through the house. She had a telephone call to make.

* * *

By 9:30 a.m. most of the television technical crew had arrived at the Museum. There was a certain sameness about their clothes, khakis, denims, flannels and baseball caps, each with a red, white and blue card pinned to their shirt or jacket front.

The first order of their day was to get a cup of coffee. To the dismay of all, no coffee table had been set up. Anyone wanting a cup had to send out to a coffee shop. There was a steady procession now of "gofers" carrying small cardboard boxes loaded with styrofoam cups and paper-wrapped rolls and donuts.

The remote control van served as a breakfast room for the crew. As they finished their coffee they left, hopping up into one of the equipment vans. Inside, each took a red, white and blue crate, moved it to the open door, jumped down to the ground, turned and pulled the crate out, and carried it through the rear doors of the museum. Just past McIlhenny's post they were stacking them along the wall. Once everything was inside, the floor managers would decide where each piece of equipment should be placed.

When Peter Mandel walked into the reception hall just before 10:00 a.m., more than half the crates had been moved into the museum. Only ten or twelve more remained in the trucks. He walked around the hall, nodding to crewmen that he knew. Charles was the one person he wanted to see. Where the hell was he? At the rear door leading out into the courtyard, the portly security guard walked towards him.

"Excuse me, sir, I'm afraid I don't recognize you."

Peter looked at the guard for a moment in complete puzzlement. Suddenly it dawned on him—he was not wearing any identification. He fished in his jacket pocket and brought out his UBS badge. The guard nodded and moved away.

Peter walked through the door into the parking area. The three UBS trucks were to his right. A crewman passed Peter, carrying another red, white and blue crate into the building. Peter stepped off the curb and walked out into the middle of the courtyard. Now he could see the ramp that led into the yard from Fifth Avenue. Just at the entrance to the courtyard was a grey Ford station wagon with Connecticut license plates. A security guard was leaning down at the driver's window. There seemed to be a rather heated conversation in progress. Peter walked towards the car. In a moment he could see an agitated Charles behind the wheel.

"Hi." Peter waved to the guard. "What's the problem?"

The guard straightened and looked at Peter. The UBS badge on Peter's jacket caught his eye.

"This gentleman says he's one of your television people, but he don't have a parking permit."

Peter came around and stood next to the guard.

"Good morning, Meyer," he nodded to Charles leaning into the window. "Glad you could get here. We almost gave up on you."

Peter straightened and turned to the guard.

"He just has to drop off a crate. He'll only be parked for a minute. Is it O.K.?"

The guard weighed this decision.

"I ain't supposed to let no one in without a parking sticker, but if it's only for a minute I guess it'll be O.K."

"Thanks a lot," Peter smiled at the guard. "All right, Meyer, just pull down next to the trucks."

The guard stepped away. Peter began to walk back towards the trucks.

Charles backed into a slot on the far side of the control van and got out. He was opening the tailgate as Peter caught up to him.

"Where's the parking pass I gave you?" Peter growled.

"I left it home," Charles answered.

"Terrific!" Peter said. "What would you do if I didn't show up—deliver the crate back to Claudia's house?"

"I probably would have dumped it in the river and gone home," Charles said as he slid the crate out of the car. "I don't know what I'm doing here in the first place."

"Oh, cut the shit and follow me into the museum. You know damn well what you're doing here," Peter snapped.

The two men walked. Peter led the way into the museum with Charles a step behind, carrying the crate.

"Just set it down here, against the wall," Peter pointed to a spot a bit removed from the other crates and partially hidden by other equipment.

Charles set the crate down, straightened and looked at Peter. "Now what?" he asked.

"Now get the hell out of here," Peter said, "and don't forget to be back right after 3:00 this afternoon."

Peter watched Charles until he passed safely out through the door into the courtyard.

Now that was easy, Peter thought, too easy. As he turned to go back into the large room where his men were setting up, he smiled to himself. Now, Claudy baby. The rest is up to you.

* * *

Claudia straightened her back and pressed forward with both hands on her hips. She wished she could smoke. The room was now orderly. The litter from the unpacking had been swept up and put in a large plastic barrel.

The larger pieces, after passing Miriam Gottfried's inspection, were placed on the floor on the foam-rubber pads which had lined their crates. The smaller pieces remained on the tables. Claudia looked at her watch. It was 10:10 a.m.

They were almost a third of the way through and not one of the five pieces had yet appeared.

A security guard placed the next crate on her table. Claudia stared at it for a moment. Her hands began to sweat. On the top, partially hidden by a strap, the familiar words Gran-Box were stenciled. Claudia thought of her now bandaged finger and looked to see where Gottfried was—far enough away, she hoped, so that the crate would be gone before she could see it.

The guard loosened the straps and lifted the top all in one motion. She needn't have worried about the bloodstain on the lid. However, the real test was yet to come. As she lifted the box gently from the crate, her hands shook.

In a moment Barnard Simms was at her side. "Are you all right?" he asked, gently guiding Claudia's hands until the box was safely on the table.

"Yes, yes. I suddenly felt a little queasy. Probably the excitement and no breakfast."

"Why don't you go upstairs and get something?" he suggested. "You've been working steadily since 7:30."

Claudia could feel her heartbeat slowing down. Nothing was going to get her out of the room now. "I'm fine, Barnard. I have some chocolate in my bag," she gestured towards the leather bag on the floor. "The sugar will pick me up. Thanks."

Simms moved away. Claudia was left with Roncalli's gold box. She flicked away the final pieces of foam and awaited Gottfried's inspection. She hadn't been able to find out about any dents and scrapes on the Egyptians' original piece. Would it become an issue?

She waited. The seconds stretched into eternity. What was taking Gottfried so long?

Finally, the curator appeared on the other side of the table and lifted up the box. "This belonged to queen Nefertiti," she lectured the workers. "It was used to hold ointments, presumably. It's one of a pair. The other is in a private collection." Her eyes blazed with hostility as she looked at Claudia, then lowered the box to the table. "The museum is thinking of acquiring it." Gottfried hadn't even examined the piece! She was so interested in being in the spotlight and needling Claudia that she didn't even check it against the list. The duplicate had passed with greater ease than had some of the originals. She had done it!

Claudia allowed herself only a moment of triumph. After all, there were four more pieces to go.

* * *

Charles had spent most of the past five days thinking about today. There was, however, one thing Charles had not thought about it. It had completely skipped his mind, undoubtedly because it represented no potential trouble. Charles had never figured out what he was going to do from the time he delivered the crate until he had to return to the museum some five hours later.

As he drove out of the museum courtyard, and turned right into the downtown traffic on Fifth Avenue, he was suddenly aware that he hadn't the slightest idea where he was going. At 10:00 a.m. he couldn't look for a movie or bar to kill the next five hours.

He continued down Fifth Avenue for several blocks and pulled over to the curb. He sat quietly for several minutes, thinking, but his mind remained a total blank.

His thoughts were interrupted by the shrill blast of a horn. He glanced up at the rearview mirror. The entire back window of his car was filled with the front end of a bus. Charles had parked at a bus stop. He moved into the traffic again. It was bumper-to-bumper, stop and go for the new few blocks. As far as he could see down Fifth Avenue, the traffic was solid. At 62nd Street he turned left and headed east towards the river. When he reached the Drive, he instinctively took the northbound entrance ramp.

"What the hell," he said aloud, "I'm going home. I'll come back later. Hope I remember the parking permit this time."

* * *

For Claudia, the intensity was growing with each passing minute. Her eyes devoured the cryptic stencils on each box that was placed on her table. If the contents were not one of her pieces, her interest flagged. She tried to eavesdrop on the other tables, hoping to hear what was being opened. At present, only two of her pieces had been unpacked. The miniature box was in her bag. She had heard them exclaim over the burial collar as it was unpacked at another table.

She was almost finished unpacking an urn when a guard appeared carrying another crate.

"I'm sorry," he said, "I thought you were ready for another. I'll take it back."

Claudia looked down at the crate. The stencil read DAG.

"Don't take it back," she fought to keep her voice relaxed and authoritative. "Put it down here, next to me on the floor, and open the top. I will get to it much quicker that way."

The guard hesitated for a moment and then obeyed. He set the small box on the floor next to Claudia's bag. He undid the straps and lifted the top. As he finished, Claudia called out.

"All right, Miriam, we have another."

Miriam Gottfried walked over to the table and stood next to Claudia.

"Ah, yes," Miriam sighed, "the golden wine urn." She ran her finger absentmindedly around the rim of the urn as she searched her book for the right page.

The older woman studied the sheet for several seconds and then bent forward to examine the urn. As all eyes followed Gottfried, Claudia stepped backwards to where the guard had left the open crate. Looking casual, but with frantic effort, she knelt down and pulled the real dagger from the bed of foam pellets, letting it sit on the edge of the crate. Quickly, she reached into the tan bag, felt for the duplicate dagger, and pulled it upward.

She took one quick look around. The staffs attention was still riveted on Gottfried. Never thinking about where the guard might be, she placed the real dagger deep inside her bag, the duplicate held in her left hand.

Miriam Gottfried finished with the urn and looked down to see Claudia kneeling with a dagger in her hand.

"What have you there, my dear?" she asked.

Claudia drew in her breath sharply. A second earlier and she would have been caught with two daggers in her hands.

"It's the dagger from the royal armory," Claudia answered. Her smiled was sickly. She had the feeling everyone knew what she had just done.

"Yes, I see," Gottfried nodded. "Since I'm right here, let me look it over, and I'll check it off my list." She held out her hand.

Claudia began to hand the knife to Miriam Gottfried and then froze. She was handing the curator a fake, and not one of Roncalli's fakes. She drew her hand back slowly. In one minute the whole thing could be over. Gottfried's rage, her own humiliation. She could see the curator's brows knitting into a puzzled frown as she held back.

"Well, come now, Claudia," Gottfried said, "we're supposed to be saving time."

Claudia slowly moved the knife towards the outstretched hand. Before she could hand it to her, Gottfried reached out and took it from her. The curator turned away towards the table, where she put the knife down and began to turn the pages in the binder. Claudia stood behind her. She could not see the knife on the table. She heard the pages stop turning. Gottfried was reading. Now she was finished reading. Claudia watched the woman's back bend over the table as she began her examination. Claudia closed her eyes, her shoulders sagged, her hands hung at her sides. She was waiting for the explosion. Any second now the gun would go off.

Slowly she opened her eyes, staring. As the curator straightened, then turned towards Claudia, she smiled. She placed a checkmark on the front sheet of the book. Once more Claudia found she could quit holding her breath.

TUESDAY, APRIL 5

The needle spray of the shower danced off her upturned face. Sharon opened her mouth, and when it was filled she pursed her lips and spit a stream at the ceiling. She was feeling giddy. She couldn't remember a time when she had felt happier or more satisfied with herself.

She reached out and adjusted the spray from hot to warm, tensed her body for the final shock, and turned the hot water all the way off. The cold water coursed over her. She hugged her arms to her sides, letting her breath out in a long whistle, and turned the water off. Once out of the shower, she rubbed herself dry with a large towel, working briskly. It was the best way she could think of to get rid of the excess nervous energy.

When she was dry, she stood for a moment, hands on hips, looking at herself in the full-length mirror on the back of the door. She twisted from side to side, bent her slim waist and flexed her knees. Today she liked her body—boyishness and all. She yanked open the bathroom door and ran into her bedroom. She suddenly remembered that Clayton was still at home. If he saw me running around like this, she thought, it would mean nothing to him. Sad, but true.

She pulled on her bikini pants, put on a robe and began to comb her still damp hair. The reflection in her dressing table mirror smiled at her.

"Ms. Hiller, her serious voice said to the reflection, won't you tell our readers what a typical day is like for a famous writer like yourself?

Why, I'll be glad to, the reflection answered.

The reflection put down the comb and crossed her arms. I may be a famous and talented writer, but I am a mother, too. So on a typical day, I get up early, help the girls get ready for school, give my housekeeper her orders for the day, and then I do some writing.

Then what happens?

Well, on a day such as this there may be some interviews or some fan mail replies my secretary wants me to sign. I may have a meeting with my publisher or with my agent and a movie producer. Or, take today for instance. Today, I have to go to the Metropolitan Museum where UBS is doing a TV show that I wrote. I may have to work on the script. After the show, I may stay over at my suite at the Park Lane. Yes, I guess that pretty much covers it...except that I am going to steal part of the exhibit.

Thank you for the time, Ms. Hiller, the interviewer voice said.

Don't mention it, the famous writer replied graciously, my public deserves it."

Sharon was laughing as she hurried down the carpeted stairs to see how

Clayton was coming with his breakfast.

* * *

Claudia was straining to either see or hear what new pieces came out of the vault. By 11:30, neither the candle holder nor the statue of Sekhmet had appeared at her table. She knew the arrival of the statue would cause a reaction similar to that given the collar. At 11:45, the reaction came. It was from the table across the room, nearest the vault door.

The statue was unpacked, examined and placed on the floor, near the other large pieces awaiting final movement up to the exhibition hall.

A guard appeared at the door. "That's the last of them, Mr. Simms." Where was the candle holder? Claudia realized that she must have missed its arrival.

Simms nodded his thanks and moved over to Miriam Gottfried, who was finishing an examination. The two whispered together. Simms took the inventory sheet from the curator and turned to face the people who idly fingered the pieces on the tables, awaiting further instructions.

"Everything's here, safe and sound," he announced, a pleased grin creased his round, smooth face. "It's just noon and we're right on schedule. Time for lunch. Please be back here at 12:30. Then we can begin taking everything upstairs."

The people began to move out of the room. Finally, only Claudia, Simms and the curator remained.

"Shall we go?" Simms was looking at Claudia as he spoke.

"Yes, of course," Claudia answered. Her mind was racing, trying to find a way to accomplish the next step of her mission.

"Come along. The guards will lock up behind us," Simms said.

The three of them walked out of the room together. Behind her, Claudia heard the guard jingling the keys as he locked the door. They started down the hall towards the staircase. Then Claudia stopped and put her hand on Simms' arm.

"How stupid of me, I left my bag in the room. I'll have to go back for a second."

Simms looked at her, his pleasant smile now slightly exasperated. He called out to the guard, who was still at the door.

"Please let Mrs. Betancourt back in for a moment, she's forgotten her purse."

Claudia returned the guard's stare with a sickly smile and stepped back into the room. The guard remained outside. She was alone. Her heartbeat quickened. She went directly to her bag and picked it up.

She stood for a moment, looking first at the Sekhmet statue and then at the golden collar on the table. Sekhmet, she knew, would have to wait. She stepped over to the table and set the bag down next to the collar. There was an instant's hesitation, then she reached into the bag, lifted out the replica and replaced it with the real one. She grasped the shoulder strap and slipped the bag from the table. As she turned, she saw the candle holder. It sat on the next table. She moved a step closer to it and set the bag down.

She reached for the candle holder on the table with one hand while the other slipped into the bag to begin its blind groping for the replica.

"Are you through in there, ma'am?"

Her heart crashed, her knees turned to jelly. The instant sweat on her hands made her lose her grip on the candle holder and it fell back onto the table. The guard took a step towards her.

The bag...close the bag. She yanked the bag from the table. It slammed against her side. She pulled the strap over her shoulder as she covered the bag with her arm.

"I'm sorry I took so long. I just can't pull myself away from these beautiful things."

As she spoke she started towards the door—slowly, deliberately—her legs had gone too weak for any speed.

Outside the room, she stopped. She was alone, save for the guard at the door. Simms and Miriam had gone ahead. She walked to the foot of the staircase, and realized she could not walk up the stairs. She turned and sat down on the steps, her legs stretched out in front of her. She twisted the tote bag around and sat it on her lap. The top zipper was open. Closing it required all the strength and concentration she could muster.

She sat there for several minutes, aware of the slowing of her heart and the quieting of the pounding in her head. Gradually, her strength returned. At last she stood and climbed the steps to the main floor.

Outside the entrance to the new 'temple,' Claudia found a scene of busy confusion.

All the television equipment had been moved into position. The red, white and blue television equipment crates were scattered everywhere, most of them now emptied of their contents. Coils of black cable lay all over, the floor. Three-wheeled light stanchions were standing about, some already rigged with the small spots and key lights they carried. Others were still empty poles waiting for a technician.

Men and women hurried in and out—some with cables, some with crates, some with clipboards. A group of technicians was busy setting up a television camera on a four-wheeled, hydraulically operated dolly.

Claudia clutched the tote bag tightly to her side. There were so many television crates, and they all looked alike. How was she to know which one was hers? Only Peter could tell her, but he was nowhere in sight.

She walked across to the camera technicians. "Excuse me," she said. One of the men turned his head.

"Yeah," he said. Seeing that the interruption was caused by a very attractive woman, he stopped his work and stepped towards her.

"What can we do for you?"

"I'm looking for Mr. Mandel, Peter Mandel."

"Pete was here a minute ago. Maybe I can help you? You look lost."

"No, I'm not lost," Claudia's tone was cold. "I just have to find Mr. Mandel."

"Let's see if we can find him." He put out his hand and reached for Claudia's arm. "I'll be right back," he called to the others.

Claudia pulled back her arm and followed him. Several feet away, in the midst of a group of people, she saw Peter. Before she could go to him, her guide called out.

"Hey, Peter, I got some lady here wants to see you." Peter turned, saw Claudia, and came over to where they were standing.

"Thanks, Sam," he nodded to the man, "get back to what you were doing. I'll take care of the lady."

"I'm sure you will," the other man said, the leer in his voice obvious as he moved away.

"How are you?" Peter asked, taking her by the arm and steering her to a quiet corner. "You look terrible—white as a ghost."

"I'm fine now, Peter. I've had a rather hectic morning."

"Oh?" His voice was urgent.

"I've switched three pieces. I have them here in my bag. I must get to that crate, Peter. Where is it?"

Her tone was matter-of-fact. But the words were heavy with emotion. Somehow, Peter had the feeling that the moment was unreal. He couldn't believe what he was hearing. He closed his eyes and shook his head, trying to clear his mind.

Claudia was becoming impatient. "Well, Peter, where is it? I haven't much time."

Without speaking, he turned away and walked back towards the place where he had moved the crate. During the morning Peter had checked repeatedly on the crate to make sure that the innocent-looking box, now partially hidden from view in its corner, was not disturbed in any way. He gestured towards it with his head.

Claudia turned and looked around. The corner was relatively quiet. No one was looking at the producer or at the woman with the leather totebag.

Claudia bent over the crate and released its two trunk-type locks. She lifted the top and pushed it back against the wall. She took out the small TV camera inside and placed it on the floor, quickly slipped the bag from her shoulder, and tucked it in the crate. With some effort, she returned the camera to lie on top of the bag and closed the lid.

The entire process had taken no more than twenty seconds.

Only when the top was down did Peter realize that he had been holding his breath. When Claudia turned, she was smiling. Some of the color had returned to her face.

"There, see how simple it is? Now, you just make sure no one disturbs this crate until Charles gets back here. I'll see you later."

She patted his arm and walked away. Peter stood motionless, watching her trim figure through the door.

Sitting alone in a corner of the cafeteria, a cup of coffee and three cigarettes, smoked in rapid succession, were Claudia's lunch. The unpacking crew had asked her to join them at their tables, but she had waved them off. She had needed a few minutes of quiet before the tension of the afternoon. And in the corner she could smoke without too much reprimand. Instead of being pleased, she was furious at herself.

When she put the totebag in the crate, the duplicate candle holder had still been in it. Now she could no longer switch that piece. How could she have let herself be so stupid? Another sip of coffee and several drags on the current cigarette made her feel a little more satisfied with her morning's work. She muttered, "Can't be greedy, can we?"

Her thoughts were interrupted by the voice of Barnard Simms. He was standing near the crew's tables.

"All right, everyone, it's 12:30. Back to work."

* * *

Crossing the grand entrance rotunda, Claudia was aware of the blue uniforms of several New York City policemen. She was also acutely conscious of the fact that she was empty-handed. Did anyone notice she wasn't carrying a bag.

Downstairs, the guard outside the unpacking room stood back and nodded to them. Inside, they grouped around the tables waiting for instructions. Claudia's eyes darted back and forth from the candle holder on the rear table to the Sekhmet statue on the floor.

Forget the holder, she snarled at herself. Concentrate on the statue.

"Ladies and gentlemen," Simms began, "we now begin a tiresome, but delicate phase of our work. The pieces that go to the furthest chamber of the tomb, will be taken upstairs first, and so on. That should keep us from falling all over each other. No one should have to make more than four trips. We won't use the stairs. The elevators just beyond the staircase will let us out just outside the temple, and I caution you, that is where we are in most jeopardy. There are cables all over the floor, and the activity is quite hectic. Each of you will be accompanied by a guard, whose first job is to see that no one runs into you. Your cargo is very precious."

He paused to see that everyone was listening. Satisfied, he went on. "Once you enter the temple, proceed directly to your chamber. Dr. Gottfried and myself will be there to indicate the proper display case or pedestal. Just set them down. We will position them properly once they are all upstairs."

Claudia was thinking furiously. If Simms held to his sequence, the statue should be moved sometime halfway through the operation. But she was convinced that meticulous Simms would have planned every detail, even who was to carry what. Her chances were one in fifteen of getting to carry the statue.

She became aware of Simms' voice, as he read from his clipboard.

"Mrs. Patterson, the ceremonial bowl." Claudia's patience was rapidly disappearing. Suddenly wildly, she wanted to pick up the statue and march upstairs with it right to the crate and drop it in.

"Mr. Lefrac," he droned on, "the gaming board, there on the floor. It's rather awkward, so gently, gently."

Prissy fool, she raged—and was suddenly interrupted by the sound of her name.

"If you would be so kind as to carry the royal scepter." His benign smile made her want to throw up. She looked around the room and spotted the piece. "Since I will be upstairs during the moving, I am leaving this list on the table here. It will tell you what you are to take on your second and third trips, and fourth trip for those who have one. Please look it over carefully. We want no confusion. See you upstairs." Simms left the room.

Claudia walked over to Simms' list and ran her finger down the names. On her second trip she was to carry the golden headrest. On the third trip it was the Lotus chalice. She had no fourth trip. She hurriedly scanned the list, looking for the statue. She found it next to the name of a Mr. Voorhies. He was to take it up on his third trip. She looked around, and saw him standing behind her waiting to check the list.

He was a tall, thin balding man with thick glasses set high on a hawk nose. Like Claudia, he was a collector. Like Claudia, he was independently wealthy. They had bid against each other at several auctions. He was soft spoken and pleasant, she recalled, and accepted being outbid in gentlemanly fashion. She remembered remarking to Maurice that the easiest way to distinguish between old and new money was the breeding displayed at auctions. Maurice had called her a snob, and she had agreed. She turned towards the tall man.

"Hello again," she smiled.

"Mrs. Betancourt," he bowed in greeting, "how are you enjoying our day?"

"I find it thrilling, Mr. Voorhies—the opportunity to actually handle these pieces. I feel like an archeologist."

"Yes. This intimate contact is very satisfying."

"It almost always is." Her smile turned coy. She could see the tall man's Adam's apple as he swallowed.

"Mr. Voorhies, there is a very great favor you might do for me." Claudia was bringing all guns to bear. "I guess my favorite piece in the entire collection is the goddess Sekhmet." She pointed to the statue on the floor. "I just noticed that you were to take her upstairs on your third trip. It would give me the thrill of a lifetime if you were to switch with me and allow me to carry her up. I'm scheduled to carry the Lotus chalice." Claudia's eyes were like saucers, her lips pursed in their most provocative pout.

"Well, I can see no harm in that, Mrs. Betancourt. But perhaps we should keep our little secret from Mr. Simms." The tall man smiled down at her.

"Of course. I'm so pleased," Claudia gushed, "and, please, call me Claudia."

She turned to collect the royal scepter. She was ready for her first trip.

They left together in a procession. Each member of the party carried one, and each had a museum security guard for an escort. One of the group pushed a rubber wheeled cart with a foam-rubber-lined basket. It was not unlike a supermarket cart. His piece was too heavy to be carried by hand.

At the elevators, the procession was forced to separate, as the car held only ten people. Claudia was in the second group to ride up from the vault area to the exhibit floor. The first group had already started for the tomb entrance by the time she got out of the elevator. Their passing had created a stir, and curious television technicians had come over to line the way right to the entrance passage to the tomb.

Claudia walked slowly, the royal scepter held in her hands, her escort a step ahead of her, one arm stretched out as a barrier to the crowd. She could hear the occasional oh's or ah's as she passed. Once at the entrance to the tomb, she paused. The guards had moved the people away from the area, and it was quiet in comparison to the rest of the museum. Together, she and the guard proceeded into the narrow passage that descended to the tomb itself.

The narrow passage was some sixty feet long. Once inside, at the first chamber of the tomb, Claudia paused again, this time to allow her eyes to adjust to the dim lighting. Bare pedestals stood waiting. The first party had passed through and were already in the farthest chambers placing the pieces according to the instructions of Miriam Gottfried and Barnard Simms.

Claudia threaded her way onward. Even with the moving party, the tomb was very quiet. Voices were hushed and the rubber-soled shoes made no sound.

In the farthest chamber, Claudia moved from pedestal to pedestal reading the white plaques, looking for the display for the royal scepter. She found it and set the piece in place. She stood quietly, waiting for Gottfried. Her escort stood next to her, his hands on his hips. For the first time, she noticed the handle of a gun protruding from under his jacket.

Suddenly, Miriam Gottfried was standing beside her.

"I see you've located the proper display, Claudia."

"Yes. It was getting rather heavy."

"You can go back now." The grey-haired woman turned away.

Claudia stared at the back of her white smock. Supercilious bitch, she thought. Even that white coat is just for snob appeal.

"Shall we go. Miss?" the guard interrupted her thoughts.

Simms was standing near the door, whispering to each worker as they left.

"Use the stairs going back down. It will keep the elevators clear and speed things along."

Worm, she thought. If I didn't love these things, I would like to see someone drop an urn and smash it right at his feet.

On her second trip, this time she was cradling the golden headrest through the museum, she spied Peter and Sharon. The young writer was still wearing her coat and hat, and had obviously just come in. Sharon saw Claudia and began to wave to her. Claudia could see Peter grab her arm and pull her back. She was relieved. The less any of them had to do with each other, the better.

Claudia deposited the headrest and hurried back to the unpacking room. She wanted to be there before Voorhies left for his third trip—just in case he had forgotten his promise.

At the unpacking room door, Claudia used an elbow to get past her escort into the room. The security man straightened up as she brushed by. She stepped into the room. By now, most of the artifacts were gone. Only about ten pieces remained. She looked down along the wall where the larger pieces had been lined up.

The statue of Sekhmet was gone.

The blood drained from her face. She could feel her arms and legs grow weak. Her eyes blurred and the room grew dim. Knowing that she was about to faint, she bit her lip and drew in a deep breath. She closed her eyes and shook her head vigorously, trying to get some circulation going.

Claudia felt a hand on her back. Her blouse felt damp against her skin. "Are you all right. Miss?" the guard asked.

She nodded, afraid to trust her voice. Then she saw Voorhies, standing off to one side. In his hands he held the statue.

He caught sight of Claudia, smiled and walked over to her.

"You're right," he smiled, "she is beautiful. I can see why you would want to carry her." He extended the statue towards her.

Claudia shook her head from side to side and pointed at the table. She was in no condition yet to touch it. Voorhies set the goddess down and stared at Claudia.

"My dear, are you feeling all right?"

"Yes," she whispered. She cleared her throat and tried again. "The excitement of the day and no breakfast or lunch seems to have caught up with me. I'll be fine in a minute. This is my last trip—I'll leave after this and get some rest before the reception this evening."

Voorhies put out a restraining hand. "Nothing of the sort. You leave right now, and I'll carry this for you." He reached for the statue.

She grabbed his arm with both hands. "No, please, it's very kind of you, but this is the high point of the day for me. I'm feeling much better now, I really am."

He stepped back reluctantly. "If you're sure," he said.

"Yes, quite sure, and thank you, you've been most kind."

Claudia turned and half smiled at the guard. Then she picked up the statue and started out on her last trip of the day.

* * *

"Will you please tell me again," Sharon urged Peter. "What did Claudia say?"

They were standing in the room outside of the tomb. It was only minutes after Claudia had passed carrying the gold headrest.

"She's switched three pieces. They were in a bag she was carrying. Now they're in the crate."

"Where?" Sharon asked.

"Come on. I'll show you."

They walked across to the comer where the crates lay. "It's this one with the gash in its side." He pointed with his foot. The end of the crate was visible among an array of other network crates—Peter had decided to add them for disguise a half hour before.

"This is so hard to believe! You mean to tell me that the real things are in there just waiting for Charles to come and carry them out?"

"That's right." Peter nodded looking around. "Don't worry."

"I'm not worrying." Lines creased her forehead.

"At least not until Chucky baby comes back. He is a real fuck-up."

"He got the crate in all right, didn't he?"

"If I hadn't come along, that crate would be in the river right now."

"Well, it's not. Everything is going according to plan."

"Look, let's get away from here. That crate makes me nervous."

They turned back toward the entrance, away from the tomb.

* * *

Claudia was carrying the statue, her legs acting independently of her brain. She was unaware of her surroundings—neither the people, nor their activities, were able to penetrate her consciousness. Every fiber of her being concentrated on the object she held in her hands. It had to become hers.

They stepped off the elevator, into the large room, looking no different from the other pairs that had been passing for nearly two hours.

Just a few more steps, and they would start down the inclined passageway to the door to the tomb. Suddenly, Claudia stopped. She uttered a low moan. The guard turned. "What is it. Miss? Are you sick again?" Claudia closed her eyes. "I feel faint. I'm afraid I'm going to fall. I must sit down." She opened her eyes and looked around. The guard held her gingerly under one arm afraid to jar her and the statue. She took a hesitant step, and would have fallen if it had not been for the guard's support. He guided her towards the wall where a radiator cover protruded several inches, providing a narrow bench.

The guard eased her down, gently. She cradled the statue in her lap. He stood looking down at her, undecided what to do.

"Please," she said, "we passed a water fountain back by the elevator. Could you bring me a drink?"

He hesitated, "Is it safe to leave you?"

"Please," she urged.

He turned, and hurried back the way they had come.

Claudia closed her eyes again. Nerves, and lack of food, that was what it was, she thought. As soon as she put this statue where it belongs, she was going to the cafeteria for a sandwich and some very sweet tea. Someone was poking at her shoulder. The guard had returned with a cup of water.

"Take a slow sip now," he urged.

Claudia took the cup and drank. The cold water tasted good. "Just give me a minute, and we'll continue."

"Take your time," the guard said. "We got lots of time."

Claudia finished her drink, and got up.

The guard held her. "How are the legs. Miss?"

"They feel better. Let's get this over with."

They moved together into the passage, and down to the door of the tomb where Barnard Simms was waiting. He recognized the statue in Claudia's arms.

"Ah!" he exclaimed, "the goddess Sekhmet. Welcome." He pointed toward the far end of the room. Claudia walked through into the next chamber, called the Treasury, where Miriam Gottfried was waiting. The curator reached for the statue.

"Let me have her, Claudia. I want to set her in place myself."

Claudia handed Miriam the statue and watched as she placed it on the black velvet stand. She turned it, first one way, then the other, checking the light from the overhead spot. Satisfied, Miriam stepped back next to Claudia, her hands on her hips.

"Yes, that's perfect. The goddess is home."

No, Claudia thought, the goddess in not home. Not yet. Not until later tonight.

TUESDAY, APRIL 5

"I don't like the way you're looking at me." Charles Green's voice was low, his eyes darting about, nervously.

"Will you relax?" Peter urged, steering him towards the crates stacked near the wall.

"Why couldn't you get someone else to move it? Why did you need me to come back? I don't like this."

God, Peter hated whiners. How would Charles take the rest of his instructions? "There's a little more to do than just move the crate," he said sternly.

"I knew it." Charles muttered self-pityingly. "I knew it!"

They had reached the stack of crates. After a second's hesitation, Peter pointed at one with his foot. "Open it, Charles," he said.

Charles Green looked at Peter in puzzlement. "Open it?"

A man passed and glanced at them. Peter gave Charles a sharp order, loud enough for the other man to hear. "Get the camera on, Meyer. And let's move. We won't have all day."

Charles, flustered, bent to open the crate. Peter lowered his voice. "Take the camera out ."

Charles stood up, holding the camera in his arms like a very big loaf of bread.

Peter whispered. "Sit it on your shoulder, there's a curved brace that goes over your arm and supports it. That's right. Now let me fasten this strap around your back."

Charles was standing still as if in a trance. Finally, the camera was in place, atop Charles' shoulder. "O.K.," Peter said, "let's move out."

"Where are we going?" Chiles whimpered.

"Just walk next to me. We're heading for the tomb to meet the dragon lady."

"Tomb...?" Charles stopped Peter grabbed his arm. "What for?"

"Act natural. Come on. It won't take long."

They walked through the passage to the door of the tomb. There stood a very nervous Claudia Betancourt chipping the polish from her thumbnail. She had put on her camel-colored blazer, Peter noted. She straightened at the sight of Charles Green with the television camera on his shoulder.

"I was beginning to worry." If she was going to say more, a glance at Peter made her stop.

There was no one anywhere close by, but Peter kept his voice low. "Charles, the three of us are going into the tomb. All of the pieces are in place now, and everyone has gone for the moment. I'm sure the grey ghost and her assistant will be back a dozen times to recheck it all, but there's no one around."

Charles was staring at Peter, blankly. Peter went on. "The entire tomb is being monitored by closed-circuit television. You'll see the cameras once we get inside. The guards in the monitoring room will think we're just a television crew testing camera angles. To make it look kosher. I'll take a few light readings with this meter." He reached into his pocket and held up a small black leather case with a photoelectric cell in it...the kind used by photographers.

"The whole idea is to look busy and natural. They can see us, but they can't hear us."

Claudia added, "The statue we want is in the Treasury. That's the room beyond the Burial Chamber."

Suddenly, Charles spoke. "If they can see us, how are we going to do anything?"

"Don't worry. We've thought of everything," Peter said as he watched Claudia turn and start down the ramp towards the tomb. Charles hesitated. Peter gave him a shove to get him moving.

* * *

In the basement of the museum, a tall, thin security guard stood near the four small television monitors on the table in front of a chubby young man dressed in a security uniform.

"Each set is a different room," the guard said to the young man. "The cameras sweep up and back to cover the whole room. If you see something suspicious, you can freeze the picture by hitting the button in front of you. Got it?"

"Yeah, I think so." The young guard whose name was Gregory did not sound sure.

"What don't ya understand? I mean, this is so simple it's ridiculous."

"Well...what's suspicious? What am I looking for?"

The older man raised his eyes towards the ceiling, as if looking for divine help with his burden.

"Suspicious is any one that ain't just walking and looking. If someone stops to pick their nose, you check 'em out."

Gregory was nodding. "Yeah...O.K., I got it. Now what if I see someone doing something wrong?"

"Hit the alarm! Bluecoats will be all over the joint like flies."

The older guard sighed. He had a vision of this punk Gregory hitting the alarm every time some guy went to scratch his crotch or grab his old lady's ass in the semi- darkness. "Hey, remember and watch close. We don't need false alarms."

"Don't worry, Mr. Hansen. I think I can handle this with no trouble." Gregory leaned back in his seat and crossed his hands over his ample stomach as Hansen turned and walked out, mumbling under his breath. When he looked back at the monitors, the one under the card which read "Chamber 1" showed three people—two men, one carrying a television camera, and a woman. They were in and out of the monitor's view. Jacob Gregory leaned forward, his hand resting on the table, next to the alarm.

* * *

Peter, Claudia, and Charles moved about in the antechamber for five minutes. They walked around the pedestals, pointing, pretending to check distances and camera angles. Occasionally, Peter would hold the light-meter up and say something to Claudia, who would dutifully write something on the small note pad she was carrying.

"How much longer?" Charles asked. "This machine is getting heavy."

"Not much," Peter said, looking at his watch.

"Do you see the monitor?" Claudia asked Charles.

"Don't look around," Peter said. "It's over the door, near the corner. The red light shows that it's on. You can see it sweeping back and forth very slowly. If it stops sweeping and the red light is still on, you know it stopped to look at something."

"Scary, isn't it, Peter?" Charles asked. "Like big brother is watching you?"

"Watch your timing," Peter looked at both of them.

Charles turned to look for Peter, but the producer had vanished.

* * *

After he left the tomb, Peter Mandel retraced the steps he had taken earlier—downstairs through the rotunda area where the reception was being prepared, and down a wide marble staircase to the first basement.

Directly across from the bottom of the staircase was a door marked "Service By Authorized Personnel Only." Behind it, a short flight of iron steps led down to a narrow catwalk suspended over the main boiler room. Now Peter stood on the iron grillwork of the catwalk. The electrical control panel for the entire museum was on the floor level of the boiler room, directly below him. Except for Peter, the boiler room was deserted.

On his trial run, the catwalk was as far as he had come. He had figured that one minute would be enough for him to climb down the iron ladder and throw the switches necessary to cut out the lights, and, hopefully, the cameras in the tomb. It was now 4:59. They were set to move into the treasury at 5:00.

He quickly climbed down the ladder and opened the control panel. Peter stood transfixed. It was much more complex than he had expected. There were dozens of switches and knobs. Behind him the steam boilers were emitting a low roar as they forced the heated water through the miles of piping that snaked around the huge room before diving through the walls and ceiling.

The fucking place was like the guts of a ship, he thought, reaching in his pocket for the diagram Claudia had given him. That woman was unbelievable, he thought. He wondered fleetingly how in the world she had gotten some building engineer to draw it for her.

The diagram indicated that four switches in the upper right-hand corner of the panel controlled the tomb. He looked at them, reached for the first switch and pulled it down. It snapped back to its original position. He pulled it down again, with the same result. "What the fuck!" he swore out loud, and reached for the next switch. It too, sprang back without clicking off. He panicked, and began to pull all the switches in the right hand corner of the board. The same thing happened. Suddenly, he saw the reason. In the center of the board there was a keyhole. Under it, in white letters, were the words "Main Control Lock." In order to operate any of the dials or switches, he'd first have to unlock the board. He looked at his watch. It was 5:02.

* * *

At 4:59 Claudia and Charles moved towards the entrance of the treasury. In the doorway between the two rooms, she put her hand on Charles' shoulder. "Wait," she said. "When the lights go out, we can go right into the treasury without stumbling around." They stood in the doorway. It was exactly 5:00. Charles glanced up at the television camera behind him, sweeping the first chamber, and the one in front of him, in the treasury. Both machines continued their lazy, side-to-side sweep, the red light never blinking. They reminded him of blood-shot cyclops.

"How long do we stand here?" he asked. There was a break in his voice.

"Just shut up and wait," she whispered angrily. Her watch read 5:02. "Peter may have run into someone. Just be patient, we have lots of time."

"Bullshit! If those lights don't go off in another minute or so. I'm cutting out."

She looked at him, and something in her eyes made him back away from her.

"Don't you dare move," she said. The words came from deep in her throat.

It took Peter two minutes of panic to find a black metal key box attached to the wall, ten feet to the left of the electrical control panel. The box was twice the size of a medicine cabinet, and when he swung open the door he saw a dozen rows of hooks, with a key hanging from almost every hook. Under each hook was a number. Peter followed each row with his finger until his eye fell on the words

'Main Control Lock'.

He snatched the key and ran back to the board. It fit and it turned. He reached up and pulled the four switches. There was a loud click. They held in the off position. It was 5:06.

* * *

"That's it," Charles whispered. "I've had it. I'm going." He started to move, but Claudia stepped around him and stood directly in his path. He shifted his weight as if he was going to go around her right flank. She edged to her right and continued to block him. They were bobbing and weaving like two boxers in a ring. The red eye of the camera began to sweep in their direction. Claudia looked at the camera out of the corner of her eye, and suddenly thrust her body against Charles. She ducked to avoid his shoulder-held camera and pressed her face next to his, burying her lips in his ear.

"If the camera catches us now," she whispered, "the security guards will have the hottest gossip in the museum."

Charles stepped back, and Claudia moved with him, keeping her face against his.

"What are you doing?" he asked, twisting his head away from her.

"I'm giving the boys in the control room a little show," she hissed through clenched teeth. "Now they know why we're not doing anything."

"I don't give a fuck, let me go!" he rasped, and brought his hands up to push her away.

She saw his hands, and knew the only thing that would make him drop them. She reached for the front of his pants. At that same instant, the lights went out.

* * *

Jacob Gregory took a Camel from a pack in his shirt pocket and lit it with a disposable lighter. For the past three minutes he had been absorbed in one of his television screens. Actually, he was more puzzled by their lack of activity. The third person in the group on camera had disappeared from view and the remaining man and woman seemed to be standing around, doing nothing. Each time the camera swept past them, they were standing in the doorway between rooms one and two. They seemed to be waiting. The guard edged forward in his chair, a puzzled look on his round face. Should he stop the camera, he wondered. The camera came back towards the couple. The guard reached for the stop button, and pushed it.

The sweep halted, with the man and woman centered on screen number one.

113

The guard pulled on his cigarette. His hand moved over the alarm. Then the woman moved around the man and leaned up against him as if they were kissing.

"Holy shit!" he exclaimed, "would you look at that!"

He leaned closer to the monitor. At the same instant, the four screens went black. What do I do now, he wondered, half rising out of his chair. Should I hit the alarm?

* * *

"Now, Charles. Let's go." Claudia tugged at Charles' work shirt, pulling him after her through the doorway, into the treasury.

The darkness was total, but Claudia was prepared.

After handing Sekhmet over to Gottfried this afternoon, Claudia had counted off the distance from the pedestal to the doorway of the treasury. It was only twelve steps but now the exact count was lost in her efforts to keep Charles close to her.

She stopped, and extended her arm. Nothing. She moved her arm in a sweeping motion. Still nothing. She moved forward, one step and searched again. This time her hand brushed something soft. It was velvet ... a pedestal.

"Stay here," she whispered to Charles as she edged closer to the pedestal and moved her hand up along the base until she felt the cold metal feet of the goddess. "Yes. Here."

Claudia reached behind her for Charles. "Here, turn your back to me so I can open the camera." Charles turned around, swinging the case into Claudia.

"Sorry," he said.

"Just stay still," she ordered.

Claudia fumbled for the four large wing nuts, loosening each one, putting them in her blazer pocket as they came off.

She lifted off the back of the camera. "Here, hold this," she whispered, passing it around to Charles' hands. Within seconds, she loosened the side of the camera, pulled out the rubber-shrouded duplicate, and placed it on the floor between her feet. Gingerly, she removed the statue from the pedestal, took the rubber covering from the duplicate, and placed it on the real statue. It took only a few seconds longer to complete the switch, and finally re-tighten the nuts on the back of the camera. Charles stood quietly as she finished her work.

"Finished," she whispered. "Let's get out of here."

Charles followed her through the doorway of the treasury into the first chamber. There she paused for a second. Which way now? The total darkness was confusing.

"Christ, this place gives me the creeps," Charles said.

"Yes," Claudia agreed, suddenly feeling shivers running down her back. She moved on. As they reached the doorway leading into the passageway, Claudia turned around quickly.

"What's the matter?" Charles' voice had a frightened edge to it.

"I don't know," Claudia answered thinking of the room where the fake statue now stood. "For a moment...I guess it was nothing ."

The oppressive silence of the tomb was broken by the shrill sound of an alarm bell.

"What the hell is that?" Charles asked.

"The alarm system. The blackout made someone turn it on. Damn it! I wish we could have gotten out of here. Whatever happens, just keep quiet and let me do the talking.

Loud footsteps sounded on the ramp, and several beams of light were moving towards them.

"Hold it!" came from behind one of the flashlights which pointed first at Claudia, then at Charles. Through the beams of light they could make out several shadowy security guards.

"Who are you and what're you doing here?" one of them asked.

"Will you kindly take that flashlight out of my eyes?" Claudia demanded.

"Not till you tell me what I wanna know, lady!"

Claudia glared at the man. "I'm Claudia Betancourt. I work here and this is one of the cameramen for tonight's show. We were back in the tomb when the lights went out."

Before the guard could ask another question, the chamber was flooded with light. At the same instant, a phone rang from behind one of the partitions.

"I'll get that." The guard who had questioned Claudia disappeared behind the wall. Within seconds, he was back. "That was Jake in the control room. Seems when the lights went out in here and the monitors quit working, he panicked and hit the alarm. Everything seems to be working now."

"Can we go then?" Claudia asked.

Charles was shifting his weight from one foot to another as the camera straps dug deeper into his shoulders. "Yeah, this thing's getting heavy," he volunteered.

As the guard stood debating, Peter walked into the room. "What happened?" he asked.

"Who are you?" the guard asked.

"I'm Peter Mandel, from United Broadcasting. Is there something wrong?"

"He was with us earlier," Claudia explained to the guard. Then she turned to Peter. "The cameraman and I were back in the treasury when it happened."

"Why didn't you stay there?" the guard demanded. "You could have knocked over something walking around in the dark."

"It was damned creepy in there," Charles was surprised at the loudness of his own voice. "How'd you like to be locked up in the dark with a three thousand year old relic?"

"Can we please go?" Claudia asked.

"What is going on in here?" Miriam Gottfried and Barnard Simms appeared in the doorway. "Why did the lights go out?"

"Someone's checking on that now. Dr. Gottfried." The guard looked at the floor uneasily.

"And what are you doing here, Claudia?"

"As I was telling these gentlemen," Claudia managed a smile, "Mr. Mandel wanted to make a last-minute check on the lighting. Since I knew the pieces better than he did, I volunteered to come with them."

Suddenly the telephone rang again. "Excuse me." The guard disappeared behind the wall. When he returned there was a puzzled look on his face. "That was the electrician in the basement. It seems as though someone pulled the main switches on the control panel."

"You mean to tell me, someone deliberately turned the lights off?" Miriam Gottfried asked.

"Looks that way."

"I don't understand it," the curator turned to Simms. "We'd better make a careful check of all the pieces. Right now. Barnard, we'll begin in the treasury. Claudia, please wait here."

Within minutes, the curator had satisfied herself that all the pieces were accounted for. "Nothing is missing," she muttered to no one in particular. "Nothing is missing."

"Maybe it was just an accident—or someone playing a prank," Peter volunteered.

"Can we be of any more help to you, Miriam?" Claudia looked sideways at Peter.

"No—nothing's missing or broken."

"May I suggest something?" Peter said, and continued without waiting for a reply. "Could you post someone near that panel during tonight's broadcast? If someone is playing a prank. I'd hate to have it happen again, especially on national television. My network would never forgive me."

"Yes, sure," the guard answered. "We'll post two men down there."

Peter smiled. "Thanks. Let's go," he added, motioning to Charles. "Let's pack this camera away until tonight."

Charles moved up the incline behind Peter. Claudia lingered behind a little longer. "You're sure there's nothing you'd like me to do down here?" she said to the curator.

Miriam Gottfried shook her head hardly even aware of the question. She looked disturbed.

Claudia nodded to the guards and headed up the passageway well behind Charles and Peter. Halfway up, she paused and turned around. The curator was still standing where she had left her. Only the guards were starting to move away.

I wonder if she suspects anything, Claudia thought. Damn that alarm! She felt the strange sensation prickling her back that she had felt in the darkness.

She shook it off, walked out of the tomb, and headed briskly toward the street entrance of the museum.

TUESDAY, APRIL 5

At 10:50 p.m. Charles arrived back at the museum and attempted to blend in with the television crew. He had been unable to shake the anxiety he'd felt earlier in the day. It was making a shambles of his nerves.

At 11:00 the show ended and the camera lights were turned off. The brightness that had moments ago flooded the tomb was gone. In contrast, the normal lighting seemed dim. The crew began to pack up. Charles walked around, pretending to observe, looking for Peter.

The packing seemed to proceed at a faster pace than the setting up. Charles had a feeling that if he didn't find Peter soon, someone was going to give him a job to do. He was already getting peculiar looks from some crew members—or so he thought.

After what seemed like an eternity, Peter appeared, smiling and shaking hands with crew members. Charles waited patiently for Peter to finish before approaching him.

Peter saw him coming. Charles' nervousness was visible on his face.

"Hey, how's it going?" Peter asked casually, smiling at him.

Charles ignored the question. "Where is it?" he asked.

Peter still smiling, answered, "Relax, everything is okay."

"All I want to do is get the crate and get the hell out of here before something happens."

"Calm down. Nothing's going to happen. Getting it out is easy."

Peter's nonchalance was having little effect on Charles.

"Where is it?" he hissed.

"This way."

Peter led the way to where twenty or thirty crates were stacked against the wall.

"Here it is, babe. All you have to do is pick it up and haul ass."

Without waiting for an answer, Peter turned away.

"Where're you going?" Charles asked.

"I'm taking some of the people out to supper. It's the producer's ritual. Sharon and I and a few others are off to Le Café. That's where I'll be in case you need me. I hope you don't. See you on Friday." He patted Charles on the back and moved off, leaving him alone in front of the pile of crates.

Charles' nervousness quickly turned to depression as he watched Peter depart. He was light years removed from the gaiety and glitter. He felt alone and abandoned. Slowly, he turned and walked towards the crates.

When he reached the stack he bent down and examined the ones at the end, looking for the raw gash he had put in the side. He found the crate quickly but several others had been set on top of it. He moved one aside, then the second, stacking it on top of the first. As he bent down to pick up the crate containing the statue, he heard a voice boom, "Hey, Mac, what are you doin'? Don't play with them, take them out to the van!"

Charles straightened up. The man who had shouted at him wore a black turtleneck sweater under a ski parka. Memories of other, possibly better times, appeared as patches on the front of his jacket—Vail, Aspen, Garmische and Cortina.

"You new?" Ski parka asked, looking at Charles' badge.

Charles nodded his head. If he tried to speak, nothing would come out.

"Those crates," the man said, "belong out in the van. Might as well start carting them out. I'll get someone to help you. Hey, Lou! Over here. Help ah ..." he looked at Charles' badge—"Meyer load these things in the trucks."

Charles' mind was racing. He couldn't simply pick up the crate and walk to the car with it. His new helper, Lou, would be right behind him. If he left it here, someone else might take it. He decided to risk the latter. Looking at Lou, he pointed to the crates at the other end of the stack and said, "Let's start with those."

The two men each picked up a crate and walked out. They carried them to the waiting vans in the courtyard and returned for another two.

Each trip they made brought them closer to the crate with the gash in the side. When there were less than ten boxes left, Charles decided to take, a chance. He hung back, allowing his helper to leave for the van without him. He stood next to the crate intently examining his hand, waiting for the right moment to seize it. As he bent down, the man in the ski parka appeared again.

"What's holding you up, buddy?"

Charles told him he thought he'd picked up a splinter.

The man murmured, "Too bad. Here, I'll give you a hand," and before Charles could stop him, he stooped and lifted the crate with the statue in it. Charles stared in disbelief as the crate and the man carrying it started for the door.

Quickly, he picked up one of the crates and followed the ski parka. By the time he reached the dark courtyard, the man was gone. There was no way to tell which truck he had gone to. Charles stood in the open courtyard behind the Museum, and sat the crate down on the wet ground. His shoulders sagged and his arms ached. He abandoned the crate and walked slowly towards his car, unaware that the mist had turned to rain. He felt sick.

* * *

It was just past 11:30. Large, round raindrops exploded against the grey station wagon, pounding the roof, racing down the windshield, turning the air inside cold and damp.

In the center of the empty parking lot, Charles Green sat behind the wheel of his station wagon, staring through the rain-streaked window. He was only partly aware of the storm taking place around him. His mind was occupied with the trucks that had just left, their cargo and the sudden realization that he had failed.

Inside one of the trucks that had just pulled away were dozens of small wooden crates. One of those crates should now be resting in his station wagon. Charles Green's responsibility tonight had been to carry out one crate and put it into his car. It was a ridiculously easy job. Now the crate was gone, and he had no idea where the truck was taking it.

"How could I have been so stupid?" He sighed aloud, but the words were lost in the drumming of the rain.

He raised his arm in a sweeping motion brought his fist crashing down against the dashboard. The pain shot upward into his shoulder.

"Stupid," he cried. "Stupid, stupid, stupid." Each cry was punctuated by a smashing fist.

He stopped and sagged against the seat. "Oh, God, what will I tell them?"

Charles Green closed his eyes and covered them with his hand. Suddenly, he sat up.

"Peter, I've got to find Peter. He'll know where they're going. He'll know what to do. He has to help."

A tiny smile appeared on his face at the thought of Peter Mandel. ''Of course. I have to find Peter. This is mostly his fault."

With the speed born of desperation, Charles Green started the car and backed out of the parking spot. The rear wheels spun on the wet pavement as he changed gears and tore out onto Fifth Avenue.

"Le Café," he said. "Le Café. That's where they went. Peter and his fancy dinner party. Bullshit! He'll choke when I tell him the crate is gone. And it's his fault."

He sped down Fifth Avenue, fishtailing away from the green lights with a plume of water shooting up from the rear tires. He turned east and slowed. There it was, Le Café, the name printed on a canopy that reached out to the curb. The street was nearly deserted. He pulled over to the curb and turned off the engine.

With his hand on the door handle, he paused. Suddenly he was afraid again. He had failed to carry out the simple task he had been given. How was he to explain it to Peter? How could he blame it on Peter? Peter had gone off and left him alone, sure, but only because the job was so simple. He, Charles, was the one who had blown it.

There was no way out. He opened the car door.

He pushed Le Cafe's heavy wooden door open and stepped inside. Peter had better be here, and he had better know a way to get the crate back, because if he didn't, Charles Green might just as well drive into the river. But it wasn't Peter Mandel that Charles Green was afraid of. It wasn't Peter Mandel that Charles would have to answer to.

"Oh, please let him know where to find that crate," Charles prayed silently as he watched the approach of a dapper headwaiter.

A five-dollar bill sent the headwaiter to find Peter Mandel, and now the two men stood facing each other in the foyer of the restaurant.

Charles was looking pale, almost hangdog in his khaki work clothes, Peter Mandel noted. He was puzzled. This was the last place he expected to see Charles Green.

"What are you doing here?"

"We have a problem."

"Problem?"

"The crate's gone."

Charles said it so matter-of-factly that Peter thought he was kidding.

"What the hell are you talking about?"

Charles put his hands on his hips and tried to look exasperated. "The crate you left me with. The one that only had to be picked up and moved out to my car. Well, one of your crew picked it up and loaded it into one of the trucks with all the others! God knows where they're off to!"

Peter ran his hand through his blond hair. "Shit! Plain old, ordinary shit!"

"It wasn't my fault," Charles interrupted. "They grabbed it before I could get to it. There were people watching the whole time. If you had hung around ..."

"Shut up, Charles, and stop bellyaching. Let me think." They were quiet for a minute. "Look," Peter began, "those trucks are headed for the studio on the Westside. They'll park them for the night and unload them in the morning."

"So?" Charles asked.

"So, if we give them a chance to get there and park, we can go over and get the crate."

Charles straightened up slightly. "It's that simple?"

Peter Mandel snapped back. "No, it's not that simple. There are watchmen all over that building and I really don't belong in the garage area. It's going to take time to find the right crate, and then we have to carry it out of there without getting stopped."

"Oh, Christ." Charles' shoulders sagged again. "It was easier to get it out of the museum."

"You bet your sweet ass it was easier at the museum." Peter Mandel glared at Charles. "Look," he continued, checking his wristwatch, "it's 12:15. I have to go back and make my excuses. Let's give them time to park the trucks. Suppose I meet you outside the studio building at 1:30."

"Yes .... O.K. Fine. It's at Fifty-seventh Street at Eleventh Avenue."

"Yes. I'll be there."

"Look." Peter tried to bolster the obviously sagging Charles. "Don't worry, we'll get it. I'm sorry I ever got involved in this thing, but I can't walk away now. If anyone else opens that crate," he paused, searching for the right words, "well...we won't think about that." Peter had turned to go back to his table when Charles' low voice stopped him.

"It's only a ten-minute drive to the studio from here. What should I do for the rest of the time?"

Peter Mandel looked at the khaki-clad man first in wonder, and then in disgust. "Why don't you look in the store windows on Fifth Avenue? Perhaps you can find a place that sells balls and brains." He turned and walked away, shaking his head.

* * *

"The museum should be proud of itself for this evening," Maurice Betancourt said to his wife as he turned the key in the lock and swung their front door open. "Whose stroke of genius was it to televise the opening?" There was sarcasm in his voice.

"The credit belongs to UBS as far as I know." Claudia slipped out of her coat and handed it to Maurice. She wanted no part of an argument. Not now. The crate at this moment should be downstairs in the basement. She had to get down there to see it. Tonight. She did not have the will power to wait.

Maurice made it easy. "I'm having a brandy in the study. Will you join me?"

"In a few minutes. I have something I want to take care of first." Claudia walked down the hallway and into the kitchen. She waited until she heard Maurice enter the study then she went to the cellar door, turned on the light, and started down the stairs.

At the bottom to the right of the staircase, was an alcove. There, eight large floor-to-ceiling wine racks were in half shadow from the dim, overhead bulbs. With a feeling of exhilaration, Claudia crossed the cold concrete floor to the main aisle separating the racks.

There was nothing in the aisle.

Puzzled, she stared at the place where the crate should have been. Where was it? Maybe she misunderstood me? Claudia turned and looked down the other aisles between the racks. Although the floor was half hidden in darkness, she could tell that the crate wasn't there. Her eyes flashed back to the spot where the crate should have been.

Nothing!

Where else could she have put it? Mrs. Britton always follows instructions.

She re-crossed the room and switched on a light in the storage area. Nothing.

"I don't understand it," Claudia said out loud. Maybe Mrs. Britton hadn't been able to carry it down those steps and left it somewhere else. But where?

The vision of Maurice coming across the crate somewhere in the house, and opening it flashed through her mind. She lifted her gown and quickly made her way up the stairs.

She searched the kitchen, the front closets, the dining room, and the library. Maurice was still in the study, sipping brandy and reading. He'd have seen it if it were in there, she thought.

Claudia dashed up the stairs to the second floor, and then the third. In ten minutes she had gone through every room, every place where the crate could be. It simply was not in the house. Claudia came back to the bedroom, and sat down. The clock showed 12:30. She lifted the receiver then punched out Mrs. Britton's telephone number.

"Mrs. Britton, I know it's late, but that crate, the one Mr. Green brought here this evening. I can't find it. Where did you put it? What? No—no—that's all right. Thank you. I'll see you in the morning."

Claudia put the telephone down slowly. A sick feeling lodged in the pit of her stomach.

She stood up, then slowly picked up the telephone and pressed the numbers for Peter's apartment. After twenty rings she hung up. Her stomach felt worse.

She went downstairs to the dining room and poured herself a glass of brandy. As she passed the entrance to the study, Maurice looked up from his book. Her face was white and pinched with pain.

"What on earth is the matter? Are you ill?" he asked.

She nodded her head. "I guess it was just the excitement and overeating. You know how my stomach reacts."

"You're going to help it with that?" Maurice nodded towards her snifter of brandy.

"I thought it would help calm my nerves. Anyway, I just wanted to say goodnight."

"Sleep well," Maurice replied, and went back to his reading.

Claudia lingered at the doorway a moment longer, watching him read, then started back up the stairs. "A lot he really cares," she said softly.

In the bedroom, Claudia tried to reach Peter again, but with no success. She changed into her nightgown and leaned back against the pillows. She'd call again in a little while.

WEDNESDAY, APRIL 6

By 1:15, the rain had stopped. In its place a fine mist had moved up from the river. Inside his car, at the corner of Eleventh Avenue and 57th Street, Charles Green sat watching the mist create specters out of the street lamps. Time and two glasses of Scotch had helped soothe his fear. Now Charles was angry. Peter knew better than anyone how those crews operated.

Why the hell hadn't he been more concerned? Why hadn't he hung around? No, he had to play producer and dash off with all the stars. Served him right. "I'm glad his plans got fouled up." Charles was surprised to hear the sound of his own voice. He turned around to see if anyone had heard him, but there was no one in sight. The street was quiet. In the distance a foghorn moaned as a boat made its way down the Hudson.

At 1:35 a.m. Peter spotted the grey Ford station wagon. When he knocked on the window on the passenger side, Charles leaned over and opened the door. Peter slid in. As he closed the door behind him he said, "I'm not going to ask how that crate got away. The only thing that's important now is to get in and get it out of there." Peter gestured toward the UBS warehouse.

"No, wait a minute now," Charles countered, "what happened at the museum couldn't be helped. You should have warned me that those guys were picking up stuff, right and left. One minute the crate's there, the next it's gone. If I had known, I would have done it differently, gotten there earlier and taken precautions."

"Just like you did this morning? With the parking permit?" Peter's tone was cutting.

"That's beside the point," said Charles angrily.

Peter cut him short. "No, it's not. Look, I don't want to fight about this. Frankly, I'd like to go home and forget the whole thing. The trouble is that now the network is involved. If that crate is discovered, the repercussions will be terrible. I can't walk away and let that happen. It's my ass on the line. So let's get the damned thing out of there. O.K.?"

"How do we do that?" Charles asked him.

"I know how to get to the garage. But the rest of it, we're going to have to play by ear. Come on."

As they walked up 57th Street, Peter explained the layout.

"The garage entrance is on the avenue. That's where the vans drove in. The office part is here on Fifty-seventh Street. We can get to the garage through the office building, and I guess that's how we'll have to get out, too."

"How do we get in?"

"I've got a key to the building. It's a badge of being a news producer. There's always late-night editing to do."

Charles looked around. From the outside, the UBS building showed no signs of life. He wasn't sure if it was the chill of the early hour or his own increasing nervousness that was making his spine tingle. Right now, in spite of his resentment, he was grateful for Peter's calm assurance. Maybe that's what came of being a race driver, a pilot and all the other crazy things Peter did.

At the front entrance, Peter opened the door. Directly, across the dark lobby, Charles could make out two elevator banks. To his right, a red-lettered exit sign looked out of the darkness. To his left, at the opposite end of the lobby, was another red-lighted exit sign.

"This way." Peter headed toward the door on their right. It opened into a stairwell. A naked light bulb protruded from the wall illuminating stairs leading up and down. The wall paint was the nauseating green that was used in hospitals.

Peter opened a door on the far side of the stairwell. Beyond was a long, wide hallway lit only by an exit sign above their heads and another one far down at the end of the hall. The entire space had a dim, fiery glow.

"You could develop pictures in here," Charles said. "We should have brought a flashlight with us."

"I had no idea it was going to be this dark."

"Where are the doors to the garage?"

"At the end of the hall."

"There must be a light switch around here," Charles said.

"Forget the lights. Stay close and follow me."

Peter moved quickly, keeping one hand against the wall as a guide. Charles hurried to keep pace, reaching out to clutch at the back of Peter's jacket.

"Slow down," Charles pleaded. "I'm not a bat."

"Sorry," Peter turned his head. "I just want to get this over with."

They came to the end of the hall and stood facing two large metal doors locked in place by metal bolts anchored into the ceiling and into the floor. Peter chose the right door to begin with, moving the bolt from the ceiling slowly, without making any sounds. Next came the bottom bolt. Peter pulled and the metal released easily, causing him to lose his balance and hit the door with his shoulder.

The clanging sound seemed to reverberate up and down the hall.

Charles lunged forward to steady Peter. The two men stood holding each other.

"Are you all right?" Charles asked.

"Yes," Peter hissed, pulling himself out of Charles' grasp.

"Did you hear anything from inside when I hit the door?" Peter asked.

"No," Charles answered. "From where I was standing I thought you hit your head."

"I'm O.K. The damn bolt just moved easier than I thought it would."

"Where are the security guards?" Charles asked.

"They've got an office across the garage, between the two overhead doors. They're usually in there drinking coffee or watching TV."

Peter had been feeling along the surface of the door.

"Here's the bar. I'm going to try to open the door a little."

Peter leaned his hands, then his body, against the bar. As he pushed down on it, the door started to open. He looked out through the two inches of space, then quickly and quietly let the door slide back into place.

"Shit!"

"What's the matter?"

"There's nothing parked between this door and the guards' booth. There's no way we can open this door without being seen. I'm surprised they didn't see me. There's two guys in there. One's drinking something, and the other's playing cards."

"What do we do? Don't you know of any other way to get in there?"

"Don't push, I'm thinking."

After a moment, Peter broke the silence. "Wait a minute. I've got it!" He pounded his fist into his palms. "If we get upstairs to the second floor and work our way back towards the garage, we'll be at the repair rooms that are on a balcony over the garage. A couple of stairways come down from there."

"Let's go," Charles urged.

Peter started off, Charles holding onto his coat. They returned to the stairwell, and mounted the stairs to the second floor. Then they were in the office section. Ahead of them a hall continued along the front of the building. To their right, another ran back towards the rear of the building and the garage area. There were no lights on in the hall or in the glassed-in offices on either side. The only illumination came from the streetlights outside, filtering through the dirty windows and partially closed blinds.

"Which way do we go?" asked Charles, "I've lost my sense of direction."

"That isn't all you've lost."

"Well, if you had been more of a help... . "

Peter cut him off. "This way, let's go." He turned to the right. Ahead of them the hall dissolved into darkness, with the distant red exit sign appearing like a bright, bloodshot eye.

Halfway down, the wall of offices gave way to an open area filled with desks and typewriters. Just as they started by, Peter stopped. He turned and grabbed Charles by the arm.

"Listen," he whispered urgently. The hairs on the back of his neck and his arms bristled.

"I don't hear anything."

"Shhhh."

They stood. Charles felt cold sweat beginning to form on his forehead.

Suddenly, Peter ducked into the nearest office and crouched down on the floor behind the desk. Charles was next to Peter in an instant. The desk shielded them from the open doorway and the hall. They sat there hardly breathing. The darkness swarmed around them like a cold liquid.

"What did you hear?" Charles asked.

"Quiet. Listen."

Then he heard it. Heavy footsteps walking, slowly, down the other hall. There was a rhythm to it—several steps, then stop. Several steps, then stop.

"Security?" Charles hissed.

"I guess so," whispered Peter.

"He didn't see us, did he?"

"I don't think so."

"Didn't you know they made rounds in here?" Charles persisted angrily.

"No!"

They waited. Suddenly the footsteps stopped. Charles squeezed Peter's arm.

In the hall, a flashlight beam was moving up and down. The footsteps started again. The light beam came closer.

If this weren't so real, thought Peter, it would be funny. How the hell did I get myself into such a situation?

The footsteps passed in front of the office where they were hiding. Stopped, then retreated. They heard the stairwell door open, then close. All was silent again.

"If we had been a few minutes later coming through that door," Charles said, "we would have run into him."

"I'm trying hard not to think about it," Peter answered. "Let's just get this over with and get the hell out of here."

Charles stood and began to massage the back of his legs. Peter looked down. On the desk was a disposable lighter. He picked it up and as he moved towards the door, he looked out into the hallway. He motioned to Charles.

"I don't believe this is happening to me," Charles said, still trying to straighten out his legs.

"Just wait," said Peter, "the best is still to come." Cautiously they started towards the red exit sign.

"They don't keep dogs around here, do they?"

"Dogs?" Peter's voice raised slightly.

"The Doberman kind. Killer dogs."

Peter sighed deeply. "Do you stay up nights thinking of ways to be pessimistic?"

"I don't have to." Charles' tone was flat.

They had reached the exit door. Peter opened it slowly. Outside was a narrow balcony which ran around three sides of the garage. Leading off from the hallway were small repair rooms used to service the electronic equipment.

"We're right above that door we tried to go through before," Peter said. "Keep back from the rail and head for that staircase." He pointed to a narrow flight of steps that led down to the floor of the garage, next to where two vans were parked.

Peter started along the balcony and stopped suddenly. He seemed to cave in.

"For God's sake, what's the matter?"

Peter shook his head. "The other door—downstairs. I forgot to reset the bolts—it's still open. God, how stupid!"

* * *

Charles had been trying very hard to keep calm. The prowl had, for the most part, taken his mind off how scared he really was. Slowly, the implications of Peter's oversight set in. He leaned against the wall, breathing quickly and sharply, a roaring filled his ears.

Peter stepped close and grabbed his shoulders, shaking him.

"You're going to pass out. Now cut it out! Breathe deeply. Slowly. All the way to your toes, and out. That's in. Again. Keep doing that."

Charles did what Peter said. The sound of rushing water subsided. He felt better. He clothes were damp, his body moist. He needed to sit down. Slowly he sank to the floor.

Peter sat down beside him. "What happened to you?"

"I don't know. Guess my nerves are just not up to this. I'm all right now." His breathing returned to normal. "I sure hope that security guard didn't find the doors unlocked. That's all we need—to have them laying for us."

"Look," said Peter, "we're almost there. I think we're really overreacting. Are you ready to try again?"

"Yes, let's go."

They stood up and moved towards the balcony railing. From where they stood the entire garage floor was barely visible. The brightly lit security booth, across the floor provided the only illumination for the entire garage. Sitting quietly below them, hoods towards the booth, were the vehicles—a control-room truck and six vans. All were white, and all bore the red, white, and blue UBS markings.

Peter tugged at Charles' sleeve, pulling him closer. "What was the license number of the van they put the crate into?"

Charles looked at him in total bewilderment. "How in hell should I know?"

"Well, Christ, you were standing right there when he loaded the thing! The least I figured you did was remember which van it was. Those damn trucks all look alike."

"Well, I'm sorry. It was dark. I don't know which one it is!"

"There are at least twenty boxes in each van."

"I guess we have to look in each one."

"Maybe not. The vans used for the special should have been the last ones in tonight, so they'd be parked at the end." Peter pointed to the rear.

The pair made their way down the steps and between the trucks until they reached the last two vans. They stood in silence surveying the identical backs of the trucks.

"Any idea which one it could be?" Peter asked.

"Sorry. . .no," Charles said with a deep sigh.

"Let's start with this one on the right." Peter moved towards the double doors. They squeaked as he opened them, then hauled himself up inside.

"Watch it, they'll hear us," said Charles standing behind the van.

Peter ignored him and pulled the disposable lighter from his pocket. In the glow of the flame, he could make out crates scattered in haphazard fashion on the floor of the van. He moved back to the rear doors.

"Do you remember anything at all about the truck, the interior, anything?"

Charles sighed, "No, I don't. I told you. It was dark. I didn't see the inside."

"Then we'd better start going through each one of these." He knelt down, pulled Charles into the van beside him, and closed the door.

"Hey, wait a minute," Charles said. "There is something. This morning, when I took the crate from Claudia's and put it in the trunk, it got caught on a jack. There's a big gouge along one side. I'm sure I'd know it if I saw it again."

Peter's only reaction was a slight smile.

"What's the matter?" Charles asked.

"Did you ever take a close look at these crates?" Charles shook his head.

"Let's start looking, you'll see what I mean."

Peter held the lighter while Charles started examining the boxes. Methodically, he looked at the sides, one crate after another. On some the paint was chipped off. On others, letters were missing. Once he thought he had found it, but the crate was filled with tools and cables.

"I have this feeling that it's not here," Charles said. "Why do things always work out this way?"

He kept moving along until he had finished all the crates.

"I couldn't have missed it. Shit!"

"Come on," Peter said. "Let's try the next truck." Peter opened the door slightly, pausing to listen. After a moment he lowered himself to the floor and helped Charles down.

They crawled over to the next van. Peter opened the door and pulled himself inside. Charles followed, closing the door behind him. Peter pulled out the lighter and flicked it on.

The crates were stacked two and three high but in a more orderly manner than the first van.

They started on the left. In a minute the lighter dimmed, then brightened again.

"I'd hate to try this using matches," said Peter. "We'd be here all night, for certain."

"Peter—I think this is it." Charles was pointing to a bottom crate. He restacked the two top boxes, then removed the straps from the bottom one, and lifted the lid. Even in the fading glow of the cigarette lighter, they could see the side of the mini-cam and, beneath it, the edges of a leather tote bag.

"My God, that's it, isn't it?" Peter said almost in awe. All right! Let's get it out of here."

"I guess we're going to have to take the whole crate," Charles said. "I'll carry, you lead the way and listen for the guards. Why do I keep having the feeling that as soon as we walk out of here, someone's going to jump out and say 'gotcha'."

Peter gave him a weary look. "Let's go."

Charles lifted the crate and walked to the door behind Peter. Slowly the door was opened. They listened for several seconds, then Peter jumped to the ground. Charles handed him the crate then slipped down to the garage floor beside him.

Charles took the crate again and followed Peter across the floor to the foot of the steps leading up to the balcony.

Peter told Charles to stay down while he made certain the guards were where they should be.

"They're talking to each other," Peter reported, "and one is sort of facing this way."

"Shall we chance it? It would only take a couple of seconds to get up the steps." Charles was suddenly feeling brave.

"Why don't we wait a few minutes and see what he does."

In silence, they crouched next to a truck. Peter suddenly wondered how the rest of his supper had gone. Sharon had certainly given him one peculiar look after he came back from his 'phone call' and announced that he had to leave. Wait 'til she finds out. This was really one for her book.

"I'm going to check again," Peter whispered.

Over the top of the hood he could see the guards. They were no longer talking but one of them still faced their direction, although his head was tilted downward.

"I don't know what to do. The longer we wait, the more chance there is of being caught."

"Let me try it," said Charles, and before Peter could protest, Charles picked up the crate and started up the steps. Peter let him get halfway to the top before he ran to catch up. When they reached the top, they stopped to give their hearts a chance to slow. A few more steps and they were back at the door leading into the hall. Peter reached for the handle and pulled. Nothing happened.

He pulled harder. Nothing. The door was locked!

"What's the matter?"

"The fucking door is locked from the other side. We got in, but we can't get out."

Charles stood holding the crate. His face drained of color. He lowered the box to the floor.

"What do we do?"

"I don't know...I don't know." There was a long pause before Peter spoke again. "If we weren't in this building, I think I would chuck the whole thing. Just leave this fucking box and go home and forget you, Claudia, the Museum, everything. I tell you true, I have had it."

"Well, you're in this building and you can't forget it. Think, big shot, think."

Before either could move they heard footsteps. Loud, steady steps coming from behind the door. Someone was walking down the hall and heading right for the door. Instinctively, they flattened themselves against the wall, just beyond the point where the door would swing open. A few feet beyond where they stood was a doorway into one of the repair rooms. Peter motioned to Charles to pull the crate into the room. In a second, Charles had disappeared behind the doorframe. Peter, waited, for an instant, then followed him.

The footsteps reached the other side of the door and stopped. Peter leaned far enough out of the repair room to see the door start to swing open. Then the guard came through and crossed to the balcony railing, letting the door go. It swung back slowly. Very slowly.

The guard leaned over the balcony and cupped his hands to his mouth.

"Hey, downstairs," he called out. "Hey, Flannery."

A muffled voice replied from the security booth.

"Before I come down, do you want any coffee from the machine?"

Peter remembered a coffee vending machine in the wide secretarial pool, halfway down the hall from the doorway. He silently prayed for someone to want coffee.

"Two cups, black," a voice called from the garage floor.

"O.K. Back in a minute."

The guard turned, reached for a huge ring of keys, found the right one and opened the door. He disappeared through the door.

In the instant that the door hung open, before beginning its swing back, Peter stepped out of the repair room and grabbed it. He caught the knob and held it just long enough to push in the 'unlock' button, then released the knob and let the door close. He reached down and turned the knob. It was unlocked. Peter slowly let out his breath and slid back into the repair room.

"Charles?" he whispered.

"Yes."

"Come on, get ready, as soon as that guard comes back with the coffee, and goes back downstairs, we can go."

"Where?"

"Back down and out of here."

"What about the door?"

"It's open."

"How?"

They heard the guard's footsteps returning.

Peter put a finger over Charles' lips.

The guard opened the door clumsily, as he was carrying a small plastic tray with three steaming paper cups on it. He turned left and started down the steps into the garage. The door banged shut.

Peter waited until he could see the guard approach the security booth.

"O.K.," he whispered, "let's go."

Charles appeared from behind a work bench.

"Charles."

"What?"

"The crate."

"Oh."

They tiptoed back to the door. Peter reached down, grasped the knob and turned. The door opened. He turned and smiled at Charles. Peter held the door open as Charles stepped through carrying the crate, pushed the button back to "lock," then let it close.

They retraced their steps quickly. Nothing was said until they were outside the building and Peter began hunting for his keys.

"There were moments back there," Charles said, "when I didn't really think we'd ever see these dirty streets again."

They walked toward the car. Fifty-Seventh Street sloped downward toward the river. The sky was still dark, and in the distance a fire engine howled, breaking the stillness of the night air.

"I'm not going to feel better until we're away from here," Peter panted. "Step on it, Charles!"

When they reached the car, Peter unlocked the tailgate, Charles pushed the crate in, and then Peter slid onto the front seat.

"Before we go," Charles said, slamming the car door behind him, "tell me one thing."

"What's that?"

"What if the guard hadn't come and opened the door asking about coffee. What would we have done?"

"I don't know. I honestly do not know."

Charles took a deep breath and looked at his watch, "I guess it's a little late to drop this stuff off at Claudia's. Can you imagine what she must have thought when she got home tonight, and the crate wasn't there?"

"She must be pretty pissed off," Peter said. "Actually, I can't say I really blame her. She pulled off one of the greatest thefts..."

"Yes, I know what comes next," Charles interrupted, "All I had to do was carry the crate out of the museum and I couldn't even do that right."

"No," said Peter, "that's not what I was going to say. But right now it's beside the point. We got it out—that's what matters. Take me home then we can decide what to do next."

They were silent as Charles drove up Eleventh Avenue. At 60th Street, Eleventh Avenue became West End Avenue and the warehouses gave way to high-rise apartment buildings. Past 66th Street, the huge Lincoln Towers complex straddled both sides of the streets. While they waited for a light to change, Peter looked up at the thirty-story buildings. Even at 3:30 a.m. lights shone through many of the apartment windows.

Peter lived on West End Avenue at 79th Street. Charles pulled up and turned off the motor.

"What do you want to do?" he asked Peter.

"I'm not really sure. Claudia was supposed to take everything and hide it."

Charles' mind started working. "The only thing Claudia really wanted for her collection was the statue. Why don't you take it and give it to her tomorrow? I'll take the other pieces back to Connecticut with me and hide them in the attic. It's warm and dry there."

Peter gave Charles a strange look. "Why do you want to take the pieces?"

"I don't want them," Charles said, emphasizing the word want. "I just thought it would be easier this way." Peter wasn't certain he followed the logic, but he was suddenly too tired to care. It had been a long day.

"I guess Claudia won't mind, as long as she's got her beloved statue."

"That's what I mean. What difference does it make who keeps the rest?"

"O.K., you're right." Peter opened the door and stepped out.

Charles opened the tailgate and pulled the crate closer. Peter lifted the lid and took out the camera. Gently, he removed the statue.

"I can't go walking into the lobby with this thing under my arm. Do you have a cloth or something?"

Charles rummaged under a pile of rags and pulled out a red plaid blanket. It was old and streaked with grease. For a moment, Peter hated to use it to shield the three thousand-year-old statue but there didn't seem to be an alternative. He wrapped the blanket around it.

As he was about to close the lid, he suddenly became aware of Claudia's totebag staring back at him. "Wait a minute. Chuck. It seems like it would be a lot easier if I just took everything upstairs with me, and gave it to Claudia tomorrow."

"You'd only be attracting more attention to yourself carrying that tote bag or the crate at this hour," Charles said.

Peter shrugged tiredly and took the blanket-wrapped statue.

"Goodnight, Charles."

"Goodnight."

As he walked into the lobby, he could hear Charles starting the motor.

Inside his apartment, Peter poured himself a drink, unwrapped the statue, and placed it on the coffee table. He sat on the sofa and stared at it, sipping his drink. I'd like to leave it out here, he thought, but the cleaning lady's coming tomorrow. Must hide it before I go to sleep.

Peter leaned back and closed his eyes.

In the meantime, Charles had turned on to the Henry Hudson Parkway, heading north towards Connecticut. He was very pleased with himself.

Sometimes, he thought, things really did work out for the best. If everything had gone according to plan, Claudia would have everything. Now, at least, he had insurance in case something went wrong.

WEDNESDAY, APRIL 6

Claudia woke with a start. She was lying on her side, looking down into two gold eyes. She stretched out an arm and patted the top of the cat's head. You must want breakfast, she thought. Breakfast! She looked at the clock. 7:45. The statue! She could hear water running in the bathroom. Maurice was already up. She got out of bed, slipped on her robe and went downstairs. The cat followed.

In the study, she dialed Peter's number and waited. Finally she heard someone mumble something, possibly "Hello."

"Peter? Peter this is Claudia."

"Claudia? Oh...wait a minute." It was obvious that she had awakened him. "Sorry, I had rather a late night and I'm just not with it."

"Yes, I know. I called you over and over. What happened to the crate?"

"That's why I had a late night. We ended up with a few problems."

"Problems? Did you get the crate?" She was almost afraid to hear his next words.

"We got it. I'll tell you about it when I see you."

"You said there was a problem."

"I'll tell you when I see you."

"Good. I'll come over and get it before you go to work."

"Claudia, give me a couple of more hours of shut eye. Be here around ten." He gave her his address, then hung up the phone.

Claudia didn't want to use the car, but the crate would be too heavy to carry all the way back across town. A cab was the answer. She'd only have to carry the crate to the sidewalk—in fact, Peter could do that for her. So all she needed was something to cover the markings of the crate. An old sheet would do. She found one and stuck it in a Saks shopping bag.

At five minutes to ten, she rang the bell of Peter's apartment.

"You're early," he said as he opened the door.

Claudia smiled as she walked in. The apartment was a lot larger than she thought it would be, but the decor left something to be desired.

She looked around, searching for the familiar red, white and blue box. "Where is it?" she demanded.

"Oh, we've got it," he answered. "You can't imagine what I went through last night to get it."

"I ... I don't understand. Didn't Charles pick it up last night after the program ended?" Her brow knitted into a frown.

"No. You'll hear all about it tomorrow night, and in more detail than you ever wanted. What it amounts to is this—Chucky let the crate get away from him. It got back to the warehouse along with everything else. I had to go bail him out. At three in the morning. I'm crawling around on the floor of that damned garage in my evening clothes. Right? Anyway, here's your statue."

He disappeared into the bedroom and returned in a minute carrying the Statue.

"Where are the rest of the pieces?" Claudia took the golden goddess from his hands, and cradled it in her arms.

"Back in Connecticut with Chuck."

"You said you had them!"

"Yeah, I know. I was sleepy. Besides, what difference does it make? I'd have let him take the statue as well if he'd wanted to."

Claudia's eyes narrowed and clouded. "Why did he want the pieces? Wouldn't it have been easy enough for you to take the tote bag and bring it up here along with the statue?"

"Look, as I said, you've got your statue. That's what you wanted. What difference does it make if Chucky has the others? If you're upset, take it up with him tomorrow night."

She took the statue, wrapped it in the sheet, and placed it at an angle in the large shopping bag.

"Can I help you find a cab?" Peter offered.

"No, thank you. I'll see you tomorrow night." She walked out of the door towards the elevator. It wasn't possible, she thought. All the planning and Charles ends up with the box and the other pieces. What could he know about how precious they were to her. This was wrong, it was not the way it was supposed to happen. The pieces were hers. She was not ransoming anything. They were always meant to be hers.

Outside Peter's building, in the warm April sunlight, the man in the raincoat waited. He found it odd that Mrs. Betancourt was up and out at that hour, considering the exhibit opening the night before.

In fact, he had been so convinced that she would be sleeping late, that he had almost missed her, arriving in front of her house just as she was making her way towards Park Avenue.

He was surprised as her cab stopped at 79th and West End Avenue. She'd never been here before. She was going to see that man Mandel, the one she'd met for cocktails two or three times.

Their meeting, for whatever purpose, was short. Claudia Betancourt emerged with a shopping bag that looked much bulkier and heavier than when she went in. She seemed angered, upset. Something was wrong. He wished he could see what was in the bag she was carrying.

THURSDAY, APRIL 7

Late afternoon sun poured through the small stained-glass skylights, bathing the golden statue in pale greens and blues.

Claudia Betancourt sat in a chair in the middle of the library, mesmerized by the elegant figure—unaware of the passage of time. Not until the room turned dark did she realize how long she had stared at the goddess with the emerald eyes. Her finger ran across the breast and down the graceful drape of the gown.

Beyond the closed door of the library, Claudia could hear the sounds of voices in the hall. She got up, placed the statue inside the wall cabinet, and pushed the door closed.

As she started across the carpet towards the library door, her husband came in. He was walking slowly and seemed preoccupied. He almost looked surprised to see her.

"I hope you're in a better mood than you were last night."

"I'm so sorry, I didn't mean to upset you. I was upset, but let's forget about it. Everything is better now." She started to walk past him, out of the library.

"Stoneham and Pawkowski are coming over around 9:00," he said. "They've got a case on which they'd like my opinion."

"Ohhh. . .that's too bad," Claudia said.

Maurice turned to face her, a puzzled frown on his face. "Why is that too bad?"

"I had something I wanted to show you after dinner."

"My dear, it's only after seven. They won't be here for two hours and dinner isn't ready. Show it to me now."

"No!" Claudia's sharpness was unexpected. Then her voice softened. "This is a special surprise and I don't want to be hurried. Perhaps I can move dinner up. I'll go see how Mrs. Britton is coming along."

Claudia's behavior at dinner ranged from non-stop chatter to equally non-stop silences. Maurice was puzzled. The usually composed Claudia was behaving in a way that in a patient, ordinarily caused him to prescribe a sedative.

Immediately after Mrs. Britton had cleared the last dish, Claudia stood and announced to Maurice that they would have their coffee in the library...or miss it altogether...she didn't care. There was an urgency in the way she escorted her husband to one of the black leather chairs which she had turned to face the wall cabinet section of the bookshelves. All lights except those in the display cases were off.

"What would you say," she began, "if I told you that I had done some collecting on my own and discovered the one piece that is now the prize of the entire collection?"

Maurice offered no answer. He gestured for her to continue.

She drew a breath, squaring her shoulders inside her blue caftan, and began talking. "Right now the Metropolitan Museum is reputed to have the greatest exhibit of Egyptian treasures as yet discovered."

"My dear," he began, and then paused as the word 'reputed' struck him. He continued more slowly. "I am well aware of the exhibition and the fight to get it here, and the lunacy every day at the museum. But what has this to do with us or with our little collection?"

"This!" She chose that moment to pull the catch on the bookshelf. The cabinet door swung open, and with the spotlight on, the statue stood revealed, staring out of the dark, felt-lined cabinet into the room. Maurice stared quietly at the familiar cat face, and emerald eyes. At last he tilted his head and looked at his wife.

"It's beautiful," he said softly.

"Yes," she answered. "Aren't you proud?"

"Proud of what?"

"Of me! Of it! Of owning it!"

The heavy brows knit. There was no smile. "What are you talking about?" His voice was hoarse.

For a second Claudia felt a tiny knot in her stomach. Then it passed. She was calm when she spoke, but the excitement of the moment was gone. "You know perfectly well what it is. And it's ours!"

"Ours?"

"I gave the museum a perfect replica to replace it. This is ours. It's real. It was all very simple, Maurice really." Claudia spoke patiently. "Yesterday, during the afternoon, I simply put a duplicate of this statue in the display and took the real one—this one—away."

Maurice closed his eyes. He was quiet. Suddenly, he was on his feet, reaching towards the opening in the bookcase. Then he stopped, his hand suspended. He was looking into the cabinet, not at his wife. "I believe you, Claudia. I believe you. What I can't understand is why. You can't, for one minute, think you can keep this." He turned and faced her.

The small pain in her stomach returned. "Of course we can keep it. I don't think anyone will know it's gone. And, if they did, so what?"

Maurice sat down. He stared at his wife and she at him.

"How in God's name do we get rid of it?"

"What?"

"Get rid of it. That's what I said. How are we going to get it out of here without incriminating ourselves?"

"I don't understand you, Maurice." Her hands were on her hips, her voice hard, defiant. "We own one of the most priceless treasures in the world and you want to get rid of it."

Maurice Betancourt sprang to his feet and took a step towards his wife. She flinched and moved back. Now he was directly in front of her.

"We don't own a damn thing," he gestured towards the bookcase, "it's not yours—not ours."

He turned and walked back to the chair. This time he did not sit, but walked behind it and stood facing Claudia with his hands on its back.

"Tell me again. How did you do it?"

After a moment's silence, she spoke. "I had the duplicate with me at the museum yesterday, and during the unpacking I just switched them. That's all."

"Who was there?"

"Who? Everyone was there."

"Gottfried?"

"Yes, Gottfried. Everyone."

"Who could have seen you?"

"No one saw me. My God, Maurice, don't you think I was careful?"

"I think you were insane. Stupid. Ridiculously rash." He punched the back of the chair with each word.

"No one saw me, Maurice. There is no danger at all." As she spoke, a picture of Charles Green flashed through her mind. "No danger at all." This time the words were soft—thoughtful.

"No, Claudia. I can't believe that something this bizarre can have happened as simply as you tell it. It's too preposterous. They must know. They will find out. It will come back to haunt us."

"Impossible." She turned and stood admiring the statue.

For a moment neither of them moved or spoke. Then he came around from behind the chair, stepped in front of his wife, and shoved the bookcase panel closed. There was a click and slam as the cabinet lights went out and the heavy, book-laden door shut. As it closed he spun to face her.

"I can understand your motives," he said angrily. "But this isn't rational. You're not rational! There is no way on earth that this piece can remain here."

He seized her arms. "Do you know what you've done? Are you at all aware of the consequences? Are you so blinded by that thing in there," he jerked his head towards the bookcase, "that you've completely lost all sense of reason?"

She glared at him, teeth clenched. He was hurting her arms.

"If anyone discovers what happened you'll spend years in jail or paying to stay out. I'll be a laughing stock! Didn't any of this cross your mind? Didn't it?" he repeated.

She pulled free from his grip.

"No! I took it because I wanted it! I didn't weigh it against your holy career. I did it because I had to! I have to have this! It's mine!"

"It is not yours! Damn it! It's not yours! It's got to go back."

He turned and strode out of the library, slamming the door behind him.

Claudia stood looking at the closed door. She rubbed absently at the red marks on her arms where Maurice's hands had held her.

"Never," she whispered. "Never."

FRIDAY, APRIL 8

On her way to Sirocco the next evening, Claudia put it all into perspective. She would get around Maurice. She always had. True, she didn't have the gold box, but she assumed that it and the other pieces were safe in Charles' possession. It would serve no purpose, at this juncture, to anger Charles. The most important consideration now was to find a way to get the pieces from Charles and keep him from doing anything that would expose what had happened. So long as no one did anything, the switch would go undetected until such time as the exhibit was re-examined. And that would not happen until it was returned to Cairo.

Weeks ago, when she first thought about what would happen after the robbery, she had never come to a conclusion. It had never occurred to her that she would not have the pieces and therefore, not be in complete control of the situation. What she eventually would do when they ran out of patience never entered her mind. But that was weeks ago and now the wrong people were in control.

Tonight at Sirocco, she had to show constraint. Charles and Peter both had prodded her for a review of her movements of last Tuesday morning. Charles, she felt, could hardly wait for her to finish telling them of her part in the adventure so that he might launch into a description of the scene he and Peter had played in the warehouse.

Sharon was playing an unknowing ally to Claudia in the latter's attempt to temper the high spirits of Charles. Tuesday had been exceptional for Sharon, too, but in an altogether different way. The excitement of the switching of the art treasures had to be shared with her pride in hearing the script come alive in the hands of a professional narrator. The lukewarm critical reception accorded the program by the press did not diminish her growing impatience to be gone.

The conversation at the table in Sirocco was, therefore, somewhat disjoined. There were four independent streams of thought. Claudia, watchfully holding her tongue; Charles, recounting each tension-laden step taken in the UBS warehouse; Peter, prodding Claudia on one hand and tempering Charles' somewhat vivid memories on the other; and Sharon's recollection of her night as a celebrity and accomplice.

"That night watchman passed by not six feet from where Peter and I were hiding." Charles' eyes were wide. He made a cutting motion, through the air, across his throat.

"It wasn't exactly that close," Peter corrected him, "and anyway, even if he saw us, I probably could have talked my way out of it."

"Only if he didn't shoot first," Charles was adamant. "Did you know that the network got over two hundred telephone calls from viewers?" Sharon asked no one in particular.

"How exciting, dear," Claudia answered, thankful for the new direction. "You may find yourself having to hire a secretary to handle your public."

"Incidentally, Claudia," Peter asked, "now that the little gold cat lady is at home in your library, does Maurice know?"

The question took Claudia by surprise. Why should Peter care if Maurice knew?

"Yes, he knows," Claudia answered slowly, but said no more.

"What does Maurice think we ought to do about the rest of the stuff?" Charles asked.

"He has no opinion." Claudia's answer was cold and sharp.

Charles decided to abandon that line of questioning. Not totally undaunted, he went on in a more sheepish tone. "I guess we should start thinking about how we are going to dispose of them."

"I think it best if we just leave everything alone for a while," Claudia was looking directly at Charles.

Each one stared at her. She went on. "No one will start to look for the pieces until we choose to tell them. That is an advantage we should not quickly abandon. Let's not be in a hurry."

"It's our own little annuity," Charles said. "We can cash it in whenever we want. Right, Claudia?"

"Yes, Charles."

"However, we don't want to let too much life pass us by before we yell bingo, do we, folks?" This time Charles swung his gaze from Claudia, stopping at Sharon and then Peter.

"Well, I'm with Claudia," Peter said. "There's nothing pushing us, so the smart move is to keep cool until we have the next steps all worked out. How do you feel, Sharon?"

"Oh, I'm for going slowly but not too slowly. Cautiously. We've come a long way and a few more days won't hurt."

"I guess it's unanimous," Charles said. "We sit quietly and begin to figure out where we go from here. That seems smart. But let me tell you all right now, I don't want to wait too long to enjoy the fruits of our labors. Sooner or later we're going to have to blow the whistle, Claudia, and as far as I'm concerned, it might just as well be sooner."

Damn Charles! Claudia nodded her head in apparent agreement. If I had those other pieces no one could force the next move. Why did that fool Peter give them to him? Perhaps Charles is smarter than I give him credit for. The best place for them is with me. I could hide them until these people were out of the picture. Then I would deal with Maurice. But that damn Charles won't let them sit for too long. He's going to demand action. A ransom letter to Miriam Gottfried would be perfect. The ultimate embarrassment. I would love nothing more than to send it, but there will never be a ransom note.

Claudia became aware of the conversation that had resumed at the table. Charles was building to a melodramatic climax, recounting his feeling when he discovered the crate had been taken out of the building. Claudia's patience was beginning to wear thin. So in order to avoid antagonizing Charles by lashing out at him, she rose to leave.

"Well," she smiled around the table, "for now the job is done. Perhaps the most difficult time is behind us. We must be patient now. We'll get together in a few days."

She turned and left.

"Remind me to use that word at home tonight, would you, please?" Charles asked of the two remaining at the table.

"What word?" Sharon asked.

"Patience."

"I don't understand," Peter said.

"Her royal highness has just requested patience of her subjects." Charles' voice was a sing-song. His face twisted into a sneer. "I just want you to remind me to say 'patience' when I go home tonight and see the pile of bills on my desk and the vacation brochures that are gathering dust on Pat's bureau. Patience, I'll tell them. It's a virtue."

SATURDAY, APRIL 9

Peter hadn't been back to Indianapolis in years. He no longer called it home, but now it was the only place he could think of where he could escape, at least for a little time, from Claudia and this crazy situation.

Two hours on a plane and a short drive north in a rented car brought him to the house where he had grown up. The aunt who had raised him after his parents' deaths was surprised and pleased to see him. She made sure he was comfortable in the same room where he had built model airplanes and dreamed of racing the 500. It was that night, in his old soft bed, under the lumpy feather comforter, that his conscience emerged to confront him.

Long after the house had quieted, when even the night sounds had disappeared, he turned with an angry wrench of body, facing the faded, flower-patterned wallpaper so indelibly inscribed in his memory that he could see it in the darkness.

How had he become a willing partner in this idiocy? No, this crime. Had he done it to impress Sharon? Did he care enough for Sharon to need to impress her? Or had he done it to shame Charles? Or had he just been bored, looking for some spice in his life?

The whys were overshadowed by the fact that he was inextricably involved in a crime. He was puzzled and frightened. He was once again the little boy who had broken a window and run to hide in the basement. No matter how long he hid, or how much he argued that the errant baseball was thrown in jest, the window remained shattered. It would not heal with time.

The warmth and softness overtook Peter, carrying him into a fitful sleep. On the drive back to the airport his thoughts remained focused on the night just past. It was funny enough to make him laugh...or cry...when a little boy's voice in his memory said, "If you forgive me this time, I promise never to do it again."

The Exhibit

WIND

MONDAY, APRIL 11

The square white card on the clipboard was a standard employment agency form. Charles Green filled in the information quickly, pausing only where large spaces asked for the position desired and salary requirements. No company ever went looking for men like him. He was just another insurance man.

He was going through the motions of looking for a job when he knew it was hopeless. The last few days had left him feeling strange. He was euphoric over the money that would soon be his and, at the same time, terrified when he thought of the consequences of discovery. He alone had four of the pieces—everything that had been taken except the large statue. The rest of them could throw him to the police, and what could he do? It was a situation he did not want to think about.

He forced his attention back to the card and the words he had just written. "Insurance agent (television broadcast specialist)." Back at his old office, they would not be hiring anyone to fill his job. They'd simply split his accounts among the other men.

What the hell.

Quickly Charles wrote 'negotiable' next to "salary requirements." He stood up and handed the clipboard, with the card attached, to the girl at the desk. She smiled, took the card, and disappeared into the inner offices.

He returned to his seat to wait. Christ, he hated employment agencies. Wait until the joker hears my request for 95G's, he thought. These bastards love telling you that you're worth less than you think. If you were older, they say, or younger, or worked longer, spoke Spanish, had a degree—oh, shit, I hate this.

The girl was back from the inner offices.

"Mr. Green, Mrs. Hatcher will see you now."

The placement specialist he had to see was a woman! That was the final degradation. Meekly, hating himself, he followed the secretary inside.

Mrs. Hatcher was younger than Charles expected. In her early thirties. By Charles' standards she was cute. Large blue eyes, round cheeks, a rosebud mouth and blond bangs. She was cute, nauseatingly cute. He smiled insincerely at the young woman.

"Hello, I'm Joan Hatcher." She was obviously playacting with that serious voice. "Won't you sit down, Mr. Green?"

This bimbo should be on the other side of the desk asking him for a filing job. How could he be expected to take this seriously?

She studied the card. "I see you are interested in insurance."

So, she could read. Probably majored in steno and typing, he thought.

"It's not that I'm interested in it," Charles' voice had an edge. "It's my field. I've been in it for fifteen years. I'm an expert."

"I see..." she continued to study the card. "It says that salary is negotiable. That's wonderful. But I need a number to know where to start. Can you give me one?"

Charles stared. Now or never. "Ninety thousand."

The woman smiled. And nodded. "You are requesting an extremely high salary. At that level, positions are not plentiful."

Charles sat back in the chair and crossed his legs. He folded his hands over his knees and looked into the round blue eyes. "Two years ago, during a strong economy, I earned two hundred thousand. Ninety is far less than I've been making." He watched her carefully. She was unmoved. "I am a producer. I build businesses."

He stopped talking. Why was he trying to sell her? How had she gotten this job? Probably married one of the owners right out of school.

"I can appreciate that you have been in the upper income brackets, Mr. Green. However, right now we have to deal with reality."

"What does that mean?" Charles was not even trying to be pleasant.

"The reality is that no company is going to pay the kind of money you want for a nonspecific job title. You say insurance with a television specialty. Can I place you at a local station? Can I place you at an agency? I don't know if you qualify for any one of those. Do you follow me?"

"Yes..." Charles' voice was a hoarse whisper. She pulled a metal tray towards her and began to flip through the cards. "We specialize in marketing positions here at Judd and Fields. Let me read you some of the openings.

"Market Manager, cosmetics," she said. "Marketing director, food. Research director, consumer products. These are all specific titles, with specific responsibilities and qualifications. Your past experience does not lead you into such areas. You are an insurance salesman who has been selling broadcast liability insurance rather than health or life insurance. Do you follow?"

"Yes."

"This is not a put down, Mr. Green. You are probably very good at what you do, otherwise you wouldn't have earned as much as you did. The problem is that your skills suggest only a sales management position with an insurance company. The problem is that those jobs are usually filled from within. Do you follow?"

The little dope had really put her finger on it, Charles thought. Blind luck.

"Have you considered applying to another insurance company, Mr. Green?"

"No, I haven't. I thought I would sniff around before ..."

She cut him short—it was a familiar speech to her. In the ten years she had been working here she had heard it many times. No one who came in ever needed a job. They were all just sniffing.

"I would suggest you consider following up on the insurance side of things, Mr. Green. That area does not happen to one of Judd and Fields' specialties, but there are agencies that deal specifically in that area. If you like, I can jot down several places for you to call."

He looked at his fingernails, then his shoes, then at her, then past her and out the window.

"Yes... please."

She took a small directory from the desk and began to write names and phone numbers on a yellow legal pad. When there were four names on the pad, she stopped, smiled up at Charles, and handed him the paper.

"Anyone of these should be able to help you." Charles folded the paper and put it in his inside jacket pocket. He arose, and extended his hand across the desk.

"Thank you for your time, Mrs. Hatcher, you've been most enlightening."

"You're quite welcome, Mr. Green. Good luck." Charles walked out of the building into the late morning sun. It was a cool, clear spring day. Under other circumstances, he would have been totally depressed by the office he had just come from, the girl, and what she had said.

So why aren't I crying and feeling sorry for myself? Hell, let's not pretend, Charles. The job hunting is a fake, you don't even care if there is nothing doing— in fact, you hope there isn't. That just makes everything else that much simpler.

Charles smiled to himself. Playing games about jobs that might pay as much as fifty thousand—wow, fifty thousand. *Well, right now, in my attic, blondie, is a box worth...millions. Yep, cutie pie...millions. So you just take your list of insurance agencies and stick it!*

Charles reached into his jacket and pulled out the carefully folded sheet of paper, crumpled it into a ball and threw it into a trash can.

Insurance agency, his ass. He had insurance in his attic. Well, payday was near. He was going home. First, he was going to get those things out of the attic and put them someplace else and then he was going to begin thinking about a ransom note. Charles Green flexed his shoulders .... *look out, Claudia Betancourt.*

Charles stood on the busy street corner, unaware of the people and traffic. He tilted his head back in the spring sunshine and laughed out loud.

TUESDAY, APRIL 12

The late afternoon sun made Sharon Hiller blink as she drove home from the station to the house on the hill. The weight of her indecision was unbearable.

This afternoon she had come very close to giving the network a definite answer about going to California. They were waiting for her to give them a date when she would begin work at their Hollywood Studios. But at the last minute she couldn't do it.

Like Charles Green, Sharon was moving back and forth between two worlds. In one world, she had her nest egg, the money that could buy her a new life, with her daughters, away from Clayton. Time to write. Time to put on paper the story she had been living for the past few weeks.

In the other world were divorce, separation from Peter, the nagging fear that she would fail. This world frightened her so badly that she froze every time she rose to walk into her boss's office and give him a definite answer.

She pulled into the circular driveway and saw her mother-in-law's car. Only then did she remember, with relief, that Clayton was out of town.

Mrs. Hiller greeted Sharon as she walked into the living room. Seeing her daughter-in-law's anguished appearance, she volunteered to get the girls' dinner. Sharon was astonished but tonight a dirty kitchen was preferable to her daughters' company. She gave in without any resistance.

Sharon wanted to be alone. To think. She wanted to take a bath. Relax. Take a nap. She wanted to clean out the insides of her mind.

It took her ten minutes to fill the tub, undress and slip into the hot water. She closed her eyes and leaned her head against the sloping back of the tub. Immediately, the stolen museum pieces marched to the forefront. God knows how much my share will be, she thought. Whatever it is, it's more than I need. What difference did it make? The deed was done and now all that remained was to collect and split.

From her standpoint it had been easy. Too easy. Somewhere, sometime, she would have to talk to Claudia about what had actually happened in the vault. She wondered if Claudia would tell her. She doubted it. She would probably have to make it all up—create the suspense. No matter. She had the framework of her story. Names, dates and locations would all be changed. She would have to cleverly disguise the plot so as not to arouse curiosity. She could do it. She would give them her answer tomorrow.

WEDNESDAY, APRIL 13

It did not come as a surprise to Claudia when Charles called two days later and suggested they all meet again. It was a meeting that Claudia, expected and dreaded. Tonight, she knew that Charles was going to make demands. She was sure of it.

Tonight, at Sirocco, the atmosphere was cold. There was an edge of expectation in the air.

Charles felt strong, assured. He knew what he wanted —what he needed. He had the tote bag safely hidden and only he knew where. He could move now, with or without their cooperation.

Sharon knew what she wanted—what she needed. And she meant to get it.

Peter wanted peace. The thrill of the crime had come and passed. Now he could wait for however long Claudia wanted. In fact, the thought of getting a very large sum of money scared him.

Claudia had to play for time. She was afraid of Charles and what he might do. She had to get those other pieces.

Greetings were perfunctory, drink orders mumbled. Charles' glass was up and moving, and he was checking each face. Claudia was fidgeting—her cigarette and lighter in constant motion.

"I was job hunting this week." Charles looked around the table defiantly. He wasn't sure they had all been aware of his situation. They would be. Tonight, there would be no foolish pride. "I guess none of you can appreciate that." He tipped the glass towards Claudia and smiled. "Have you ever gone job hunting with your back to the wall?"

There was no response.

"Can I tell you what it's like? You sit in a room with someone you've never seen before. You're in trouble and they know it. You're vulnerable, at their mercy. The night before, you could have been at the country club, dancing with your wife. You could drive home in an expensive sports car to a beautiful home and walk across your plush lawn into your plush living room. You can put on an a designer suit and shoes, and walk into the agency office, and then do you know what you are? You're nothing. You're a piece of meat to be sniffed over and told you don't smell fresh. That's what it's like. And I don't like it. Most of all, I don't like not having money to do what I want to do! I don't intend to wait..." he looked directly at Claudia, "much longer."

"I'm sorry, Charles," Claudia said. "I truly never realized that you were having a rough time. You know that if there is anything I can do to help ..."

She caught herself, but it was too late. Sympathy and charity were two things that Charles didn't want.

Charles' eyes blazed. "What you can do, Claudia, is help me turn our treasure chest into money!"

"Yes, you're right," Claudia said. "It would be best to wait, but I guess we had better begin to explore all the possibilities."

"What do you mean all the possibilities?" Peter asked.

"There's more than one way to dispose of them," Claudia answered. "You know that. The easy way, through a private sale, or the ransom we talked about."

"Which is best?" Sharon asked.

"Each has its disadvantages, but I think a private sale would be the best. With a private buyer, you hand over the piece and collect your money and you're done. In this case, the museum isn't even aware anything is gone—at least not for some time."

"So, where's the problem?" Sharon asked.

"The problem is that before a buyer will give us the immense price we'll ask, he or she will want to see the provenance."

"The what?" Peter asked.

"Papers, documents, testing—anything substantiating the origin of the pieces. So that anyone buying them would know their history."

"Any other problems?" Sharon asked.

"If you can't find one buyer for all the pieces, then you've got too many people involved."

"It still sounds better than trying to sell them back to the Museum," Peter said.

"Oh, it definitely is," Claudia said. "The only advantage in going back to the museum is that they would know immediately that we were telling the truth, and they would act quickly to get everything back."

"What's the fastest way?" Sharon asked.

Peter jerked his head in her direction while Charles secretly grinned behind his glass and Claudia put on a puzzled look.

"The fastest way?" Claudia repeated. "I'm not sure. That depends on however long it would take to prove to the buyer that the piece or pieces were genuine. I would guess it to be a matter of weeks."

"What about the museum?" Sharon asked. "They would know immediately that they had fakes."

"Well, the museum would have to get all the parties involved to agree on what to do. Don't forget, the Egyptian government has a say, and the insurance company," Claudia smiled at Charles.

"It would be even longer with the museum."

"What's your rush?" Peter asked Sharon.

"I want to get moving. I'm afraid if I drag my feet any more about going to California, the network will take back the offer or I'll change my mind and stay here."

Charles put his glass down on the table and rubbed one finger across it, leaving dark smudges on the wet surface.

"It seems as though Sharon and I have pressing problems. How about you?" He looked at Peter.

"No, none here. I'm in no hurry," Peter answered, looking at Claudia.

"Then it's settled," Charles said, slapping his hand on the table. "Sharon and I want to move ahead now, Peter doesn't care, and Claudia isn't getting any money."

Damn Sharon. Claudia thought. I didn't think she would be a problem.

"All right," Claudia said, "I hadn't realized how urgent your needs were. So tomorrow I'll begin to make some discreet inquiries about a buyer. I'll have to go through a third party, a dealer."

They all nodded. Claudia continued, "I don't know how long it will take to line up a prospect. As I said, we'd be best off with one buyer. Incidentally, once there is a buyer, he's going to want to see the pieces before he buys them. I guess you can bring them in, can't you, Charles?"

Charles had been wondering how long it would take Claudia to ask him for the crate.

"It's very safe where it is," Charles said, trying to sound casual. "I can't see risking another move. As soon as someone wants to see the others I can deliver them. But how about a timetable?"

"Yes, that's a good idea," Sharon said.

Charles leaned forward. "Tomorrow, Claudia contacts a dealer. Let's give the dealer three days to round up a prospect. That should be enough time."

"Well," Claudia began to protest, "I'm not sure ..."

"Nonsense, that's more than enough time. Hell, all the guy has to do is pick up the phone and call his customers. In three days he could call the world and ask them if they're interested in some hot Egyptian junk. Yes or no, that's all, no crap. If a guy says yes, and he knows it's a big transaction—bingo, we're in business." Charles paused to catch his breath. "No," he continued. "Three days is sufficient."

"What happens then?" Peter asked.

"If there's a buyer, Claudia calls me and I bring the pieces. If she or her dealer strikes out, we meet again and start composing a ransom note. How does that sound?"

The table was silent. Flushed with his own power in moving the group along, he opened a new subject. "How much shall we ask?"

Claudia thought of the tote bag and its contents. There were three priceless original pieces and the replica of the candle holder. She couldn't guess as to their value. But since she had no intention of selling anything, she could make up a member.

"They are priceless," Claudia said. "I thought of offering the entire package for two million. I'm sure the dealer has prospective buyers who would find that a reasonable price."

"Two-thirds of a million cash," Charles said.

"How much?" Sharon asked quietly.

"Six hundred and sixty-six thousand dollars for you," Charles answered.

"I guess I can go to California, buy a house, hire some help, and go to work."

"And whatever is left, you can invest," Peter added.

"It's not really all that much," Charles shrugged.

Claudia cut in. "Then you all agree the two million should be the asking price?"

"You tell us, Claudia," Charles said. "Would you pay that much for them?"

"I certainly would, if I could, but that would be too steep for me. Don't worry, though," she added quickly, "there are many buyers to whom two million dollars is nothing."

They sat in silence for a moment, contemplating the money. Claudia needed to make the first break. She had to get away, to think. "As soon as I hear from the dealer. I'll call you," Claudia said to Charles.

"That should be no more than four days, is that right? One day to contact the dealer and three days for him to get a buyer."

"Yes, that's right," Claudia said. "And now, if you'll excuse me, I have to go decide on the right dealer, one who won't take too big a cut."

"Hey, wait a minute, we forgot about that. How much does this go-between get?"

Claudia threw out a figure at random. "About ten percent."

"That cuts our take down to an even six hundred thousand each."

"Easy come, easy go," Peter answered as he nudged Sharon towards the end of the bench. "I think it's time we went home and practiced being rich."

THURSDAY, APRIL 14

The green numerals on the bedside clock cast a sickly light on Claudia's face. Her eyes had not closed at all since she lay down. It was 3:20 a.m. The solution would not come.

At first, she thought it would be easy. She could tell them she had found a dealer and a buyer. She could have Charles bring the pieces to her for delivery to the buyer. She knew Charles' cowardice would keep him from delivering them himself. But that, in itself, was the risk. Suppose she lied, and suppose Charles insisted on meeting the dealer or the buyer. She couldn't take that chance. If Charles discovered her lie, he would act on his own. And that would be disastrous.

Charles, she thought, Charles. He was the problem. If not for him, she could handle the others. Sharon was full of romantic nonsense, and Peter would wait forever. But not Charles.

As she lay motionless in the darkness, she remembered the little jeweler in Brooklyn. How convenient his heart attack had been. If he hadn't had that seizure he, too, would have been a problem. That had been luck. Now she had to make her own luck. She had to have a plan. But what? A heart attack for Charles ... a plane crash for Sharon...a car accident for Peter. Those were not plans, they were fantasies.

Four days. In four days she had to report on the dealer and the buyer. Four days to plan. Four days to save her statue and the rest of her treasure. Four days to satisfy Charles and get him off her back.

Only handing the money over to Charles would satisfy him. She could put him off for one day, maybe two, but in the end nothing but money would work. Charles had to be paid or... Claudia's rambling thoughts stopped. She became aware of the faint street noises that were never completely absent in mid-Manhattan, of the light on the clock, of the movement of the cat curling up at her feet. These were real things. Everything in her mind was a dream. Accidents didn't happen on schedule. Roncalli was a fortunate coincidence. Could she be that fortunate twice?

Charles was a man under stress. A family man who had lost his job. He was overweight and middle aged. He drank and was in poor physical condition. Charles was a prime candidate for a heart attack. Charles could drop dead at any time, and no one would be surprised. Roncalli did it, why couldn't Charles?

She knew that with Charles it was different, but she had the feeling that everything was going to turn out well. It was as if her life was being guided by someone else. Someone with the power to make things turn out well. She knew she was destined to possess the Sekhmet, and all the other treasures. Yes, she knew that. It was written. She was merely a tool.

Tomorrow she would begin to look for a way to remove the problem of Charles. And she would find it. And tomorrow she would speak to Sharon. She could put her off until she found a solution to Charles.

She smiled in the dim greenish shadows. Within seconds, she was asleep.

THURSDAY, APRIL 14

"Come in, Sharon. Thank you, Mrs. Britton," Claudia rose from the couch in her downstairs sitting room to greet her guest. Once again seated, she patted the couch beside her and Sharon moved around the coffee table and sat down tentatively. Sharon remembered their last meeting in this house—the closeness of the woman and the faint odor of her perfume. At that time, Sharon had been anxious to see the library. Now she hoped they would not go in there.

Claudia poured brandy from a crystal decanter and handed the glass to Sharon who leaned back into the far corner of the couch. She turned towards her hostess, found a cigarette and lit it.

"I'm glad we could meet here," Claudia said. "I'm getting a little tired of Sirocco."

"I was, too," Sharon said following the thread of smoke as it rose towards the ceiling. For the first time, she noticed that the ceiling had a hand-painted border design—geometric patterns running around the entire room. "And your house is convenient. A quick taxi ride and I'm at the train." Sharon looked at her watch. It was five thirty.

Claudia looked at the younger woman for a moment. "You won't be doing that much longer, will you?"

"Doing what? Oh, you mean riding the train? No, not much longer." After a pause, she added, "Thanks to you."

"Thanks to all of us," Claudia said. "That's why I asked you here tonight."

"Why me?" Sharon asked. The question sounded foolish, almost naive.

"I need your help. Yours and Peter's, as a matter of fact."

Sharon sipped her brandy and kept quiet, waiting. Claudia breathed deeply. "As honestly as I can put it, Sharon, I'm scared."

Sharon was shocked. Claudia Betancourt was a woman who knew no fear. She waited for the rest.

"We've been very lucky so far. Everything went even better than we could have imagined. No mistakes. I don't want to push our luck."

"How would we do that?" Sharon asked.

"By trying to turn our exchange into quick dollars. Right now, we have the pieces and no one knows it. That means nothing can happen. I have a feeling that the minute we try to do something, all hell will break loose. Even if we go through a dealer for a private sale, the museum is going to find out."

"So what?"

"Investigations. That's what. Investigations when events are still fresh in people's memories. I'm sure there is no way for any of us to be implicated, but why take the chance that a jewelry store clerk will still remember the woman who bought the Sekhmet statue, or Gottfried will remember finding Charles and me in the tomb after the lights came on?"

"Aren't you being afraid of shadows?"

"The longer we wait, the less chance anyone has of making these associations."

"You're right," Sharon sighed. "But how long do you suggest waiting?"

"At least until the exhibit is closed and moved."

Sharon sat forward. "That's three months from now!"

"Three months isn't a lifetime."

"Three months is too long, Claudia."

"You're afraid of losing your opportunity to go to California?"

"That's right."

"If you could go now, would the three months seem so long?"

"Of course not," Sharon replied.

"Well, suppose I advanced you some money against what you'll get when we sell the pieces? Enough money for you to go to California now and take your daughters with you?"

"It would be fine for me—wonderful! But there's Charles. He wants it all now. He won't settle for a little now and more later."

"I think I can convince him to wait. I don't think he'll act on his own. Charles isn't that brave, we all know that." Claudia drew a breath, she had made it sound reasonable. Reasonable enough, she hoped, for Sharon to agree.

"Do you think so?"

"I think so. It's in his own best interest to wait. Charles is greedy, but he's also practical."

That was it. Claudia had pleaded her case and now the jury of one was deliberating. Sharon had extinguished one cigarette and was lighting another. Claudia refilled her brandy glass.

"Look, Claudia," Sharon said after several moments. I'm not a troublemaker. I just need to know what to do."

Claudia was listening intently.

"I've got to get away from here," Sharon continued. "I've got to begin to build a new life for myself, and I can't put it off. My greatest need is not whatever we get from the sale, but enough to get started and make the move. If you want to lend me enough to do that, then I'm satisfied. I certainly won't screw up the rest of you."

Claudia swallowed her brandy and closed her eyes. The fiery liquid burned her throat. The heat felt good. One down, one to go.

"I think that's very wise," Claudia said as she rose from the couch. "There's cash upstairs. Would thirty thousand be enough for now?"

Sharon stared at her blankly. "Let me think. I've some money of my own, and I will get a salary and travel expenses from the network. What I need is money to cover living expenses until I rent a house. So thirty should cover it for a few months anyway. That's what we're talking about, isn't it, just a few months?"

"No more than that," Claudia called over her shoulder as she left the room.

Sharon got up and walked to the bookshelves next to the fireplace inspecting book titles until Claudia returned and handed her a large envelope.

"Here's your down payment." Claudia said.

Sharon looked at it, then clutched the envelope as though it might get away.

Claudia sensed her uneasiness and changed the subject. "Tell me, how's the writing coming? You're still planning to do a mystery for television, aren't you?"

"Yes, yes." Sharon brightened. "It's coming nicely. All I have to do is keep track of day-to-day events, so I can build them into the story."

Claudia was puzzled. "I don't follow that, Sharon. What events?"

"This," she swept the air with her arm. "All this. The story of our escapade at the museum. It's the story line for my movie. Four amateurs switch a priceless treasure. It's so unbelievable it could sell."

Claudia had been standing next to the fireplace while Sharon spoke. Now she reached out to grasp one of the bookshelves. Slowly, she closed her eyes and waited until her heart returned to a normal beat. "That's a bit close to home, isn't it?" she asked.

"Not if it's properly disguised," Sharon answered.

"Has the network seen any of this yet?"

"God, no." Sharon gave her one of her quirky looks. "I've been making notes as we go. I haven't put it into outline form yet. That will have to wait until I get to California."

Claudia stood in the living room long after Sharon had left. Brains was the last gift God gave to these people, she thought. While Sharon's money issue was solved, another, new, complication rose to take its place. What could she possibly be thinking of. It would have to be dealt with. But right now, she needed to take care of Charles. She had set up a meeting with him for tomorrow.

FRIDAY, APRIL 15

Claudia did not want to meet with Charles in her home. She couldn't stand the thought of him being there. And for some inexplicable reason, she didn't want to go back to Sirocco. She had to come up with a place quiet and out of the way.

It was Charles who had suggested the bar where they now sat facing each other. The high, wooden-backed booths gave them the privacy they sought—that, and the fact that there was only a handful of people in the room.

"I like this place," Charles said when they sat down. "It's loaded with atmosphere. All it needs is a slow turning fan and sawdust."

He was right, she thought. The other patrons were sitting at a long, dark, wooden bar. She and Charles were the only people at a table. There was no waiter. Charles had brought their drinks from the bar to the table.

Claudia came to the point quickly. "I've put off talking to a dealer until I could speak to you alone," she began. "I want you to change your mind."

"About what?"

"About going ahead with a sale right now."

Charles' frowned. She gave him the same argument she had given to Sharon, finally recommending that they wait until the exhibition closed.

"It's out of the question," Charles said. "I have debts now and more coming. I want to go away. I have investment opportunities now that will be gone in three months. No. We have a deal. What about the other two?"

"I spoke to them both. Peter had to go out of town, but he said he would wait, he was in no hurry."

"What about Sharon? She was all hot to trot two days ago. What about her?"

Claudia was down to her trump card. "She thought it was a good idea not to push ahead now. I advanced her enough money to go to California. The money is to be paid back when we sell the pieces." She plunged ahead. "I'm ready to make the same deal with you Charles. I'll advance you money to tide you over for three months until we collect."

Charles leaned forward, both hands on the table, until his face was as close to hers as it could get.

"So you bought off our little friend," he said violently. "I always suspected her talents were for sale. Well, I'm not for sale. I put my life on the line for you, and it's payday!"

Claudia realized that he believed what he was saying.

"I hope you realize," he went on after gulping his drink, "that I can go ahead on my own. I can, you know. I haven't been sitting around waiting for you. I've been doing a lot of thinking. I had an idea you would pull some kind of shit!"

Claudia drew back. She wondered if the fear and disgust she felt were obvious.

"I thought about a ransom. I came up with a way that will get us in bed with the Arabs."

He drew out the first A in Arabs.

"Egyptians," Claudia corrected softly.

"Same thing. No matter what you call them. There's no doubt about it, in my mind. Ransom is the way to go."

"Why?"

"When you're dealing with the government, money is no problem. National pride and all that crap."

"Then it's only because you think you can get more money from a ransom."

"That's the name of the game."

"But ransom exposes the substitution immediately," she said. "That's why we decided to go the other way!"

"So what if a ransom note blows the whistle? Where will they look? They'll probably spend six months tripping over each other while they try to make up the rules for the investigation. Who had jurisdiction? Is it the New York Police, FBI, CIA, Interpol, the Egyptian police? It will be a real circus.

"We can ask a fortune from the Arabs. I've thought about the amount. At first, I said a nice even ten million. That would have been two and a half apiece when there were four of us. Then I remembered you wouldn't take anything, so I said let's give them a bargain—nine million among three people. That's three each, easy come, easy go."

He laughed. Claudia stared at him in horrible fascination. He mistook her gaze for rapt attention.

"But that's all academic now. With Peter not caring, and Sharon willing to settle for peanuts. I've got to rethink this whole money thing. Would you like me to tell you about the money transfer?"

"Yes," she whispered.

"The biggest chance of getting caught is during the pickup of the ransom money. So we won't pick it up."

What can this madman be up to? Her mind screamed.

"I see you're intrigued. Well, my financial training came in handy. It's so simple, it's criminal."

He stopped. The double meaning struck him, and he burst into loud laughter. Several heads at the bar turned. Claudia smiled back at the room, pretending to share the joke.

He hiccupped and continued. "We'll instruct the authorities to transfer the money into a numbered Swiss bank account. The name that goes with the number is something known only to the bank, and is never divulged, unless there is evidence of a crime against the Swiss government."

"I didn't know you had a Swiss account."

"I don't."

"But ..."

"You do ... or at least your husband does."

"How do you know that?"

"Oh, come on. He makes a fortune in his practice and you both buy a lot of high-priced art. I would imagine that much of his income is cash. He's a doctor, isn't he? So to hide his cash and screw around in the art market, it would stand to reason that he has to have a Swiss account."

The glint in Claudia's dark eyes could not be disguised. She was sure Charles could read the anger. He could not read its depth. At this moment, she could pull a trigger, easily.

"Once the money is in that account, any part of it can be transferred to your bank in England. Oh, yes, I checked Maurice's bank references through my old contacts. With the money in the Betancourt account in England, you can buy stock for me, open savings accounts for me in small-town banks. Oh, I can think of many things I can do with three million dollars. Well? What do you think?"

"It is clever," she said aloud. Her mind was racing. It was impossible!

"I want to show you something," he whispered. He took an envelope out of his pocket and handed it to her. The upper left-hand corner bore the name Perkin & Stevens, his former employer. Inside, a white piece of letterhead bore the same company name.

Claudia read the penciled note.

I am in possession of four articles from the Golden Age exhibit now on display in the New York Metropolitan Museum of Art. The articles in the museum are fake. I have a collar with hinges on it, a small gold box, a gold knife, and a candle holder. You have ten days to check on this. After ten days I will send you further instructions.

Claudia folded it and replaced it in the envelope. She closed her eyes. It was more horrible than she had thought. To draft a ransom note on letterhead—oh, God, what an ignoramus he was! He couldn't send this letter—it was out of the question!

Charles put the envelope back in his pocket, and sat back smugly. "That covers it, doesn't it?"

"The descriptions are not exactly precise."

"Oh, who gives a shit? They're going to tear that museum apart when they get this. They'll know what's real and what's fake."

They would find out about Sekhmet, too, she thought.

"May I comment now, Charles?"

"Be my guest."

"First of all. I'm not sure that my husband has a Swiss bank account, and if he does, he will never cooperate." She held up her hand to keep him from interrupting.

"Secondly, the Betancourt account in England is in my husband's name. He is the only person who can transfer funds."

"A technicality," Charles blurted before she could go on.

"Nevertheless, a complication."

"Are you through?" Charles asked.

Through? Claudia thought. She wouldn't be through until she was free of him and his interference.

"You'll get him to cooperate," he said, a hint of menace in his tone.

"I do not want to do that."

"That's just too bad," Charles' voice was not pleasant. "It's the way we're going to go unless you come up with something better."

Time. She needed time.

"All right, Charles." Claudia leaned back. "Call it personal problems or fear. Call it what you want. You know where I stand, and where the others stand. All I want is three days. I want to pursue the private sale. If I don't have a prospective buyer by Monday, we'll proceed another way."

"With the ransom," Charles shot back.

"Yes, with the ransom."

Charles savored his victory. Weeks ago, when he had first walked into her office with Peter Mandel, she had given him no more than a quick glance. She had dismissed him as some inconsequential little insurance man. Someone of no more importance than an errand boy. Now, he had her frightened, ready to do his bidding.

"I'll call you on Monday, in your office. I'll use the name Meyer. Charles Meyer, just like on the passes Peter got. I'll tell you where and when to meet me on Monday evening. If you have someone set up by then, we will go on with it. If not, you can walk with me to the nearest mailbox and we can both drop the ransom letter in."

"Monday, you say?"

"Yes, Monday. That gives you the whole weekend to find your buyer."

The Exhibit

* * *

A thin spiral of grey mist rose from a burning cigarette, joining the cloud of stale tobacco smoke which floated over the dimly lit sitting room. On one end of the sofa Claudia Betancourt sat thinking. Cigarette butts filled the ashtray. She had looked at her nails at least a dozen times, each time chipping away at the paint along the edges.

No avenue offered a clear way to rid herself of the danger Charles had summoned up earlier that evening. Whether or not she had the artifacts no longer mattered. There was a dead end wherever she turned. Charles Green was there blocking every route.

Claudia got up and went into the library. She needed help, inspiration. The bookcase opened, revealing the shimmering golden statue. Claudia's thoughts drifted to Maurice, working on an article upstairs. She felt anger, revulsion, love. What did he feel—anything? She didn't know any more. If he wanted her to get rid of the statue, why hadn't he brought it up again?

She stared at the statue. *Where do I go from here, she asked. There has to be a way out. You must help me find it. You must! If I don't come up with an idea by Monday night, I will lose... everything.*

She went back to the desk chair and sat, looking at the statue. Eventually, the idea of disposing of Charles rose from the depths of her mind, where it had smouldered for some time, to the surface where she could feel its presence. Maybe it had always been there, waiting for the opportunity to be released. No, that wasn't possible. Two weeks ago, she hadn't cared whether he lived or died. He was inconsequential. But now she cared...she more than just cared. She had no future, she had nothing if he persisted. His existence was a threat to her security, to her happiness. Yes, that's what she had to do. What about the other pieces? Where were they...in Charles' attic? She shrugged her shoulders irritably. She would worry about getting the pieces later. Afterwards.

Now the anxiety that had been with her all evening was gone. She knew what she had to do, and she was almost certain of how she was going to do it.

Upstairs, she smiled at her reflection in the dressing table mirror as she loosened her hair before retiring. It was a calm smile, satisfied. Almost serene.

SATURDAY, APRIL 16

Even through the drawn draperies, Claudia could tell the sun was shining. She had fallen asleep content with her decision. And now, fully awake in the new daylight of Saturday morning, there were no feelings of doubt or guilt. She was exhilarated, excited, looking forward to the day and what she had to do.

Maurice was already up. Even Karma wasn't around. Mrs. Britton had probably fed him hours ago, she thought.

Dressed, she went downstairs for coffee. Mrs. Britton told her that Maurice wouldn't be back until late afternoon. He had said not to forget about their dinner engagement later. Good, she thought, that gives me the whole day. The kitchen clock showed 9:30.

Upstairs in Maurice's book-lined study, Claudia began her search. One of these books, she hoped, would hold what she was looking for. There were books on mental disorders, physical diseases, the history of psychiatry. She took one out, looked through it and put it back. And another, and still another. The fourth was what she was looking for, but the fine print made her realize that she had, at least, a couple of hours of work ahead of her.

Claudia took the book, along with a pad and pencil, into her bedroom to work. She settled against the pillows and opened the book to the first chapter: "*Introduction to Poison and Poisonings.*"

She read, trying to match the right symptoms to the right poisons. This would take even longer than she had anticipated. The poisons were not cross-referenced in any way, so she had to go through each description of a substance and the clinical findings.

Charles' death had to look like something else. Not an accident, but natural causes, A heart attack would be perfect. And the poison had to be slow-acting. Not so slow that it took days for him to die, but slow enough that she was far away when it happened. It couldn't look like murder. Murder...ugh! What an ugly word, she thought. It had to look like a simple heart seizure. After all, he had been under a great deal of stress. It would be plausible. The police wouldn't investigate. No! There could be no autopsy. If there were, there must be no way to connect her with it.

She rubbed her eyes, then stood up to stretch. To her horror, she found it was 2:00. She'd never get this done before Maurice came home! And she had planned to choose a substance, go to his office and check through his cabinets, all this afternoon.

She ran down to the kitchen for coffee. It was then she remembered that she hadn't eaten at all. She took a container of cottage cheese from the refrigerator and brought it back upstairs with her.

It was impossible! One poison would give the right symptoms, but Charles would have to breathe it in. Couldn't be done. Another took only thirty seconds to act. That wouldn't do either.

By 4:30, her pad had two words on it. She wished there was more time to check, but time was the one thing she didn't have. One was really risky. The book admitted that the fatal dose by ingestion was not known, although it provided the amount that would cause marked symptoms. But she couldn't chance Charles merely becoming ill.

The second substance was better, with complete dosage information. It was actually a drug, and chances were very good that Maurice would have it in the office. But it was fairly quick acting.

"Claudia?" Maurice's voice as he climbed the stairs made her panic. She had left the bedroom door open. Oh, my God, he can't see these. Quickly she placed the book and notes under the bed, then lay on her stomach pretending to be asleep.

"Claudia," the voice was nearer. Finally she heard him stop in the doorway. She rolled over, blinking her eyes.

"Are you all right?" he asked.

"Yes, I'm fine. I was up late reading last night and I guess I'm still tired."

He stood in the doorway a moment, then turned and went into his study.

Claudia had to put the book back before he missed it.

"Maurice," she said as she entered his study, "let's go down and have a drink out on the patio before it gets too chilly. The garden looks perfectly beautiful."

He hesitated. "All right," he said reluctantly, "just one. Then I've got to get back up here and finish writing this report. I'll just have time before we go to the Kleinmans."

"What would you like?" he asked, as they went downstairs.

"Gin and tonic. And put some lime slices in it, please."

"I think I'll have the same. Tonic's in the kitchen, isn't it?"

"Yes. Oh, I've left my cigarettes upstairs. I'll be right back."

Claudia trotted up the stairs, grabbed the book from under the bed and returned it to the study shelf. Back in the bedroom she took the paper and stuffed it in a drawer. Then took her cigarettes from her pocket and walked downstairs.

SUNDAY, APRIL 17

With as little noise as possible, Claudia slid out of bed. Maurice was still, sleeping. Even though it was Sunday, Maurice might decide to go to his office, he sometimes did on Sunday to catch up on his paperwork. But he never went until after noon.

She'd be there and back well before that.

She dressed quickly in the bathroom, took a large handbag, and crept down the stairs. The weather was warm enough that she didn't need a coat.

Fifteen minutes later she entered the building on Park Avenue and Sixty-Third, unlocking the office door with the spare key Maurice kept in his study.

The office suite consisted of four rooms: a combination reception-waiting room, a consultation room, his office, and a laboratory. She headed for the laboratory. What she wanted, would be there, if anywhere.

In the laboratory, bottles stood on all the shelves and counter tops. As she examined each, she kept alert for sounds of someone opening the front door. She didn't expect Maurice to come barging in, but each passing minute...not finding what she needed...was making her more and more nervous. Finally, she found the first substance name on her list. She'd take it if she couldn't find the one she really wanted. She set the bottle off to the side by itself and continued searching. She had almost finished searching the entire laboratory. All that remained was a cabinet. Claudia knelt down and slid back the door. Inside were dozens of boxes, each containing sample-sized bottles. She began to open them.

The fifth box contained an assortment of multicolored bottles, some pills, some liquids. Resigned to the fact that it wasn't there, she almost missed it. As she turned the bottle over, only the last part of the word caught her eye. She had moved on to the next bottle when it registered. She picked up the bottle, carefully matching the spelling on the label with the word on her paper. Her hands turned moist. She had it!

The front door slammed shut. She was no longer alone. Maurice—it had to be him. Then she heard footsteps in the hall. Had she been here that long? She looked at her watch. It was almost one o'clock.

Quickly she put the lid on and she shoved the box back inside. After sliding the credenza door shut, she darted to the corner of the room away from the door.

She heard the door to Maurice's office open and close, then the creaking of his desk chair as he sat down. Then she heard a female voice. Who was it? Maurice's low tones came in answer. Claudia could not make out the words. She could not stand it, she had to try for the door. She took her bag and crept to the doorway. The female voice was still talking.

She looked out into the hall. The door to Maurice's office was closed. She tiptoed down the hall, past his office, pausing for a moment to listen. The female voice continued, and then was cut off in mid-sentence, followed by the sharp click of a tape recorder. She wanted to laugh. Maurice was listening to tapes.

She hurried through the reception room, opened the front door and silently closed it behind her. Outside, she breathed a sight of relief. It was a beautiful, sunny, Sunday afternoon. People were emerging from buildings to enjoy a stroll to Central Park. Claudia shared their jubilant mood, but for an entirely different reason. Her thoughts were focused on the small bottles in her handbag, and the relief it would bring to her life.

Later that evening, while Maurice was out—'a conference' he said—Claudia searched for a container to put the poison in. She needed a small watertight bottle. The cabinet in the bathroom held many small, plastic containers of pills.

Claudia dumped the pills out of one of them, filled it with water and replaced the lid. She knocked it over and watched. The water began to seep out. No good. She dried it out and replaced the pills.

In the back of the second shelf was a small bottle of aspirin. It had a screw-on lid. Perfect!

The next part was more difficult. The poison was in three ampules. She had to break off the tops without losing any of the liquid. Since she didn't know how much was enough, she dumped the contents of all three into the small bottle. She replaced the cap tightly and placed the jar in a small plastic bag. There! Finished! She was pleased with herself. The kitchen clock showed 9:00 p.m. She put the plastic bag in her pocketbook, together with the other accessories. Just twenty-four more hours.

* * *

The warm weather was, perhaps, here to stay. The detective found a seat in an outdoor café and ordered a beer. The one thing he had discovered in the months he had been on the case was that Mrs. Betancourt's movements were totally unpredictable. She went about at the oddest hours to the strangest places. There was no routine. Take this morning for instance, her going to her husband's office, and him showing up a little later. Then she comes out again by herself, scurrying as though she didn't want to be seen. Chances are he didn't know she was there. What the hell was she up to?

There was something about this woman. An instinct was reacting, sounding an alert. He knew that if hung around her long enough, something would happen. Whatever it was, he wanted to be there.

The Exhibit

FIRE

MONDAY, APRIL 18

Claudia Betancourt stood at the door of the unfamiliar restaurant, searching the dimly lit tables for Charles. After a few moments, she began to feel awkward. A thin young man with dark hair approached her.

"May I help you?"

Claudia started at the sound of his voice. She looked at him for a long moment before answering.

"I'm looking for someone."

The deep, cultured voice did not go with the short, black leather coat and blond bangs. She could see that the young maitre d' began a more interested appraisal of her. Where was Charles?

She walked towards the rear of the restaurant. Monday nights were notoriously slow in most places and tonight was no exception. Even here. Only three tables in the rear were occupied. Then she spotted him, in a booth near the back. She approached cautiously. What if it wasn't Charles? She saw that it was him. Her intake of breath was audible. He turned at the sound and looked at her. There was a flicker of uncertain recognition.

"Claudia?" It was a hesitant question.

"Good evening, Charles."

He half rose, then sat back and watched her slide onto the bench opposite him. His puzzled stare was gradually replaced by a broad smile.

"This is priceless. You're a regular Mata Hari! I would never have recognized you."

"I'm so pleased." Claudia settled herself into the seat and set her purse on the bench next to her leaning it against her hip.

"But why the wig? I guess it's a wig. No one knows you here."

"Yes, it's a wig. I'm acting out my fantasies. The international art thief is now the woman of mystery. You must let me play my little scene."

"If that's what turns you on... " His voice trailed off as a waiter approached. "Scotch again," he pointed at his glass, "and for the lady ..."

"White wine, please," she spoke without looking up. They were both silent now, looking at each other. A game of cat and mouse was about to take place. Who was the cat, and who the mouse?

Charles felt strong and secure. One way or another, within a very short time, no more than a week or two, he would be rich.

He was in control. He had the treasure. This woman, no matter how rich and sure of herself, was now doing his bidding. If she had a buyer for the pieces so much the better. It would be easier, and the risks would be all hers.

If she had no buyer, then the ransom note, addressed to the Egyptian ambassador and resting safely in his jacket pocket, would be mailed tonight. The payment of the money would be more complicated this way, but again, he would be clean. Claudia had to handle her husband. That was too bad, but it was her problem, especially if she wanted to keep that statue she worshiped so much.

Charles was pleased with himself. He had gone over the situation time and again during the weekend. There was no way he could get hurt.

But Claudia was another story. She could be hurt. And Charles suddenly wanted to do so. He wanted to humiliate her, burn the aloofness out of her. She had never hurt him, and he had never felt oppressed by the very rich. In fact, he had tried to emulate their style—and yet, he hated her now. Perhaps it was the realization that she was human and subject to pain and uncertainty just as he was. The shattering of his images could have brought on the anger. He knew he wanted to make her squirm.

He took the ransom letter from his pocket and tapped it on the table. Claudia's eyes riveted on the letter, following its every movement. Charles was pleased that she looked uncomfortable.

"This is the little bomb," he nodded at the envelope. "It reads just like 1 showed you on Friday. When this little note hits the ambassador's desk tomorrow, or Wednesday, what do you think the first thing is they'll do?"

The skin had tightened around Claudia's mouth. There was an almost imperceptible tic in her eyelid.

"They'll ask their own people, Mr. Ali and Kamil, since they're here to verify everything in the collection." Her voice was lifeless.

"And then what?" He was prodding her, making her twist and turn. She couldn't escape. His groin tightened.

"They will probably fly their own experts in from Cairo."

"How long would that take?"

"A few days."

"They'll check every piece, won't they?" He wanted her to think about that statue of hers. He wanted her squirming.

Claudia took over. Now for the lie. "I don't think we have to worry about that letter." She essayed a half smile. The tic in her eye persisted.

"You found a buyer?"

"I'm pretty sure I did."

"Pretty sure?"

"I have found someone who is terribly intrigued. This person knows the pieces and would be willing, in fact, happy, to pay two million for them."

"Well, then, what's the hangup?"

"The prospective buyer demands a provenance."

"So what do we do?"

"We have to let this person have the pieces so he can verify their authenticity."

"No way. They're not leaving my sight."

"Then you go with them." She would make up anything now, any way he wanted it.

"I'm not going with anything. Nobody's going to know I exist!"

"If you were going to buy them, wouldn't you want to know if they were real?"

He thought for a moment.

"I'll hand over one piece. They can check that one. If they're satisfied with one, they can hand over the money and I will give them the other three."

"I think that will be all right." She had him. He had bought the story!

He was asking her a question. She hadn't heard him. "I asked you who the buyer was."

She was ready for this. "He prefers anonymity, just as you do."

"It's like a black market adoption," he laughed. "Only the lawyer knows the buyer and the seller. I guess it's best that way."

"Yes. Next step. I tell the buyer that I can give him one piece for authentication and when he's satisfied, he will get the others."

"After paying."

"After paying," she agreed.

"When do we do it?"

"I'll call him tomorrow and arrange to deliver the piece to him as soon as he has set up the authentication process."

"Will that take long?"

"No, no more than a few days."

"Well, when you need the piece you call me at home, at night, and I will bring it to you somewhere here in the city. We'll pick another place to meet. You can wear another wig. Do you think you'll need it by Wednesday?"

"Probably." By Wednesday, she thought. I'll be able to breathe.

"O.K." He picked up the letter and slid it back into his pocket. Claudia followed it with her eyes. "You won't need that any more."

"I hope not. I don't want to throw it away here. I'll take it home and burn it."

"Why not let me do it?"

He looked at her, suspiciously. Then he smiled. "Why not? It will be a relief to you, won't it? Just remember, if anything goes wrong with this sale, it will take me no time at all to write it again and mail it. This time, no questions."

He handed her the letter.

Her time had come. He was ready to leave. She had to act now.

"Let's drink a toast."

He gave her that same suspicious look, and then signaled to the waiter for another round.

The drinks came. Claudia opened the zipper of her purse, put Charles' letter away, and continued to rummage in the bag until her hand found the small bottle in the side compartment. She took it out, keeping it hidden below the level of the table, and turned the cap until it came off.

"Charles, will you catch the waiter? I need a package of cigarettes."

He turned. The waiter was nowhere in sight, as she had known.

"Would you?" She began to rummage in her purse for change.

"Certainly," he slid out of the seat. "Forget the money. In a few days I'll be as rich as the Betancourt."

He laughed as he walked away.

She reached across the table towards his glass, the small bottle in her hand. Suddenly Charles stopped, turned and started back towards the table. She froze, her arm lying on the table, her hand next to his glass wrapped around the bottle, hopefully covering it.

He stopped several feet short of the table.

"What was it you smoke?"

"Benson & Hedges." All of the air in her lungs escaped in a long, low hiss.

He turned and left. She looked at the bottle. Her hand was steady. It was warm and dry. She smiled at her lack of nerves and as the smile faded, she turned the bottle over, dumping the contents into his drink. For a moment, she tried to follow the path of the poison as it descended into the amber-colored liquid. Then she turned the bottle upright. As she did, the last drop of liquid ran down its side, dripping onto Claudia's hand. She stared at it, fascinated, then returned the bottle to her purse. The drop was still on her knuckle when Charles returned to the table. Quickly, she took the wet napkin from under her drink and wiped it away.

Charles lifted his glass. "To our success. To my new fortune, and your new toy in the library."

"To the toys in your attic." She lifted her glass.

"They're not in the attic any more. I had to find a better place to hide them. But I'll drink to them anyway."

Her wide-eyed shock was lost on him as he gave Claudia the Charles Green salute, staring at her for a moment through his glass. She had seen this gesture many times before. He then finished his drink in two swallows.

On leaving the restaurant, Charles Green was floating in a warm ocean of pleasure. Everything had worked out perfectly. Claudia was a tame kitten. There was no need to send a ransom note and set in motion an international circus. A private sale was simpler, cleaner, less risky.

He walked towards Grand Central Station. Two million dollars. He did interest multiplications in his head. The numbers were big and very comforting. His major problem was going to be the story he must invent for Pat to justify their new wealth. He already had several ideas. The invention would be pleasant work.

Charles had to run the last few yards down the ramp and across the platform in order to catch the 8:05. As he fell into his seat, his shortness of breath was accompanied by a burning sensation in his chest. He closed his eyes, waiting for his pulse to return to normal and the burning to stop.

He opened his eyes several minutes later as a clack, clack signaled that the train had emerged from the tunnel under Park Avenue and was racing above ground, heading north. He did not feel better. The beating of his heart seemed to be more regular, but the burning was still there. He reached under his jacket and rubbed his chest.

He tried to think about the money. He tried to work on his story for Pat. He tried to picture Claudia in the blond wig. Nothing worked—his mind would not forget the burning. His heart was on fire.

He took a deep breath to ease the pain, but it didn't work. He looked at his watch—thirty more minutes, only a half hour. When he got home he could take something or, if it hadn't eased up, he'd call a doctor.

He tried leaning forward, shifting his weight, then leaning back against the seat. The pain reached his arm and fingers. He couldn't move them. He shut his eyes tightly, fighting the nausea that swept over him.

The conductor leaned over him, shaking his shoulder. "Hey, mister," he asked anxiously, "are you all right?"

Charles looked up at him. "I don't...I don't feel good." It was an effort to speak. "I feel terrible! Feels like heartburn. I can't breathe." Charles was struggling for every word.

The conductor frowned. "I can call ahead and have a police car at the station to meet you. They'll take you to the hospital. I don't think you should fool with this. What's your stop?"

The conductor had to lean down to catch the word, "Darien." Charles reached up and grabbed him. It was harder for him to breathe. Was he having a heart attack? No, that wasn't possible. "I'll be all right."

The conductor freed himself and walked forward to make the call. He looked at his watch. It was 8:55. They were due in Darien at 9:02, and they'd be on time.

The train arrived in Darien precisely at 9:02. Charles tried to raise himself out of the seat but fell backwards. The conductor held him quietly until one of the policemen arrived. Together, they helped him out of the train and onto the platform.

There, another policeman was hurriedly setting up an emergency oxygen unit.

The conductor helped the now sagging, gasping Charles down onto a stretcher and then stepped back towards the train. He hung on the steps as the train began to move out, shaking his head as he watched the uniformed men working over the prostrate form. "Heart gets them younger all the time," he muttered.

The pain Charles felt was almost gone, or at least his mind could no longer accept it. Now he was battling for each breath. He bit at the air as if it were food passing before his face. Only a trickle of air found its way into his chest, and he collapsed into the arms of the policemen. Again and again he repeated the act, the intervals growing longer.

Charles felt the plastic cup of the oxygen mask on his face. One more time he lurched forward, shaking his head from side to side, like a dog, worrying a bone. Then there was a gurgling sound from deep in his chest as his legs and arms surrendered the battle. The last mortal thought of Charles Green was of a white, eight-year old Volkswagen, standing in the station parking lot not fifty yards from where he lay. How will the car get home? Pat can't drive a standard shift.

The policeman relaxed his grip on Charles. The two uniformed men looked down and then at each other.

"Radio the ambulance—it's just a pickup and delivery now. I'll check his clothes and find out where he lives. We'll have to notify his next of kin."

One of the policemen rose and walked towards the patrol car. He turned and shook his head sadly.

"No matter how long I'm on the force, this is one part of the job I'll never get used to."

THURSDAY, APRIL 21

"Yes, Charles died suddenly Monday night. Yes, his heart. She's holding up ...very sad...boys are with friends..."

A cousin of Pat Green made the call to Peter Mandel. Peter, in turn, called Claudia, and Sharon. There was no one else he felt he had to notify.

Claudia did not attend the funeral but Peter and Sharon did. It was short. They approached Pat before leaving the cemetery and made the appropriate sounds, promising to visit when things were quieter. It was a visit neither wished to make. Sharon hoped she would be in California before Peter decided to go.

SATURDAY, APRIL 23

William T. Pilkington, also known as Billy Jive, was more than just annoyed at the assistant golf pro, he was mad. It was almost 5:00, and he was due to quit work in a few minutes. He was sure it would take him an hour to drive from the Country Club of Darien to Thelma's apartment in Manhattan, and he had promised to be there before 6:00.

The assistant club pro had found William just five minutes ago.

"William, I guess you heard that Mr. Green died of a heart attack," the pro had said'

"Yeh, man. Tough."

"I want you to find a carton and empty his locker. Then go by the pro shop and get his clubs. Put it all in the back of my station wagon so I can drop it off at his house."

"You mean now?"

"Yes, now."

"Sheeit."

William pulled open the tall, narrow steel door of the locker, and stood staring at the contents.

"Oh, shit. Green's old lady ain't gonna look at this stuff anyway. I just dump it in this box, however."

On the top shelf was a peaked hat with a pine tree emblem and the letters D.C.C. There were two, three packs of golf balls. William shoved those into his back pocket. "Where Green is, he don't need 'em."

From the hangers, William removed a blue sweater and two pairs of bright plaid slacks. He sat down on the wooden bench in front of the locker in order to get at the things on the bottom. A pair of white golf shoes. A rolled-up plastic rain suit, both pants and jacket. The rain suit was lying on something. Willie leaned over and stuck his head into the locker.

"What in hell?"

He pulled out a large leather totebag, set it on the bench, and dove back into the locker. A small metal tray set in the door was all that was left—several score cards, a bag of wooden trees, one loose golf ball and a comb.

Willie tossed it all into the carton and turned to the leather bag. Suddenly, he remembered Thelma and the long drive ahead of him. He threw the totebag into the top of the carton, picked it up, and headed for the parking lot.

SUNDAY, MAY 1

"Did you have any idea that he was sick?" Pat Green asked. "Did he complain about his heart?"

Sitting in the Green's living room, Peter thought back. "No, I don't think so."

"He was under a terrible strain these last few months," Pat added.

Peter said nothing.

Pat continued, "When he quit his job, he thought he would connect right away. I imagine he found it frustrating. A man of his ability not getting rehired right away. He did so much for Perkins and Stevens—that was his company, you know—and they really acted badly at the end, ungrateful."

"He was preoccupied the last few times I saw him. I could tell he was upset about something," Peter replied.

"He mentioned you often. He was very much involved in that television program you did from the museum. I guess it was his last job with the company, and he was nervous about it."

Pat said nothing for several moments, then spoke hesitantly. "You said he seemed upset. That may be your nice way of saying he was acting strange, irrational."

"Why do you say that?"

"He seemed so odd those last few weeks. He was secretive. He made me leave town for a few days, as if he had to be alone. And then after that. I'd see him sneaking up to the attic and staying there for some time. There's nothing up there. I just don't know what got into him. And then last week."

"Something happened last week?"

"Last week," Pat explained, "a man from the Country Club came by to give me the things Charles had left in his locker. I really had no interest in any of it, but there was something very curious in the carton."

Pat left the room. Peter had a sudden premonition just as Pat returned, carrying a large leather totebag. The sight brought Peter forward in his seat, fighting to control his emotions.

Pat sat down and opened the bag. Slowly and carefully she put its contents on the floor, next to her feet—a dagger, a collar, a small box and a candle holder.

Peter's heart began to race. There they all were, together, in one place. What in God's name was he to do? If he denied any knowledge of what they were, Pat would continue asking questions, and eventually someone would recognize them. Who knew what disastrous chain of events that would set in motion?

He had to invent something, anything, to get the pieces away from her—to protect this woman—to protect himself.

"You seem to recognize these things, Mr. Mandel. Why did Charles have them in his locker? I called the club and there's no mistake, the boy found them in Charles' locker."

"Oh, yes, Pat, I've seen them before." Peter was inventing on the spot. "Charles showed them to me the last time we were together."

"What are they?"

"They're replicas of the pieces on display at the museum in New York. You know, the Golden. Age exhibit. The one we did the program about."

"Oh." Pat nodded. "But why would Charles have them?"

"He was trying to set up a sales organization." Peter paused, fitting the lies together into a plausible story. "You said it yourself, Pat, he was getting desperate— anything to earn money."

"God, yes, he was scared." Pat sighed.

"He met this man in Sirocco, a guy who always finds a way to turn a buck, you know, a real promoter. This guy is an opportunist of the first order—I've known him for years. He sold JFK pictures after the assassination and models of the Andrea Doria after the sinking. Well, anyway, with all the publicity, the exhibition was getting, this guy decided to go into business selling these replicas. These things are not junk. They're gold, and quite valuable."

"I can see that." Pat was holding up the jeweled burial collar. The wall behind the table lamp was aflame with the reflections. Red and blue bright spots danced on the ceiling as she turned the collar from side to side.

"Charles and this man made a deal," Peter went on. "Charles was to see if he could line up some people to act as salesmen up here in this area. You know, get some woman to talk up these things at the bridge club, or get some guy to pitch them to his friends as great gifts. Whoever sold them got a commission, and Charles got a commission, and this other man got his profit. You didn't have to sell too many to make money, since they are expensive. These few pieces are worth over a thousand dollars each."

"Oh, my," Pat drew in her breath. "I didn't know. But why would he keep them in his locker at the club?"

"I guess he was ashamed, Pat. In his mind, he was no longer a respected member of the working community. He was a huckster, a jewelry salesman. I guess he just didn't want you to know how far he had fallen."

"I wouldn't have cared, I loved him."

"He cared, and that's what mattered. His self-respect was on the line. He had lost a lot, he didn't want to lose that, too."

Pat was biting her lower lip. Peter sat quietly and watched as tears formed on her cheek.

He hated himself and, at the same time, was proud of his story. If he could get these things away from there, that night, then the lies were worth it.

"If they're valuable, what should I do about them?"

"I believe Charles had them on consignment from this guy—you know, borrowed, to see if he could sell any. They were his samples. I would imagine that our man from Sirocco is looking for Charles, and for these pieces. He probably doesn't even know about Charles."

"Peter, take them with you tonight. Give them back to this man. I don't want him thinking Charles was a thief."

"I'll be glad to, Pat, since that's what you want. Glad to."

On the drive down from Connecticut, Peter's mind was racing. He needed to sort out his options.

There were really only two. Any way he turned, it came down to a choice between Claudia and the museum. He looked down at the leather tote next to him and shook his§ head, "What a god awful responsibility you are..."

In the silence following his words, he heard a little boy's plea. "If you forgive me. I'll never do it again." It was clear that he had only one option.

SATURDAY, MAY 7

Claudia felt that she had simply rid herself of a pest, much as one eliminates a flitting mosquito. It was not an act that required no afterthought or remorse. Murder? Not at all.

Her one regret was that she hadn't acted sooner. When he took the objects back to Connecticut with him, she had known he was up to something. He had taken them as insurance, in case things didn't go his way.

As much as she disliked her next move, it was absolutely necessary. She had to drive to Connecticut and pay a condolence call on Pat Green. There, she would—she must—discover what had happened to the objects. It was the last piece of the puzzle to be put into place.

It was another weekend, and Maurice was out of town. As a result, she found herself free on that Saturday morning to drive to Connecticut, without offering an explanation to anyone. She merely told Mrs. Britton she'd be away visiting friends. As awkward as calling unexpectedly might be, Claudia found it preferable to a long explanation over the phone. So she decided to go to Darien without calling ahead.

* * *

The sky was a cloudless blue and traffic sparse, but her mood grew darker as the miles rolled by. Hard determination gave way to increasing uncertainty. She hated being in this position. Charles' wife had to have them. Claudia went over her story. It was real enough, she though. Pat would give them to her. But what if she didn't have them ... damn! This was so unnecessary.

The next exit was Darien. She turned off, went north to Middlesex, a left and then a right on Ridge Road. She couldn't believe how easily she had found the street— now she had to find the house. She remembered Charles saying it was near the country club, but she'd already passed that. Driving slowly, peering at the mailboxes, she finally found it. It was a nice neighborhood...typical suburbia so far as Claudia was concerned. She pulled into the driveway. Ahead of her was a grey Ford station wagon. No other car was in sight.

She got out and rang the bell. Within moments the front door was opened by a dark-haired woman.

"Mrs. Green?" Claudia asked.

"Yes?" she responded.

"Mrs. Green, my name is Betancourt, Claudia Betancourt. I was acquainted with your husband."

Pat Green stood there, dressed in jeans and plaid shirt, staring at Claudia. Her dark hair pulled tightly back off her face, and she wore no make-up. Then she moved aside, allowing Claudia to enter.

"I was very sorry to hear about Charles. We were...acquainted. I met Charles through my work at the Museum."

Pat Green's face brightened a little. "Your name—I guess I may have heard Charles speak of you—or perhaps it was Peter Mandel. Forgive me. The past few weeks have been very difficult. I'm really not thinking too clearly. Won't you please come in?"

Pat Green led the way into a colonial-styled living room. It was pleasant enough, thought Claudia. Everything in its place. Dull, but pleasant.

"I'm sorry I didn't call before coming, but explaining in person is easier than over the phone. As I said, I met Charles through the museum. One evening, not too long before...well, not too long ago...I stopped after work to have a drink with Peter Mandel and to ask a favor of him." Claudia flicked a piece of lint off her navy-blue linen slacks. "Charles was with him." She paused again, as if giving the other woman time to absorb each part of the story.

"My husband is a collector of rare Egyptian art, " she continued. "I had purchased four objects that I planned to give him on his birthday next week. I needed someone to hide them for me. Peter was leaving for an out-of-town job. Charles graciously volunteered to keep the pieces for me. I dislike bothering you at such a difficult time, but I'd like to get the objects back."

Claudia noticed that the expression on Pat Green's face had begun to change. Her forehead had come together in a frown. Claudia began to feel terribly uneasy. "What did the objects look like?" Pat asked.

"There were four of them, all gold." She described them in detail. "I put them in my leather bag when I gave them to Charles." Claudia hesitated, then asked, "Is something wrong?"

Pat shook her head. The story she had just heard was so totally different from what Peter had said. Someone was lying, but who? Why? This woman didn't look like she needed money. Maybe she was the person Charles was doing business with? No, Peter had said it was a man.

Suddenly Pat stood up. "Would you like something to drink, some coffee, or a soda, perhaps?"

Before Claudia could say no, Pat went into the kitchen. Claudia followed her. "Mrs. Green, you know about the pieces. What happened to them?"

Pat Green fumbled with the cream and sugar, without answering.

"I wish you'd tell me what's troubling you. All I want is to get the objects back. They're for my husband. I realize they're not real, but they are part of the limited edition the Metropolitan Museum produced to commemorate the exhibition. So, in a sense, they are quite valuable."

Pat quickly whirled around, spilling coffee as she did. "I don't understand."

Claudia's patience was at an end. This woman was as idiotic as her dead husband. She knows where they are. Claudia wanted to shake it out of her.

"You heard me, Mrs. Green, or weren't you listening?" Claudia's voice had become sharp, her anxiety was beginning to show. "I said they were copies, but valuable copies. Now where are they?"

"Look," Pat Green said, as she sunk into a kitchen chair, "I haven't been able to handle Charles' death very well."

Claudia watched the woman impatiently.

"The day after Charles died, his country club returned the things that were in his locker, among them was a leather bag. I knew it wasn't Charles'—I thought maybe he had bought it for me—then I looked inside, and didn't know what to make of the whole thing."

Tears began swelling up in her eyes. "Then, last week, Peter Mandel came over. We talked about Charles, and then I showed him the things that were in the bag. He told me a story about Charles—and a man he met in a bar. They were going into business together to try and sell these things—these replicas or whatever they are. Peter said he would return them to this man, and I was grateful. Now you tell me about your husband's birthday present—I just don't know what to make of the whole thing. Your story and his don't go together." Then she looked up at

Claudia. "I just don't understand any of this."

Claudia thought fast. "If I know Peter, he was probably trying to avoid telling you that Charles was doing a personal favor for another woman. He thinks he did a good deed by inventing the other story. Don't worry about it any more. I'll call him when I get back."

"But—but what he said about Charles ..." Claudia had gone into the living room and retrieved her handbag. Now she walked towards the front door, saying, "Mrs. Green, if you loved him, it shouldn't make any difference."

Pat looked at her and shook her head, "No, I guess it shouldn't."

Within ten minutes, Claudia was on the Thruway heading back to New York.

Her thoughts centered on one person only. Peter Mandel. He probably wants them for himself. Yes, that's it. Well, Peter is clever, but he doesn't know that one of the pieces isn't real—that it never got switched. He wants to steal them from me! Claudia kept pressing harder and harder on the accelerator, oblivious to the world outside her car.

The blue morning sky had turned to thick grey clouds which grew heavier as she approached the city. Before long, drops of rain began hitting the windshield, quickly becoming a downpour. Claudia turned on the wipers. Suddenly, and without warning, a car pulled out of the right lane, and directly into her path. Claudia hit the brakes with such force that she skidded off of the wet pavement, narrowly missing another car, and came to rest on the dirt shoulder.

For a moment, she couldn't breathe. She touched the windshield—then looked at her arms and hands. Everything seemed to be in one piece. No blood. No cracks. She sank back into the seat and reached for a cigarette, but her hand shook so badly she couldn't get one out of the gold case. She gave up and just closed her eyes. The rain continued pounding the car. She turned off the wipers and sat in silence.

Ten minutes later Claudia started the car. For a few seconds she was terrified to even touch the gas pedal, then she pressed down on it and moved out into traffic. She drove slowly at first, the memory of the car from nowhere still very vivid.

Twenty minutes later she pulled off the East River Drive at 72nd Street and headed for home. She was not surprised when there was no answer at Peter's number. She replaced the receiver slowly. This whole situation was getting out of hand. She felt drained. A warm bath. A glass of wine. That's what she wanted. Then she would think about what she had to do next.

MONDAY, MAY 9

For Claudia, the hours from Saturday afternoon until Monday evening could have been measured in years, but they had finally passed. At last, it was Monday evening. Peter's secretary had said he'd be back in the office tomorrow, which meant he'd probably be at home tonight. Ever since Claudia got home from work, she'd been dialing his number every fifteen minutes.

At 9:30 she tried the number again. This time, he answered. .

"Peter, this is Claudia Betancourt. I've been trying all weekend to reach you." She was trying to sound calm.

"Claudia? What a surprise. I just got in from L.A. I saw Sharon. She's in the process of unpacking. It should take a year," he laughed.

"How nice." Claudia spoke coldly. "Peter, I have to speak with you as soon as possible. When would be a good time to get together?"

"How about tomorrow night after work? I'll meet you at the Four Seasons at 6:00. If I'm going to be delayed. I'll call you before 5:00. All right?"

This was not what Claudia had planned. She wanted to meet him now, tonight. She wanted to meet him at his place, but there wasn't anything she could do about it. She agreed.

TUESDAY, MAY 10

At five minutes past 6:00 on Tuesday, Claudia walked into the cocktail lounge at the Four Seasons. Peter was waiting for her, watching her make her entrance. He noticed the eyes in the room move in her direction. She is beautiful, he thought, elegant and aristocratic. Even in a place like this where they see beautiful women every day she is special. He had the feeling he knew what Claudia wanted. He didn't look forward to this meeting, but it had seemed best to get it over and done with.

"Claudia," he rose to greet her.

"Peter, it's good to see you." She extended her hand.

"It's been too long."

"Sitting here with you now, it seems hard to remember those interesting evenings in Sirocco."

"Yes," he said, "things have a way of changing, don't they?"

A waiter came and took the drink order, returning a few minutes later with a glass of wine and a Scotch and water.

They sat in silence for a few moments.

"Did you go to the funeral?" Claudia began.

"Yes," he answered. He looked at her curiously. "It was damn sudden, I guess."

"Well...Charles did have a lot of problems, and maybe the stress built up to a point where his heart couldn't handle it." She sipped her wine. "I paid a call on Pat Green last Saturday."

"Oh? Why did you do that?"

Claudia looked at him. She couldn't fence with him any longer. "You know why," she said angrily. "I went to get those four pieces that Charles took home from the museum."

Peter leaned back in his chair and returned her stare. "And Pat told you that I took them."

"Yes, she told me. Are you going to tell me the rest?"

"What do you mean, the rest?"

"What you did with them. Where are they? What are your plans? I find it hard to believe you've taken them for yourself. That would be stupid."

Peter smiled. "Claudia, you're wrong, very wrong. I did take the pieces, but not for myself. I didn't want to leave them with that poor woman. God only knows what would have happened if anyone had found out what they really were. I took them and did what I should have done in the first place—I returned them." The words fell on Claudia like blows.

"Returned them?" she repeated. "Where? To whom?"

"To the museum, to Gottfried. I put the bag in a locker and sent the key to Gottfried."

"No! You couldn't have done that. You wouldn't have done that. I don't believe you!"

"Claudia," he said angrily, "listen to me. This has gone far enough. The robbery was crazy, but it's over and done with. The pieces, except for yours, are back where they should be."

"No, Peter. You don't understand. You shouldn't have done that. It's not over with. You've just made matters worse."

"Claudia, I really don't want to listen to anything more about those pieces. Finish your drink. Let's go."

Claudia almost seemed to be in a trance. Her eyes seemed very far away.

Once they were outside, Peter took Claudia's arm and looked at her. "I'm sorry it had to end this way, for all of us."

"But it's not over, Peter. Wait and see." With that Claudia pulled away from his grasp and started walking up Park Avenue toward her home.

THURSDAY, MAY 12

Miriam Gottfried reread the letter for the tenth time—or was it the twentieth? She had lost count. It was typed on a sheet of yellow tissue ... the kind of paper used for office memos:

Dr. Gottfried,
This key will open a locker on the Vanderbilt Avenue side of Grand Central Station.
The locker contains some objects that are of great value to you and the museum (and the Egyptian government).
Please go yourself, and do so immediately. If the locker is opened by anyone else it will be an embarrassment to you and the museum.

There was no identification other than a New York City postmark. The postmark read May 2. The letter had been in her mailbox for over a week awaiting her return from a seminar in Boston.

Objects? What could they be? Could it be a prank? The parts about the Egyptians and 'embarrassment' were curious. For some reason, the note had the ring of truth about it.

She looked at the key, turning it over in her hand. She had to go. If it was someone's practical joke, then no one would be the wiser. The trip would take no more than a half hour, there and back.

A short taxi ride left the curator at the Vanderbilt Avenue side of the cavernous station.

There were hundreds of lockers. It took much stooping and squinting before she matched the key number to a door. She was about to insert the key when the vision of a bomb exploded in her mind. There had been horrible killings at LaGuardia Airport when Serbian patriots left a time bomb in a locker, and it seemed to her that she had read many times of dismembered bodies found in public lockers.

She shook off her momentary terror, thrust the key in and pulled open the door. There was no blinding flash, no drip of blood. There was only a leather totebag. She pulled it out of the locker and let the door swing shut.

The bag was not heavy. Her black brows pinching together in a frown, she opened the zipper, spread the sides of the bag apart and peered in. She widened the opening and brought her head closer.

"*Mein Gott! Was giebt's.*" Her lapse into her native German was a sign of total surprise. She closed the bag and shook her head slowly. There were benches several feet away. She walked to them and sat down.

She opened the bag again. This time she slipped her hand in, then suddenly withdrew it, as if the contents were hot. It was several minutes before she got up to leave.

Back in her apartment, she put the totebag on her coffee table and sat down on the sofa. The bag itself fascinated her. There was something about it. It was not a common bag, perhaps she had seen it before.

With sure, determined movements she unzipped the bag and took out the contents, aligning them on the table in front of her.

For a long time, she just looked at them. Then she went to the bookcase wall of the combination living and dining room. She returned with several volumes including the catalogue of the exhibit.

Gottfried quickly turned pages, read, picked up the dagger, compared it to the color plates, read more. She returned the dagger to the table and repeated the process with the box.

Then she examined the golden candle holder, a glint of recognition in her eyes. The remainder of the time her lined face was serious, the expression puzzled.

Some time later, she put the collar down, closed the book, and leaned back. She removed her glasses and rubbed her eyes, the candle holder is not real, she mused. It has a manufacturer's mark on it. The others do not carry any marking. If these are real, how did they leave the museum? How did they get into that locker? Into that bag—that bag. Why do I think I have seen it before? It is beautiful—very expensive.

The curator burst into laughter. "Expensive? What about the value of what is in it?"

Miriam Gottfried did not eat dinner. It was after 10 p.m. when she made a cup of tea—and even then she returned to the pieces. She paced in front of the table, sipping from her cup, trying to find any hint that would tell her why these four pieces were sitting here.

She sat down, elbows up on her knees, chin resting in the palms of her hands. She stared. No explanation came. She turned her attention to the tote. Inside the upper corner, under the zipper, was a small silk label. It had curled up. She unrolled it with her fingernail and read the small red-embroidered name. "Venezia."

"Venezia. Venezia." She hurried to the front hall closed where a Manhattan phone directory lay buried in a corner.

Bottega Venezia was listed with a Fifth Avenue address. She jotted the street number down on a small note pad.

By midnight, Miriam Gottfried was exhausted. Several times she caught her head nodding forward, fighting for sleep. She got up, went to her bedroom closet and rummaged through the suitcases stacked on the upper shelf, returning with a lockable overnight case. She returned the pieces to the tote, put the tote in the suitcase, and placed the suitcase back in the closet, with several cartons and pieces of luggage in front of it.

She set the alarm one hour ahead of its usual time and went to bed.

FRIDAY, MAY 13

The curator of Egyptology arrived at the museum an hour earlier than usual, at 8 a.m.

After a few minutes in her office, she proceeded downstairs, directly to the entrance to the tomb. Two museum security men were standing near the entrance. Their conversation stopped as she approached. They touched their caps with respect, or was it fear? Gottfried's lined face and usual grey pallor gave no hint of her troubled thoughts.

"Good morning. Doctor," one muttered.

"Good morning," she nodded as she strode down the passageway.

Inside the tomb there was no night or day. The overhead spotlights stared down at the pieces on their black velvet beds. She walked directly to the golden dagger, picked it up, and began to turn it slowly in her hands, squinting at it.

Suddenly, she stopped. There it was, the tiny manufacturer's mark. If she had not been looking specifically for it, and hadn't known where to find it, it would have gone unnoticed.

She moved on to the burial collar. The test was repeated, with the same result. Only at the small granulated box did she remain for a long time—searching, turning, touching, turning—but no mark appeared. The box did not have that minute signature that identified it as a reproduction. The box was real.

Miriam Gottfried left the tomb slowly, pensively, almost sadly. Back in her office, she looked small and frail behind her large desk in her high backed swivel chair. She stared at the papers in front of her. Several minutes passed.

"Can I get you some tea. Doctor?"

Gottfried looked up startled. "Oh...No. Ah...yes, thank you."

The secretary turned and was about to leave when the doctor called after her.

"Do you know a store called 'Venezia'?"

"Yes. It's a very exclusive boutique on Fifth Avenue, in the fifties."

Miriam Gottfried replied with a nod as she thought of her next move.

* * *

Each red traffic signal was a personal affront to Miriam Gottfried. The Fifth Avenue bus was moving much too slowly. The curator was not entirely sure what she would do or say in the boutique, or what she hoped to learn. Now she was reasonably sure that three pieces from the exhibit were in her closet at home. The totebag was the only clue she had. The untrained eye could sense it was expensive. Even Venezia could not sell many like it.

The grey-haired woman got out of the bus at 57th Street on that part of Fifth Avenue that housed most of the best stores in New York City...Cartier, Steuben,

Gucci, Tiffany...they were all there, in a line, a jet-set flea market.

There was Venezia. In the quiet, luxurious interior, Miriam Gottfried had to wait while a saleswoman finished with a customer. When her turn came, she tried for pleasantness. It did not come easily to a woman who rarely smiled. The saleswoman appraised this potential customer with a practiced eye. Older women were definitely the worst customers. The two women were now prepared for the over-the-counter confrontation.

"May I show you something?" The smile was warm and shallow.

"No, thank you, but you can help me." The smile was cold and forced.

The saleswoman's smile was replaced with a frown.

"I found a leather bag at Kennedy Airport. To be quite honest, I didn't want to turn it into the airport people—I don't trust them. So I took the bag home."

The saleswoman listened, not very patiently.

"I'm afraid there was no identification in the bag, no way I could find out who the owner was. The only thing that gives me any clue is your label. The bag came from this store."

"We also have shops in Paris, Rome, and Beverly Hills." The tone was matter-of-fact.

"Oh. I didn't know. Perhaps if I described the bag to you, you might remember it. I don't imagine you sell many of them."

"Madam, I..."

"No, wait, just a moment, please." Miriam Gottfried proceeded to describe the totebag in minute detail. Her training in the cataloging of artifacts made this, task simple.

The saleswoman's interest was captured by the grey haired woman's incredible detail, including even the dimensions of the gold buckle. She began to nod her head.

"I think I remember the bag," she said, and stepped away for a second, only to return with a large looseleaf binder.

"Yes. Yes," she mused, as she turned the pages. "The 19-inch tote with the shoulder strap. A beautiful bag. Here it is. Style 307B."

She looked up at Miriam Gottfried and smiled. This time, the smile was real. She spun the book around and pointed to a picture. Miriam nodded. It was the bag. "Let me check our inventory control sheet."

The saleswoman disappeared into the rear of the store and Miriam Gottfried was left to look at the merchandise or the other customers. Neither was of interest.

She closed her eyes, absorbed by the memory of those pieces as they sat on her coffee table last night. How warm and radiant they were. How they changed the atmosphere of the room. How good it was to spend those few hours alone with them, unhurried, unwatched. Just she and them.

The saleswoman returned holding a slip of paper. Now her smile was one of complete self-satisfaction. "Our record-keeping is very complete and accurate."

Miriam Gottfried wanted to shout. Tell me the bag came from some other store! Tell me you sold it to Mrs. Jones or Mrs. Smith! But tell me, you officious twit! She bit her lip.

"We have sold three of those bags since they first came in last December."

The saleswoman paused.

"Well?" The curator wanted to grab the paper from the woman's hand.

"One bag was sent to a Mr. Burden in Chicago. It. was ordered over the phone."

Miriam Gottfried reached into her own purse and took out a pen and small scrap of paper.

"What did you say that name was?"

"Burden, B-U-R-D-E-N."

"And his address?" Miriam Gottfried asked.

"Oh, I'm afraid we cannot give you that information. However, we will contact each of the customers and ask them if they have lost it. We will call you as soon as someone gets in touch. May I have your name and phone number, please?"

The curator sagged. A dead end, she thought, a waste. She dropped the scrap of paper back into her purse and flicked the button on the ballpoint pen.

"My name and phone number? Yes...let me give you my business card."

She began to rummage in her purse.

"The other two bags were sold over the counter right here." The saleswoman was looking at her piece of paper again. "One was sold to a Miss Dreyfus and the other to a Doctor Betancourt."

The curator's had shot up.

"Doctor Betancourt?" she whispered.

"Yes, Doctor Maurice Betancourt."

Miriam Gottfried dropped her business card back into her purse, and pulled the zipper closed. She turned on her heel and walked to the door. Before the saleswoman could voice a question, the grey-haired woman, was out the door and into the street.

The curator strode up Fifth Avenue, arms swinging, legs pumping. Past the stores, the hotels, the super chic apartment houses. Block after block, head slightly bent, watching the sidewalk in front of her. It took less than thirty minutes to cover the distance from the boutique to the museum, but Miriam Gottfried had no conception of the time. Her mind was on fire. She knew where she had seen the leather tote before.

MONDAY, MAY 16

As the cab inched along the expressway from Kennedy Airport, heading into the city, Sharon Hiller gazed out at the slow-moving cars and buses.

She had to keep reminding herself that she was here as a visitor, and not heading for her home in Connecticut after a business trip. She wondered what Clayton was doing. Was his mother catering to his drinking? The thought made her furious. But then, thinking of her mother-in-law usually did.

She was looking forward to tomorrow morning and her first storyline meeting with the network brass. She was excited over the outline. It had been approved back in L.A. Now it had only this last hurdle to pass.

Her thoughts drifted back to Clayton and the other reason for her trip to New York. She was settled now in California, and it was everything she had imagined it to be. She could breathe again. She had been able to throw herself into her writing. The work on the series was formula pap, but the story of the robbery was good, it was intriguing. Now she wanted a legal separation. She hoped there would be no hassle over the girls. That was a battle nobody won. Even Clayton had to realize that. She was already getting herself tensed up over her meeting with him before she left.

The cab crawled over the 59th Street Bridge the skyline of Manhattan stretched out before her. Behind the skyscrapers the sun was sliding into the New Jersey hills, sending a last burst of color into the sky. The red glow changed into orange, then to rose, pink and finally into a deep purple. She found that the scene was still breathtaking.

It was just past six by the time she arrived at the Park Lane Hotel. She quickly unpacked then called Claudia. Finances were getting tight and she needed to know if Claudia had done anything with the remaining four pieces.

"Claudia? It's Sharon. Sharon Hiller."

A pause. "Sharon. Where are you?"

"Here," she laughed, "in New York. Feels funny being a visitor."

"How are you doing, and what are you doing?"

"I'm fine. I'm here for some network meetings. They're reviewing my outline for a television movie."

"That sounds exciting. I'd love to hear more about it. How long are you going to be in town?"

"Well, that kind of depends on how well the meetings go tomorrow. And I have to talk with Clayton about the girls."

"Sounds like you have a full schedule."

"Sort of. That's why I called you now. Do you have any time to get together?

Can't tell what tomorrow's going to be like."

"Yes. If you're not too tired, why don't you come over here. We can have a drink, and you can tell me what you're doing."

"I'd love to. I can't wait to tell you about the movie."

"Do you remember the address?"

"Yes."

"All right—see you in a little while."

Sharon hung up the phone and checked her make-up. It was a warm evening and she didn't need a jacket. She started to leave without it, then looked in the mirror. Would Claudia ever go out looking half-dressed? She put on her jacket and left the room.

On 74th Street she was greeted at the front door by Claudia who was dressed in a long, pale blue silk robe. Her hair was brushed back off her face and fell softly to her shoulders. Sharon was glad she had worn her jacket.

"You're looking better than ever," Claudia said in greeting. "California obviously agrees with you."

"Thanks. I think it's the change in lifestyle more than the climate."

Claudia led the way into the sitting room.

As Sharon entered the room, she said, "Being here brings back a lot of memories."

"Memories?"

"Don't you remember? This is where we plotted our trip to buy the reproductions."

"Oh, yes. I'd forgotten. I...ah...guess so much has happened since then. Still drinking the same thing?" Sharon nodded and Claudia disappeared into the hallway returning a few minutes later with two glasses of white wine.

"How's Peter?" Claudia asked as they sat down.

"Doing very well. He's been staying with me for a while. He's still producing news specials, but there's some talk of international assignments."

"Where are you living?"

"Right now I'm renting near Malibu. The house looks out over the ocean. It's lovely but pricey. But I think I'd like to move a little further south. How have you been?" Sharon noticed tiny lines in Claudia's forehead and around her mouth. They hadn't been there before. Something has been bothering her, Sharon thought.

"I've had my ups and downs. Poor Charles—I guess everything was too much for him."

"I missed you at the funeral."

"I didn't think it would be appropriate. I wasn't exactly a friend of the family."

"Yes, I see your point." There was no point beating around the bush. Sharon came right out with her question.

"What happened to the pieces, Claudia? Charles had them, but where are they now? Did you get them from his wife?"

"No," Claudia said calmly.

"No?" Sharon almost shrieked.

"No. There was no way to get them from him. And I couldn't exactly go up there and ask his wife for them."

"So—what happened to them?"

"Mrs. Green found them and gave them to Peter."

Sharon sat with her mouth open. "Peter? He's never said a word about them. I can't believe it."

"He returned them, anonymously, to the museum."

"He did what? I don't believe it! And you're so calm about it!" Sharon was aghast. "How can you not care? You must."

"No. I have the statue. The other pieces don't really concern me."

Sharon didn't believe her, but there was no point in saying so. She sighed deeply. "It's incredible. He knew how much the money meant to me." She stared off into space. "I don't understand him."

"Tell me how your job is coming along," Claudia said. She understood Sharon's anger. She shared her outrage. But there was something she needed to find out. "What are you working on?"

"So far, about half my time is spent in brainstorming sessions to come up with ideas for new series. The rest of the time I devote to the mystery movie." Sharon was beaming. "The outline has been tentatively approved by the L.A. office, pending what happens here tomorrow."

"I think that's great! Is this the one you were doing about the robbery?" Claudia was afraid to hear her answer.

"Yes. Remember I told you I was keeping a diary of our adventure?"

"How could I forget?"

"I've taken it as far as I can, based on what's happened. But Peter's little twist with the artifacts throws me."

"What do you mean?" Claudia's pulse spiked.

"I've written a plot outline based on the actual robbery—although, of course, no one will ever know that," Sharon laughed. "But now I don't know what to do."

Claudia's expression was beginning to change as Sharon continued.

"My idea was to take the robbery as we actually did it, switching the fakes for the real. The people involved were going to be something like all of us— it's much easier to write from what you know. I've kept the occupations the same, although the network may object to having an employee involved in a crime."

"You mean, you are really serious about telling this story on television?"

Sharon mistook the tone of Claudia's voice. "Yes. It's a great idea?"

Claudia looked at her, eyes hooded. "I don't know what I think."

"Well, let me tell you where I was going from there. After the robbery, the thieves sell the objects back to the Egyptian government. But in the end, and this was really blue sky, they all die in some way or other, usually under mysterious circumstances. That made it look like there was some supernatural force at work, dooming the robbers."

Claudia shook her head.

"And you say the outline is approved?"

"Not for sure, not until tomorrow." At last noticing Claudia's troubled expression, she asked, "Why, is something wrong?"

"You're coming a little close to home."

"Don't be silly." Sharon reached over and placed her hand on Claudia's arm. "You're imagining things. No one would suspect that it's based on fact."

Claudia knew better. Maurice would know. Even the people at the museum might start wondering. "Sharon, do you really think that it's a good idea to draw so much on what really happened?"

"Well, to tell you the truth, I handed in two versions of the robbery and this is the one that was selected. They think the idea is unique and they like the characters."

Unique, thought Claudia.

Sharon looked at her empty wine glass. "Claudia, I'm sorry. I didn't think you'd get upset. Peter thought it would be a lot of fun. Of course, poor Charles doesn't really have a vote in it. But it can't make any difference to any of us. It's all over now."

No, Claudia thought, it would never end.

"It's been a long day," Sharon said, "I'd better be going. My first meeting is at 8:30." She stared at Claudia's unsmiling face. "Look—maybe they'll turn the idea down tomorrow then it'll be all over and done with."

But what if they didn't turn it down. What if they really did like it? Claudia wanted to scream out at her. "Why don't you call me tomorrow and let me know how you made out? I have more than a passing interest in the project."

"I'll do that. It'll probably be late. In between network meetings, I have to try and meet with Clayton to discuss the separation."

"Do you think he'll give you any problems?"

Sharon sighed, "I hope not. I'll call. It was really good seeing you."

"Maybe we can get together again, before you go."

"I'd love that," Sharon squeezed Claudia's hand. "Talk to you tomorrow. Good night."

After Sharon left, Claudia refilled her glass and returned to the sitting room.

"I thought I heard voices," Maurice said, standing in the doorway.

"You did. A woman I know who is now living on the West Coast writing scripts for UBS came back to town for a couple of days. She dropped by." Claudia didn't feel like mentioning Sharon Hiller's name.

"What's the matter?" Maurice asked. "Did she say something that upset you?"

"No, why?" she gave him a startled look.

"I don't know. You seem pensive. And nervous."

"No, no. I'm fine," Claudia said. "I've just got other things on my mind."

"Are you coming upstairs?"

Claudia shook her head.

"No, not just now. Goodnight."

Claudia waited until she was certain Maurice had gone upstairs then went down the hall to the library. She loved the room at this time of night. Everything was so perfectly still. Not a sound. She opened the bookcase to look at the statue, then sat and lighted a cigarette.

Sharon occasionally had a way of being naive. Claudia was never certain if it was real, or just a way of getting to people. But this was not the time for it. Couldn't Sharon see the disaster her script would create should it ever be produced? Obviously not. Or else she just didn't care. How could Peter have encouraged her!

Tomorrow Sharon would have to change her mind. There must be a way Claudia could persuade her to alter the outline.

* * *

It was after nine thirty by the time Sharon finished dinner. Ordering room service was better than sitting in a restaurant alone. She had gone from being furious at Peter to just being angry. She just saw Peter. And he never said anything about returning the pieces to the museum. How could he have done that? The money Claudia advanced her was nearly gone and there would be no more. Thanks to Peter.

She called his phone and he picked up on the second ring.

"I was hoping to hear from you tonight. Miss you," he said.

"I miss you, too, but I have a question. I met with Claudia about an hour or so ago. And she tells me that you returned the four artifacts to the museum. How could you have done that? You know how much I needed that money."

"You may need money, Sharp, but not *that* money. Charles is dead and I know I can't prove it, but I will swear that Claudia had something to do with it. I know she was somewhere else that night, but I swear she was involved. Charles had problems. But not heart problems. Not the kind to cause a fatal attack. That woman's dangerous. Stay away from her. Besides there's nothing more she can do for you, but there is something I can do for you."

"I hope it's good.

"You have no faith. I know your finances. I know putting a roof over your head is pricey. That place you liked in Brentwood?"

"Yes?" Her heart was beating so loudly she could barely hear her own voice.

"I put a down payment on it and in the next few weeks it'll be ours. At least that way, you won't have to worry about rent."

Happiness welled in her chest. She sobbed into the phone. "Thank you."

"Go do great tomorrow. Sell them that movie. You're on your way."

TUESDAY, MAY 17

Claudia rang the bell on the Park Lane door marked 1601—3 and waited. Before she could ring again, Sharon Hiller appeared and threw open her arms in greeting.

"Hi, come on in, I just got here myself."

Claudia stepped through a small entrance foyer into a huge living room. There were several couches and chairs arranged in conversation groups. There were tables, lamps, a breakfront, a bar cart and a TV, yet the room was large enough to accommodate it all and still remain uncluttered.

The far wall was a floor-to-ceiling window overlooking Central Park.

Sharon swept her arm around the room. "Do you believe this? I mean, talk about plush. My bedroom's through there," she pointed at an open door, "and the kitchen is that way, and next to the kitchen is a walk-in closet full of booze. The network brass keeps this on a year-round lease. Can you believe it?" She looked at Claudia and her face brightened. "Yes. You can believe it, if anyone can."

Claudia offered no response. Sharon continued her running monologue.

"I'm on a treadmill. They've got me running so fast you'd think there was a deadline to get me out of town. Our story conference just broke up and we pick it up again at dinner. I'm really sorry about not having a lot of time to spend with you, but I guess I'm lucky to have from now until 8:00 to relax and put myself together. I'm going to sink into a hot bath."

Claudia noticed that Sharon was shoeless.

"I'm going to mix us both a drink, and then we can talk while I start the repair job." She went to the bar cart and Claudia heard the glasses and ice come to life.

"What can I make you?"

"Nothing, thanks."

Sharon mixed a light Scotch and water for herself and carried it into the bedroom.

"I spoke to the girls this morning." Sharon was speaking loudly, her voice carrying from the bedroom. "Clayton is not making any waves."

Claudia only half listened to Sharon's chatter. She walked over to the window wall and looked out at the dusk settling over the park. To her left, the sky was red and streaked with grey. The grey could be high clouds— more likely, just pollution. To her right, the sky was dark. Lights had begun to twinkle on Fifth Avenue.

Claudia heard the water running from beyond the bedroom.

"Claudia? I can't shout from the bathroom. Come in and keep me company.

We'll talk while I soak."

Claudia turned just as the curly, brown head disappeared back into the bedroom. She walked to her purse and took out a cigarette, lit it and went into the bedroom. Sharon's clothes were thrown all over the bed. Her shoes were on the floor. A pair of pantyhose was on a chair near the bathroom door. She could hear Sharon splashing into the tub.

"Oooh, oh, it's hot."

And then a contented sigh as she settled into the water.

Claudia went to the bathroom door and hesitated. There was a strange knot in her chest as she thought of Sharon in the tub.

Sharon was talking again. "I'm sorry, Claudia, I go on and on. I never asked you what it was you wanted to talk about."

Claudia hesitated, frozen in the bathroom doorway. Finally, she stepped into the room. It was hot and steamy. The pink and grey tiles on the walls were perspiring, the little beads running into the grout cracks.

Claudia took a towel from the wall rack and folded it lengthwise, laid it on the ledge of the bath tub and sat down.

Sharon was stretched out, with soapy, opaque water covering her to her chin. Below the surface of the water, Claudia could make out the faint outlines of Sharon's body—the slightly darker color of her nipples, the dark triangular patch between her legs and the coloring on her toenails. The knot in her chest persisted.

"I really wanted to talk about the show. How did your story conference go?"

"They've given me a go-ahead. Isn't it exciting? At least from where I'm standing it is." Sharon smiled.

"That's just it, dear. Doesn't your point of view worry you?"

"Why should it?"

"Eventually, the substitutions are going to be discovered. It's inevitable. And, when that happens, won't your script be too coincidental for comfort?"

Claudia sounded like a patient mother.

"It's just coincidence, that's all. Even if anyone ever remembers the show and makes the connection with the museum, there is no way they can point a finger at me. I'm just an imaginative storyteller, that's all."

Claudia reached over and flicked her cigarette ash in the sink. She kept her eyes averted. She did not want to look at Sharon.

"Don't you think that when you do the show, you will arouse the suspicion of the people at the museum?"

"Oh, goodness no. Those people never watch television, and if they did, no one believes what they see. It's make-believe, remember?"

"Sharon, I wish I could make you understand." Claudia's voice showed the slightest bit of steel. "This lark of yours is putting everything in jeopardy. If they get the slightest bit suspicious, they'll examine everything in the exhibit and the switch will be discovered. You're handing them the crime and the solution on a platter. And there's no need to."

Sharon was silent.

Claudia began to hope that she had gotten through to her.

Finally, Sharon spoke. "Claudia, do you know what I think? I think you're getting paranoid. I think you're beginning to see boogie men under the bed." Sharon's words were light, but there was an edge to her voice. "Every day there are murders and robberies on television, in the movies, in books and every day there are murders and robberies for real. So what? If UBS puts on a movie about a plot to steal some museum treasures, no one but you is going to get excited about it. Everyone will accept it for what it is. Fiction! Just good clean fun."

"You foolish girl," Claudia was looking directly at her now, "your good clean fun will end up putting all of us behind bars."

"How can they associate any of us with it? My God, Claudia, there are only three of us left, and none of us will ever talk about it."

"Sharon, I beg of you, please don't do it."

"It's too late, Claudia. The boss O.K.'d the outline and gave me a deadline to deliver a treatment. And they're going to get it." Sharon was now irritated. "I guess my bath is ruined."

"I'm sorry," Claudia whispered, her voice husky. Sharon stood up, her waist level with Claudia's eyes. Apparently being naked in front of a stranger didn't bother her.

Claudia stood up. She held her hands out in a pleading pose—then she reached up and grasped Sharon by the shoulders. "Listen to reason, Sharon. Don't do this. Too many people will be hurt." She shook her.

Sharon pulled back to break Claudia's grip, but the soapy water gave her no support. In an instant, her feet shot out from under her and she pitched sideways. Her legs slid along the bottom as she fell, her head slammed against the side. The room echoed with the dull, metallic thud. Her head left a bloody trail along the side of the tub as she came to rest under the water.

Claudia gasped. Both hands went to her mouth, her eyes staring as the body slipped beneath the water. She bent down, reached towards the blurred face—then stopped. Sharon's knees were up, her torso and head completely submerged. Claudia could hardly distinguish her features under the soapy water. A thin stream of bubbles rose from Sharon's mouth and nose.

She stared at the column of bubbles and did nothing. Her brain registered what she was seeing, but it sent no messages to her muscles—there was only the fascination with the stream of bubbles.

After a few more seconds, the bubbles stopped. A few more came. Then they stopped. And then there were none.

Claudia bent closer. She put one hand to her lips and bit down on her fingertips. She ran the other hand over the surface of the water dipping it under the surface to touch Sharon's head. Then she moved her hand over the face, touching her neck.

Too late for an ambulance.

She picked up her purse and strode to the door. No one paid any attention as she rode down in the elevator and left the hotel.

MONDAY, MAY 23

Sharon Hiller was buried quietly in the First Episcopal Church cemetery. Green Haven Manor, Connecticut.

Because she had died accidentally, in New York City, an autopsy had to be performed. Death by misadventure was the finding. She was found to be, prior to the accident, very healthy and definitely pregnant.

Clayton's first cousin went through the Hiller phone book informing the immediate family and friends. The crowd he drew was small.

The first to find the body had been the hotel maid. She, in turn, informed management, who informed UBS, the apartment lessee. One of the UBS' secretaries called Clayton and called Peter in Los Angeles, so they wouldn't have to read it in the newspapers.

Peter flew back to New York in a state of shock. He didn't even consider propriety. He called Clayton and was told where and when the funeral would be. Again, just as in the case of Charles Green, Peter called Claudia. They attended the funeral together. Afterward, Claudia returned to her office to spend a restless day, while Peter flew back to California to an empty house.

WEDNESDAY, MAY 25

"I wanted to see you for two reasons," the curator began. "Some weeks back, the last time you were here in my office, we spoke of the scarab."

"I recall." Claudia could not keep the bitterness out of her voice.

"You don't seem to take warnings to heart. I repeat, the scarab is mine, and I won't tolerate any persistence in the matter on your part. Is that understood?" Miriam Gottfried leaned back against her desk, arms folded in front of her.

Claudia said nothing. This was a startling degree of rudeness. The rhythmic tapping of her foot was the only evidence of the nervousness she felt.

Miriam broke the silence. "Have you and Maurice added anything to your collection recently?"

Claudia frowned. Gottfried's tone was peculiar. "No... nothing."

The grey-haired woman folded both hands under her chin. Her mouth was a straight-line. "I would have thought this exhibit would inspire you to great things." The words were venomous, icy! Claudia was past caring. If this woman knew something, she wanted to hear it. She could tolerate no more games.

"I've known you too long, Miriam. We don't like each other. Is there anything specific you would like to say to me, or may I leave?"

"You may leave any time you want, Claudia. However, I thought you might want to stay and talk about, some of the pieces from the exhibit." Gottfried paused to gather the full dramatic effect from her words. "Like the dagger, or the granulated box or the burial collar."

Claudia sank back against the couch cushions. Gottfried watched her closely. She was aware of the change, in Claudia's eyes. The dark, flashing anger of a moment ago was now hunted animal fear. The curator rose and walked to a corner of the office where a silver tea service gleamed against a background of manuscripts and dusty cartons.

She poured two cups and turned to look at Claudia.

"Cream and sugar?"

Claudia said nothing as the curator approached the couch and handed her the cup. Gottfried sat down in a chair on the other side of the coffee table.

"Do you wonder why I mention just those pieces? No, of course, you don't. But you do wonder how I know? I'm very curious, Claudia, about two things. How did you do it? Did you just walk in with the duplicates and walk out with the real ones? And more important— what happened? Why were they returned?"

"Miriam, I'm sure I have no idea what you're talking about." The words sounded hopelessly stupid to Claudia. Any denial would be ridiculous.

"You know damn well what I'm talking about."

The curator had her glasses off—the cold, grey eyes were slits.

"I want to know why they came back. Who sent them? I know it was not you. Once you took them, you would never give them up."

Claudia put her cup on the table and stood. She was looking down now, directly at the top of the Curator's grey head. Gottfried had to lean back to look at her.

"All right, Miriam, I did take them. I took them right out from under your nose. How they got back is of no consequence, but you are right, it was not me. I would never have returned them. However, they are back. You can't prove they were ever gone, or that I took them. What do you intend to do?"

Claudia walked away from the couch. She stopped next to a dictionary stand and turned, one arm leaning on top of the stand.

"I have asked myself that question many times since I learned of your little peccadillo. I do not intend to let this little knowledge go to waste. I also do not intend to use it hurriedly and unwisely." Gottfried's words were measured.

"In the world in which you move, my dear Claudia," she continued, "even a hint of scandal will destroy your name. I do not have to prove anything. You would have to prove me a liar, and in defending yourself you would become tainted. The stink would cover you and your husband. The art world would close its doors to you. Here comes Claudia Betancourt, lock up your valuables. Ha, ha, ha, ha, ha, ha."

The laugh became a shriek. Claudia closed her eyes, trying to blot out the sound and the words.

Gottfried walked back to the desk. She sat down again in her tall swivel chair and leaned down to open the bottom drawer of the desk. Her head disappeared below the desk top. Claudia could not see her, only her words were audible.

"But as it happens, I can prove everything," she shouted.

She pulled the leather totebag from the drawer and stood up, slamming the bag on the desk.

"Here is your bag, Mrs. Betancourt—the gift of your husband. Here is how the pieces left the museum." She placed both hands on the desk and leaned forward. "Deny it," she said.

Claudia's arm had begun to tremble on the stand. She stood erect, heart pounding. "I repeat, Miriam, what do you intend to do?"

Miriam Gottfried left the desk and returned to the couch. She folded her hands in her lap. Claudia's eyes followed her.

"First, as I said before. The scarab is mine! From now on you will never engage in another bidding war with this institution." The wrinkled, grey face was determined, the lips compressed. "Second, I think it is time the Betancourt made certain tax-deductible gifts from their private collection to this museum." Claudia's discomfort was something Gottfried could see and feed on. She continued.

"I also want to prevail upon your name and friends in the publishing world. My manuscript on the early kingdom is almost finished. I'm sure it will bring a very good price from a publisher especially with your wholehearted endorsement."

She paused, a smile crossed the stony grey mask. "You see, dear Claudia, some of us must worry about such mundane things as money. I'm afraid the museum is not in a position to pay me very well, and I must begin to plan for my later years."

The curator got up, took the totebag from the desk top and returned it to the bottom drawer. She did not sit down but remained standing, looking at Claudia. "Come, come, my dear, have you nothing to say?"

Slowly Claudia was regaining her composure. Gottfried at least remained ignorant of Sekhmet. But the cold, hard truths were not to be denied. Gottfried would find out sooner or later, and then what? She was breathing now in long, deep draughts. She approached the desk. The two women now stood facing each other. Claudia smiled at the curator. It was a smile that Gottfried had never seen.

"I see I must pay for my indiscretions. What you ask isn't unreasonable. I'm lucky to be released with such a light sentence."

"Perhaps there will be certain other penalties. Who knows?" Gottfried began to look pleased.

Claudia turned and retrieved her purse from the couch. She started for the door. A thought struck her as she was about to walk out, and she turned back to the curator, who had seated herself at the desk.

"A question, Miriam. My own curiosity is aroused. How did you return the pieces to the exhibit and remove the replicas with no questions or repercussions?"

The older woman closed her eyes for a moment. She saw a suitcase in the back of her bedroom closet.

"Ah, yes," she sighed. "There are certain privileges that come with this office. It enables me to do things that would be difficult for anyone else."

Claudia looked at the older woman. The answer was no answer at all. Except she was willing to bet the woman had never returned them. She turned and let herself out.

Gottfried watched the door close. She was immensely pleased with herself. Claudia's speech at the end was a show of bravado. She had her, and she did not intend to let go. She would hear from Claudia very soon about a gift for the museum. Claudia was a woman of principle. She would give the museum its due. She would want to pay the first installment of her fine.

* * *

Upon leaving the museum, Claudia went immediately to the red brick and granite building where Maurice had his office. He wasn't seeing patients which was perfect. But one of the nurses would still be there to let her in. Thank God for the interminable paperwork.

There was no slinking around corners or tiptoeing past closed doors, this time. The nurse who answered her ring went back to the folders on the reception desk while Claudia disappeared down the hall using some pretext which was immediately forgotten. It took only a few seconds to locate the box containing the poison and drop more ampules into her purse.

Claudia was moving with a drive and determination surprising even to herself. She had always been direct when there was something to be done. But now, as was the case with Charles Green, she felt a magical strength and coolness. She had to get rid of Miriam. The curator was just one more person trying to separate her from her statue. She could not allow that. It was written that she should have the goddess Sekhmet.

THURSDAY, MAY 26

Miriam Gottfried heard from Claudia much sooner than she expected. The day following their confrontation, Claudia asked for a meeting that evening. The curator agreed, telling Claudia to come to her home.

The evening had turned cool as Claudia walked towards Lexington Avenue. To insure anonymity, she pulled her shoulder-length auburn hair back from her face, pinning it in an unbecoming knot at the nape of her neck. She wore a neutral-colored suit and a neutral hat which shaded her features and hair coloring, and had scrubbed her face clean of makeup.

She found a cab and rode across town to 79th and Central Park West. She would walk the last couple of blocks to the curator's apartment building. She clutched her bag tightly under her arm and strolled slowly, almost casually.

When she reached the apartment building, which was north of 82nd Street, she paused for a moment. Then she walked quickly across the great expanse of lobby to the elevators, got in and pressed the 20th floor button. No one had seen her.

At Miriam's apartment, halfway down the long, dark hallway, Claudia took a deep breath and pushed the buzzer. The door opened. There was no polite exchange of greetings. Instead, she followed the grey-haired woman directly into the living room.

"Miriam, I'm not going to rehash what happened. How it happened, and why it ended the way it did really have no further place in our little...negotiations."

Claudia hoped that Miriam Gottfried would be disarmed by a straightforward approach. It would be unlike Claudia to crawl. The old lady might become suspicious if she did. "What you said yesterday is correct. The Betancourt name is important in the art world. Any hint of scandal, proven or not, is to be avoided."

The grey-haired woman sat on the couch, listening, waiting. She was not sure where Claudia was going.

"You know how much my collection means to me, and to Maurice. Donating any part of it to the museum is a severe punishment—but the alternatives are more severe."

Gottfried smiled. "A correct appraisal."

"We will take steps in that direction as soon as it can be arranged."

"I'm so pleased."

"We will also try not to interfere with any of your acquisitions in the future. We'll just have to keep closer track of what you are pursuing."

"Yes, you will," Gottfried agreed smugly.

"And finally, as soon as your manuscript is ready, please let me have it."
Claudia's beautiful speech was ended.

Gottfried got up from her chair and rubbed her hands together. "Good, good. I am pleased with you, my dear."

Claudia's head rang with hysterical laughter.

"Miriam, shall we have a cup of tea? We must seal our bargain somehow."

The grey-haired woman smiled, agreed and disappeared into the kitchen. Claudia heard the sounds of water running and the rattle of cups and saucers. In a few minutes, the curator returned with the cups on a tray. The tea had already been poured. There was no milk or sugar.

God! thought Claudia. She probably even uses tea bags.

Gottfried sat down in the chair facing Claudia, who remained on the couch.

"Miriam, might I trouble you for some cream for the tea? Milk will do, if that's all you have."

Again the curator rose and went into the kitchen. She returned with a small pitcher of milk. During her absence, the bottle that Claudia had carefully filled was now empty and returned to her purse.

"I am so pleased," Gottfried spoke, "that you are able to see the wisdom in my little compromise. It's a more pleasing word than 'punishment'."

Claudia could not leave it at that. "It was not easy to swallow, Miriam, not half as easy as swallowing your tea. It was something I had to do. It really changes nothing between us."

"Oh, but I beg to differ with you, Claudia, my dear. It changes things immensely. It clears the air, and leaves no doubt in anyone's mind who is the boss."

Claudia looked down. Both tea cups were empty.

"More tea?" Gottfried asked.

"No, thank you. I must be going now."

They walked together to the door, and as Claudia was about to leave, the Curator stuck out her hand, grasped Claudia's, and shook it.

"Good night, Claudia."

"Goodbye, Miriam."

Claudia walked down the hall, a clear image of the way Miriam lived indelibly etched. If Miriam had the remaining artifacts, she would have brought them out to gloat. Therefore, she didn't have them. They were returned.

When the door closed, Gottfried walked back to the living room. She rubbed her hands together again in a gesture of satisfaction. She spoke aloud.

"It is good, everything is good." She clapped her hands together. "One thing is needed to make a true celebration."

She headed for her bedroom. From the top shelf of the closet she pulled down a small suitcase. She laid it on the bed, opened it and took out the four golden objects. One by one she carried them back to the living room coffee table. She sat back on the couch and took a deep breath. There was a slight burning sensation in her chest.

The coffee table held an interesting display. First there was a burial collar, then a golden candle holder and a golden dagger. Next to the dagger were two empty teacups. Next to them was a small gold box. It looked, at that moment, like a coffin. The burning in her chest persisted.

* * *

The evening with Miriam had gone as she hoped. Except for the missing pieces. But she had the statue and Miriam would no longer be around to blackmail her. She walked calmly across the marbled lobby floor of Miriam's building and out onto the sidewalk. She breathed deeply, taking in the coolness of the night air.

At 83rd Street, she turned away from Central Park West, going over to Columbus Avenue before she hailed a passing cab. Once at home, she went right to bed, and fell asleep soundly and peacefully.

She had not noticed a car parked alongside the curator's apartment building. Inside was a large man in a tan raincoat. Earlier in the day, the curator had called and told him, rather mysteriously, that his services were no longer needed. The job for which he had been hired no longer existed, and the problem with the Betancourt —conflict of interest, he was told—had been solved. His check would be mailed to him.

Having spent months watching Claudia Betancourt, he had begun to know her. Miriam Gottfried was no match for the Betancourt woman, regardless of what the curator said. Besides, he had that gut feeling that he had stumbled onto something much bigger than the curator knew. At first, he had figured, it centered around Claudia. Now, especially after today's phone call, it involved the curator. He was determined not to be left out in the cold. These people dealt in a world of big money. Thus he had taken up watch outside Miriam Gottfried's building.

He had spotted Claudia Betancourt walking in and had felt his suspicions were confirmed. He thought about following her upstairs, then decided against it. Three could turn out to be a crowd.

Now, forty-five minutes later, Claudia had turned the corner into 83rd Street. He got out and went inside. He was determined to find out from the curator what was going on.

His first ring of the apartment buzzer went unanswered. As did his second. He was sure the curator was home. The odds of the Betancourt woman visiting someone else in the same building were too absurd. He pushed the buzzer a third time. There was noise on the other side of the door. Probably the old woman was checking him out through the little spy window. He waited. The knob turned, but the door was not pulled open. He pushed against the door, and it began to swing in. Miriam Gottfried was on the other side, holding onto it for support.

The detective stepped inside and took the grey-haired woman by both shoulders. He half-dragged, half carried her to the living room and sat her in a chair. She was gasping for breath. Her face was ashen white.

"What's the matter, Mrs. Gottfried? You sick?"

The curator nodded.

"Look, I think I should call a doctor or an ambulance."

Again she nodded, and grasped at the front of her blouse.

"Is it your heart?"

His question was met by a blank stare. He got to his feet.

"I'm going to call."

She waved her arm, trying to catch his attention. She was pointing at the coffee table. He looked down and, for the first time, noticed the golden objects.

"What in hell are they?" he said half aloud.

She was waving that clawlike white hand, beckoning for him to bend down, close to her. She was trying to talk.

He bent over and put his ear next to her mouth. He could feel her shallow breath.

"Hide. Take away. Don't leave."

He straightened up and looked at her. "You want me to take these things away?"

She nodded.

"Hide them?"

She nodded again.

"You don't want them left here?"

She was nodding vigorously.

"All right, but first we've got to get help."

In the kitchen he found the wall phone, dialed 911, and asked for an ambulance. He told them he thought it was a cardiac case, and, yes, he would wait there till they arrived. When he returned to the living room, the old lady had slumped over, her breathing very shallow and irregular.

"I don't think she's going to make it," he whispered to himself.

His attention turned to the things on the table. He could tell that they were a lot more than just coffee table decorations. He wondered why the old lady wanted him to take them away and hide them. The whole situation was intriguing. He went back into the kitchen and began pulling open drawers and cabinets. Finally, he found what he was looking for, a large brown paper shopping bag. It had a large red star on the side and the words 'thank you for shopping Macy's.'

Back in the living room he picked up the things and put them into the bag. He picked it up. The objects were hitting against each other. He returned to the kitchen found a small stack of newspapers. He took a few sheets back to the living room, took the pieces out, and wrapped them. Then he returned them to the bag.

The old woman was very quiet. Her eyes were closed. Only an occasional movement of her chest showed that she was still breathing.

When the door buzzer rang, he admitted two ambulance attendants with their rolling stretcher. In a matter of minutes, she was on the stretcher, on her way out the door.

"You want to ride in the ambulance with her?" One of the attendants looked back to the detective.

"No, thanks. I'm just a neighbor. I'm going to have to locate a relative. What hospital?"

"Roosevelt."

After the door had slammed shut, the detective walked around the living room.

"Books," he muttered to himself in disgust as he surveyed the wall of bookshelves.

"Where does she hide the booze?"

The liquor supply was in the bottom of a breakfront—an almost full pint of apple brandy, a fifth of Canadian Club with less than one drink remaining, and a still sealed bottle of something yellow with a Spanish name that had a rock sugar tree growing in it. He grimaced, took out the Canadian Club bottle, and gulped down the remnants.

"Good luck, old lady," he said.

He picked up the shopping bag and surveyed the room. The two empty tea cups reminded him that the curator had a visitor. "Betancourt comes in and leaves," he spoke aloud. "Then I come in and find Gottfried with a heart attack, and on the table are some very interesting *objets d'art*. Curious," he said. "Curious."

He looked at the cups and hesitated. Then he took them to the sink and washed them and left them to drain dry. One had to belong to Claudia Betancourt. Better that he know that than the police.

SUNDAY, MAY 29

On Sunday morning Peter was sitting at the kitchen table drinking coffee, browsing in the Sunday *New York Times*. In the Arts & Leisure section he noted that Memorial Day Weekend opened the summer programs. The Metropolitan Opera House was running a summer of dance, which he didn't particularly care about, but the new City Jazz Festival was something else. He ripped out the page listing the events.

Now for Sports. The Yankees were in first place, and why not? Someone he didn't know had the pole position for the Monte Carlo Grand Prix. It made him think of his own racing. He'd have to think about getting back into it next year.

Finally, it was time for the front page and the news. The president was up to more skullduggery and the mayor had another asinine statement. He skimmed through the ads for Tiffany's, Bergdorf's, Bloomingdale's, Macy's. He took another sip of the coffee, which was now almost cold, and quickly leafed through the remaining pages. On the next to the last page was the obituary section. He was about to close the newspaper when a headline caught his eye. *"Dr. Miriam Gottfried, Curator at the Metropolitan Museum of Art, dead at sixty."* He knocked over the coffee cup.

According to the *Times*, Dr. Gottfried had died in Roosevelt Hospital of an apparent heart attack. She had been stricken while at home. The story went on to outline her achievements at the museum, the new Egyptian wing, the Tutankhamun exhibit and the current Golden Age of Egypt exhibit.

The coincidence was gnawing at him. There it was again.

Charles...Charles had died of a heart attack. But he had never complained of heart problems. Sharon slipped in the bathtub, hit her head and drowned. Those things happen, too. And now Gottfried dies of a heart attack? He didn't believe in coincidence. He didn't know the curator. But he knew someone who did. That same someone also knew Charles and Sharon. He had suspicions about Charles' death and here it was again!

He saw that the coffee had dripped onto the rug. He cleaned it up, got himself another cup, dove into the Business/Finance section. After five minutes he found he hadn't read a word. But he simply couldn't shake the idea.

He got a pencil and pad. Across the top he wrote three names: Charles, Sharon, Gottfried. He wrote Claudia under each of them and stared at the page. He crumpled it up and started again. This time he wrote four names across the top: Charles, Sharon, Gottfried, Peter. Under each of them he added the name Claudia.

Under each name he wrote robbery. Of course, he told himself, Gottfried got the pieces he sent so she knew about the robbery. But how had she connected it to Claudia? Had she?

He leaned back against the sofa. He was getting nowhere.

He tried a different angle. Charles had the pieces and Claudia knew that he did. Gottfried eventually had the pieces and Claudia knew that she did.

Peter wrote treasure under the two names. He stared at it. He then wrote heart attack under Charles and Gottfried and under Sharon he added 'drowning'. He could see a pattern being formed. It had to be more than just coincidence.

For a while, Peter recalled he had also had the pieces. So he added treasure under his name.

Peter stopped for a moment, staring at his list. Then, under Charles' name, he wrote money. Now suppose, he thought, Gottfried knew Claudia had taken the pieces. What would she do about it? Turn her in? No. Something more subtle, probably blackmail of some sort.

He added money under Gottfried's name. The pieces began to fit, and yet there was no evidence of foul play with either Charles or Gottfried. They died of heart attacks without a doubt!

But what about Sharon? He looked at the chart. She hadn't had the treasure, and her death was unlike the other two. Maybe it had been accidental. Then again, perhaps she had been involved in a way Peter didn't know about. She was in New York working on her script of the robbery movie.

The robbery movie.

He wrote risk under Sharon's name. And added it under Charles and Gottfried's. It hadn't been money at all. It was the threat of exposure. Charles, Gottfried and poor, wonderful Sharon. Charles would have risked exposure for money. Sharon would have risked it for security. And Gottfried would have exposed her just for revenge. It was frightening. The pieces fit, without a doubt.

But how did one produce a heart attack in perfectly healthy people? A drowning—he shuddered—was simple—but a heart seizure? If Claudia had found a way to do it, then she was far more cunning and dangerous than he had ever imagined.

At the moment, the police were out of the question. Even if he could convince his friend on the police commissioner's staff that Claudia Betancourt had all the wrappings of a serial killer, it all came back to the museum theft and his complicity in it. He wasn't ready to do jail time. There had to be another way.

WEDNESDAY, JUNE 1

The problem swirled around in Peter's mind since Sunday. The only thing that came to mind was having a discussion with Maurice Betancourt. How involved was he with the incident at the museum? One way to find out.

After creating various scenarios, he decided that visiting the doctor at his office was his best option. All he had to do was call to find out the doctor's schedule. As it turned out, the psychiatrist kept a somewhat erratic schedule except for Tuesdays and Fridays when he was there until 6 p.m. With luck, he could call on Maurice Betancourt before he closed his office today.

* * *

The receptionist gave him a friendly but puzzled smile. "May I help you?"

"Is Dr. Betancourt in?"

"Yes. He's with a patient."

"Well, it's extremely important that I see him. I'll be glad to wait as long as necessary."

"He'll be out in about a half hour."

Peter nodded, and settled into a chair.

The room was comfortable, the floor covered with a blue oriental rug and the walls painted a matching shade. The oils that hung on the walls were of flowers and a landscape of Central Park. It reminded him of other doctors' offices, except a bit more plush. Nothing in the room hinted of the Betancourt' fascination with ancient Egyptian art.

He was thumbing through an art magazine when an inner door opened.

"Goodbye, Mrs. Carson. See you next week." The woman walking past Peter was a total blur. His entire attention was focused on the balding man who stood in the doorway, his expression not entirely friendly. Obviously, he didn't like unexpected callers.

Peter rose. "Doctor Betancourt, my name is Mandel, Peter Mandel."

There was a flicker of recognition in the psychiatrist's eyes.

"We were introduced several weeks ago at the museum reception."

Maurice nodded slightly.

"I'm an acquaintance of your wife's. I would like to talk to you about..."

Peter stopped in mid sentence and turned his head slightly in the direction of the receptionist. Maurice stood aside and spoke to the woman.

"Mrs. Stern, I believe I'm free for the next thirty minutes. Please hold my calls."

He turned and motioned for Peter to follow him.

The psychiatrist's office was dimly lit. A large antique desk stood in a corner with two leather chairs facing. At the other end of the room, in front of the bookcases, were a sofa and two large, comfortable looking chairs separated by a coffee table.

Once inside with the door closed, Peter felt more comfortable. When he saw Maurice head for the desk, he said, "Doctor, would you mind if we sat over there?" indicating the sofa. "I think we'd be much more comfortable." He disliked "over-the-desk" relationships, as he called them. Conversations beginning that way usually ended up as confrontations, and today's was too important for him to let that happen.

Maurice Betancourt turned around, looking surprised and agreed to the request. Once they were seated, the psychiatrist said, "What is it that needs my attention?" His voice was sharp.

"This is not going to be easy for me." Peter leaned forward, looking directly at the doctor. "It isn't easy because it involves myself, several other people, and...your wife."

Maurice's eyebrows raised, then lowered. His eyes narrowed slightly. He said nothing.

"I mentioned that we met at the museum reception in early April."

"Yes, I remember."

"What I'd like to tell you goes back some time before we met."

For the next ten minutes, Peter gave Maurice Betancourt a summary of the events leading up to the opening of the exhibit, naming names and ending with the statement that on the next day Claudia Betancourt had in her possession the statue of the goddess Sekhmet, while four other pieces, which she had taken, were in the possession of a Mr. Charles Green, in his home in Connecticut.

Peter looked for a reaction, but there was none. He decided to take some of the coolness out of the doctor.

"I must assume, Dr. Betancourt, that you are, and were, aware of the robbery...at least of the statue."

Peter waited.

"I'll refrain from interrupting until you're finished, Mr. Mandel."

"Not long after the robbery, the four of us met and Charles Green proposed ransoming the pieces back to the Egyptian government.

"Both Sharon Hiller and I wanted to wait, to do nothing. We were overruled by Charles Green. That left only your wife and Charles to arrange the sale, which was totally against your wife's better judgment. On Monday evening, April 18, Charles Green died of a heart attack. Prior to that night Charles was in perfect health."

He looked at Maurice, half-expecting a response. The doctor remained poised, attentive, yet noncommittal.

"I retrieved the four pieces from Charles Green's widow and returned them to the museum through Dr. Miriam Gottfried."

Peter leaned forward. "Last Monday evening, Sharon Hiller came back to New York. She visited Claudia at your home and told her about a television movie she was writing. The movie was based on the robbery. Claudia's switching the pieces and so on. The next night, Sharon Hiller died in her hotel in a bathtub accident."

Maurice's face visibly began to sag.

"Last Friday, Miriam Gottfried died of a heart attack. Now, I know you can say, so what? What does any of this have to do with Claudia? Well, I'll tell you my theory. I think Claudia was directly or indirectly involved in all three deaths. I can't buy coincidence. Why would she have done it? How about to protect herself? We don't know what kind of ransom plan Charles had in mind. Maybe with only Claudia and him left, he simply decided to blackmail her—or perhaps it was something much more complicated that she didn't want any part of.

"Let's go to Sharon Hiller. Claudia probably couldn't handle the idea of her robbery story flashed on the screen in front of millions of people.

"Then there's Gottfried. Could she have connected those objects with Claudia? Let's say she did. Would she turn your wife into the police? No! She would set up some form of blackmail. Last comes the real question. Two of these three people died of heart attacks, and their deaths weren't even questioned. Is it possible to induce a heart attack? It must be, with the proper poison. Could Claudia have gotten hold of some? Yes. You probably have it right here in your office."

Peter sat back. He had meant to take Maurice through the facts and suppositions one at a time, allowing each to be digested and discussed. Once started, he hadn't been able to stop and the story had spilled out. It was the opening of an emotional floodgate in Peter's mind. Now it was the doctor's turn.

Years of training and practice had taught Maurice Betancourt to listen and absorb without betraying emotion. It took every ounce of his conditioning to meet Peter Mandel's stare with cool composure.

"If you're so convinced of the story, Mr. Mandel, why have you come here and not the police?"

"That should be obvious to you. Dr. Betancourt. Even if I was not directly involved in the robbery, I couldn't escape the scandal. I did nothing more than supply a crate—the means by which the artifacts were removed from the museum—but I'm involved, and knowledge of that could ruin me. Then there are the families of the dead. Does it help them to know that their loved ones were murdered? And last of all, what about you? What would happen to all of this, should Claudia be found out?"

"What is it, then, that you want from me, Mr. Mandel?"

"I'm not sure. If Claudia is guilty, as I believe, then something definitely has to be done, but I don't know what. I need to know that she's not going to be out there looking for the next person who seems to threaten her safety. That next person could be me." He paused for a moment, "or you."

"Suppose that I don't believe your theory. Then what?"

Peter hadn't thought beyond this point. He really didn't know.

"You have the facts and theories now, just as I do. I can't ask you to tell me what you intend to do about it. Obviously, right now, that would be unfair. You'll want to think about it. Judging by your reaction, you don't doubt the truth of what I've told you. You may disagree with the conclusions, but the facts are there. You can conclude what you want. I'm sure that when you are ready, you'll do what's right. And one way or another I'll know about it."

"Thank you, Mr. Mandel."

Peter got up and walked to the door. He looked back at the psychiatrist sitting on the couch. Neither of the men had even considered shaking hands or prolonging the goodbyes. It had been the shifting of a great weight, from one set of shoulders to another.

FRIDAY, JUNE 3

The detective was whistling. Today was warm. It was sunny. He was going to see a man who was rich, famous, married to a beautiful woman and in a lot of trouble. Actually, the detective was going to tell this man the last fact, a fact, he was sure the man didn't know yet.

In the week since his unfortunate ex-client Dr. Gottfried's death, the detective had done his homework diligently and well. He had identified the objects in the shopping bag, and he had spent hours going over his notes on Claudia Betancourt's movements.

They presented a curious set of coincidences. It was time to find out how much the doctor liked his practice, his lifestyle, and his wife. Not necessarily in that order. It was time for a one on one. He called Dr. Betancourt's office and got the last appointment of the day. Inside the plush Park Avenue offices, he had only a short wait to see the doctor himself.

Maurice looked up from a file on his office desk as the door to his office opened. The size of the man in the tan raincoat was a surprise.

"Don't get up, doctor." The detective waved Maurice back into his seat and eased his large frame into a dark maroon leather chair facing Maurice's desk. He looked around the office.

"You are ..." Maurice reached for a card with the patient's name.

"I'm Fred. Fred Burkhart."

"What is it I can do for you, Fred?" Maurice was wary.

"Dr. Betancourt, how much do you love your wife?"

The detective had chosen the question carefully, and rehearsed the tone and the look in front of his shaving mirror. The question was intriguing, unanswerable, not open for further probes. He was proud of his choice. Before Maurice could formulate any sort of response, he went on as he had planned.

"You don't have to answer that. We both know that you love her very much, and certainly want to protect her."

The detective had expected an outburst here, some show of outrage, but the doctor sat quietly, staring. The detective knew he had to be careful. This was a cool one.

"I've been following your wife, Mrs. Betancourt, for a long time. It doesn't matter why. I know how interested she is—you both are—in Egyptian things. You collect them."

He thought he caught a flicker of response in Maurice Betancourt's watchful eyes.

"Go on."

"All right. In my travels I've picked up a pile of loose ends. If I dig long enough I'm going to put them all together. In the meantime. I've got a funny-looking picture with your wife right in the middle."

"I don't know what you mean."

"Well, Doc, I'm going to level with you. I'm going to spell out all these unconnected little pictures I have, and then maybe you and I together can work them out."

Again Maurice was silent.

"First, I see your wife in L.A. She's disguised like a floozy and she's buying a reproduction of something from the Golden Age exhibit. From there she goes on to Chicago and buys something else."

"My wife travels a lot in our collecting." Maurice decided that excuses were not needed. He gave it up.

"Yes, she does. But not for reproductions. Anyway, here the story gets jumpy. Your wife has some friends that she sees regularly, in a joint called Sirocco. OK? In the past few weeks one of the friends, a young guy, dies of a heart attack—right after he and your wife meet for a few pops at another dive. Incidentally, the good lady is wearing her floozy costume again. Maybe just a little hanky panky, but I doubt it."

"I'm sure she would appreciate your confidence." Maurice's sarcasm went unnoticed.

"Not too long after this guy kicks off, another one of your wife's friends buys it accidentally in a bathtub. Real tragic stuff, young mother, and everything."

He paused to make sure his vignettes were having their proper effect.

"Next, your wife's good friend. Dr. Gottfried, the museum curator, dies of a heart attack, again right after a visit from the Mrs. And now for what's really intriguing—in the curator's apartment are a couple of pieces from the exhibit. They're the same pieces your wife bought on her trip west, only the ones that old lady Gottfried has are the real thing, and not reproductions."

The detective stopped talking.

Maurice watched him for several moments. "Are you through?"

"Mostly."

"What am I supposed to make of all this? Several of my wife's friends have passed away, and you have positive proof that she purchased several museum reproductions. My dear Mr. Fred...so what?"

The detective was ready—this was the long shot he had to play.

"Here's the 'so what', doc. I have become the sole possessor of the objects from the collection. The ones that the good Dr. Gottfried had the night your wife was there. The night she passed away.

"I have a very strong feeling that they are very valuable. The Egyptians would pay a lot to get them back, and I bet the museum would, too. They'd want to know who had them. I guess I'd have to include your wife in my story, since she was there with the old lady and the pieces. The museum would be very interested in knowing. Oh, I forgot. I'm sure the police would be very interested, too. I bet they'd love to talk to your wife about why people tend to get heart attacks after they see her."

"Blackmail, is that what we have here? A simple case of blackmail?"

"Yep. Only not so simple. Come on, doc, this is a beaut. It's got stolen art, rich people, hints of foul play—it's got everything."

"Including blackmail."

"We've all got to live as best we can."

Maurice formed a tent of his fingertips and drummed them together.

The detective began to look impatient.

Maurice broke the silence. "May I ask exactly what it is you want?" Before the man could answer, Maurice continued. "Please bear in mind that the price you are asking is merely to keep you from starting unsubstantiated rumors. It's like saying a girl is pregnant. It takes only a little while to prove you right or wrong. However, in the meantime, she is suspect."

"Rumor or not, doc, what I've got can leave a big stink around the Mrs. I can clean this whole mess up for a hundred thou."

"One hundred thousand dollars?"

"That's the number."

"And what does that buy?"

"My silence and my gratitude."

"What about the museum pieces you claim to have?"

"Oh, I've got them all right, but that's another deal entirely. They're worth more than you can raise."

"I have no safeguards in this whatsoever. What's to stop you from making me a habit?"

"You've got to trust me, doc."

Maurice smiled. The detective smiled back.

"Well, doc, what do you say?"

"I'm not prepared to say anything right now. This package of innuendos is, I'm afraid, hard to swallow in one sitting. I want to think about it, and I want to explore my options. And finally, Mr. Fred, I want to think about those museum pieces you say you have. They intrigue me as a collector."

"Are you stalling me?"

"Yes, but only for a few days. I would hate to buy a car one fender at a time."

"When do we talk again?"

"Why don't you come here on Sunday at noon? There's no office hours and we can be alone."

The detective heaved himself out of the chair. He stood in front of Maurice's desk and waited. When Maurice remained seated, the detective jammed his hand into the raincoat pocket and lumbered out of the room.

"Sunday," he called over his shoulder just as the door closed.

* * *

Long after the detective had gone and the nurse, too, had said goodnight, Maurice sat quietly at his desk. It was a time to sort options and plan.

At age fifty, Maurice Betancourt had spent more than half his life as a student of the human mind. Mental aberrations should be as easily recognizable to him as a rash to a dermatologist. Yet the information he had received from "Fred" and Mandel left him doubting his own abilities. There was something terribly wrong with his wife and he had not seen it. Had the signs been there? Had he missed them because he wasn't looking? What did he know about his wife?

Their ten-year marriage was a puzzle to him. On the surface, theirs was an idyllic relationship, yet it was all surface. There was no depth. They appeared together in public, worked together in private, shared a house and bed, and did so with a total absence of passion.

His meaningless affairs, were they a punishment for Claudia rather than a satisfaction of his own needs? Was his resentment of her wealth so deep that it made him hit back?

He thought of the goddess Sekhmet. Was the statue Claudia's unborn child, or long-dead mother? Were Claudia's actions those of a protective mother? Yet where had she lost perspective? Obviously, she had crossed over into a world where the slightest threat to her possession—her statue, her child—had to be met with strong, final defenses.

It was not a surprise to him. He must have known, subconsciously, that if he tried to take the statue away, or tried to make her do so, his own life would be in jeopardy. He realized now it was why he had ignored the problem. When faced with a problem case, the doctor almost always began his analysis with a pragmatic review of the facts. The "what" was usually more easily available than the "why."

In this case, the "what" was terribly clear to him. Claudia Betancourt was a thief and a murderess. He marveled at the ease with which his mind accepted those facts. Something had to be done about Claudia.

Other people were aware of her crimes. If only he knew, would he act? The question was unanswerable, yet disturbing. He shrugged it off. Peter Mandel knew. And Fred was closing in.

Fred. He represented the most pressing problem.

Peter Mandel wanted only that steps be taken to neutralize Claudia. He did not demand an eye for an eye, only a quarantine. The detective, on the other hand, demanded money. The detective could be placated now, but only for the time being. The pig's lifestyle would require periodic infusions of cash.

Maurice considered his options. He could simply do nothing. That would bring down the wrath of all parties. He could pay the detective. This option had no end, good or bad. He could bring Claudia to justice. Maurice's mind rebelled. "Bring to justice"—in Claudia's case, what did that mean? He could see this proud, beautiful woman, his wife, stand trial, to be judged by whom—some filth from the ghetto? Never! What would they do to her? Find her criminally insane and send her to a state institution? Never!

Maurice's thoughts turned to himself. Public exposure of his wife would obviously taint him, too. There would always be suspicion of collusion. He did not want to spend the rest of his life as a curiosity piece, the object of the scandalmongers. The hierarchy of international psychiatry was fine-tuned to the conservative lives of its inhabitants.

He needed a solution that was quiet and, if at all possible, final. It was late when Maurice finally admitted to himself what he must, at least, try to do. There were only two things to be done.

He must take whatever steps were necessary to keep Claudia from continuing in her current homicidal behavior. What he did with her must also placate Peter Mandel. That man would have to be satisfied that amends had been made, and that nothing like it would happen in the future.

He must also do whatever was necessary to eliminate the persistent threat of the detective. Too many important lives were threatened by that inconsequential pig. He had until Saturday to decide how best to do these things. Perhaps all ends could be met through a single act.

SUNDAY, JUNE 5

"Instead of paying you a paltry one hundred thousand dollars now, and take the chance that you will be back in six months after a disastrous sojourn in Las Vegas, I've decided to establish a short-term partnership with you."

"I don't understand, doc." The detective was in the leather chair again.

"You said you had certain items from the collection —the original items, not duplicates. These are the items you claim my wife took from the museum."

"That's right. I've got them."

"I have something else that was part of the collection, by far the most valuable item."

"Oh? Your old lady really did a job!"

"I don't want the piece. With it gone, and your pieces disposed of, there's no more evidence connecting my wife to the robbery. I suggest that we pool our resources. I will arrange a private sale, out of the country, Hopefully, to one buyer."

"Hell, doc, in my business, I know about dealing in stolen art. I already intend to sell the pieces I have."

"Yes, but I'm offering you a chance for a bigger payoff and a chance to stay out of the picture entirely."

The detective wasn't buying it, but he was intrigued. "Just how is this going to work?"

"I just told you. We take your objects and mine, combine them into one big package, and sell it."

"To who?"

"I have several people in mind—does that matter?"

"How much?"

"Together, at least five million."

The detective let out a long, slow whistle.

"You get it all, Fred. One hundred per cent."

The detective stared at Maurice in disbelief. "Why, doc? What do you get?"

"Freedom for my wife and myself. You see, with the pieces gone, you no longer have any evidence that can connect my wife with the robbery. We don't need the money, and with five million dollars, you will never need to come to us again with threats of exposure."

"Five million should keep me away forever, doc."

"If you come back again, it will be without any concrete evidence, and you will be more of a nuisance than a threat. But, if you should return, I'm afraid I will be forced to kill you."

Maurice smiled.

"You know, doc, I think you mean it."

"Don't test me, Fred."

After several minutes of silence the detective asked, "How's it gonna work?"

"I want you to pick up the item that I have and keep it safe until I consummate the sale."

The detective looked puzzled. "You trust me with it?"

"Yes. You have a lot to lose if you run. You can't get as much as I can for the pieces. You don't know the right people and—I'm sorry to say it, but people just wouldn't trust you as much as they would trust me."

The appraisal was accurate, yet the detective pursed his lips. He seemed to be pouting as if Maurice had hurt his feelings. Finally, he asked, "What's this about me picking it up? Why can't you deliver it?"

"My wife would never voluntarily let it go." This much was true, Maurice thought, as he continued. "The only possible way to get it to you is to have it stolen."

"By who?"

"You, of course. We will stage a little break-in, and the thief will get a very precious statue and one or two other items to make it look good."

"What about your wife and the police?"

"She can't very well call the police about the statue, but I will call them about the other items. Our insurance will cover some of it."

"So you want me to rob the place?"

"Can you handle it?"

"With the cooperation of the owner, it's a cinch."

"I will get you a set of keys. You'll have to do something to the locks on the way out in order to make it look like a forced entry."

For the next hour they went over, in detail, the steps to be taken to make it look as though the Betancourt had been burglarized.

Maurice drew a diagram of the house and the library, including instructions on how to open the secret display case. He promised that his wife would be asleep upstairs and would not hear a thing.

They decided on Thursday night as the best time for the robbery. As the detective rose to leave, he was surprised and pleased at the offer of Maurice's hand to seal the bargain.

The detective left happily. Everyone was getting a good deal. The doc's wife would lose her statue, but she'd get away scot free with the whole robbery, and no questions ever about the Green guy or old lady Gottfried. The doc would get his wife back and they would live happily ever.

And he himself would get five million dollars. Just for opening a door, picking up a statue, and going home. It was the kind of deal that came once in a lifetime. Suddenly his euphoria fled. Careful, he said to himself. Careful. It was too good to be true. He had to walk slow and keep his eyes open. Nevertheless, he began to whistle as he left the building, turning to his right down Park Avenue.

THURSDAY, JUNE 9

From somewhere under Lexington Avenue, a subway rumbled to a stop. The doors opened and closed, and it moved on.

The time was 2:30 a.m. By this hour on a Thursday morning, most bars and restaurants were closed. There were few cars and fewer people to be seen, especially on the upper east side of Manhattan.

The night was cool, a faint damp mist in the air. It was the kind of night that reminded New Yorkers they were indeed in a sea-coast city.

The man wearing a tan raincoat mounted the steps to the street. For a moment, he paused, breathing heavily from the exertion of the climb. He then ducked into a drugstore doorway, out of the mist, in order to pull up the collar of his coat and lower the brim of his hat. He was carrying a large metal suitcase.

He walked north on Lexington Avenue. The street surface shone as though sprayed with black enamel, reflecting the blurred image of the street lights and occasional neon signs.

He turned and started along 74th Street past Madison Avenue towards Fifth. He checked the address then climbed the black wrought-iron staircase. From his raincoat pocket, he extracted a ring with several keys on it. The top lock was the large security type. When it opened, the click seemed to reverberate against the side of the building. The second lock was smaller and quieter. As the door swung open, the detective picked up the suitcase and stepped into the entrance foyer.

He set the case on the marble floor and stood leaning against the wall, listening, allowing his heart to slow down. His eyes were becoming accustomed to the darkness. All was quiet. After a minute he pulled a flashlight from his raincoat and turned it on, using his hand to shield the full glow of the light. The polished black-and-white floor stretched from the foyer, past the staircase, and into the dark recesses of the house.

He began to move along the hall, pausing briefly at the staircase to listen for movement from the upper floors of the house. He could hear nothing.

About three-quarters of the way down the hall, past the staircase, he stopped. Here were the double doors to the library—at least on the diagram Maurice Betancourt had drawn. He tried the right-hand door. It was locked. He had forgotten. The key was on the ring with the others. He found it and the door opened.

He walked in silently, closing the door behind him.

He turned on the flashlight once more, illuminating a section of deep red carpet, and stepped hesitantly towards the center of the room.

The oval of light moved along the floor, danced around a chair, and began to climb the front of a display case. The glitter of several golden objects held it for a moment, and then the light moved on.

After sweeping the room once, the light came to rest on the desk. He stepped over to it, put down the flashlight and turned on the desk lamp. In the dim light from its green shade, he could take in the full room with its display cases and bookshelves.

"There's more books here than a regular library," he whispered to himself.

From a suit pocket under the raincoat he took a folded sheet of paper which he spread open on the desk top. He oriented himself to Maurice's sketch, figuring which of the bookshelves held the catch for the hidden cabinet.

Just as he was about to move towards the bookcases, there was a muffled noise. It came from the hall, just outside the library doors. He snapped off the lamp and stood frozen, one hand resting on the desk's leather surface.

The noise came again. It sounded like a soft fabric rubbing against the bottom of the door. The intruder could feel the cold sweat forming in his armpits and on the small of his back. His hand moved across the desk and touched the cold metal of a letter opener. His fingers curled, as if in reflex action, and lifted it from the desk top.

There was a slight bump against the door. The detective felt a hammer like blow in his chest. Suddenly the rushing of the blood through his body sounded like a hundred waterfalls. Then there was a small "meow" from outside the door. The waterfall stopped; his eyes closed; his body sagged; his hand uncurled and released the letter opener.

A fucking no-good, cat!

The detective turned the light on again and moved toward the wall of bookcases. He began to search the shelves, looking for the catch. At the far left-hand end, his hand stopped. There was a space of about six inches between the last book and the end of the cabinet. His fingers probed further, diving into the empty space. He felt blindly along the wood until one finger slipped into a narrow opening cut into the side of the bookcase. The finger curved under a lever and pulled. There was a sharp click. A portion of the bookcase swung outward until it stood perpendicular to the wall. As it came to a stop, two small fluorescent lights blinked on.

The detective stood absolutely still. He was transfixed, his eyes wide, his mouth partly open—his attention riveted on the burnished golden figure.

Suddenly, he remembered where he was. He reached out and lifted the figure from its base. For a second he stood holding it, then he moved to the desk and sat it down.

On the desk was his list of the three other items Maurice had told the detective to take. The first two were in free-standing cases near the desk, the third in a wall cabinet on the far side of the room. He put the last of his booty down next to the large statue.

He felt pleased. Everything was in order. The secret cabinet door was open so that the doc could convince his old lady that her statue was ripped off, and so were the other display case doors. He was a sloppy, but very selective thief, a connoisseur.

He chuckled under his breath and turned to gather up the rewards of his night's work. He was so intent, he failed to hear the library door open. As he turned to leave, Maurice was standing just inside the library doors. He still wore his suit pants under a short silk smoking jacket. One hand was thrust into the pocket of the robe, the other held a cigarette.

"What in hell are you doing here, doc?" the detective breathed heavily.

"Just a slight change in plans, Fred."

Even in the dim light, the detective could see the beads of perspiration on the doctor's upper lip as he moved slowly into the room. The detective put the statue back on the desk and slumped into one of the black leather chairs.

"What the hell are you talking about?"

"I'm talking about a change of heart on my part," Maurice said. He was now standing next to the desk, facing the chair with its large raincoated occupant.

"I don't understand, doc. Maybe you can spell it out."

"Quite simply, Fred, I've decided to dissolve our partnership."

"I don't think I'm agreeable to that, doc."

The large man moved in the chair. Maurice tensed and pulled his hand out of his pocket. In his hand was a pistol. The detective opened his mouth slightly. "What do you think you're going to do with that?"

"I told you. I'm going to dissolve our partnership."

"But why? I'm playing it your way. I've got nothing to gain by crossing you. Hell, you're my ticket to easy street."

There was loathing in Maurice's voice when he answered. "The fact that you exist is an annoyance to me. What you know, or think you know, is dangerous. I don't think I will ever be rid of you. There isn't enough money in the world to satisfy you. But your tragic death, here in my home can serve several useful purposes."

"Are you really crazy enough to use that thing?"

"Yes," Maurice whispered.

The two men were quiet, each staring at the gun. They both heard the soft, rustling sound at the same time. The detective recognized it immediately. Maurice was momentarily startled. His eyes moved from the gun and the detective, to the door behind him.

The detective moved with speed that belied his bulk. He stood and lunged forward, chopping down on the doctor's arm. The gun flew up, landing softly on the carpet near the door. Maurice stared at it, but did not move. The detective sat back in the chair now and, with a slower, more deliberate motion, drew a gun from his raincoat.

"Don't you know your own pussycat when you hear it, doc?" The detective laughed. "I think, doc," he continued, "it's time for a little renegotiating. What do you think?"

* * *

Upstairs in the master bedroom, Claudia Betancourt opened her eyes and looked at the green glow of the digital clock radio. The numbers were a smear, she could not make them out. She lay in bed moving, listening, straining for a sound—any sound—that could have awakened her. But the house was silent. She tried to remember whether she had been dreaming. Maurice had given her two pills to take. She remembered taking only one. She looked at the clock again—it was no use, her eyes would not focus. It was an effort to reach for the reading lamp and locate the switch. Her arms were heavy and her fingers clumsy. The light came on just as her cat appeared around the slightly open bedroom door. Karma ran across the floor, leaped onto the bed, and stared at Claudia, meowing softly. She raised her hand to stroke his head, but she missed. Her hand fell heavily on the bed.

The cat leaped from the bed and went to the doorway. There he sat, waiting for her to follow.

Claudia slid her legs out from under the covers. She stood with one hand resting on the bed for support. Her head was spinning, but after several moments it stopped.

At the door she leaned on the doorframe. Every step down the hall was an effort. At the head of the stairs she grasped the rail with both hands and began to move down sideways, one step at a time. Her progress was slow and uneven. At the bottom of the stairs she stopped to listen. There was the muffled sound of voices coming from the library.

She stood still, allowing her head to clear. Then she moved down the hall to the library doors. There were men's voices inside.

"You look lousy, doc. You look like you're going to fall down. Why don't you sit in that chair?"

Once Maurice sat down, the detective got to his feet and leaned against the table. He took the sleeve of his coat and wiped the perspiration from his forehead.

"Know what, doc? I've just put us back in partnership. I think the best thing to do is go right ahead. Don't you agree?"

Maurice did not answer.

"Well, I don't really give a shit whether you agree. What I'm going to do is gather up all these goodies and walk out of here. And I don't think you're going to do a thing. If you blow the whistle on me, I'm going to blow it right back. And this time, I take you and your old lady with me. The same crap I had on her before still goes. Only now, I got you, too. You set me up to do this. You gave me the keys." He patted his pocket. "You gave me a diagram. And I got it all."

Maurice stared at his tormentor.

"On second thought, doc. I'm just going to take the little golden lady here. That's all I need to make my collection complete. Hell, I can sell her and my other goodies for a pretty good price. I don't need you. And you know what? I won't ever bother you again. You're lucky, doc, you got just what you wanted. No more statue. No more blackmail."

The detective was intent on Maurice as he stooped to pick up the statue on the desk. He was so intent at keeping the gun on Maurice that he failed to see the door open slightly, just wide enough to allow Claudia into the dimly lighted room. Her bare foot struck a cold, hard metal object. She looked down, saw the gun, and bent to pick it up.

The detective stood with the statue under his arm and his gun pointed at Maurice. "I'm all set, doc. Time to go," he said as he turned toward the library door.

"Put my statue down." The words were soft, almost slurred.

Both men jumped.

Claudia stood with the gun held tightly in both outstretched hands, pointing at the detective. "Put my statue back," she repeated.

"Well, well. If it isn't the museum ripper."

"Claudia, this thief broke in and is stealing your statue."

The detective looked at Maurice, and then back at Claudia. "Lady, I'm just taking something that isn't yours anyway."

"Put my statue down," Claudia insisted.

"He told me he only wants the statue," Maurice said.

"What are you doing, doc?"

"He says he's going to sell her."

"Put her down," Claudia said venomously. "She is not for sale."

"This is crazy. You're both nuts. You've been locked up in this room too long. I'm getting out of here."

The detective started towards the door—towards Claudia.

"He's going with your statue, Claudia."

She straightened her arms and bit down on her lower lip. Her eyes closed as she pulled the trigger. There was a sharp crack. The pistol jumped up and to the right, the bullet hitting the detective above the center of his chest. The impact sent the man staggering backward into the black leather chair. Both the chair and man went over backward, tumbling to the floor, coming to rest next to the desk.

Claudia stood frozen, the gun still pointing to the spot where the man had stood. She unclenched her lips, opened her eyes and forced herself to look down. The detective's legs were bent at an awkward angle, the toes of his shoes pointed in. One arm was out from his side, the other was still clutching the statue. bent under his body. The statue lay next to the body where a dark puddle was beginning to spread outward on the carpet.

Near the statue, the white cat sat quietly, licking his paw, his tail flicking back and forth, brushing the hem of the tan raincoat. The cat's tail was the only movement in the room. There was no sound. The smell of gunpowder filled the air.

"Maurice," Claudia said softly, "Maurice, is he dead?"

The doctor knelt down and reached out to touch the mound on the floor. Grasping the shoulder, he tried to roll the body over but succeeded only in moving it part way, scaring the cat. He stood and pulled on one arm. The body rolled up onto one shoulder, balanced for a second, and fell over onto its back. Claudia dropped the gun to the floor, and covered her mouth with her hands.

The pale light bathed the face of the fallen man, allowing Claudia to see his features for the first time. Her mind screamed. The last shreds of drug-induced sleep vanished in that instant. She saw again that fat face, sitting atop its tan raincoat, there in Los Angeles and once again, for a moment, in Chicago. The same heavy jowls and puffy eyes that were now staring sightlessly at the ceiling. What was he doing here, in her library, with Maurice? Her mind raced. Maurice knew him. Maurice sent him to spy on me. No, it was Gottfried. Gottfried and Maurice. They both spied on me. But now they can't, because Gottfried is dead, and I've shot their spy.

Claudia wanted to laugh with relief. Instead, she threw herself into a chair and watched her husband hunt for a life sign in the body on the floor.

Maurice slowly moved his hand across the chin and nose to the eyes and pressed the lids together. He turned to look at his wife.

"He's dead."

"I killed him. Isn't that funny, Maurice? I killed him. Who is he?" Claudia felt very clever.

"A thief. He broke in and I caught him here. He got my gun away from me, and was about to leave."

"Did you ever see him before?"

The question was asked almost coyly. For a moment Maurice was flustered.

"No. Where could I have seen him before?"

Liar, she thought. "What shall we do with him?"

"Do with him? There's nothing we can do, except call the police."

"No!" Claudia was on her feet. The white cat leaped at the sound. "No police. Not in my house." She stood directly in front of Maurice, her hands on her hips, her face thrust into his.

Maurice reached out to stroke her cheek. She reached up and hit his hand, slapping it away from her, face.

"Don't touch me!" she snarled. "I told you no police. They'll ask questions and find her." Claudia pointed to the statue.

Maurice knelt and lifted the statue from its dark pool next to the body and, in what would later seem to him the most cold blooded act of all, wiped the base of the statue on the raincoat. Then he carried her to the cabinet and set her back into the velvet lining. Claudia's eyes following his every movement. He reached out and pushed the panel closed, the sound of the lock snapping filled the room.

"There, now," he said gently, "no one need know."

Claudia remained standing. Her breathing was deep, and more even than it had been. She became aware of Maurice's voice.

"I suppose the police would be most unhappy if we touched any of the other things on the desk. We should leave everything alone."

Claudia surveyed the room now, looking from the pieces on the desk to the open display cases around the room.

"You do agree that we must call the police?" he asked again.

Claudia looked down, and then back at her husband. "No, I don't agree," she answered.

She stepped around the body and sat down in one of the black leather chairs. The cat jumped into her lap and Claudia began to scratch his head. "But I suppose we have to. I wish we could keep them away. I don't trust them."

"Claudia, when the police come it's not going to be pleasant. There's going to be endless questioning. Are you up to it?"

She looked up at her husband. Why was he suddenly so interested in her well-being? She guessed he was worried about what she would say. But she was too smart for him. And for them, too.

"I'm up to it," she said. "I'm much stronger than you think."

"The best thing for you to do is go up and lie down," Maurice tried to sound sincere. He had to get her out of the room. He had something to do before the police came. "When the police come, I'll tell them I had to sedate you and perhaps they'll be briefer and gentler. As long as the statue is safe, you needn't worry."

She rose, started forward, then stopped. "How did the thief know that I had the statue?"

"I don't know. He said he wanted it to go with some other pieces that had been stolen from the museum."

Her thoughts were jumbled as she stared at Maurice. That meant Miriam never returned the pieces to the museum. She did want them for herself. But how did this man get them? And where were they now? She would deal with this later. "Karma and I will go up now."

Maurice stared at the closed door after she had gone. His mind ran over their conversation. Not more than ten minutes ago she had killed a man, and there was no hysteria, or remorse, no self-recrimination. There was no emotion of any kind. None, that is, until the statue was mentioned. Then she became paranoid, almost hysterical. My God, Maurice thought, could Peter Mandel be right?

He knelt down next to the body and reached into the raincoat pocket. He found the key ring and set it on the floor. Next he searched until he found the paper with the diagram he had drawn. Satisfied, he put the key ring into a desk drawer, and the paper into his pocket.

From the desk drawer he took a screwdriver and walked out of the library to the front foyer. He saw the metal suitcase the detective had left and decided to leave it where it was. It looked like a natural thing for a thief to do.

The next part was the most dangerous. He opened the front door and stepped out into the dark night. There was no one in sight. He pushed the screwdriver into the crack between the door molding and the doorframe and twisted the blade until he heard wood splinter. He moved the blade down to a spot opposite the lower lock and repeated the action. He wanted to give the police some evidence that his front door locks had been tampered with. Let them figure out what the thief had finally done.

Satisfied that the doorframe looked slightly mangled, he went back to the library and repeated his tampering with the library door. He put the screwdriver into the dead man's pocket and picked up the phone. It was time to call the police.

SATURDAY, JUNE 18

On the second floor of the 26th Police Precinct house, the detectives' day room was seldom quiet. The phone rang day and night, weekend or holiday. People came and went, stopping only to drink a cup of coffee, type a report, answer the phone, or take a statement.

On this particular Saturday afternoon, there were only two occupants. A well dressed police officer was sitting near a dirty window, jabbing a keyboard with four large fingers. Next to him, a thin nervous man fidgeted in the straight-backed chair that faced the desk.

"It s all a technicality, Mr. Burkhart." The detective's exasperated tone was obviously meant for the visitor, but his attention remained focused on the computer. "Your brother was shot while in the act of committing a felony...an armed robbery."

"Yes, yes. I know all that," the skinny man said. Nervousness had left dark stains in the armpits of his short-sleeved, plaid shirt. "I just want to know when I can pack up his belongings and take them back to Denver. I can't be away forever."

"Look, Mr. Burkhart," the detective turned to face his visitor. "The district attorney called a fact-finding committee—like a coroner's inquest, only less formal. They found that your brother was shot while in the middle of committing an armed robbery in this couple's home. It's referred to as 'home invasion'. Even if he had no intention of shooting anyone, the fact that they felt threatened in their own home was justification for protecting themselves. Do you understand?"

"Yeah. Can't imagine Fred doing that, but, guess he did. So after this I can go to his place, pack up whatever is worth packing, and take it with me?"

"Yes. And you also take his personal effects. The items he had on him. Now that the hearing is over, you can pick them up. All you need is a release. Get it Monday at the D.A.'s office. I'll give you the address."

FRIDAY, JUNE 24

Harry Burkhart leaned back in his kitchen chair and pulled the tab on a Coors. The Burkharts, Harry and Francine, were finished with dinner in their two-story, semidetached frame house on the outskirts of Denver. The remains of the meal, resting on the table between them, were rapidly solidifying in the grease. It was not a neat house, nor was it clean. And its inhabitants were not, by any measurement, pretty people. Harry's hair had thinned when he was in his late teens. Now, almost twenty years later, a reddish-grey fringe circled his bony skull, passing over two protruding ears. Harry looked emaciated, except for a potbelly in which six to ten Coors per day found refuge. Harry Burkhart was ugly. Yet Harry Burkhart had found a wife. Francine. A small, nervous sparrow of a woman.

"You never did tell me much about New York," she said.

"Dirty place," he snorted from behind the beer can.

"You stay in Fred's place?"

"Hell, no. I took the bridal suite at the Waldorf."

"Just asking, Harry."

"Course I stayed at Fred's."

"What kinda place was it?"

"Just a place. Wasn't much. Bedroom, living room kitchen. Real plain, like Fred."

"What's all that stuff you brought back?"

"Everything of Fred's."

"Anything nice?"

"I don't think so. The clothes is all too big. Fit my car better than me. The furniture was ratty, and there was a few other things, suitcases and such, in the closet. One bag was filled with the filthiest magazines you ever seen. There was some junk in another bag. Looked like stuff you win down at Vet's Hall on Bazaar night. A big letter opener, and a pencil box covered in some cheap gold or brass covering, and some other junk. I just threw it all into the cartons that's out in the garage."

"Doesn't sound like much. Too bad Fred couldn't have left us more." Francine Burkhart got up from the table and smoothed the front of her apron, which needed washing. She turned on the gas jet under a saucepan filled with water, and went about putting instant coffee into two mugs. One mug had a red, white and blue stripe on it and the numbers 1776-1976. The other mug had the brown letters DAD on it. It was Harry's special mug.

The thin woman stood next to the stove, waiting for the water to boil. "Well, maybe later, if I get the ambition I'll go through it and see if anything is usable."

"Sellable, you mean."

"Whatever."

TUESDAY, JULY 12

"Maurice, don't thank me for my professional courtesy. We've known each other too long for that."

The speaker put his pipe back in his mouth. He was a man in his fifties, short, with broad shoulders that supported a large head. He had short, curly grey hair and a neatly trimmed grey beard. On the lapel of his white lab coat, a black plastic name tag read "Dr. Beringer."

The two men were seated in a white-walled office. Through the partly closed blinds, behind the desk, Maurice could see the tops of pine trees, and beyond them the hazy outline of mountains.

Dr. Beringer got up from behind his desk and came over to Maurice's chair. He placed his hand on his shoulder. "I've known you for what...twenty years? And Claudia for ten. I'm like family, *mein freund*. I want to help. Now that Claudia has been with us for a week, I know I can."

"Thank you, Albert."

Maurice was silent for a moment. Then he turned to his friend. "I want to beat my breast shouting mea culpa, mea culpa. I am guilty of blindness." There was a slow sadness in his voice. It was a tone he had rehearsed often.

"She was a troubled woman for many years, Maurice. She made adjustments in her life to fit the needs. The problem is that as the years passed, the adjustments, the little fantasies she had created, became real. Her art became her family."

Maurice spread his hands. "Albert, I should have seen."

The bearded man patted Maurice's shoulder. "It was impossible for you to see. You lived with it every day, and the changes were gradual. It's not like a case history where the evidence of years is on one sheet of paper, easy to see."

Maurice smiled at the doctor. "You are offering excuses for me. Is this my therapy?"

"Do you need it?"

"Now I can look at you and say 'no', but tomorrow, when I return home, back to America, to my empty house, the answer will be 'yes'. I will begin to remember too much—little hints, things I should have seen."

"Have you told Claudia when you are leaving?"

"Not yet. I wanted to talk to you first. I had to make sure you understood."

"My dear Maurice, you helped me build this clinic. Have you no faith in our work?"

Maurice got up and began to pace the room. "Yes, of course, I do, but...look, after the robbery at my home, when the police decided not to bring any charges, the police psychiatrist suggested I find help for her. She saw that Claudia was on the verge of a breakdown. I suggested this trip for the sole purpose of bringing her here to you."

The short-bearded doctor nodded. He had heard all this before. Maurice obviously just needed to talk.

"Once we were in Switzerland," Maurice continued, "I talked her into spending a few days here, to see you again, to relax and enjoy the beauty of this place. But I'm afraid of her reactions when I suggest—no, tell her that she must remain."

"How do you think she will react?"

"I'm not sure, Albert, you have already heard her classic paranoid fears. Her fantasy of a robbery where she, Claudia Betancourt, steals part of a golden treasure from the New York museum." Maurice paused to stress the enormity of Claudia's fantasy.

"Her haunting fears began with that fantasy. She felt that men were spying on her. Then, when three of her friends died tragically, her deterioration accelerated."

"To be brought to a head by the shooting," Beringer interrupted.

"Yes. The shooting. It was an act of passion. That man was a chance thief, but to her he was a kidnapper. I must admit, had he not overpowered me, I might have shot him. But she was a mother lioness, protecting her cubs. The shock of the killing brought it all to the surface."

"Her interviews with the police must have exacerbated her condition."

"Yes. Of course. Claudia was excused. The gun was licensed, and Claudia was in peril, so the shooting was considered justified. But I'm afraid the findings did not help her. She began to insist the treasures were being watched, that there was a conspiracy against her. She even...she even fantasized that there was infidelity on my part. That is when I decided to bring her here. I didn't know what else to do. My lovely Claudia..." Maurice studiously assumed an expression of helpless grief.

"You did right, Maurice. We will help her."

"I know you will treat her decently. Here she will maintain her dignity. That is important. I could not take her somewhere where they would lock her up, or worse."

"She is a patient and a friend, Maurice. What more can I say?"

"Nothing. I must go to her now, before it gets dark."

"When will you be back?"

"Several weeks, a month. I'm not sure. There is so much to catch up with at home, and she will be here a long time, I'm afraid." Maurice got up. "Goodbye, Albert. Be kind to my lovely Claudia."

"Auf Weidersehn, my friend."

It was just a short walk down the white-tiled hallway from Dr. Beringer's office to the patient's wing.

Maurice knew he had achieved the best possible situation, and yet his mind was not at rest. So long as Claudia remained here under treatment, Peter Mandel would be placated. And with Claudia here, he would be totally free to continue his work and his collecting, in his own way, and his own style. At home, in the library, the statue waited, at peace.

Maurice smiled briefly at the turn his mind was taking. He sounded very much like Claudia.

Poor Claudia, resting now behind one of these oak doors. They all looked alike, he thought, not at all the style of the individual spirit that was his wife. She could never come home cured. How could she be cured of being a cold blooded murderess, of being rich, beautiful and possessive?

This was the best way, the only way.

* * *

Claudia had spent the past hour in deep thought. For the first time in weeks, she had been able to think quietly and clearly. The peaceful surroundings and the kindness of Beringer had enabled her to review her actions in sharper focus.

The little jeweler, Roncalli, was simply happenstance. Charles had been her first big problem and she had solved it brilliantly. Sharon had been a different kind of problem. Thinking of Sharon was both exciting and sad. Claudia had never come to grips with her feelings about Sharon and now, in retrospect, they were all confused. She pitied Sharon's unhappy married life and envied her ability to give herself to Peter. It would have been so fulfilling to give oneself to someone. Sharon was young and refreshing. She could have loved and protected her. But it just wasn't to be. It was a pity.

Gottfried had been an annoying problem. It was good riddance to an old fool. How dare she think she could frighten Claudia the way she frightened everyone else?

Finally, there was the detective Maurice had hired to watch her. He was eliminated most unpleasantly.

She stood at her window, looking out at the sanitarium grounds.

One person remained a problem. Maurice. He did not love her. He was unfaithful. And he envied her fortune. And—most important of all—given the chance, he would keep the statue as his own. Not while she, Claudia, could help it!

Thinking of Maurice made her feel sad as she had when she remembered Sharon. It was a sadness for what could have been.

She knew that Maurice was in Beringer's office, discussing her. "Dear

Maurice," she said half aloud. "How I must embarrass you. How happy you would be to have me disappear from your life. I know that is why you had me come here. It is what you are plotting with Albert this very minute. How sorry I am to have to disappoint you."

Claudia turned from the window. On the dresser her purse stood next to a tray with a bottle and a glass on it. She began to speak again, whispering. "Maurice will be here soon."

She turned her purse over, dumping its contents onto the dresser. From the small pile she took her cigarette package and took out a cigarette. She lighted it and began to replace everything in her purse when she saw the small, familiar bottle. How well it had traveled. Not a drop had spilled since she refilled it in Maurice's office before their trip began. It made her smile—for the first time in a long time.

Maurice stopped in front of the door and its small one-way glass panel. He fought back the impulse to look through the glass. Instead he breathed deeply, knocked, and without waiting walked in.

Claudia was standing on the far side of the small, neat room looking out through a large window, at the last rays of the afternoon sun as it set behind the mountains. Now in midsummer, the view was a wash of browns and greens. Soon the upper levels of the mountains would be dusted with the white of the first snows.

By Thanksgiving there would be no browns in the picture. The green of the Swiss pine forest would be frosted with ice crystals. The mountain would be pure white with deep snow, and the blue-black lake would be a solid, icy grey.

The room was frighteningly familiar to Maurice—it was like so many he had worked in. The furnishings—bed, dresser, night stand and club chair—were spartan.

Claudia turned from the window. She was wearing the pale green lounging pajamas he had given her last Christmas. She was smiling. He could not judge what the smile meant. There seemed to be suspicion in the dark piercing eyes.

"I was wondering if you were coming." Her tone was light, friendly, yet an edge was there. "Have you and Albert finished discussing me? I feel better just having talked to him. He is a very reassuring man. You were right, dear Maurice. He is warm and very understanding."

"Yes, he is. He feels that your talks have gone well. He would like you to remain."

Claudia tensed. No, dear Maurice, I know who wants me out of the way.

"There is so much more he wants to talk about, Claudia. Your friends, your fights with the museum. I'm sure he will be able to help you, but it takes time."

"What kind of help do you think I need?"

"Help..." he was thinking quickly, "help you realize that your fears are groundless."

"Are they?"

"Of course they are! You have nothing to fear."

"Not even you?" Her dark eyes were large, innocent.

"Claudia, I'm your husband. Why should you fear me?"

Claudia turned and walked to the dresser. She looked down at her pursue and the tray next to it. Suddenly, she spun and faced Maurice.

"You stopped being my husband a long time ago. You ignore me, use me, despise me, tolerate me, placate me, pacify me, patronize me " She paused to catch her breath. "You do everything but love me. You are probably my worst enemy. That's why I should fear you."

"Don't be foolish Claudia. It's true I feel resentful, at times, when you spend your money on things I can't afford."

"It's our money."

"No, it's yours. The way you spend it makes me feel impotent."

"Ha!" Claudia's laugh was an explosion. "Not physically impotent. I'm sure. Or should I check with some of your patients? You know, the ones you give that special personal therapy?"

"Oh, God!" Maurice turned from her and sat heavily on the bed. "I don't know what you're talking about."

"You've been having affairs with half the women who come into your office. Don't lie to me!"

He rubbed the back of his neck, his eyes closed tightly. "You are sick, Claudia. Beringer is right, you must stay here. There is no other way. God knows what you will imagine next."

"Must? Must? Beringer be damned!" Her voice rose as she walked towards her husband. "It's not Albert, it's you who want to keep me here. You want my statue, my collection, my money and your women. Your adoring little sluts."

She looked down at him. Maurice saw that her lower lip quivered, as if she were going to cry, yet no tears were visible. A slight tic became visible in one eyelid.

"I needed you to be strong, Maurice. I wanted you to be strong. But you were weak. I had to be the strong one. I had to decide where to go, when to go, whom to see, what to buy. Oh, how long the resentment must have burned in you, until it became jealous hate."

Maurice started to get up but she held him down, her hand on his shoulder.

"There was no hate, Claudia," he offered quietly.

"Of course there was hate, and now there is revenge. Now you don't have to ignore me to hurt back. Now you can forget me altogether. Now you can leave me here to rot."

Maurice got to his feet. She prodded his chest with her finger.

"Don't think you're rid of me, Maurice, because you're not. You can go home to your precious whores, but it won't be for long. Beringer doesn't know everything yet, but I want to tell him. He'll be shocked, but he'll agree with me that I had no choice. Everything that happened was forced on me and once he sees that he'll send me home.

"That's when you had better start to be afraid, dear Maurice, because when I get home..."

"Then what, Claudia? Will you kill me too?"

His lashing remark made her step back, away from him. They stood looking at each other. The coldness was almost tangible.

She stooped slightly as if he had hit her in the stomach. She had to tilt her head back to look at him.

"Why did you say that?" In her mind there were flashes of memory. She saw the small, glass bottle tilting over Charles' drink. She could feel the coldness of the vial in her hand.

She saw a cup of tea on a dark coffee table. Tea made with a teabag, not loose tea.

A dark, curly patch of pubic hair, underwater. A fat lump under a huge raincoat. Pills in a pill bottle, tumbling, tumbling...a teabag.

Claudia brought her hand up to cover a smile. Her eyes were dancing. A tiny giggle escaped her mouth, and she bit down on her fingers. But even this self-inflicted pain could not stifle the next giggle, nor the next, nor the deep laughter that followed. She threw back her head, planted her feet wide apart and laughed. "It is crazy," she said to her husband through the laughter. "It is hilariously crazy. With all that has gone on, do you know what bothers me most?" Maurice watched her, stone-faced. "What?"

"That old bitch Gottfried used teabags instead of real, loose tea."

"Is that why you killed her?" Maurice threw the question at her. He wanted to bludgeon her with shocking accusations until she could take no more and retreated into a shell that Albert Beringer would find hard, if not impossible, to break.

Claudia had stopped laughing and was trying to regain her breath. "Dear Maurice," she gasped, "I'm afraid you have formed an opinion of me that will be very hard to change. I'm sure your fat friend, whom you hired to spy on me, made many accusations. I'm equally sure you believed them."

She lay down on the bed, one arm thrown over her eyes.

Maurice did not speak for a moment. She was indeed a puzzle. Her behavior fit no pattern.

"I'm sure you are right, dear Maurice," she said, eyes hidden by her arm. "Staying here with Albert will do me a world of good. Perhaps I can even forget poor Miriam's tea habits." This time her laugh was just a throaty chuckle.

Maurice started to agree, but thought better of it. Silence, at this point, was his best tactic.

"Before you go, let's have a toast to the future." She rose and went to the dresser. "I have a bottle of sherry. Albert most kindly provided it to help me fall asleep."

He stood waiting.

"Maurice," she said, her voice steady, "we have one clean glass. Would you get another? The pantry closet's just across the hall."

"Yes, of course. I'm delighted to toast our future."

He was back in a minute, putting the glass down on the dresser and waiting while Claudia poured sherry into it.

He took the glass she offered. "To us. To the future." He clicked his glass with hers and took his first sip. Claudia groped in her purse for the cigarettes. Her fingers touched a cold, small bottle, the kind that aspirin came in. It was a bottle that Claudia had found useful in the past, and most useful only seconds ago. There was no fear of spilling its contents now. It was empty.

Maurice took another sip. Claudia looked down at her glass standing untouched on the dresser, walked to the bed and lay down. She reached behind her to adjust the pillows. The rays of sun were almost horizontal now, piercing the window in hazy streaks. She closed her eyes and a smile crossed her face. Her mind drifted back to more pleasant moments.

MONDAY, AUGUST 8

On this warm, humid evening, as Peter Mandel left his office, his thoughts had no focus. He was drifting, as he had been for weeks. His program responsibilities were light. His social life was virtually nonexistent—an occasional dinner with friends, male or female, which was quickly forgotten.

Sharon's house in California was a distant memory, re-rented after Sharon's belongings were returned to Clayton Hiller. The deposit on the house in Brentwood was returned to him. The sadness and loneliness he had felt at Sharon's death was becoming more distant. Now when he thought about it, he felt sadness at the loss of what might have been, rather than of what was. He occasionally thought of Claudia and Maurice, remembering his one attempt to reach the doctor after their meeting.

"Left for an extended stay in Europe," the maid had said in her British accent.

Suddenly his mind emptied of all memories. There, on the newsstand he was approaching, was a bold headline, staring at him. MUSEUM ROBBERY UNCOVERED. The three words covered most of the front page. And below them, in smaller type, Egyptian Treasures Missing—page sixteen.

Peter took the top copy of the tabloid, thrusting coins into the vendor's hand. Oblivious to the street around him, he read the brief text.

As usual in the evening paper, the information was no more than wire service copy. A routine examination of the Golden Age exhibit by Egyptian experts, prior to the packing for return to Cairo, had uncovered the fact that four pieces were duplicates. The loss was unexplained. It could have happened, the experts said, at any time since the last examination, which had been months ago, prior to the exhibit's leaving Cairo. In typical news fashion, there was a fruitless attempt to put a value on the loss. A museum source said that all the pieces were priceless. The fact that there had never been a ransom attempt left little doubt that they had disappeared into a private collection.

Peter re-read the story and searched through the rest of the paper. There was nothing else. Obviously the story had broken late in the day.

Peter signaled for a taxi, got in and lay back against the seat as he headed home...for refuge.

Once inside the apartment, he sat down on his couch and dropped the newspaper on the coffee table. The front page stared up shouting to be read and understood. Peter had no knowledge of the passing of time. His mind raced through every detail of the robbery. He heard the voices in Sirocco, the deep, hushed tones of Claudia in the tomb, the whining of Charles in the warehouse. Only Sharon's voice failed to make its presence known.

An hour had passed when he stood up. He made himself a stiff Scotch and sat back down, his legs resting on the coffee table, his feet covered the damning headline. Why were the four pieces missing? Only the statue should be gone. And he had thought that, after his conversation with Betancourt, the statue, too, would have, somehow, been returned. His whole purpose in going to Maurice had been to put an end to it all. Were the Betancourt together in this, he wondered? Or had the statue been returned and not the others?

He turned the liquor glass slowly in his hands, the ice tinkling softly. What had happened to the four pieces in the tote bag? He was sure that Gottfried would have retrieved them from the locker in Grand Central and returned them to the museum. But somehow they had never gotten back to the museum. Somehow, their trip had been interrupted. Claudia, he thought, Claudia again. She had gotten to the old lady. The alleged 'heart attack'. Claudia had gotten to the old lady before she had a chance to return them, killed the old lady and took the pieces home. It made sense. The timing was right.

And it was not too long after that, he was thinking, that the Betancourt took a trip. They must have been working together.

"Christ, was I a fool!" Peter said aloud. "That doctor must still be laughing at me."

Again Peter questioned the empty room. "Now what?" He swung his feet to the floor and began to pace. First to the window, then to the sofa, then to the kitchen door.

Weeks ago he had thought of calling his friend on the police commissioner's staff. He still wasn't ready for jail time but he was getting closer.

He stopped near the telephone table. The small leather address book sat next to the phone, tempting him. He found the Betancourt number and dialed it. His adrenalin was flowing. Where were they? Busily murdering someone else? Stealing? He had to know.

After several rings an English accent came on the line.

"This is Peter Mandel," he said, and the brusqueness of his tone surprised him. There was a touch of anger in his voice. "Are either Doctor or Mrs. Betancourt at home?"

There was a long pause before the woman's voice answered, slowly, hesitantly. "I'm sorry, Mr. Mandel, the doctor died quite suddenly in Switzerland several weeks ago. He was buried at his family home in Belgium. Mrs. Betancourt remained with friends in Switzerland, but she's on her way home now. We expect her in a day or two."

Peter's breath came up short. "Could you tell me what he died of? I was acquainted with the doctor and thought him to be in good health."

"Heart attack," came the answer.

A chill like Peter had never known ran up his back.

"Did you hear me, Mr. Mandel?"

"Yes."

"There was no warning. It was very sudden."

I'll bet it was, Peter thought. "Thank you."

He heard the voice say, "I'll tell Mrs. Betancourt you called when she returns. Goodbye."

Peter walked into the kitchen. He put his Scotch glass into the sink and stood staring at the dirty breakfast dishes. Some egg yolk had hardened on one of the plates. It'll be a bitch getting it off. he thought. He picked a soggy crust of toast out of the sink and , dropped it into a plastic garbage bag. He turned and pulled open the refrigerator door. He stared into the white interior. Its contents failed to register on him. He closed the door and walked out of the kitchen, past the telephone table and into his bedroom. He sat down on his bed and kicked off his shoes. As the second shoe landed in the corner, he lay back on the bed. His lips formed words.

"She did it again," he whispered into the room. "Maurice must have gotten in her way. So now she's coming home to all of her treasures. No one will ever suspect her. Charles, Sharon, Gottfried and now Maurice. There's no one left to give her a problem. No one but me."

TUESDAY, AUGUST 9

On his way into his office, Peter thought of an old cliche 'when in doubt, punt.' Claudia was coming back and the robbery was no longer a secret. And an investigation driven by the Egyptians was underway. There were only two people now who knew what happened. He needed time to think. Consider his options. Talk to an attorney? He could only imagine the kind of punishment to be exacted for stealing national treasures. Still...his part was insignificant compared to Claudia's.

Would the law care?

He needed to get the hell away and come back strong.

Peter's boss, the network news chief, listened to his plea for a change of scene. Any short term assignment—out-of-town, overseas, anywhere.

Girl problems, his boss concluded. Peter's in over his head with some broad.

"How do you feel about Palestine?" the news chief asked.

"What about it?"

"We're doing a story on the border incidents between the Israelis and the Palestinians. You interested?"

"When do you need me there?"

"Immediately. The crew is there already."

Back in his apartment, Peter finished cleaning. Not wanting to come back to an ant and roach filled apartment, he washed, vacuumed, and dusted. It looked the best he could remember. Then he began to pack. There wasn't much to take. The khaki work-clothes were strewn over the bed ready to be jammed into an old flight bag. He worked with deliberate speed. The plane left from JFK at six the next morning.

SATURDAY, AUGUST 13

Claudia lay back on her bed, smoking. The white cat approached. She put out a hand to touch the white fur but the cat backed away.

"I'm sorry. I know I was gone a while. I missed you."

The cat sat erectly and stared. Not returning Claudia's try at affection.

Three suitcases stood near the foot of the bed, waiting for Mrs. Britton to unpack them. The green numbers on the bedside clock read 7 p.m. On the bed lay Mrs. Britton's list of all those who had called to offer condolences. Claudia had just finished reading through it. The last name disturbed her. All of the other calls had come in weeks ago. Peter Mandel's was dated several days ago. Mrs. Britton said he called and was not aware the doctor had passed away. He offered his condolences.

But that wasn't the reason he called. It had to be about the news of the museum theft being discovered. He had to know the pieces he put in the locker never made it back to the museum. Thanks to Miriam. Thanks to the detective. But where were they now? It was time to find out. Maybe that's what Peter was calling about.

She looked up Peter's phone number and dialed. It rang and rang then went into the answering machine.

MONDAY, AUGUST 15

Lieutenant Joel Shulman sat on the tailgate of the truck, swinging his legs and chewing the tattered remnants of a cigar. He was a thirty-two-year old sabra, a blond with a ruddy complexion. He looked ten years younger and entirely too Irish for the green fatigues of an Israeli reserve unit. He glanced at the scratched face of his Rolex Oyster and shook his head sadly. 4:00 should be the time when a handsome bachelor lawyer begins to think about closing the office in Tel Aviv and meeting a delightful teacher named Tova, who taught romance by night.

Joel Shulman sighed aloud. Why this idiocy? he wondered, looking around at the men and equipment. It was such a waste. On the day he was born, the Jews were fighting here in the desert. Now, thirty-two years later, where were they" Back to the Nile again. Fighting again—or still. And thirty-two years from now—where would they be? Joel Shulman was afraid he knew.

He could no longer get his juices flowing in patriotic zeal every time a border settlement was raided, and his reserve unit was alerted for a retaliation strike. After fourteen years he found it a frightening bore. Every time he thought he could see more than twenty-four hours in advance, somebody lobbed a shell across the Nile and it landed in the middle of his plans. And this boring repetition could kill him. It was senseless.

Many Israelis of his own age, the second-generation people and the new settlers, seemed to think they had something to prove. They would not settle on a safe lane and work to create a lush oasis out of the desert. No, they had to settle on a desolate strip of desert, right on the border, or near the Nile, under the noses of the Arabs. These settlements were spite kibbutzes, Joel brooded, and the people who inhabited them were hard nosed and obstinate fools who never knew when to leave well enough alone.

Not that the stubborn stupidity was all on the side of the Jews. The Arabs had their share. Instead of leaving the crazy Israelis to bake their brains out in these border settlements, the Arabs whipped themselves into a frenzy to drive the Jews from what was a practically uninhabitable sand box.

If Lieutenant Shulman were in charge, he'd end the idiocy. First, he'd build an immense soundproof debating chamber. Then he would install in it the scraggly-bearded, sweaty leaders of all the political groups. He would turn on the air conditioning, turn off the sound and let them call each other whatever they wanted for as long as they wanted, just so long as they stopped to observe the Sabbath.

Next, he would abandon the border settlements and put the Jews and the Palestinians to work building hotels along the Nile. He'd establish the next Miami

Beach or French Riviera right here, where he, Joel Shulman, could participate in his own small way, as a real estate lawyer.

Shulman threw the cigar butt away in disgust. This whole war was making him neurotic. He had better shape up or Tova would find a new pupil.

His thoughts were interrupted by the arrival of a Jeep. The lieutenant stared at it sadly. The garish red, white and blue shield of the United Broadcasting System was painted on the doors and hood. The lieutenant knew that Americans were a proud lot, but why, in God's name, bright colors in a battle zone? The Palestinian gunners didn't know one network from another. But they knew the bright sign proclaimed that some correspondent was covering the battle, and correspondents made far-reaching public relation targets. A reporter was worth ten foot soldiers any day.

A khaki-clad man swung out of the Jeep and walked towards Shulman's truck. His appearance was a startling surprise. He looked very much like Shulman himself—his ruddy skin freckled from the desert sun. The two men could have been brothers.

Peter Mandel stopped next to the tailgate and extended his hand to the lieutenant.

"Shalom, lieutenant. I'm Peter Mandel of the United Broadcasting System."

"Shalom. Mr. Mandel."

"You don't look like you expected us," Peter remarked, gesturing towards the Jeep and its two other occupants.

"No. I'm sorry."

"Oh." Peter hated reciting the litany of his work every time he moved to a new location, but it was always necessary. "We're filming a series on the border fighting," he began. "I've been following it for several days. Now the action seems to have moved down here."

"I see—you like to be where the action is." The lieutenant's tone carried a slight edge of sarcasm.

Peter picked it up on his sarcasm. "I need to be where the action is. It's my job. Can't have a war without the press as you know. What's happening?"

"Maybe we have a war because of the press." He stared at Peter. "Nothing out the ordinary, Mr. Mandel. Last night, the Palestinians came across the river and hit this kibbutz with a mortar and small-arms attack. Several people were killed, including a woman and two children. Tonight we will cross the river and strike back at their camp. It is all very simple, as I said. Nothing out of the ordinary."

"You said a woman and two children were killed." Peter had a pad and pencil out and was making notes.

"Don't be carried away with the horror of innocent civilians being killed, Mr.

Mandel. The woman was probably firing a rifle that she was trained to use, and the children were undoubtedly carrying ammunition."

"And that makes them fair game?" It was Peter's turn to sound sarcastic.

"In the stupidity of these little skirmishes, Mr. Mandel, everyone is fair game, including television reporters. You, the Brits, and everyone else."

"I take it, lieutenant, you're not too happy to have us along."

"Mr. Mandel, whether you are here or not is inconsequential to me. As you said, we all have a job to do."

"I thought all the Jews—Israelis," Peter corrected himself, "were patriots."

"Oh, I'm proud of what we've done in Israel. Very proud. I'm just tired of this senseless warring—these spite camps. Maybe years ago it was necessary to fight, to give this country a heritage of blood. But now—enough already. Why must we continue to fight? I think if the rest of the world stopped reporting every little incident, every skirmish. It would be better off."

The Israeli hopped down from the tailgate. He was shorter than Peter, and heavier.

"I'm feeling quite sorry for myself today. I am even more sorry for what I have to do tonight, and it bothers me that you have come to observe it for the purpose of providing two minutes of war movies for your indifferent viewers."

Peter watched the broad-shouldered back of the young lieutenant disappear around the side of the truck, heading towards another vehicle with a dirty canvas tent extending from its side. Under the canvas, the Israeli strike force was sitting down for the evening meal. Peter walked back to the UBS Jeep and the two men sitting in it.

"Well, I guess we're all set. Let's get over to that mess truck and see what's cooking."

"I bet it ain't ham and eggs," one of the television men laughed.

* * *

The moon was full and unblinking, a silver eye watching the movement on the river. Its light picked out the tiny wavelets, giving the entire river a rippled, fluorescent glow.

The flat-bottomed motor launches of the Israeli strike force were drifting towards the western bank. Fifty yards from the shoreline they had shut down their engines. Now, bobbing gently they were silently nearing the tall reeds along the shore. The water lapping against the boats was the only sound disturbing the heavy, hot silence of the night. The first and second launches carried armored Jeeps, the third, the UBS television Jeep, the fourth, a crowd of armed men. The moonlight washed the UBS shield and lettering, making it shimmer a brilliant silver.

It was not a good night for a raid. The commandos all agreed: it was too bright.

The four launches struck the bank at nearly the same moment. The Jeeps were pushed off the front ramps onto the sand and stones of the river bank. Once ashore, the soldiers melted into the shadows, and Peter and his two crewmen were left to wait.

Randy Patton, the camera man, had dragged a camera through the waist-deep mud of the last tsunami. To him, this assignment was simple. But the sound man was young—a recent graduate of Northwestern School of Journalism. Young Arnold had this assignment because his father was high up in UBS financial management. Peter had jokingly predicted that Arnold's next assignment would be to co-anchor the evening news.

"Randy," Peter whispered, "this light—I hope you can pick up the action."

"We'll get something, with this moon and the fires they'll start. Don't worry."

The Israelis started their Jeeps and began moving slowly, parallel to the river. The newsmen followed along behind the last of the soldiers, who were moving at half trot after the Jeeps.

The lead Jeep, Lieutenant Shulman's, turned inland, moving away from the river. They all followed. Ten minutes later, the men trotting in front of Peter's Jeep suddenly stopped and crouched. They were waiting. Randy Patton panned his camera back and forth. None of this footage was going to be usable but he had to keep moving. Arnold poked his microphone out from the side of the Jeep. There was no sound. The needles on the sound recorder were still.

Suddenly from up ahead came the growl of accelerating car engines and the squeal of tires spinning in gravel. The foot soldiers sprang from their crouches at some unseen signal and began to run, some straight ahead, others fanning out to right and left. They had arrived at the camp. The attack had begun.

The sharp crackle of light-arms fire filled the air. Arnold spun his dials. The needles on the recording equipment jumped in and out of the red zone. A flare burst into brilliant life and began its lazy descent. Ahead, to the right, Peter could see tents. The Israeli Jeeps were heading straight for them, machine guns hiccoughing and spitting fiery tracers.

Peter drove the Jeep forward, slowly closing the distance between himself and the army vehicles.

One of the Israeli soldiers to the left of the Jeep screamed. He lifted in slow motion and floated backward, landing in a sprawling heap in the sand. The attack group was under fire.

The Israeli unit had ringed the camp and continued to pour rounds into the tents and the surrounding trees. Several of the tents were ablaze, their red glow combining with the phosphorescent flares and the silver radiance of the moon, to give the entire scene a surrealistic illumination.

After several minutes, the fire slackened. The lieutenant signaled his men to turn and begin evacuating the enemy camp. Peter turned his Jeep around and started moving slowly back along the direction from which he had come.

He had gone no more than a hundred yards when Shulman's Jeep motioned Peter to fall in behind him.

"They're probably waiting for us, between here and the river," the lieutenant yelled.

Peter slowed and let the Israeli move ahead of him.

Soon, through the trees, Peter could see the silver ripples. The lead Jeep began to pick up speed, and Peter followed suit, Randy and Arnold desperately holding on to their equipment as the Jeep bounced over the rocky terrain. A white flash and a column of smoke and sand erupted ahead and to the right. The small vehicle passed the spot. The plume of dirt and sand showered the men with debris.

There was another explosion from ahead and, at the same time, one on the right.

Peter accelerated, following the lead of the lieutenant's Jeep. They had broken out of the line of trees and were now racing along the rocky shore of the river.

Peter pulled his head down. The Jeep hit a rock and leaped into the air, all four wheels off the ground. Randy Patton clutched the underside of his seat with one hand, the other clenched on the web strap around his camera.

Arnold held onto the Jeep seat with both hands.

The Jeep slammed back to earth, the impact almost tearing the wheel from Peter's hand before he wrestled it back under control—only to have another rock send the machine careening into the air again.

Two shells fell simultaneously on either side of the Jeep. Peter felt a sharp pain in his cheek as a stone hit him below the eye. He reached up to touch the cut—and in doing so almost lost control of the wheel. The vehicle began to tip up onto its left side, the right wheels slowly lifting from the ground.

At that same instant, a shell landed not more than ten feet to the right of the Jeep. The vehicle passed the point of balance and began to slip, almost lazily onto its left side.

The forward speed and weight dug the front left side into the beach sand. The Jeep stopped in midflight and stood straight up on its front end, then cartwheeled forward, once, twice, another half turn, and the vehicle landed on its back. It slid for twenty more yards and stopped half in the water. The wheels spun for a moment, and then the gasoline tank exploded.

Ahead, Lieutenant Shulman looked back. He slowed but did not stop. He shook his head angrily from side to side. "That damn shield had been such a beautiful target."

TUESDAY, AUGUST 16

In the Valley of the Nile, daylight came quickly, as it always did.

On the bank of the river, a blackened Jeep lay upside down. It had been on fire. The paint had bubbled and discolored along its bottom and partly visible sides. Only very near the sand, where the river water had kept the flames away, could the marking still be seen. Part of a red, white and blue shield and three white letters.

Twenty yards from the Jeep, Peter Mandel sat on a rock. His blond hair was matted with blood from a wound. Tears in his shirt and pants where his body came into contact with the rubbled surface as the Jeep went sideways. He faired better than his companions. For the longest time, he stared at the vehicle and at the two bodies floating beside it. He had taken this assignment to get away. To think clearly. To find his place in life again mentally and physically. He had done that. But at what cost? Randy and Arnold had not bargained for this.

Their bodies were rag dolls in a tiny inlet at the river's edge, caught by the stones of the bank, their heads towards the opposite shore, moving gently in the slow river.

A red stain seeped from the inlet into the river itself. It grew larger and less distinct as it was caught up in the northward flow of the current. The rich, dark crimson turned to brown as it mingled with the muddy waters. Soon it disappeared as it became one with the eternal Nile.

SUNDAY, AUGUST 28

It was nearly noon by the time Claudia finished her coffee and completed her morning ritual. Since her return from Switzerland and Maurice's funeral, she felt a freedom she had never known possible. The mental and emotional imprisonment she had experienced during their marriage was now over. Her usual routine when she returned was to unpack and put everything in its place. Without his overpowering presence, she had left things languish. Clothes were left on chairs. Makeup and perfume bottles were scattered on tabletops. Eventually, she'd get to it. But not now.

While she was still in the bathroom, the white cat moved across the top of the antique table with its gold inlays and uneven legs, sniffing at the jars and bottles. Each new scent was a signal to the twitching nose and tail. The sounds of the woman in the bathroom next door were of little interest compared to the sights and smells of this new play area. Everything had to be examined...sniffed, licked, touched. With one hesitant jab of his paw, the cat sent a crystal perfume decanter tumbling onto its side, knocking the stopper loose, sending a small puddle of liquid onto the polished wood.

For an instant the cat tensed and pulled his ears back against his head. The scent was strong, filling the bedroom with a lingering muskiness. He then smacked a second, then third bottle watching them fall and create a domino effect with other bottles as they tumbled.

The bathroom door opened, allowing a steamy cloud to float into the bedroom. At the sound, the cat spun to face the woman, sending additional bottles crashing into each other.

The woman started into the room, hugging a large towel to her body. "Karma," she demanded, "what are you doing?"

As she approached him, the cat jumped down and headed under the table.

Claudia looked at the floor surveying the mess. "What's wrong with you?" Her voice at an angry high pitch as she examined the debris. Then she looked at the bottles on top of the table, laying on their sides, failing to notice that a small, blue, glass bottle so carefully brought back from Albert Beringer's laboratory in Switzerland was among the fallen...its delicate stopper snapped so that the colorless poisonous contents seeped out in a trickle heading toward the edge. Its contents were meant for Peter Mandel in case he disagreed with her quest.

"What have you done?" Claudia said. "Bad cat. Look at this mess."

She reached under the table to grab him.

At the sharper voice, the cat hissed and struck out. It claws finding the soft, white skin of Claudia's arm. Then it backed further away under the table.

Awestruck, Claudia stared at the long streaks of red surfacing on her right arm. She looked at the white cat hunched against the far legs of the table. Ready to strike.

"How dare you. Come here." As she reached under, the cat moved again, bumping against the leg. The paw struck out scraping her arm again.

"What's wrong with you?" She pulled back and at the same time, the blue bottle which had been dislodged by the jolt to the table's leg, moved toward the edge. With the stopper now separated from the opening, the remaining poisonous liquid dribbled over the end of the table dropping into the open wounds of her arm.

At first, so furious at the cat, Claudia didn't pay attention to the dripping liquid until it began to burn in the crevices of the scratches. She looked at her arm knowing she had to stop the bleeding, then she looked at the table's surface and froze when she saw that the liquid causing her pain was from the blue bottle.

For a moment, it felt like her body ceased to function as fear replaced rational thought. Closing her eyes, she tried to remember if the information contained in Maurice's manual included the consequences if the poison entered the body by other means. As far as she could remember, it only spoke of ingestion. She went into the bathroom, washed the wound, applied an antibiotic dressing, then covered it with gauze to stop the bleeding.

She slipped on a dressing gown and left the bedroom, turning only once to look for the cat. Karma was nowhere to be seen.

Downstairs, inside the library, she opened the secret cache where the goddess Sekhmet was housed. Now she could gaze upon the culmination of a lifetime ambition. She could look upon the statue. Uninterrupted. So many years, so many had stood in her way. But no longer.

She walked over to the window and parted the draperies to let a stream of light in. As she turned toward the statue, a pain stabbed her arm. Then a feeling not unlike indigestion coupled with nausea rose from the depths of her stomach. *That's what I get from too much wine and not enough food.* Maybe she needed something other than coffee. As she gazed at the statue, the pain in her stomach and the throbbing in her arm became more acute. Each breath she drew was more and more difficult. She found herself gasping each time she tried to inhale.

"We are together as we were always meant to be." As she gazed into the green eyes, she felt the goddess calling her. She tried to take a few steps toward the gold outstretched arms, then suddenly unable to breathe, she lost her balance and pitched forward. Unable to stop her fall, her head struck the edge of the nearby table, and she crumbled to the floor.

SUNDAY, AUGUST 28
2:30 P.M.

On that same Sunday afternoon at a little past two o'clock, Peter Mandel left the restaurant and stood on the corner of Third Avenue and 72nd Street. Hot, humid air intensified the afternoon sun as it beat on his head and the back of his neck. For the last two hours he met with members of the news department where he was asked about his trip to the Middle East. He always thought most on-air news people lacked sensitivity. But after the trauma of the last few weeks in the war zone and the deaths of his companions, he could see why a heavy, sometimes prickly outer shell was developed.

It took all he had to put that trip behind him. And nothing helped more than wondering why Claudia Betancourt called. Her phone message of a few days ago said she wanted to meet claiming she had a business venture to discuss. He knew he was the loose end. The only person left who could tie her to the theft. Was she lying in wait with her bag of tricks to get rid of him? Or did she really need his help?

She had to be referring to the missing pieces. And in a way this was all his fault. He had no idea if Miriam Gottfried ever picked them up. But if he hadn't been so blind to everyone elses needs, he wouldn't be the last man standing. It was the guilt. The ghosts. The memories. The knowledge that if he had done something different, anything different than what he did with the remaining artifacts, the outcome for Sharon, Charles, Miriam, Maurice could have been different. In a way, he was as guilty of their deaths as Claudia was.

Only one way to make this right. The light turned green, he crossed the street and kept going.

He walked east on 72nd Street, then went north on Madison. At 74th Street he turned left. The street of three-story single family homes was shaded by tall elms and maples. Leaves, stagnated by the ninety-degree air and lack of rain, fell to the sidewalk and were crunched into small pieces by his leather loafers. Sweat trickled down his neck and into the collar of his one and only clean polo shirt. Since returning, laundry hadn't been a high priority. Tomorrow everything went to the cleaners.

The Betancourt home was in the middle of the block. He climbed the five steps and rang the bell. The door was opened by a woman perhaps in her sixties wearing a dark, short sleeved dress.

"Mrs. Britton?"

She nodded.

"I'm Peter Mandel. We spoke a few weeks back. I was wondering if Mrs. Betancourt was in."

She stepped aside allowing Peter to enter the foyer with its polished marble floor and glittering chandelier.

"Please have a seat in the living room and I'll see where she is."

"Thank you." Peter followed her into a room where landscape paintings dominated the walls and Louis the Sixteenth furnishings provided seating. He knew the time period because of a program he had done. Amazing the useless information that's accumulated in a lifetime.

While he waited, he was conscious of the silence. No voices or music from a radio or tv. No footsteps or sounds of animals. Even the outdoor noises were dulled by the thick walls. Suddenly, a shriek broke the solitude. He hesitated, then hurried in the direction of the sound. As he neared the rear of the house he heard his name called. The voice came from behind a room guarded by double, dark oak doors. Stepping inside, he knew this was the library that housed the famous Betancourt collection of art and antiques.

At first, all he saw in the dim light was the gold statue of the goddess Sekhmet—the spotlight giving its emerald eyes an ethereal glow. Perched on a pedestal, inside a niche in the paneled wall, the arms were stretched out as it gazed over its domain as it did thousands of years ago.

Mrs. Britton stood several feet away by the window, head bent as she stared downward. As he got close, he gasped. Claudia Betancourt was on the floor in the shadows created by the partially closed draperies that blocked the heat of the late afternoon sun. She was her side but her left arm was extended outward and covered in blood that had seeped through the silk sleeve of her bathrobe. Her eyes were open but her features were contorted with pain.

For a moment, nothing seemed real. Claudia, dead? He bent down and felt for a pulse. There was none but her skin was still warm. He tilted her head to look at the head wound. She had slammed into the edge of the table with some force. That could be the cause of death...or...he lifted the sleeve and could see several long gashes on the arm. Could that have caused her death?

"Is she dead?" Mrs. Britton asked.

"Yes.

"She killed the doctor, you know. How ever she did it. This is only just."

"Any idea what happened?" He stood and looked around.

"None."

Near Claudia's feet a white cat gazed contentedly. Then the cat turned a pair of gold eyes in his direction and gave him one of those all knowing stares that cats do. Then it padded across the floor to sit by Mrs. Britton. He wanted to say, 'the cat did it', but thought better of it. "You need to call nine-one-one," he said instead.

Mrs. Britton nodded then left the room. As Peter followed, he saw the chance of discovering what Claudia wanted, perhaps some insight into the location of the missing pieces, slipping away. Claudia must have known what became of them. It was hard to believe this was the end.

When they reached the central hall, a reckless thought took hold. It was worth a try. "I don't mean to be insensitive to Claudia's death," he started, "but she called a few days ago while I was out of town and left a message about a business proposition she wanted to discuss. That's why I'm here. Do you have any idea what she wanted?"

"No. But...perhaps it had something to do with the robbery that took place here in early June."

"Robbery?" Peter's eyebrows raised.

"In the library. Some thief broke in. I guess he intended to steal part of the collection. Maybe that gold statue. He was holding the doctor at gunpoint when Mrs. Betancourt came in. There was a struggle. She ended up with the gun and shot the thief."

Peter stared. "I was in California at the time. I knew nothing about it."

"The doctor did his best to see that it didn't make the papers. Publicizing it wouldn't do anyone any good."

"How'd he get in? The thief. He'd have to bypass the house alarm system and I noticed that the library has one as well."

"I don't know. I guess the same way he found out where the gold statue was kept." Her look said she knew the answer but wasn't sharing it. "Mrs. Betancourt's office is on the second floor in the back. You're free to look around."

Peter started for the stairs, then stopped as he heard his name called.

"Mr. Mandel. I've been with the doctor and his family for years. With his first wife until her...unfortunate skiing accident. Then here with the doctor and Claudia Fielding who proved to be most peculiar and extremely difficult to work for. Please search thoroughly. I cannot have anything around that will embarrass the doctor's memory or his family."

"Thank you. If I don't find it within ten minutes or so..."

"She's not going anywhere," she interrupted.

Startled by the coldness of the remark, Peter hurried up the stairs. He found Claudia's office at the end of the hall. Walls painted a pale turquoise. A small striped sofa and comfortable chair. Dark wood bookshelves housing books, photos, and Egyptian art and artifacts. The first place to start was her desk at the opposite end by the window. The dark surface with its gold inlay was cluttered. Knowing that Mrs. Britton probably never came in here and that Maurice was dead, Claudia didn't need to worry about someone snooping.

What he wanted should be out in the open. It was. Off to the side were three by five inch photographs of the missing artifacts. A small gold cat used as a paperweight held them in place. He moved the cat and picked up the photos. It had been several months. He had forgotten which ones had been taken. Under the photos was a notebook with a letter tucked inside. Her attorney had written her with information about a private investigator named Fred Burkhart who appeared to be the person Claudia shot. What was a private investigator doing in the Betancourt's house?

The letter had marked her last entry in the notebook. It answered his question.

"I couldn't believe it when I saw the same man Miriam had hired to follow me standing in our library. Although he denied it, Maurice staged that robbery to get rid of the statue. How stupid. He hired that detective to steal it and probably a few other pieces. Didn't Burkhart see the flaw in the plan? Did he really think Maurice would let him walk away then be at the mercy of a blackmailer? I was slow in getting Burkhat's home address. By the time I got there his brother Harry from Denver had cleaned out anything of value undoubtedly taking the pieces with him. That was back in June. Which means they're with a man who has no idea of their value...or worse. I need to get to Denver soon. I hope Peter will help."

He closed the notebook, slipped the photos inside then placed it inside the leather cover of his ipad. For a moment, he thought about telling Mrs. Britton what he found then decided against it.

Next, to be sure he covered all the bases, he went through her desk. The pencil drawer contained nothing except pens and pencils. The other drawers were empty except the bottom right where files were kept. There were maybe two dozen folders marked 'exhibit' and 'museum business'. He quickly viewed the contents which were interesting as they detailed Claudia's relationship with Miriam Gottfried and setting up the exhibit to come to the Met. It could be damaging to the doctor and the museum. He needed to convince Mrs. Britton to dispose of the files. But there was nothing in there on the missing artifacts.

As he stood to go, he wondered how Claudia knew where to find the missing pieces. Maybe Miriam had them after all and told her. But how did they get to Fred Burkhart? And if Burkhart had them, how did Maurice enter the picture? Blackmail. Peter took one last look around the room then headed down the stairs. He found Mrs. Britton in the kitchen cleaning out the refrigerator.

"Did you find what you were looking for?"

"No. I searched her files, even checked the bookshelves. There was nothing about why she called." Maybe the housekeeper knew he was lying. If so, nothing in her expression told him that. "But there are files in her bottom desk drawer that should be destroyed. While they have nothing directly to do with the doctor, they detail her work at the museum, including various acquisitions and how they were accomplished. It could prove damaging. Perhaps a shredder might be the best solution."

Her eyes grew large and her mouth dropped open. She nodded. "That's not something for the doctor's family or the police to find."

"I agree."

"I will take care of it."

"The doctor's family, are they here in New York?" Peter couldn't remember what Claudia said about them.

"Yes. They're in the diamond business, from mining to retail so they have offices here, in Antwerp, in Johannesburg, and a few other cities."

She thanked him profusely, then Peter left, not breathing deeply until he was outside the house and walking toward Fifth Avenue.

As he caught a cab and headed to the west side and the network, he thought about Claudia. He knew she was dead but it didn't seem real. He also wondered about the gold statue and what Mrs. Britton intended to do with it. Then again, not his concern.

When he reached 70th Street and Columbus, he got out of the cab and rather than going directly to his office headed to his favorite bar. Dark paneling and air conditioning shut out the heat of the afternoon. He found a seat in the corner.

"Got something new in," the bartender said. "Those microbreweries are turning out some fine beers. Try this one." He placed a frosted mug with a light colored foam dripping over the side in front of Peter.

Peter sipped it and nodded. "You're right. Are you going to carry it permanently?"

"Everyone who's tried it, likes it. Yours was the final approval."

Peter laughed.

The bartender went onto another customer and Peter took out his ipad and went through his work schedule for the coming week. Three projects were in various stages. And again he thought about Claudia's notes and the missing pieces. Was he being naive in thinking he was the only one who might have a handle on where they were? No telling who Fred might have told. And there was no assurance that his brother Harry ever saw them or took them back to Denver. It was only an assumption on Claudia's part. She had to know more than she wrote in her notes.

Assuming she was right, the people in pursuit of the pieces could be numerous and considering the value—dangerous. Certainly the museum had its investigators. Then there was the FBI, Egyptian police, Interpol, and what about Maurice Betancourt's family. And an assorted number of strangers along the way. Did he want to be one of them? And even if he found the artifacts, what next?

"Any more adventures coming up?"

Peter closed his ipad and looked at the blond haired woman who sat down next to him. "Nothing like the last."

"Another war or something else?" She smiled.

"Just a trip to L.A. to catch up on some odd and ends. And maybe work on ideas for new programs." The woman was a member of the weekend news production department. The less said the better.

"Whatever happened to that movie about the museum heist?" she asked.

"It went big time. One of the major studios took it over."

"Wow, the writer must be excited."

"She's dead." The words came out before he could stop them. They sounded weird. So hollow. So strange. The trip to the Middle East had eroded some of the pain, but here it was back again. He suddenly thought of her face. Her touch. As he did, a sudden jolt of guilt and sadness filled him. She had died because of him. She died because of the missing pieces. He was at fault. For everything.

He suddenly knew what he had to do. Let someone else find them? No way. He owed it to Sharon and to Charles, and to himself.

"I'm so sorry. I didn't know that." She picked up her wine and sipped it. "What happened to her?"

"Stupid bathroom accident." Peter signaled for the bill and bought a drink for his companion. "Don't mean to rush off. Just need to get some things in order before I leave."

"Thanks for the drink. Will you be in tomorrow?"

"Not sure." He slid off the stool. "If I don't see you, I'll be back in a few weeks."

Outside, the August sun was still burning. But he knew winter came early to the Rockies. Peter headed south on Columbus to the network. He would turn over his projects and put in for leave of absence.

He had to find the artifacts before anyone else. But Claudia's note said Fred's brother came in June. Two months is a long time. Maybe someone else had gotten there. Or they could be sitting in his brother's garage.

Peter had no thought of what he would do with the artifacts once he got them. If he got them. But he needed to get moving. Ahead lay a road he had never traveled. And he had to get started.

www.ingramcontent.com/pod-product-compliance
Lightning Source LLC
Chambersburg PA
CBHW061608170626
46811CB00001B/355